Apart from th distant commerce it w on the bare heights of no light worth the me whirling, writhing light t set his teeth on edge and made him ake, for, as he saw the thin grey-haired woman who'd screamed, her wide-eyed face terrified as she swayed on the edge of the fatal fall he'd meant for himself, he also saw (and a groan froze in his throat) how, shadowed in the cold blue light of the wind that beat at her, was the wavering apparition of a man kitted out as outlandishly as himself, in Elizabethan fancy dress, complete with lace ruff, doublet, baggy hose, sheathed sword and pheasant-feathered hat.

The spectre also had two mouths.

Also by Stuart Gordon from Orbit:

ARCHON: The First Book of the Watchers
THE HIDDEN WORLD: The Second Book of the Watchers

STUART GORDON

THE MASK

The Third Book of the Watchers

An Orbit Book

First published by Futura Publications, a Division
of Macdonald & Co (Publishers) Ltd
London & Sydney

*All characters in the publication are fictitious
and any resemblance to real persons, living or dead,
is purely coincidental.*

ISBN 0 7088 8324 9

Typeset by Leaper & Gard Ltd, Bristol, England
Printed and bound in Great Britain by
BPCC Hazell Books Ltd
Member of BPCC Ltd
Aylesbury, Bucks, England

Futura Publications
A Division of
Macdonald & Co (Publishers) Ltd
Orbit House
1 New Fetter Lane
London EC4A 1AR
A member of Maxwell Macmillan Pergamon Publishing Corporation

This one's for Jim

CONTENTS

Prologue:
The Sinking Ways

How long has the dream lasted? *This* dream, of floating deep in the glowing, ever-living Elohim ocean, deep in the delight of the subtle dream-body, without pain or fear or memory – until NOW, without warning, a great voice suddenly rings through the entity that was – *is* – Sam Joyce; a voice vibrating with the hard righteous joy of one forcibly shaking another from sleep which has lasted too long – a rhythmic voice, ironically quoting:

> The loathsome mask has fallen, the man remains
> Sceptreless, free, uncircumscribed, but man
> Equal, unclassed, tribeless, and nationless,
> Exempt from awe, worship, degree, the king
> Over himself; just, gentle, wise, but man
> Passionless? – no, not yet free from guilt or pain –

Guilt and pain? With a start, threshing in confusion, Sam awakens. To find hirself still in the dream, in the ocean depths, in the glowing halls of the Elohim. In the subtle body. *Hir* subtle body. For here there's androgyny, no *her* or *his*, only –*What? Where am I? What is this?*

The giant voice laughs as memory, like a bursting dam, floods hir with brilliant, burning images. All hir past life at once. Diane and Chrissa and Tiy and Dion and . . . that poem. Those lines. Feverishly sifting through a chaotic whirl of images. *Shelley*? Where? And angrily remembering in a rush of naked thought. Guilt and pain and fear. *Yes! Those idiots in London quoted it. When they tried taking over GRYP. So-called anarchists! Beast-owned fools! Before Tiy hijacked me through the Gate and Chrissa and Pierre and I beat the Beast! And we came here through the Starchamber! To sleep, perchance to dream. Hah! You fool, Sam! Azazel's not easily beat; he bounces back every time; infects us with complacent sleep in the hour of victory. He's got the Last Days wrapped up and we just sleep here? Kings over ourselves? Delusion!* Thus scolding hirself Sam sees it plain like a picture before hir. Those fools in black, disrupting the public meeting in Crouch End Town Hall called to decide the fate of the Greystoke Road Youth Project. Their voices loud, their eyes agleam, as if a dose of romantic poetry could justify or hide their banal, Beast-encouraged egotism. *The loathsome mask has fallen.* Sam laughs silently. Oh yeah? *Shelley! What a joke! Saturated in sentiment, masking reality with high-flown delusion. Romantic lies. Azazel owned them even as they thought they fought him.*

But the great voice – maybe hir own, maybe not – cries:

Cynic! You did better? Think: Shelley saw the rot the Beast sells to kill the world, so Azazel murdered him, disguising his death as accident or extravagant suicide. Why? Because the true poets have always threatened Azazel's plans – ever since the last Shift. Wake up, Sam Joyce!

And at thought of the Shift hir subtle body ripples with chill. *Is this why I'm waking up? To return to agony?* And fearfully Sam cries:

Chrissa! Pierre! Where are you?

But before either can answer the signal comes. The signal they've long awaited. All of them. All the many thousands of the Company, waiting deep in the rainbow halls, lining the deep magnetic roads that link the bright cellular cities where the wise old Grey Ones glide, where the exiled Great Souls of the Hidden World have long planned return to the sphere of their birth to fight Azazel. And where the voice alerting Sam from sleep was as strident as an early-morning alarm, the signal comes as soft as a breeze.

'*The shift is near!*' it whispers, '*Time to meet at the Emerald Gate!*'

So, both joyful and sad, Sam responds, responds with Pierre Belot and with Chrissa who was once hir daughter. Like tongues of flame they leave their place of rest and join their comrades of the Company. Along winding shell-encrusted ravines and through fertile ocean forests the transformed Lullu flow to meet in fiery rivers amid the brightest ocean deeps where the dance of the Great Grey Ones, the Elohim, never ends. Under the gaze of these ancient shape-shifting Shining Ones they enter the deepest hall where the ever-open eye of the Emerald Gate, set in its wall of pink and yellow coral, awaits them. The Emerald Gate. The door to the Sinking Ways.

And despite hir best intentions Sam groans, seized by vertigo. *No, not yet free from guilt or pain.* For sight of the Gate awakens fear. Through this shimmering crystal each of them came at one time or another during the ten Earth-millennia since the last Shift. Through it they were freed from time, death, gravity. Through its fire they were transformed. But *now*, in the depths beyond it Sam sees, coiling smokily, the Sinking Ways . . . and, at the bottom of one avenue of probability, their poor Hidden World itself.

There it is! Deep in dark, clenched against the light, a black nest of bad dreams – their Shift-threatened, Beast-ruled world! To which *now* they must return. To guilt and pain, gravity and desire. And even as Sam feels its mad attraction Chrissa cries incredulously: *We have to go back to that?*

Feverishly Sam replies: *Why must we? We all feel the same. How can we succeed where the Elohim had failed for longer than time can tell? Beat the Beast on his own ground? It's a trap! It's worse than crucifixion! I'm no hero! I'm no Christ! I like it here! Why go back to that hell?*

And many others broadcast the same desolate terror as the Beast-face of the Hidden World confronts them, mocking them through the Emerald Gate, so that their dance grows ragged and dim, and the mad night beyond the Gate seems to rush through it to envelop them, terrifying them further.

Yet even as fear threatens to defeat them before they've even faced it the great voice of a glorious Flaming One amid them rings through them:

'*We return because we choose! We came here to prepare a war, not to sleep! So wake up! Stop acting like children! Our own children need us!*'

The Company wavers. Like a sea of wind-blown flame it listens, shamed. But doubt and fearful resentment remains apparent in its unsure dance.

'Thank you!' the Great One cries ironically, and Sam's struck by a vision of a little red-brown man, simply robed under a flat-topped hat, seated on a cedar-wood podium under a baking blue sky, receiving messages and giving orders even as in the hazy hot distance a great construction slowly rises. In his dark eyes dances a bright hypnotic flame. 'So we face night and pain again,' the voice continues. 'So what? The Shift is due again: all that's been won or lost since the last Shift is in the balance. We must weight the balance towards Light so that our world may redeem itself and take its place in the Work that we call "The-Knowing-Of-All-By-Itself".'

Rubbish! whispers another voice as Sam, drawn to stare through the Gate into a mad face, to hir horror hears himself crying with cynical mockery:

'"*The loftiest star of unascended heaven, Pinnacled deep in the intense inane.*" Shelley said that! And I say your talk of redemption is inane!'

At this the disturbed Lullu dance ripples with increased agitation, an agitation now for the first time reflected in the dance of the Great Grey Ones beyond and about the simpler Lullu flames. But before the grinning Beast-face reaching so hungrily through the gate can more deeply invade Sam and the rest of them, the Great One responds with bright, forceful humour:

'Yes, my Beast-ridden friend! Inane and void all will remain – if we fail to fire our world with light! For we face a world about to Shift. Is this so terrifying? Is not Shift itself as natural as the need of water to flow downhill in a sphere of gravity; as inevitable as the dance of death-and-life; as holy as the procession of the seasons, the precession of the equinoxes? Is the Shift's outcome predetermined by the Beast's mad desire for death? No! There's a choice, and we're the harbinger of it!'

There's a murmuring, a brightening of the dance. *Out of me, Azazel!* Sam snaps at that mocking face, now ashamed of hir crass weak pessimism.

'Once,' the Great One goes on, 'it's said our world was a Garden, pure, without evil. For without knowledge there is no evil. Without knowledge there is only the blind striving of nature. But we Lullu were bred from the apes by our hosts here. We were granted vision of our own reflections. We gained self-knowledge and choice . . . and pain. We were put in the Garden to bring Light out of Darkness. But this . . .' – there's new irony in that voice now – '. . . is hard. Even the Elohim find it hard – especially in the Hidden World, with its bewildering luxury of biological variety and choice! Even before my time on Earth they found it too hard and left us, their fine creation, to our own devices.' The irony increases. 'They left us. But some of us remembered them . . . and found them here. Through philosophy and use of the wit they'd bequeathed us we fought through the gates they'd left open . . . and escaped the Beast's domain! But we cannot stay here. For now they give over to us this work of our world which we alone can continue.'

Now the dance of the Great Grey Ones all round the Company in the Hall of the Emerald Gate is one of slow, perhaps unsure, agreement. Feeling this, the Company draws closer in parochial unity. 'We can no longer ask them to do what we won't try ourselves,' the voice of the Flaming One goes on acidly, 'And if now we know that our *gods* are bound by Law like us, and can fail, like us, is that cause for pessimism?' There is a sense, now, of mutual encouragement in the Lullu dance. 'The duty's ours. It's our own world. Light is easily corrupted in Darkness. Even the Elohim are subject to the Law. And – I repeat – it is *our* world we face and must fight for!'

At this there's an increased shiver in the dance of the Shining

Ones, a sensation of mounting unease – but the speaker laughs, and continues:

'Remember: the Beast too was once a Shining One . . . and it is Azazel we descend to fight. See him there, through the Gate? He's scared, though he waits for us on the ground he calls his own. He grimaces at us: he squats on *our* world like a child on its mudpile, sticking out his tongue, daring us to take it away from him. And that's exactly what we're going to do!

'Yet to win back our world we must enter it; to enter it we must find flesh and form in it; to do that we must be invited back by those embodied in it. For they're the front line: the battle's won only where it's fought most fiercely. It's no use talking about it from these heights. We must reach those who live in these Last Days before the Shift; we must contest Azazel's manipulation of them, and convince them that we're not just ghosts and delusions, but their own ancestors, friends, and lost relations, come back to help and guide them in finding their own unknown strength.

'The Beast is an egotist. His own life being miserable, he finds all life miserable. He wants to die, to know his miserable self no more. For his sins he was locked up in *our* world – until it dies. Then he can die. So he works to kill it. But he can do that no more than we can save it. The Garden's fate belongs to the Gardeners. The Shift is deadly only if Azazel persuades our people that their trials are unconquerable; that the peace of death is preferable to the joys and sorrows of earthly existence. I repeat: the world's fate is in mortal hands – hands of flesh and blood!

'But be under no illusion. Azazel is sly. He has prepared his ground. He invades Last Days minds with glamorous new sciences preaching emptiness disguised as fullness. He fosters soul-withering art that denies the Great Chain of Being. He says that what can't be seen doesn't exist. He makes brutality respectable, claiming that the Garden is no Garden but a jungle deadly to Gardeners who don't "tame" it, "control" it, or "profit" from it. In short, he has worked so potently to separate the minds of the Gardeners from the heart of the Garden that his triumph is almost at hand.

'His triumph!' cries the voice, its contempt withering, and Sam (still shamed) sees that little man on the cedar-wood podium raise his hand in a way that fills hir with new hope. 'We deny it! We chose exile here not to rest forever, but to learn how to defeat him. It is *our* world he wishes to undo. So we freely leave our freedom! We have laid our plans. Some among us recently arrived from Last Days . . .' – Sam feels those fiery eyes pierce hir: again hir shame surges – '. . . are in touch with friends left behind. They know of the Shift. They await us. They are ready. But – are we?'

And even as the name and face of a woman in the Hidden World, a woman called *Diane*, comes simultaneously to Sam and Chrissa and Pierre Belot (and there are three other faces too; faces known as if in dream), the light of those who face the Emerald Gate grows intense, a new warmth in it, and the Great Grey Ones nod and duck in their philosophical dance as the Company surges forward, ready now to take the plunge. But the voice cries again:

'Remember: we can't reach the world uninvited. We lack solid form. To descend in subtle body is to be torn apart before we reach the battlefield. But there's a station at the threshold of the world which once the Elohim used as a halfway house. They called it the Whirling Castle. There they changed the subtle body for the dense body needed on the Earth. We can use it. It's untenanted, forgotten, invisible to human eyes. It's also beyond reach of the worst of Azazel's delusions . . . but within range of Shift-energy – energy we can use to materialize it to human senses, thus encouraging the positive Shift! For . . .' – Sam gratefully senses the Great One's humour – '. . . we too have tricks up our sleeve! We weren't born there for nothing! In subtle body we can't affect matter, but dreams and mental energy we can harness – and we surely will! So remember our plans! Remember those we must reach, and the signs we must give them. Remember the telephones!

'Again, before we go, I say: our worldly contacts must invoke us before we can help. If they reject us, Azazel wins . . . for this battle is fought in the hearts and minds of those who live in the world. Only they can choose. We can't force their choice. But neither can the Beast.

'Now. It's time. Don't forget our plans. Let's go!'

So in a blazing river of light the Company plunges through the Gate into the Sinking Ways and back to the Hidden World. Down the roads of probability to the thickness of gravity. And the pain of weight and time, merely abstract in the ocean heights, soon grows so intolerable that their memory and plans are threatened long before the threshold of the cloudy sphere below is even reached. For already the Beast's laughing in them.

Hard, getting back to shape, Sam mocks hirself in agony, plunging into the violent rapids of the shivering, Shift-threatened darkness looming ever denser below. It's the last chance; Sam knows it, yet it's so hard to do or even want to do! For it hurts so much, wild tides of time and gravity striking up from that shrouded globe to tear hir subtle body and assail hir with the cracked song of a world in pain. Already hir spirit's fainting into the scream of its mad jangled harmonic; hir sense of connection with those about hir falling under the mounting weight of hate and fear as the world's claws strike up to drag hir down into forgetfulness . . . striking so fast now that not for a moment did Sam have time to wonder what was lost.

And then he was back in time, back in gender, back in isolation.

I don't want to go back, a fading voice wailed.

But too late. Much too late already.

For already he'd forgotten whatever it was and wherever he'd come from as chaos seized and enveloped him in a poison cloak of weight and night.

Unbearably crushed, he lost his senses. There was nothing. Then there was the Scream. And he became the Scream – a thin, drawn-out ululation of desolation that shivered through the darkness, in places parting it by the intensity of its vibration to admit a smoky, lurid red light emanating in dull shafts from the hurricane clouds that hid the globe below. *Thought it was just a dream?* howled a mad voice even as, aware again of his fall, he saw the looming Hidden World below as a mouth opening wide to swallow him, and as he plunged wailing towards it he saw how those shifting beams of bloody light splaying up from it defined a terrible face that grinned at him in fiery triumph, its eyes erupting volcanoes, its mouth a poisoned ocean, its mind the turmoil of seven billion Lullu-souls locked in self-destruction games and pulling him down to join them. And he saw all the powers of the world released in countdown to the Shift. He saw ice-caps melting; he saw operations of mining and drilling and forest-chopping; he felt the magnetic field wavering; felt the storm of convection currents in the core and mantle of the world; felt the shifting of tectonic plates and the subterranean bubbling of lava; smelled too much carbon dioxide in the air; sensed the shudder of radioactivity . . . saw the thought-forms of fearful folk rising up like a poison shroud over all the globe . . . *The Beast!* cried a faint flicker of Sam-self that died even as he tried to guard it, *Azazel*!

Yesss! We all like company in hell! the Beast roared cheerfully as Sam plunged into the cannibal smile, and though (or maybe because) he hated all Azazel stood for (or hid behind), Sam knew as he fell into it that the smile was a mirror; that wailing mouth was his own mouth, and that voice – of course! – was his voice. *Thought you had me beat?* it crowed, delighted by its own cleverness, *Eh, Samjoyce?* – and now Sam saw a crabby old man in rags, bottle of cheap hooch at its slobbery lips – *Thought you had me beat when you and your tasssty little girl tricked me at the Starchamber Gate, eh? So you got to Heaven but found it so boring that now you just want to get back to Hell, eh? Back down to Dada Azazel, Eh? And jusst in Time!* the old bum hissed, prancing delightedly as he offered his bottle. *Jussst in time to join the Last Days party and have some real fun! Wanna slug?*

And Sam shrieked as the clouds writhed into monstrous forms, as Azazel drank again . . . drank Sam down, screaming as he did: *Here's tae us! Wha's like us, eh? Damn few, an' they're a' deid!*

Yet even as Sam was swallowed and began forgetting he heard Chrissa's voice. *Watch out!* she cried. *Hold on! We're almost there!*

What? Tumbling through roaring tides, Sam shuddered.

The Beast, Dad! We're going through him. Remember!

Amid his daze Sam now saw shifting, multiple images of Chrissa before him – the child-Chrissa his daughter in Hidden World London before their journey through the gates; Joana-Chrissa who'd joined the Cathars even as he'd been snared by that old Watcher Tiy and been sent to fight the Beast – but most clearly he saw the potent new Chrissa, fired by the martyrdom of those at Montségur, who with Pierre Belot had come through the Tarascon gate to join him in the Starchamber on the earthquake-rocked Sunken Isle, absorbing Tiy even as Azazel had killed him. But Pierre had absorbed Azazel: together they'd beaten the Beast and migrated to the world where the Great Grey Ones swam, where the Lullu Company prepared their return to their home, the Hidden World. THIS Return!

I remember! Sam wailed, wishing he did not. *I see you!*

So he did – and not only Chrissa, not only Pierre, but, plunging into the tumult with him he sensed the entire Company of great souls from every human age, all returning to the pain of the Hidden World; swallowed as the darkness grew. Swallowed – but not, Sam now dazedly realised, consumed.

Even as he knew this the Scream ceased: he found himself amid the calm of a realm unmanifest and without specific form, though form was latent in it. Here they drifted above the battlefield of the Hidden World. Sudden flares of violent light shot up at them, each bringing pain, but he found that now he could bear it. And amid his confusion he realised:

We've reached the threshold. The orbit of the Whirling Castle.

We're all here, Chrissa whispered. *We're going to beat the Beast.*

But how? Sam demanded. *This is his world. We didn't really beat him last time. We only escaped him. Now we're back, and . . .*

Good friend! Pierre whispered, and Sam saw him as darkened with pain as he was himself. *No despair! We must start work. We have to get down to Earth. We must locate your wife, and the others who . . .*

Then the Beast attacked again and Pierre's face fell away as the Scream returned, its pitch so shrill that Chrissa cried in desperation –

Dad, remember Diane. Faintly Sam heard her. *CALL HER NOW, SAM!*

In agony Sam fought amnesia. Amid the chaos an unsure image formed. He seemed to see a drab lonely room, and in it a grey-haired woman abed, tossing and turning in the Hidden World little death called sleep.

Diane! he called, and heard the woman moan in her sleep.

Mum, wake up! he heard Chrissa shriek through the Scream. *We can't come back without you. You have to wake up and call us down!*

But that frail-looking woman didn't seem to hear.

She can't do it alone, Chrissa yelled. *We must reach the other three; they'll help her get us down – if we can bring them together in time.*

What other three? Sam asked dully, scarcely able to think.

Come on, Dad! Don't give up! Remember! We dreamed in the ocean, and we saw them and our part of the plan. Look harder now.

Again Sam fought to look through the clouds masking the world. *The other three?* Groaning with effort he saw a handsome blackhaired woman.

She stood behind an empty bar, tv jabbering behind her, drink on the counter before her, rain hammering the roof above her, and in her hand was a brass belt-buckle at which she stared with a tragic face.

Leave her to me! Sam heard Pierre laugh. *I can manage her!*

Then do it! Chrissa cried in a steely, wounded voice even as another vision swam out of the clouds and grew briefly clear.

Look! Sam insisted. *There's the second one!*

He saw a bright-eyed young man, his hair as black as the woman's in the bar. The youth wore a leather jerkin and stood by a table with a Solomon Seal drawn on it, facing an old man wearing a black robe and skull cap.

Doctor John Dee, said Chrissa dully, and Sam saw the old man look up alertly as if he'd heard her. *He knows about us*, Chrissa went on, sounding hurt, *Enoch told him. But the boy doesn't know. He went through a gate too, but not all the way. Yet we'll need him too. In London. The Doctor knows. He'll help. But we must . . .*

Her voice faded with the scene. *And the third?* asks Sam, sceptically thinking: *So the loathsome mask has fallen? No chance!*

Stop being so cynical, Dad! Chrissa was angry. *Look again!*

Wearily Sam did . . . and saw a florid, fiftyish, shirtsleeved man with sleepless bags under his eyes. The man sat at a desk before three VDU screens, whisky bottle and framed holographic photo atop one of them. He stared sadly at the photo. It showed a fresh-faced young woman.

An English politician, said Chrissa scathingly. *His name is Agutter, Philip Agutter. He's Home Secretary. But he lost his daughter like Mum lost us. Gillian. She's with us here. She's confused and doesn't know what's going on but we have to leave him to her, at least for now.*

He's our ally? Sam demanded incredulously.

Yes! Chrissa insisted. *Pierre! Sam! Don't give up! We had a plan to bring them together with Mum! We have to remember it!*

I'll find the woman, Pierre repeated with a lusty confidence Sam knew Chrissa didn't like. *You two deal with Diane and the boy.*

Images and voices swirled. The mouth below waited to swallow them. It took all their energy not to fall into it. Then they heard Khufu cry:

We're coming home! We will not be beaten by this pain and chaos. This is our home: we will win it back! Remember that! Now let's start work!

Then all sense was lost as Sam, fighting the revolting forms that Azazel took in his effort to hold them off and ensure the negative Shift, flared with Chrissa and Pierre and the rest of the Company down into the Hidden World . . . the Last Days world tonight . . . December 20th, 1999 . . .

Part One
Shasta

But all, indeed, in descending, drink of oblivion; though some more, and others less. On this account, though truth is not apparent to all men on the earth, yet all exercise their opinions about it; because a defect of memory is the origin of opinion.

Macrobius, from *Commentary on the Dream of Scipio* (4th to 5th century AD), translated by Thomas Taylor

1.
The World Tonight

'. . . okay . . . we're on the air? Sure . . . okay . . . we're on right now, burning in the dragon's mouth, my friends, and it's gone midnight so now we're into the 20th of December, Anno Domini 1999 . . . or maybe you've signed up with the Mahdi and date it Islamic . . . up to you, but until the Hand of Allah grabs us I for one will stay with the good old Christos calendar and its sweet sound of apocalypse round the corner . . . and I'm Marc Lamotte, saying hi from Radio Shangri-La out here in the deep deep ocean of *The World Tonight*, thanking you for tuning in wherever we are tonight. You know we have to stay slick here at Shangri-La with the Beast breathing up our backsides; you know it keeps us active, right? But it's worth it, be-caause we bring you the real news you won't get nowhere else . . . and tonight we have something so big even you dead schmucks'll be dancin'! But first, the weather report, the inside one for all you people that think you think for yourselves and don't like what the Met serves up by way of a climate. Okay. Over to you, Blue.'

'Thanks, Marc. Hullo, everyone. This is Blue Jones bringing you the weather without the blether. Here at Shangri-La we try to give you truth, however foul . . . so if you don't want to know, you've got . . . from now . . . just five seconds to switch off and . . .

three . . . two . . . one . . . still with me? Right. Here we go. Sorry, but it's not cider and roses like the Metman paints it. Think the lows are almost over? Nope. Lows are heading in all over and there's no let-up, whatever they say. Blame the trans-polar vortex if you must: just don't ask me about ozone or the Amazon . . . and whatever else you do, stay inside tomorrow! UV got the dinosaurs and it'll get you too . . . if you let it! Some blame it on our negative psychokinetic interaction with the biosphere; others say it's 'cos we're a bunch of greedy shits that don't know any better – but whatever, just stay inside tomorrow, 'cos that Hole's right over our glorious dis-united kingdom this week, probably next week too! So stay inside, and don't let your kids drag you out to kick a ball – what'll you do when they start itching so bad they cry all night? – 'cos that UV's no good. And before you say I must be some kinda ecoperve I want you to know I'm a daddy too, and I don't want your kids, my kids, *anyone's* kids, to catch the Big C just 'cos the crooks that rule us can't face facts. So watch it; the next week's bad . . . and that means for all of us: Union *and* Met. So see in the New Year *inside.* Okay?

'Now from elsewhere. If you're thinking of a trip to California, *don't.* Shasta's been rumbling for days, and when he decides to blow . . .'

'Hey! Sorry Blue, we've got . . . Hey, we're being . . . *What in the hell* . . . Oh my God! Listen everyone, we're being . . .'

. . . *ssssss-sssssssrrrrrr-sssssssssssssssrrrrrrrrrrrr* . . .

Two wild nights later Philip Agutter, Home Secretary of Metropolitan England – he was still officially styled *Home Secretary of Great Britain and Northern Ireland*, but then he was also dignified by other titles, such as *Privy Councillor* and *Knight Commander of the British Empire* – was up late in the antique book-lined study of his armoured Georgian mansion deep in semi-rural Sussex. Open-necked in shirtsleeves at his baize-topped desk he was a florid, fiftyish, fit-looking man, but his eyes were tired, and as he leaned with head in hands over the green baize he looked less like a man of power and responsibility than an aging snooker player faced with a hopeless final pot to save the last frame at the Crucible. And that's how he felt. On the way out. For he was squinting not at the half-full whisky bottle perched atop the ISO monitors before him, but at the gilt-framed holo that stood by the bottle. Out of the sparkling holo depths a young woman, fair and freckled and bursting with health, was smiling at him from a sunny mountain meadow . . . and the more he eyed it the more dejected he became, until at last, shaking his head, he reached again for the bottle.

'What happened?' he asked – ritually, flatly, sadly, not in hope of answer. And Gillian just went on smiling gaily, silently, from the holo. He poured a stiff one with a shaky hand, knowing the bottle would be dead when – probably after dawn – he finally got upstairs to crawl into bed by Carol. She'd be awake by then, soured by another lonely night, ready to start into him again for doing too little to find their missing daughter.

'What'll I tell her?' he asked the holo, 'That you're just one more Disappeared One? That ghosts kidnapped you?' And he laughed, and drank.

Six months now since Gillian had disappeared in the French Pyrenees. She'd gone there to research her MA thesis on some old medieval heresy – Catharism. She'd left her Foix hotel one morning; driven her car to a ruined castle called Montségur. Three days later the car was still there. Locals from the village below remembered seeing her climbing the crag to the castle. But the Ariège police had found nothing. No body. Not a hint or clue. Agutter had flown out. 'Une autre Disparu,' the Prefect had said, shrugging with fatalistic sympathy. 'C'est terrible, mais . . .'

Agutter had understood him perfectly. The man had meant that Gillian was just another Disappeared One, meaning nothing could be done, but pray – if you were religious, which Agutter wasn't – or hadn't been. For in the last year reports of missing people had soared tenfold all over the globe. All vanished as if fallen through newly-opened cracks in the hitherto-solid world. Some witnesses were willing to state on lie-detector oath that they'd seen their nearest and dearest vanish before their very eyes!

Into thin air! And this inexplicable phenomenon was only one among many others, all apparently unrelated, which lately had begun to plague and upset an already upset world. A huge increase in events which, rationally speaking, could only be explained as *hallucinations*. Reports of UFOs, the Virgin Mary, the Loch Ness Monster; of the return of King Arthur and Charlemagne and Jesus Christ himself. Reason breaking down under pressure from the collective unconscious? Who knew? There were already a million theories . . . but as yet no adequate political response . . . especially not in Metropolitan England. *Ignore it*, said Agutter's colleagues, *and it'll go away*, But how, Agutter wondered, could you ignore the fact that mental hospital admissions were doubling every month; and that so were suicides and violent crimes?

Whatever the cause, the effects could not be ignored. Yet that was what the Met government was doing. Ignoring it.

Agutter would have ignored it too, given all the other demands on his time – but as it was his child, his only child who'd fallen prey to what otherwise he'd have dismissed as a statistical curiosity, the Disappeared Ones had come to obsess him. He knew his Cabinet colleague and especially Police Commissioner Rae were telling the PM that he was losing his grip. He didn't care – or rather, there were other things he cared about more – now. Such as his missing daughter. Such as the reports flooding his monitors. Such as the tape seized from Radio Shangri-La two nights ago.

'Okay,' he muttered, tearing his gaze with difficulty from Gillian to eye instead the monitor on which the holo stood. Linked to International Security Organization databanks in London, Moscow, Washington, Tokyo and elsewhere, it was feeding him classified updates on the latest glitches and freak events. *Rome*: an unexplained surge in power had blown every fuse in the city and started a dozen major fires. *Sydney*: Aborigines described as being in 'dreamtime mode' had been seen by a huge crowd to levitate the . . .

He couldn't concentrate. There was something else.

'The Shangri-La tape,' he said harshly. '*Play* again.'

And as the crackly voice began its impossible tale he wished he'd never got into politics. For though he was no fool, just now he felt like one, and even though the tape had been seized before it could be broadcast in the Met, he felt increasingly helpless as he listened to it again.

How long can we keep this under wraps? he wondered.

'I am John Robinson,' declared a tense American voice, 'and I make this tape publicly available in the full knowledge that by so doing I put myself, my family, and my associates at great personal risk.

'The risk must be taken. A year ago I made a discovery so important that everyone must know it . . . but the powers-that-be – and I mean not one government or agency, but many – have tried to stop me talking. My family and I have been threatened with ruin or worse. Now they think us cowed – but they're fools. They've let me live long enough to realize that they serve what I must call Evil – and that Evil is, essentially, stupid.

'Not stupid in terms of the world as we know it.' The voice laughed. 'No. Stupidity has ruled the world so long that from the cradle on we're trained to call it wisdom. But enough. I must tell you what Khufu told me will happen soon to this world of ours – this fine green world of ocean and mountain and green grass! For what is going to happen is something we must not allow! And the only way we can stop it is by waking up!

'Khufu! Do you know who I mean? I refer to the legendary king of ancient Egypt said to have commanded the building of the Great Pyramid.

'Now I've spent much of my professional life researching the mystery of the Great Pyramid, but I'm no Von Daniken or UFO-nut. I offer hard fact. They know I can prove what I say! But *"History is the lie commonly agreed upon"* – and never more than when we face what we don't understand – such as the pyramids of Egypt, the great walls of Baalbek and Sacsuahuamon, and the other antediluvian structures that don't fit the neat theories of history. Yet now here we are in a time when it's clear to anyone with eyes in their head that the existing definitions are just –

excuse me – total bullshit!

'Yes, I can say this now. *Professor* John Robinson! What a joke!

'Why a joke? Because for years I bought it. I studied at Harvard and Oxford. I became an *expert* in my field, spent years deciphering cuneiform inscriptions on Sumerian clay tablets . . . which turned out to be no more than tax demands. That was Joke Number One. Then I got involved in a more . . .'

Agutter sighed and asked for *Fast Forward.*

What am I doing, he asked himself, *listening to stuff like this at 6 am on a Sunday morning? Trouble is, I'm beginning to believe it.*

'*Stop,*' he said wearily, thinking of Gillian, moodily reflecting on the dreams he'd had of her lately. '*Play.*'

'. . . long time only three chambers were found in the pyramid,' Professor Robinson's voice crackled on. 'These are the Upper, or King's Chamber; the Middle, or Queen's Chamber; and the Lower Chamber, or Pit, located in the bedrock under the pyramid and reached by the so-called Descending Passage.

'Yet for centuries men have suspected the existence of other, hidden chambers within the huge body of this, among the most enigmatic and exactly engineered structures ever conceived and built by human hands.

'Belief that such chambers exist is eminently reasonable in the context that the purpose of the pyramid remains unknown. It exists not only as a mystery in itself but also as a telling blow to scientific hubris. Faced with it we remain like Pacific cargo cultists faced with the superior magic of the airplane or radio . . . and the theories advanced to explain it say more about the world-view of the theories, than about the structure itself.

'Thus until lately the *experts* insisted that in its entirety it was built as a tomb for the Pharaoh Khufu, said to have reigned for twenty-three years *circa* 2,600 BC. They justified their theory by reference to the Greek historian Herodotus, who in 440 BC mentioned a legend suggesting that Khufu was buried somewhere in or *below* – mark that – the pyramid. They claimed the empty granite coffer found in the so-called King's Chamber was the looted tomb of this pharaoh, who thus apparently wasted his whole reign employing the entire resources of his nation preparing for his own death!

'In pursuing this ludicrous theory they chose of course to ignore the hint given in the fact that the name 'Khufu' is phonetically similar to the old Egyptian word for this pyramid, 'Khuti', which means 'Glorious Light'.

'They also chose to ignore the entry to the King's Chamber of two air ducts – the last thing you need in a tomb – and ignored too the findings of Prince Abdullah Al-Mamun, son of Haroun Al-Rashid, who in AD 820, failing to find the door in the north face mentioned by Herodotus, tunnelled into the pyramid until by chance, hearing a stone fall, his men found the Descending Passage. Al-Mamun then found the King's Chamber, but it was as empty of the Pharoah's mummy as it was of the treasure he hoped to . . .'

One of Agutter's phones rang.

'*Code Blue-Nine-Zero*,' the recep-voice whispered.

That meant CSU, the Chemotronic Survey Unit, personal priority.

'*Stop* tape,' he snapped, '*Answer* and *Record* call. Agutter here.'

The screen to his left lit up, framing a grey-haired uniformed Met officer with a squashed face that suggested acquaintance in earlier life with the boxing ring. The man's eyes were hooded and watchful.

'Chief Superintendant Macdonald, CSU Liaison, Sir.'

'Yes. I know you. What is it?'

'Intercity Peterborough ticket inspection, Sir. A Five-Oh-One.'

'What the hell is that?' Agutter barked.

Macdonald looked offended. Agutter realized his whisky glass was visible. 'To be specific, sir, a Five-Oh-One-Alpha-Zero-Five.'

Agutter sighed. 'Remind me – what is a Five-Oh-One-Alpha-Zero-Five?'

'You set the code yourself. Sir.'

If you don't know, you shouldn't be in charge, was the undertone in the Chief Super's voice, and Agutter wondered: *What if Rae's got into the CSU?*

He made a mental note to watch the Police Commissioner. Lately Rae had been pulling far too much weight, especially with the PM.

'We have a lot of codes,' he said wearily. His daughter smiled at him from the holo. 'Be specific. What are we talking about?'

'Woman by the name of Joyce, Sir. Diane Emily J . . .'

'Oh? Do I know her?' Agutter asked, sarcastic.

'Alpha-Zero-Five refers to the . . .' – Macdonald paused.

'Say it, man,' Agutter insisted, 'The line's safe.'

'The . . .' – Macdonald was having difficulty – '. . . *Ghost* Project, Sir.'

'Ah.' Agutter's heart leapt. He eyed Gillian again. 'And?'

'Her name is Diane Emily Joyce, Sir,' Macdonald rattled out. 'She's on the Intercity. No Met visa, ID, or credit. Scottish papers. Lives in Edinburgh. Widow, aged 55. Resident in London N6 1977–1986, emigrated north before the Split. We ran her records as a routine measure and got an Alpha-Five-Zero. That's why I'm calling you, Sir.'

Philip Agutter leaned back, face blank.

'I see what you mean,' he said slowly.

Macdonald allowed himself a flinty grin.

'Exactly, Sir. She's the first we've picked up.'

The Home Secretary nodded. 'What's her story?'

'Husband and daughter, Sir. Reported in the Aberdeen Press and Journal, 13 July 1985. Said to have vanished in front of her on a moor in north-west Scotland. Two other witnesses. Never solved. Fits Alpha-Five-Zero like a glove.' Macdonald made a face. Plainly Alpha-Five-Zero offended him. 'No other relatives. Nobody to ask questions if you decide to . . .'

'She's told you that? About her husband and daughter?'

'Nossir. Says she's visiting the Met for old time's sake, wants to see where she lived, look up old friends, that sort of thing.'

'Does she know you're onto her?'

'Probably hopes we think she's harmless. She probably is. Sir.'

'Any Chancer connections?'

'Nothing obvious, Sir.'

Agutter leaned back. 'You're sure she suspects nothing? And coldly wondered: *Can I trust you, Macdonald? Who do you serve? Me? Or Rae?*

'She's not the only one, Sir. Standard on that run. Dozens every day try to sneak in from the Union. Half we send back. Those with credit get temporary permits on signing no-claims. As for her . . .'

'Do it,' said Agutter. 'If you're sure . . .'

Macdonald grimaced. 'You want *me* to be *sure* about it? Sir?'

Agutter sighed. He thought about the Great Pyramid and the message from a long-dead pharaoh. He thought about ISO reports coming in from all over the world; reports suggesting that humanity and the planet itself were going crazy. He thought about Chancers, about Radio Shangri-La, about the storms. He thought about Carol asleep upstairs . . . and about Gillian.

Gillian. Vanished, just like this poor bloody woman's . . .

A sharp pain stabbed his head. *I shouldn't do it*, he realized, fearing what the Ghost Project might bring. Not just politically. Morally too.

If Rae learns about it, he knew, *my goose is cooked.*

'Do it,' he repeated. 'ESB trackers. And pacifiers in case she . . .'

'I'll need it formally,' said Macdonald quickly. 'From you. Sir.'

'Oh for God's Sake,' Agutter muttered. 'Alpha-Five-Zero order on Code Blue,' he told his recep. 'Brain-implant surveillance on . . . who is it?'

'Diane Emily Joyce, Sir.'

'Diane Emily Joyce. Right.' But before giving the authorization code he eyed Macdonald coldly. 'You want *me* to be sure. But are *you* sure?'

'I just do my job, Sir,' said Chief Super Macdonald of the CSU.

'So do I,' Agutter muttered, 'It's called carrying the can.' Pouring another scotch, he said harshly: 'Go ahead. But if anyone outside the CSU learns about it . . . You know the consequences.'

'I just do my job, Sir,' Macdonald repeated, his eyes veiled.

Agutter cut the call . . . and with foreboding returned to the seized tape that claimed to deliver a long-dead pharaoh's message to the world.

He was still at it well after dawn when news came from California.

Mount Shasta had blown its top. Thousands were dead.

He could only shrug. *Thank God that's nothing to do with me.*

He didn't know how wrong he was for another nine nights.

2.
The Hitcher

Some hours earlier and 6,000 miles away an insurance agent named Daniel Boone Brown made the strange mistake that ruined and saved his life.

For that wild afternoon as he drove through the Mendocino logging town of Willits en route from San Francisco to Garberville he was not only about to break two state laws: (1) leaving Grid-flow on manual and (2) picking up a hitch-hiker; he was about to pick up a hitch-hiker who didn't exist.

Rain, pouring for days, poured still; the hills were hidden; the local radio babbling anxiously about mud-slides and most of all about the threat from Shasta as, cool on automatic (hair slick, shirt neat, slacks creased) Dan slid out of town on Highway 101, his UV-proofed flame-red company Audi programmed to make Garberville by dusk; he had a meeting there, and though Garberville was a good hundred miles south-west of Shasta, Dan was scared.

'So what's eating you?' he demanded as he cruised north amid the Grid-locked flow, 'It's safer in the Bay Area? Hell, man, it could all go, just like that. So forget it. Think about the bonus you get when you pull this one off.' And thus consoling himself he yawned wide and lay back, lazily drumming his knees in time to the Watchers' latest global smash hit: *'Aw ma mind's bin murdered by Mars, But I don't put no faith in them stars . . .'*

It was then he spotted the hitcher.

The man standing under a tree by the highway with his thumb up looked like a drowned water-rat in the murk. From the Audi's warmth Dan eyed him with mixed amazement and contempt. Lank and tall, he wore a soaked olive-green cape over teeshirt and blue jeans tucked into scuffed cowboy boots. His face was shaded by a battered hat, pulled low, that sported two eagle feathers tatty enough to have been dug out of the Tim Leary Museum of 1960s Antiquities. His eyes were invisible. *Another old bum too wasted to know hitching's illegal,* Dan decided. *Maybe he thinks he's invisible to cops!*

Then the hitcher pushed back his hat . . . and their eyes met . . . and without thinking, Dan did what he'd never done before, except on a road-simulation course at Berkeley his company had sent him on: '*On-grid emergencies: how to do it by hand.*' He overrode automatic and cut in manual. His hands and feet and head worked as smooth as if he'd done it for years. Brake and clutch and gear, foot on the gas! Exhilarated, he left the grid. Then it struck him. *You asshole!* His eyes leapt to the mirror; the Audi swerved, the horns of traffic ahead and behind automatically blared. *No cops yet!*

But they'd register it. Too late already. He could see it all.

Off-Grid! Off-Grid! Manual Alert! Red Audi 829 SSF Cal. Off-Grid 101 Willits North Limit: Reg. Owner Daniel Boone Brown, 35, Male, Cauc., 95 Guerrero Apt 3 SF94110, (415)282-7911: On-Grid Destination: Garberville. Call in Grid Patrol Alert Paramedics Check Driver Insurance Credit . . .

Real fear hit him. The wheel bucked in his hands as the Watchers wailed: *'An' I don't like to drive in my car no more, Since they made it illegal to open the door . . .'* Wrestling with the wheel, he cursed and cut them off. Again horns blared. Behind the one-way windows of Grid-bound cars, invisible people panicked as the manual freak bucked in and out of them, desperately clamping his foot on what he hoped was the brake.

It was.

Amid a shower of mud the flame-red Audi shuddered, with a final jolt, to a halt off the road. The hitcher watched with interest as the Audi's driver, very agitated, leapt out in the rain and shouted:

'Hey! You wanna get us both busted?' And when the hitcher still didn't move, Dan beckoned furiously. 'Come *on*, ya moron!'

In no hurry the hitcher shouldered his pack and started up the road. Impatiently Dan scanned the drenched grey sky for the Law. 'Come *on*!' he cried again, scrambling back behind the wheel. He'd stopped in gear: the engine had stalled. Still on manual, he tried to start. The Audi jerked, stalled again. *The gear!* Neutral. He pumped gas. The engine screamed. 'Automatic, asshole!' he yelled, 'What are you doing? Get outa here!'

An angular shadow fell over his face.

With a shiver of wholly biological terror he looked up . . .

'. . . And his eyes, man, I swear to God!' he gabbled down the phone that evening to a friend in Oakland. 'No shit, the eyes of a guy who's been waiting centuries, like eternally patient! And nobody ever saw him before but me, or if they did they just drove on! But *me*, man, I *stopped*!'

Dan tried to break his eyes clear of those sombre grey depths. *Tell him you made a mistake!* he told himself frantically.

'Hey!' he heard himself say, 'Get in if you're getting in!'

'Thank you, friend.' The hitcher smiled. His voice was deep, his accent . . . Dan didn't know. European? And as the hitcher rounded the car and ducked to the passenger door Dan licked dry lips. *Just some old dope-growing guy*, he told himself, horrified at what he was doing as he found himself reaching over to unlock – manually – the passenger door.

The hitcher slid in, pack dripping on his lap. He smelled of other earth; the weathering round his deep eyes said he'd slept more nights under the stars than a roof. And as Dan met those eyes again he sighed.

It felt like suns bursting soundlessly in him.

'Watch the door,' he muttered, cutting back to automatic. The Audi's doors shut smoothly: without ado or trouble from the law they slid back into northbound Grid-flow. Only later he wondered at the calm that came on him when the hitcher entered his car. 'Been waiting long?' he asked.

'Long? Yes.' The hitcher smiled, and Dan, though looking ahead, felt that smile. 'Oh yes. Very long, you can say.'

'Going far?' Dan asked, and the hitcher's grin broadened, showing teeth which had never known US dentistry. Dan saw them and flinched. The man's grin grew broader still. 'Not far,' he said in his odd accent. 'Asbill?' He eyed Dan questioningly. 'Fifty . . . *kilomètres*? Thirty-five . . . miles?'

'About that.' Dan relaxed. *French! That's why he doesn't know the law! It gives me a line too, if the cops . . .* He frowned. 'You French?'

The hitcher's face darkened. He shrugged. They swept past a billboard selling a local God-show. '*The Lord my God will come, bringing all the angels with him*' (Zech 14:5) it informed in giant red letters above a lurid image of Celestial Light hovering above a world convulsed in nuclear fire.

'What is that, please?' he asked, indicating the billboard.

Dan groaned. 'Aw, man! Mean you don't know about the Twice-Born? The assholes that run this land all the way from the Pentagon to Puget Sound?'

'Twice-Born?' The hitcher's brow crinkled. 'What is Twice-Born?'

'Assholes that want the world to end!' Dan snapped. 'Creeps that hit folk with the fear of Armageddon, saying it's all in the Bible, and if you don't pay up for *their* Heavenly Cause, then you'll miss the Rapture and rot in hell for all eternity when *they* drop the Big One to prove Scripture!'

The hitcher made a face but said nothing. Ahead, dark forested hills rose into the mists. The traffic was heavy but on automatic there were no crises. 'You French?' Dan asked again, more evenly.

The hitcher scowled and again remained silent. Dan said:

'You know it's illegal to hitch? Bad trouble, right? I'll drop you at the Asbill road – then you take care – you hear me?'

'Take – care!' The hitcher eyed the sky gloomily. 'You ask: am I French? Where I was born is now called France. So I suppose I am French.'

'I've been in Paris,' said Dan brightly. 'What part you from?'

The hitcher shot Dan a look that cut. 'You know . . . the Pyrenees?'

Dan shook his head. 'I hear it's great country. You from there?'

'Oh yes.' The hitcher nodded. 'You can say that.'

'I'm Dan. Dan Brown. Who're you?'

'I am Pierre,' said the hitcher. 'Pierre Belot.'

'And what're you doing here in the States, Pierre?'

'I see how things go. I came today from Point Reyes.'

'Point Reyes?' Dan laughed. 'Talking to the whales, right?'

'That is right.' Pierre nodded, apparently deadly serious.

Oh Jeeze! thought Dan. This time his laugh was edgy. 'Sure!' he said. 'Listen, I'm not a fool, the whales aren't around this time of year, so . . .'

'Oh, but they are,' said Pierre, 'If you know how to see.'

'Right!' Dan paused. 'And you're going to Asbill?'

'Oh yes!' Pierre smiled. 'And you. What are you doing?'

'Selling insurance in Garberville.' Dan laughed self-consciously. The hitcher's eyes, so cool and calm. *Who is this guy?* he wondered anxiously. *Gets me to risk my neck and pick him up and listen to junk about whales! Crazy!* But then Pierre smiled: his rebellion faded without him knowing it – then. 'I gotta live. So I work for the company. It's not so bad.' He was angered by his guilt. '. . . you can do a lotta good. I counsel small dope farmers. Quite a few gettin' ripped off and blown away,' he babbled, unable to stop. 'They got wives and kids; getting high don't give 'em protection. We can. Premiums are *high* too – get it, huh? – but they can afford it.' He shot the hitcher a narrow look. 'You in the dope game?'

'Dope?' The man called Pierre looked genuinely puzzled.

'Yeah!' Dan shook his head disbelievingly. 'You know!'

Pierre shrugged. Hills were closing round them, the highway winding between craggy bluffs streaming with water. The road shone slick in the rain. It was hard to see. 'No,' he said. 'I do not know.'

'Sinsemilla! said Dan, puzzled. 'Best grass in the world grows right here.' He waved vaguely. 'Still technically illegal, sure, but since the Crash folk depend on it. Dope's the number one cash crop in this state. Worth $30 billions per annum.' He frowned. 'You *sure* you don't know?'

Pierre shrugged. 'As you say, I am from . . . France.'

'Yeah,' said Dan unhappily, 'But you have dope in France!'

Pierre shrugged again, staring at the rain.

'Okay!' Dan went on. 'Yeah, I've heard! The hard stuff there, right? Electrohits, all that Sensory Identification brain-implant stuff like in Metropolitan England – but you mean to tell me nobody knows about smoke?'

Pierre sighed. 'I know nothing of what you say.'

Impulsively, feeling oddly outraged, Dan flipped open a dashboard pocket and took out a ready-rolled ZigZag spliff.

'Here. Try a toke of this. You'll see what I mean!'

'A toke?' The hitcher eyed it with scant interest. 'What is a toke?'

'I don't believe you!' Dan lit up. Even as he did he cursed. He'd need his head straight at Garberville, just sixty miles on. Smoking prime weed wouldn't help him make his pitch to a bunch of scared dope-growers who still hated the idea of *insurance* as a betrayal of their ideas. Blowing out smoke he thought uneasily, *He never saw a joint before? What if . . . ?*

Suddenly paranoid, he sucked breath and turned.

'You weren't sent to . . . . You're not a Fed, are you?'

'I am not a what?' enquired the hitcher.

'Forget it!' said Dan savagely. 'Wanna toke?'

Pierre smiled. 'I do not mean to offend your customs . . . but no.'

'Okay!' muttered Dan, and drew deep again. His mind swam as the Audi, following the Grid-line's winking gleam, swept through a curve, flowing round a tree-lined bluff down to a wooded valley by the banks of the Eel. Some hundreds of yards ahead, the turn-off to Asbill was posted.

Dan sighed. 'Here's where you get off,' he said, programming *Stop at next intersection* into the automatics. This time the Audi slowed down and left the Grid legally. *Why didn't I do that before?* he wondered as it drew in to the side of the road. Across a metal bridge the Asbill road weaved away along the river-bank and up into the hidden, rain-drenched hills.

The Audi stopped. Dizzy, Dan eyed the hitcher.

'Have a nice day!' he said savagely, hiding his fear.

'Thank you.' Pierre's grey eyes burned into Dan Brown as he took his pack and got out. 'But does your dope help you to face Truth?' He smiled. 'Soon the Whirling Castle is seen again. Soon the telephones all ring at once. The Shift approaches, my friend. Dope will not help you then.' He showed his terrible teeth. 'Au revoir.'

Dan just nodded. It was only when he was already back on-Grid and down the road that he looked into the rear-view mirror. And cursed.

For there was nobody at the intersection at all.

He was still shivering five miles on when, at Laytonville, the Law rode him off-Grid. He never got to Garberville. Instead he was grilled for hours on why he'd violated Grid procedure by going manual at Willits.

They had it all on video.

The one thing they didn't have on video was the hitcher.

Dan Brown saw his Audi screech to a halt under those trees, saw himself jump out and shout at thin air, 'Hey! You wanna get us both busted?' And beckon furiously. 'Come on, ya moron!'

'But he was there,' he said, bewildered. 'He really w. . .'

Then he realized the score, and shut up.

'Guess you're a Vacaville case, boy,' said the Laytonville sheriff, not unsympathetically. 'You wanna make any calls?'

Dan Brown never again drove the flame-red Audi; never went back to work for Insuracoun. Yet due to a freak of human charity, (or maybe God's Will, who knew?) he not only escaped trial and the Vacaville wards, but when the fire came that night, he lived and the sheriff died.

Until that hour, which involved no Rapture for anyone, he lay in a cell obsessed by the smiling face and terrible teeth of the hitcher who didn't show up on video screens, who didn't know about dope or the Rapture.

3.
Jessica Bright

But at 10 pm California time that night of the 22nd, with Agutter locked into the Khufu tape and Dan Brown in Laytonville jail, the hard rain still clattered the roofs of Asbill (pop. 1389; alt. 1218), with Jessica Bright alone behind the bar of the Rock Inn on Main Street, the old 2D tv (tuned to KRCR Redding near Shasta) on the shelf above her playing Monty Clift as Freud. She was into her fifth marguerita of the evening, staring across the empty room past the window with its blinking Coors sign to the door of the bar. So far tonight it hadn't opened at all. Licking salt off the rim of the glass she sipped without tasting. 'Don't sweat it, Jessica,' she muttered sarcastically, 'you know how you feel about them. Shasta could bury us all ass-deep and they'd still be praising the Lord for His mercy.'

Her head ached. With sleek fingernails she ploughed her black hair. She was proud of her hair. It was still as glossy as on that night fifteen years ago. That terrible night. The grey streaks? They'd come that night too, bringing the pain that never left her dark eyes. But her figure was still good. Asbill's macho guys should have been thronging the place. But the Rock Inn was empty. Those macho guys – boots shined, shirts open, guns racked across the back windows of their four-wheel drive trucks – had stayed away ever since she returned to Nome Valley a year ago to buy the bar and a place out past the Poh Ranch. She'd got some trade at first – mainly from the Reservation – but lately? Hell, the way those creeps in the Buckhorn had put it about that good Christians should avoid the Rock Inn! So, she was an evil sinner, but surely in America even an evil sinner had the right to make a buck to live? No? So why didn't she go back to the city? Her lip curled. She sipped tequila. Because she'd hate to please those tight-ass Christians and their Jesus-humping wives, that's why! Not to mention sister Clara and her mother. No way was she running just to please them!

But she knew that she couldn't stand the ostracism much longer.

For everyone knew about her. Mother and Clara had made sure of that even before she was back. Back *home*. She could hear Clara's voice now; see her sister, thin face clenched with piety that afternoon, a month ago now, when Jessica accused her face-to-face of rumour-mongering.

'You can't ask us to hide the truth!' Clara had looked and sounded so shocked. 'In the eyes of the Lord, omission's as evil as commission.'

'Clara, you wouldn't know the truth if it shat on you!' Jessica had cried. 'Jesus, girl, you're meant to be my *sister*'

'And I am. And I am, Jessica. And the Lord will forgive you.' Those bitter sheep's eyes. 'But first you must show contrition.'

'Contrition? *Contrition?* What the fuck for? For suffering?'

'Only you can know that, sister,' Clara had said so primly.

'And that's why you tell folk I murdered my son and got away with it?' She'd been flabbergasted. 'In the name of – I didn't kill Jim. He . . .'

But she still couldn't say it out loud. Not even to herself. And of course Clara had regarded this inability as proof of her guilt.

'Sister, nobody gets away with anything in the eyes of the Lord,' Clara had declared ringingly, 'But do good works and ye shall be blessed.'

'You mean join your church,' Jessica had muttered.

'We pray for you, sister,' Clara had said, pronouncing 'sister' so as to make it clear that it was sisterhood in Christ, not blood-sisterhood, she meant. And more. *When we were kids I hated you 'cos you had the fun and I didn't,* Clara was also saying, *Now you're down don't think you'll get my sympathy! And don't bother Ma. You've caused her enough grief already.*

Argument was futile. She'd known that for years. She'd been a fool to think folk back home would be different – kind, maybe – or *Christian.*

She drank again, sighing. Fifteen years now since Jim had . . . vanished. Ben had vanished too, but not like Jim. He'd deserted her, blaming her for everything. Only once the heat had died down had she filed an uncontested divorce. Fifteen years! Her eyes dimmed. Maybe by now it should have been water under the bridge. But tonight, with hard rain drumming the Rock Inn's tin roof and nobody to take her mind off the past, she had only the booze and the tv to distract her from the pain and the guilt.

For tonight it was a reopened wound. Because of that dream.

She often dreamed of Jim, but last night it had been so clear, as if she was actually there, behind him, calling him to him, but he didn't hear: he was too busy talking (in a broad accent she couldn't pick up) to an old guy in a black robe and a skullcap. They were in a dark room, standing by a table with a book on it, with a latin title – *Monas Hieroglyphica* – and Jim in clothes like in one of those costume dramas where Bette Davis plays Good Queen Bess. Most weird of all, he was grown up. Lean, tall.

She'd never dreamed of him grown up before. She'd woken up shaking, clutching in her hand the only thing he'd left behind. His belt-buckle.

Now, staring at the tv, unconsciously reaching into her handbag where the belt-buckle lay, she grimaced at Monty Clift's agonized face.

'He was a miserable prick too, poor bastard,' she said sadly.

She switched off and stared at the blank screen, remembering

She was born and grew up in Asbill. That was her first mistake.

Asbill, with one dusty main street, two bars, a supermarket, and three churches (Adventist, Baptist, Presbyterian) sprawled on the flat fertile floor of Nome Valley amid the Coastal Mountains two hours' drive north of San Francisco amid wild steep country, hot all summer and wet all winter, rich in oak and madrone; richer still in marijuana since the collapse of the logging. Now the big Louisiana Pacific rigs no longer hauled redwood out along the narrow road high above the Eel to Highway 101 and the world beyond. Times had changed in more ways than one. Thirty years ago, she recalled, young guys tearing up Main Street on Saturday nights, gun in one hand, Coors can in the other, risked – if they were red – leaving the jail in a pine box. So many had died, the jail had been removed to Willits. But times had changed. Children of the Tribes had got out of the Valley. Some had got education. Some had made money. And some, like Jessica, had come home and begun buying the place. *Their* place. Where their naked acorn-eating ancestors had once roamed, praising Taikomol, until the white man came and in a decade reduced them from ten thousand to five hundred, using whisky, pox, and the gun. Mostly the gun. And then sold them the Church.

Who'd forget a history like that? The answer? Everyone.

The children of the rednecks who'd killed the Yuki then overgrazed the land – they agreed with Henry Ford. History is bunk. Only money counts. By now it seemed the rest of the community agreed. Even the hippies had given up. They were almost all into serious business now. Meaning dope-growing. Meaning guns. Meaning: *So what's new?* The hairy philosophers and buddhists were all gone . . . or converted into churchgoers. Now nobody got by in Asbill who didn't go to Church. Which was another reason Jessica was ostracized. *So what?* she wondered grimly, mixing another marguerita. *It wasn't all bad. Remember your seventeenth birthday? 1972? Jesus!*

That was where it had all started. Everything.

She'd gone with Eddie Floyd in his new Fork pick-up, up into the hills to a commune called *None of the Above.* 'They're trash,'

Eddie had sneered, echoing what they were told in the Adventist school. Yet he'd taken her, and what she'd found had kept her there even as Eddie fled back to Asbill to spill the beans. Ma had come up with the deputy. She'd hid behind an oak, stoned and giggling, as the other guys told the deputy that she'd gone to the holy mountain, Shasta, to meditate. *Shasta* . . . no joke now, but . . .

Now Jessica thought sadly as, unknown to her, Pierre Belot approached: *If I hadn't stayed up there Jim wouldn't even have been born.*

But stay she had. For it wasn't just wide-eyed hippies she'd found up there. There were blacks and Chicanos and guys from places she'd never heard of. There was José, who said he'd been with Ché Guevara (a leftist hero of the time) when Ché had been offed by the pigs. She hadn't believed it, but it was good to hear. And there was Iron Dog. That fierce man!

Iron Dog was why she'd stayed. He was also the reason Eddie Floyd had fled so quick. Because Iron Dog, despite and maybe because of all the pain on his twisted Sioux face and in his twisted Sioux heart, was real. Within minutes of her arrival on the burned high hill, he'd eyed her pressed-jean ponytail Christian neatness and said: 'Bullshit. That's not who you are.'

Iron Dog was a Lakota from Minnesota. He was into knives, peyote . . . and sweet young things. Like her. And that first time she saw him she was hooked. Willingly. She knew he was playing her up, coming on like a real tough Sun Dance warrior. But even then she'd had a confidence that came not so much from her good figure and pretty face as from the Irish half of her . . . though she'd never known her father. Sean Devlin had dropped dead outside the Buckhorn one Saturday night when she was two. He'd been on a five-day binge after returning from a fruitless gold-hunt up Mad River.

So when Iron Dog tried on her his Crazy Horse hype that he often tried on sweet young things, she'd just laughed. 'Why live in the past?' she'd demanded. 'You want me to get hung up about being Indian – sorry, *Native American* – but I don't care if I'm Indian, Irish, or bug-eyed and green!'

He'd grinned as they lay there under the stars, tossing his bowie knife up and down, up and down. 'The past?' He'd laughed harshly, caught the knife, stabbed the poor dry earth. 'Kid, that's what you get in your white Christ school! White man's past! Where's spirit in that? Movie trash! Movie lies! Them Christians told you nothin' 'bout Taikomol – right?'

And the white long-hair kids laughed, irritating her. She didn't think they had the right to this talk between her and Iron Dog, who, even as he spoke, was fondling her tits through her poplin blouse. She'd drawn back, shaking her head, with the bite in her of an uncertainty she'd never known or admitted before. 'Taikomol?' she'd demanded, angrily defensive, 'What's that?' And Iron Dog had turned to one of the hippies and said, grinning:

'Tell this ignorant Yuki chick 'bout Taikomol, white boy.'

The kid was not much older than her. He had a sweet face.

'Taikomol,' he told her, straight out, 'is the name your people give to God, to the creator. It means: "He Who Walks Alone."'

'So what? I'm Irish too, and I don't know their old gods either!'

But it struck home, deep. That was when her change began. Soon she didn't look so neat or Christian any more, and when she did go down to the valley again, it was in the back of the VW bus that went all the way to San Francisco. And she hadn't come back for a quarter of a century. No wonder her mother and Clara never forgave her. Because she'd *enjoyed* herself. And in the city she'd done fine. Found work in a coffee house and a room in a pre-Quake Victorian on Dolores Street. She'd loved that room. Its window, crowned by a Moorish horseshoe arch, looked over stubby palms to Dolores Park, where chicanos hung out with their pit bulls. She never had trouble. Not then. She never knew what trouble meant until that terrible night in Arizona years later. She was too busy. After a year she enrolled at SF State, where she met Ben. Ben Bright. Jim was born a year later. Ben and she didn't marry – then. Marriage was for straights. Ben dropped out to look after Jim. She studied law and Native American history. As for Iron Dog, she met him again at the Black Hills International Survival Gathering in '79. And there she heard Russell Means of the American Indian Movement. She was working for an MA then: she heard Means say that degrees in 'Indian Studies' only turned Indians into 'mental Europeans'. He said a lot more, too. Back home she told Ben she was abandoning her MA. He was outraged.

'I've been looking after Jim just so you can turn soft on making money? Christ! You're looking at $100,000 a year five years from now!'

'Was Christ looking at $100,000 a year?' she demanded, knowing his real objection was to her activism. His radicalism had waned; he wanted to open a fashion store in Noe Valley – *Clothes Encounters*, he meant to call it.

She joined a law firm representing blacks, chicanos, filipinos – anyone off-white getting a bad bite of the American Dream. And they got married. A bad mistake. But they did it. For Jim, they said. He was six then, a sharp kid, the apple of her eye. Four years later she and Ben were barely speaking and Jim was running wild with a Mission gang. She got worried. 'What do you expect?' Ben exploded. 'You're never here and when you are you just denounce the System!' Then he suggested a vacation. In Arizona. He wanted to see a crafts wholesaler in Flagstaff about marketing Navaho medicine shirts, woven belts, you name it, in *Clothes Encounters.* 'Okay,' she said tightly, 'You want to do business. Me too. There's a conference at Oraibi. Six thousand Navaho and Hopi are being run off their land so utilities can strip-mine. You take a day off for me, I'll take one off for you.'

Ben agreed reluctantly. Jim just shrugged. 'Arizona? Sure, Ma.'

They packed the camping gear, got in Ben's new VW Rabbit, and drove. They never got to Arizona. On the way they stopped in Death Valley. Fifteen years later Jessica still can't face what happened there.

4.
The Fire Strikes

'Fifteen years, six months, and thirteen days, to be exact,' she told the blank tv screen mordantly, another hour gone and still nobody in the Rock Inn, nobody drinking, chalking up cues, feeding the juke or climbing into the Reely-Show booth her predecessor had imported from London England – though, if she'd heard right, it wasn't London England now; but London *Metropolitan* England, due to a crisis that split the Brits some years back – but so what: crisis was everywhere these days. So what? Shrugging, she finished yet another marguerita, hard rain still rattling the roof, her memories up against the edge beyond which they couldn't or wouldn't go.

That second night in Death Valley when the . . .

With an oath she hit the bar with her fist. Yet as she did she saw, as if he faced her, Jim's dark face in her dream last night, puppy-fat gone to show the leaner lines of the man he'd have become by now if only . . .

'Stop tormenting yourself,' she whispered, 'it's dead and gone!'

But it wasn't. Fifteen years she'd held it at bay. Now it was pushing again. Bad dreams. She eyed the empty bar. Why not lock up and go home?

She knew why not. Back to another lost night in an empty house with the country music station whispering now *Love Hurts* while she took a shower to wash off stains that wouldn't wash off? Back to her lonely bed to dream again? And what if Shasta blew while she slept? What if . . .?

'Come on,' she muttered, 'What if you ran and it didn't happen?'

She eyed the tv, turned it on, heard chatter about why skin cancer had doubled since 1990, switched to the Chico station even as a head urgently said: 'Now to Shasta for the latest. We hear that the evacuation of folk from Weed, McCloud, and other towns under threat has been completed . . . but let's learn the current situation from our man on the spot – Ron Byers!

Cut to a chopper above Weed, hovering in the shadow of Mount Shasta, infra-red lens panning from empty streets up to the sullenly smoking holy peak, ready to blow off two or three thousand feet of its 14,162-foot top just like Mount St Helens nineteen years ago.

'Below me the town of Weed lies deserted tonight,' rasps Ron Byers, his voice so taut it suggests he only took the job because if not he'd be out of work, 'and latest estimates suggest that we've got an hour or two before the big blow that's building up . . . I can tell you we're ready to get out the moment it looks like we'll need a choir if we hang about! You bet! Now here with me I have Doctor Ephraim O'Brien, who'll explain just exactly what we're seeing, and why we can say that within the next few hours we'll experience here an eruption from the – excuse me – guts of the earth to equal or even surpass Krakatoa in 1883!' With a shaky laugh he added: 'Hot stuff! You bet! But right now it looks like we'll be here a while longer before the action starts, so here's Ron Byers returning you to the studio for a message from our . . .'

And that was when everything changed.

'Pardon . . . me,' said a quiet, oddly-accented voice.

'What?' Jessica, shocked, jumped round from the tv.

'A beer, please,' said the man who'd come in unheard and unseen.

Jessica's mouth was suddenly dry. She turned down the sound. 'A beer?' she said, faltering, for something about him.

'Yes.' The stranger grinned. 'This is a bar? Yes?' Dumping his pack on the floor, he sat on a stool, stuck his elbows on the scuffed bar-top, propped an unshaven chin on the heel of his hand, and grinned. 'A beer.'

'A beer,' she said, staring back . . . then dropped her eyes, feeling struck and confused. She'd not heard the door open; she had sworn she'd never seen him before . . . yet there was something familiar about him that . . .

'Yes,' he repeated gently, the rain pouring down, 'A beer.'

'Any beer?' she asked, looking up to see nothing but his deep grey eyes. The rest of him was oddly blurred. 'I mean, do you . . .?'

'Any beer.' He nodded encouragingly. 'Just a beer, Jessica.'

She swallowed, again ducking her eyes as she uncapped a Coors. Pouring the half of it into a schooner, she set bottle and glass (both rattling in her unsteady grip) before the stranger. 'How . . . how do you know my name?'

He frowned. He took off his battered, eagle-feathered hat, and set it on the bar. She stared at it. Still frowning, he took a gherkin from the courtesy bowl on the bar, bit into it, and grimaced as if its sharp taste surprised him. He set it carefully down and took up the schooner in the brown sinewy hand of a man who'd lived outdoors all his life.

'I have a message from Jim,' he said slowly, gazing into the beer.

She froze, staring at him, the room about suddenly insubstantial.

'Jim,' she heard herself say, 'Who do you mean? Jim Who?'

'Your son,' said the stranger. 'Jim. Who went through the Gate.'

For a moment she thought she'd faint. Then, still gripping the bar, she leaned forward and shouted in his face: 'Get outa here! You cheap sonuvabitch! Who are you to come in here and give me shit like this?'

He didn't move. There he sat in drenched olive cape,

untouched beer and the eagle-feathered hat before him, grey eyes meeting her furious gaze.

'I am Pierre Belot,' he said, slowly and deliberate in his odd accent, and through the roaring in her ears she heard his every word as if each were a separate incident, a million years between each. 'I am not from this land or time. I come to say that Jim is well. He will see you soon – but not here, not yet. Jessica,' he went on as if reciting from an ancient book, 'tonight you will go to San Francisco, and later to London. You will not return here. You will join those who bring our Company down to Earth.'

Staring in consternation she saw his eyes crinkle into a warm smile.

'I ask you only to do what you were born to do,' he said gently.

'What?' The thick voice, she realized dully, was her own. Vaguely she saw shaking fingers grip the bottle of José Cuervo, spin the cap off, and start the marguerita mix again. 'But Jim's dead,' said her voice.

'No.' The stranger smiled. 'To you it seems he must be dead – since he went through the Gate in that place where . . .'

'The Gate?' she whispered, agonized by the hope she felt.

'The Gate.' He nodded. 'Jessica, there are many gates in this world – gates to other places and times. You saw Jim go through one of them.'

'What?' she cried again, still unable to face that terrible night. She shut her eyes, bit her lip. *Stop it!* she told herself urgently, *Don't let him do this!* 'You bastard,' she whispered, years of guilt welling up in her. 'Who put you up to this? Clara? My mother? If you . . .'

Tenderly he reached forward, and with a fingertip he . . . almost touched her hand. *Almost.* For, deliberately, he avoided physical contact.

Yet the shock made her jump. It was like touching a live wire. Her eyes started open. She stared at him. 'Who are you?' she whispered, her heart pounding so fast she feared it might overload and stop forever.

'I was a shepherd' he said gently, 'Until I tried one of the gates that join this world with others.' His voice was a caress; an erotic force; she felt it melting her. 'We who go through the gates,' the soft voice went on as the rain outside went on falling, 'need you who have not to bring us back . . . in time for the Shift. We must all fight the Beast. Do not blame yourself. It was not your fate to follow Jim. It was his to go, yours to stay. For we who go through these fearful higher gates . . .' – his laugh was harsh; now she sensed pain in this . . . man? – '. . . are lost if we cannot alert you to the threat and promise of the Shift. Do you know what I mean?'

'No!' Jessica muttered. She felt a crawling terror now.

'You are not stupid,' he appealed, his gaze piercing her. 'You know this world; how it has never been what those who live in it wish to see . . .'

'*What* do we wish to see?' she demanded, shaking.

'Where we all go,' said Pierre, and shrugged, 'Where Jim went . . .'

Then, surrendering, she let his eyes catch her back to . . .

. . . that morning so long ago, sun a giant eye peering over the wind-rippled dunes amid the arid ancient hills that rimmed Death Valley. That last morning she ever awoke with a glad and contented heart.

There was no *conscious* premonition.

It was only afterwards she knew she'd felt it coming.

It was just two nights since they'd left the Bay Area, driving east through baking heat to the Sierra foothills. The first night they'd camped high in a sequoia grove under Yosemite stars, lit a pine-cone fire that crackled and roared in the night, fried giant burgers and drunk a quart of Almaden, Ben vamping old Dylan songs on his Hohner until at last they'd turned in under the stars and the old moon's cockeyed gaze, sleeping bags warm, all happy for once . . . and no hangovers next morning as on over Tioga Pass they'd gone, twisted ancient bristlecone pines dark against gleaming snowbanks melting in the sun. Then down the huge bare slopes on the east side, Jim and Ben screaming exuberantly,

Jessica laughing with them all the way to the junction with US395 by the bare saltscapes of poor Mono Lake.

The day had grown hotter still as they cruised south past Mammoth Lakes; the epicentre a year earlier of quakes violent enough to shake cups off their kitchen table so far away in San Francisco. And on for hundreds of miles down the road they'd gone, continuous 10,000-foot Sierra walls to the west leaping from the bare plain, Ben on about how the pioneers must have felt a century earlier when, after struggling over mountains and deserts, salt-pan and sage-brush, they'd met this huge barrier of jagged peaks, and no easy way over at all. 'Sure,' Jessica had muttered tartly, 'No wonder when they got to California they wanted to kill injuns!' – at which Jim in the back, wearing his forty-niner's cap and chewing gum, had laughed raucously.

Ben had taken offence, sulking the next fifty miles to Bishop, where at the snowline they'd found sulphur springs, stinking but delightful, so that in them he'd regained his good mood. Jessica and Jim had exchanged knowing glances. Then on to Lone Pine, where, in the shadow of Mount Whitney (it looked just like in the Paramount movie logo) they'd eaten and tanked up.

It was late, but they'd agreed motels were out, so they took off east, past the salt wastes of Owens Lake, singing together as night fell and the stars shone, 'Death Valley or bust!' . . . and so on over more ranges and the Panamint salt flat, shining white under the moon, until at last they came 6,000 feet down to sea level, into the hot night air of Death Valley where, stiff and tired but happy, they found an empty picnic site complete with benches and trash bins in the desert by Stovepipe Wells.

Real sand-dunes stretched for miles in all directions. There was no movement and not a sound: the atmosphere was so surreal that, though Jim whooped as soon as he was out of the car, his voice scared even him.

'Don't go too far!' Jessica cried as he ran along knife-edged sand, Ben frying steaks they'd got in Lone Pine . . . and as night deepened the silence and stillness grew amazing. They spoke in whispers and left the radio off. Later Jessica went walking on her own with the ghosts; ghosts of Shoshone who'd lived here; ghosts of white pioneers who'd died here in ignorance of the water-holes . . . and Taikomol himself breathed in her, drawing her back to the beginning of things before Man or Bird or Beast were moulded . . . and no evil did she sense, no premonition of horror, only a huge ancient sadness.

And that night on the sand was awe-inspiring: the cloud-wreathed old moon shining misty-bright on white dunes marching in broken waves to the scrubland and hills lurking like bare primeval monsters, asleep yet maybe ready to awaken again if, thought Jessica just before she fell asleep, the Great Spirit should breathe the correct, huge, earth-shattering word.

Maybe, though she didn't know it, that was her first premonition.

Next day they explored a canyon. Through it once a river had carved its way down to a lake in the valley. In the canyon walls Jim saw what Ben told him were fossils, white against the horizontal bands of rock . . . and it was while staring at these eroded walls that Jessica became suddenly, fully aware of the vast forces which had formed them. This torn land, broken so many times! Global chaos, forgotten save in myth, was written in these tortured walls, and as they walked the canyon's winding gravel floor she grew so silent that Ben asked what was the matter and Jim – Jim plucked one of the little yellow flowers that grew in bushy clumps, and gave it to her.

'Here, Mum,' he said sadly, and his look said he knew how she felt.

She shivered. 'What's the matter?' Ben asked again.

'Let's get out of here,' she'd said, 'It's oppressive.'

Ben, who'd wanted to go on, shrugged. 'Getting hot, too,' he said.

So back they went, keeping an eye out for sidewinders, seeing none – but Jim suddenly shouted, and ran to pick up something black which –

'Don't touch it!' Jessica cried, her heart thumping.

'Aw, Mum, it's dead!' carefully picking up the dead tarantula,

Jim carried it back to the car, to Jessica's disgust (and now, for the first time, a hint of foreboding?) But when they started driving again, the bumpy road jarred it so much its legs fell off and Jim threw it away.

On through the waste (playing Ry Cooder and Talking Heads) they drove forty miles to the bizarre emerald of Furnace Creek's palm-oasis, where gleaming Winnebagos and fat Angelenos lumbered like satisfied dinosaurs. That was a shock. So were the baked dunes of Zabriskie Point further on.

The disaster came that night.

Later Jessica knew she'd felt it coming. She hadn't wanted a second night in Death Valley. She felt *watched*, much as she'd sensed the night before that those nameless hills watched them. Something waited. She knew this was stupid. When Ben and Jim overrode her, she made no objection. So as night fell they again camped on sand flats, at another empty picnic site with benches and trash-bins . . . and as they cooked supper the clouds began to gather and a wind began to rise – puffing, tugging, whispering.

The sky to the south blackened. The air grew electric; the wind too.

Then the lightning began. They were at the wooden-and-metal table, Ben ladling out the stew he'd made. It began flashing from cloud in the south. Thick white bolts fastening sky to earth, striking vertically down, four and five at a time. No thunder, only the wind, and an eerie murmur, as if the desert itself was coming to life – humming from every side even as they realized that the lightning was marching at them. Bugs crawled over the glass of the lamp on the table; their flesh tingled in the wind. Then Ben folded away his spectacles as he always did when he was tense. Jim held up his hand and gasped. 'Mum!' he exclaimed, 'my hand's on fire! And I . . .'

Abruptly he bit his lip and shut up, but there was a wild agitation on his face, a naked *fear* as he eyed the lightning-split night. She'd never before seen *fear* on her boy's face; it struck fear in her . . . but before she could ask him he'd turned to Ben. 'Could it . . . ?' he asked dubiously

Jessica and Ben exchanged covert glances.

'Maybe . . .' Jessica began, indicating the car.

'No,' Ben said quickly, 'Metal. Safer here.' He laughed nervously. 'In any case the chance of it hitting us is about as high as the chance of a . . .' Unable to find a simile, he ended lamely, '. . . not very high.'

'A kid at school got killed by lightning last year,' said Jim promptly, his voice excited. 'He was out on a golf course with his Dad, and . . .'

'Jim, don't!' Jessica stood up. 'I think we should . . .'

'And there was a guy playing baseball somewhere,' Jim interrupted her, 'He was out on the field, second base, someplace last year, and he got struck by lightning, right on the top of the head, and . . .'

'Jim, please shut up!' Jessica nervously cried, her whole body dancing and tingling with the electricity and the wild wind slapping.

'No, the point is he lived,' Jim rushed feverishly on, 'He had a burn-mark on top of his head, and a burn-mark on the bottom of one of his feet, and the chain round his neck and his belt-buckle were totally melted – he had burns where they melted – but he just went unconscious, totally, and woke up later in Emergency without knowing what had happened . . .'

'Is he the Bionic Man now, Jim?' Ben cracked, apparently in control of himself again . . . and they all laughed, Jessica too . . . but then they fell silent, watching as the dazzling bolts marched ever closer to them down the valley floor. *Do you think this is it, Jessica?* hissed the wind, *What does Jim hear us tell him? But don't worry, dear. It won't happen to you!*

As she shuddered Ben said, in an awed voice: 'This is really charged up. See how the clouds are changing colour over there . . . over the top of the hills . . . just going . . . pfft . . . pfft . . .'

'Maybe we shouldn't be sitting here.' Jessica nervously tapped the metal struts of the picnic table. 'Maybe we . . .'

'Aw, when it gets *here I* won't be sittin' down, I can tell you that right now!' Jim exclaimed, rubbing his hands together in a mad glee.

'Then where . . .?' she asked him tentatively.

'In the middle of the sand!' he cried. 'In . . .'

'Ben, maybe we should get out right now!' she cried, sure now that something dreadful was about to happen. 'We should turn on the radio in case they're telling everyone to get out of Death Valley . . .'

'The *radio*?' Ben demanded incredulously, 'You won't get anything on the radio in the middle of *this*! Hey, hey, now, just stay cool and . . .'

'I *am* cool, goddammit, I just think we ought to . . .'

'Oh, look at *that* one, Dad!' cried Jim – and Jessica saw his face stand out in sharp blue-white relief, and fear tore at her heart, for it was not Jim's face she saw, but a mask concealing something ancient and dreadful, something old when this valley was still young, something which . . .

Don't ever ask to see my face, Jessica, whispered the wind.

'Four bolts!' agreed Ben, impressed. 'Jee-sus H. *Christ*!'

The humming . . . the humming in her head was like a storm of maddened bees. She felt paralysed as the lightning flashed closer. She wondered if, when it came to it, she would be able to move at all.

Move to do what? a quiet cold voice inside her asked, *Jump aside and save yourself? Or grab Jim in the moment that it . . .*

'I can still . . . Gosh, I didn't even see that one!' Jim shouted, rubbing wind-blown grit out of his eyes as another flash struck the desert maybe three miles away, 'Dad,' he cried, his voice quavering, 'it's like we're in a *Galaxians* game, actually in the screen, no bigger than ants, and God or some huge space-giant's taking potshots at us.' His finger shot up at the sky. 'See him? He's pressing the button . . . right . . . now!'

And at that very moment – her heart pounded so hard that briefly she feared it would burst – the sky lit up blindingly. She heard Jim scream in triumph at the success of his prophecy; she saw his stark, uplifted face.

The look of chill expectation on it terrified her.

Then only after-images danced on her retinas as the wind swooped so hard it rocked the heavy hurricane lamp on the picnic table.

'It's veering away a little,' said Ben in the practical voice of a man firmly anchored no matter how desperate the crisis, 'I *do* think that . . .'

'Betcha five bucks he can't hit us!' Jim shouted, and stood up from the table so abruptly that metal plates clattered. Grabbing the lamp, he swung it in their faces, making them flinch and leaving them staring as, laughing wildly, he danced away from them into the night, further and still further, spinning now, swinging the lamp so that it threw his elongated shadow over the wind-whipped sand like the shadow of some wizened old shaman, chanting his challenge to the sky as he went – yet behind his incantatory voice and through the wind she heard his terror and knew he knew what was coming for him even as he tried to deny it.

'Betcha five bucks!' he screamed back at her. 'Ma! Betcha five bucks he won't hit us. Why're ya lookin' so scared, Ma? He's just some crazy ole asshole that can't shoot straight! An' even if he does hit us it'll just probably zing us through to another world like in *ET* or *Poltergeist* or something really weird like that, and . . .'

There was a blazing flash, the brightest and closest of all.

Jessica never heard herself scream as she felt the air burn, saw the fire from heaven earth itself blindingly not ten feet behind Jim where he danced. In that dazzling moment she saw her son, his arms waving above his head as the lamp fell from his hand. Crucified and flaming he danced amid the unearthly fire that fed on him; outlining and backlighting him like a pantomime demon king on a stage. She must have screamed again; certainly Ben did as the wind roared about them, tossing her hair so that coils of it slapped her face, hurling showers of grit and sand in their faces and into her wide-open, screaming mouth, for she was sure that Jim had been struck and killed, sure that . . .

Then all light faded. A black wing swooped over her and . . .

5.
Monkey Business

Fifteen years later she swam out of that horror to find herself gripping the Rock Inn bar, the grey-eyed stranger's gaze fixed on her, and the shock of his gaze told her plainly that he knew it all; knew everything that had happened that night, everything that had happened to her since . . .

She stared back. Her open mouth shut. His lips moved. She realized he was speaking. 'Jim was right.' She heard him from a long way; saw him grimace as if trying to . . . see it more clearly? Read her mind? 'He was hit, and they . . . how to say . . . *did* zing him . . . through the Gate to . . .'

'Who's *they*?' she whispered, wits in a spin.

'The Elohim,' he said calmly. 'The Shining Ones.'

It was too much. Tears spilling from her eyes, she backed up against the 2D shelf. 'Get away from me, you . . . vampire!' she cried in sudden fury, 'You came for a beer, so drink up and *go* before I call the law!'

Turning blindly, not looking back, she stumbled through the *Staff Only* door to the john, where she sat raking at her scalp with her fingernails as if to tear out the memories and throw them bleeding away.

But all she did was arouse them further.

For hours later she'd swum out of her faint. A still grey dawn grew over the desert. The wind had fallen. Silence sang in her ears. She lay on her back, knowing nothing . . . yet gripping her was a horror so intense and phantasmagoric that she thought: *Please God I'm asleep at home.*

But slowly she realized she was half-buried in sand which had drifted over her in the night, entering her mouth, ears, nose . . .

Sand? *Sand? Yes, Jessica.* Death Valley!

It came back. The lightning. It all came back. Jim!

'Jim!' She gagged on the grit in her mouth. Her head was pounding. She heard someone nearby moan. With difficulty she raised her head. She heard Ben cursing in a low, frantic monotone. 'Matches,' he was muttering, 'Where are those god-damned matches?' Blinking sand out of her eyes she saw him through her tears, dark in the grey light, crawling on hands and knees in the sand, his eyes tightly closed. But he was all she saw.

She began to laugh hysterically.

He raised his head but still didn't open his eyes.

'Fool,' she croaked, 'It's dawn now, you don't need matches.'

He stopped crawling; at last opened his eyes, and she wished he hadn't, for when he looked at her, it was with grief . . . and hatred.

'What did you do with him?' he rasped.

'What?' she asked feebly, 'What are you on about?'

'What did you do with our son? Where is he? Where's Jim?'

Ben had gone crazy, but he knew what he was talking about.

For they were alone in the desert. Alone with, some way from the table where they'd been sitting when the lightning struck, an oblong patch of dark, fused sand. Lying amid that fused sand, like a sick joke visiting card left behind as the only evidence that Jim had ever existed, was the buckle of the belt he'd been wearing when the fire came down from heaven.

And that was all. But now . . .? The *Gate*?

After a while she stopped attacking her skull with her fingernails. The memories, like escaped birds, were out. Insane questions were left. Exhausted, she went back to the bar, knowing she had to ask them. The stranger was still there, his beer untouched. Nobody else had come in.

'All right,' she said dreamily, 'What is the Gate?'

'Monkeys,' said the man who insisted Jim was alive; whose near-touch was like an electric shock. Rain still pounded the roof; the Coors sign still blinked on and off; on the 2D a talking head yammered soundlessly; on the street of the real world just feet away outside a truck swished past without stopping. 'Consider *monkeys*, Jessica.'

'Monkeys,' she echoed in a dull, strangled voice. Briefly she met his eyes . . . and a shock made her flinch. It felt like hot steel bands crushing her chest. Gasping, she stared down at the dim reflection of his face in the polished gloss of the bar-top. But even the reflection . . .

'What do you mean, monkeys? What about this . . . Gate?'

She felt his gaze shift off her. She sighed in relief.

'It is a question people must answer before the Shift comes,' he said, placidly eyeing his beer. 'Are we Spirit trapped in Monkey . . . or Monkey reaching for Spirit? Do we go *down* through gates, or *up* through gates? Or can we go both ways? Down *and* up?'

She said nothing. He looked at her.

'Your son is well,' he said quietly.

She caught her breath. She didn't dare face him.

'The fire took me too,' he went on, watching her, 'A long time ago. It has taken many. There are many gates, and at many levels . . .'

'Excuse me,' she heard herself say, 'I want to check something out.'

She twisted round and turned up the tv volume.

It was another late-night news broadcast:

'. . . Well, that's all from Shasta for now,' said the announcer. 'Now an item in from New Beirut. President Al-Khash of Hezbollah today warned Pope Peter – one-eleventh since the first Peter, for fans of prophecies by St Malachi – that if he endorses the proposal to enlist US and Russian aid in building

POP, the Papal Orbiting Platform, then, quote-unquote, "We will take steps to stop this infidel insult to the honour of Almighty God."

'Al-Khash, head of a hundred million Shi-ite Moslems, also today met the generals of his "Liberation" army at Izmit, only minutes from Istanbul. Reaction from other world leaders suggests that any attempt by . . .'

Jessica, heart pounding, turned it down.

'Okay,' she said wearily, 'You're no crazier than the news. So maybe you're really here . . . so carry on with the monkey business.'

But at his look she felt the bands round her chest grow tighter.

'No,' she said giddily, 'Wait again.'

She turned up the volume again:

'. . . the break we'll be back with items about New Zealand's immigration quota reduction; and how Dr Flora Menendez, Buenos Aires cytologist, today became the first human being to cycloplane the Atlantic alone; and also we have an item about the controversial so-called "Black Hole" experiment that MIT physicist Morris Abramel has claimed may well set off an uncontroll . . .'

She turned it off. She laughed breathlessly.

'I guess this news is by and for monkeys going *down* – right?'

'Yes.' Pierre leaned forward . . . and at his smile she felt herself melt. She blushed like a teenager. 'Old monkeys,' he said, 'can learn new tricks when they go through gates. Like me. Like Jim. Maybe like you too.'

It was then, numb, she realized: *He's glowing! And his . . .*

'I dreamed I saw him last night,' she said hoarsely, 'Jim, I mean.'

Parfait!' But as he said this Pierre frowned, as if at sad memory.

'Him and an old guy in a room with a Solomon Seal on the table; they were both dressed weird like in history movies,' she cried in a rush. 'He talked weird too, sorta like English but I couldn't . . . but there was a book on the table too; a latin title, *Monas Hieroglyphica*, I think, and . . .'

'The priest-tongue.' Pierre nodded. 'Was the old man a priest?'

'Don't you know?' She eyed the bar. 'You can read my mind, right?'

Shrugging, Pierre indicated the tv screen. 'When you think of Jim, your mind makes a picture I see as clear as the pictures on that.'

'Oh, great!' Angrily she began mixing another marguerita. But her eyes were still downcast. 'So tell me more,' she demanded. 'You walk in here and I never saw you but you know stuff about what happened that . . .' She stopped. Her reckless pouring of tequila faltered. She felt so dizzy. 'All this would make a shrink wail with delight,' she muttered. 'I'd say you're crazy, or I'm crazy . . . but . . .'

'But what?' Pierre asked quietly.

Steeling herself, she looked up and met his gaze.

'Show me!' she said, her teeth chattering.

'It is signs and wonders you want?' The stranger made a mock-sad face. 'Are you not a Christian, Jessica? Do you lack faith?'

She laughed sharply. 'Don't bullshit me!' she cried.

He laughed with her and not at her. His laugh was light.

'Very well. But . . .' – his smile faded – '. . . I cannot touch you.'

'Well, goddammit, who said I wanted you to touch me?'

His look stopped her. 'You misunderstand. You want *proof* of what I say about Jim. You want to see and hear him. So, I can show you! Yet for that there has to be touch. But, you and I, we cannot touch. We are not of the same substance. I have been through the higher gates and you have not; and what you see before you, though it *is* myself, Pierre Belot, it is not the body of the Pierre Belot that walked the hills from Roussillon to Flix seven hundred years ago, it is . . .' – he shrugged mournfully – '. . . But no matter. If you have from Jim something, that he wore, maybe, or . . .'

Seven hundred years? Shock jolted her again. *What is this?* But part of her knew . . . and wanted . . . and feverishly as she turned and felt in her handbag she said, 'Yes! I have something. I have . . .'

She found Jim's belt-buckle and pushed it over the bar, her eyes fixed on it and on the work-worn, calloused fingers that closed round it.

There was a . . . flash, a . . . scent of dry desert wind . . .

'Look,' cried a voice that echoed, 'And hear!'

There was a sense of being turned inside-out. A sense of . . .

Dazzled, she looked . . . and over by the pool table she saw . . .

Where she knew there was nobody she now saw the same high-cheekboned young man she'd seen in her dream the night before, standing not a dozen feet away, apparently as real and solid as herself.

Her mouth fell open. She felt utterly stupefied and unable to move, and yet a part of her mind that observed her own reactions remained clear, looking down, as if observing a play on a stage.

He's not really there, she told herself in disbelief, *But he is! That's definitely how he'd have looked if only he'd . . .*

It was impossible. She knew it was impossible. There was a roaring in her ears. She shut her eyes then opened them again. He was still there. In those weird clothes. Rough leather jerkin and leggings, handkerchief knotted round his grimy neck, black hair a tousled mess, his face ruddy with sun and wind. Sturdy and strong he stood facing that pale old guy in the black robe and skull-cap over the table . . . not the pool table but the table from her dream, the table with the Solomon Seal on it, and on the table lay the book with the latin name – it was all as it had been in her dream. They were in that dark room. Heavy wall-hangings, leather-bound books piled everywhere. And more. In her dream the periphery of the room had been vague. Now she saw clearly beyond them and the table a window of leaded glass that let in sunlight but which also distorted the view of what lay outside. She made out green lawns rippling down to a willow-fringed river. But that was peripheral. She shook her head in anguish but . . . still she saw them. Where the Rock Inn's pool table should be. And a third man was there too – a bearded, youngish, magnificently-dressed man. He wore a black, high-crowned, wide-brimmed velvet hat; the lace of his ruff was immaculate; his black full-skirted fur-trimmed robe was rich with gold brocade down the sides and round the hem; the sleeves of his black doublet were of silk, and the lace at his cuffs was as fine as that at his neck. His neatly-bearded face was narrow and pale, but sharp and intelligent.

All this she saw clearly – too clearly.

'What . . .?' she started to say.

'Quiet!' hissed Pierre. 'Look! Listen!'

Hardly daring to breathe, she did. And she heard them . . . and slowly she realized that they were speaking a weird English – nothing like the talk in Bette Davis Queen Bess movies, but – she realized she was understanding it.

The old guy in the moth-eaten robe and skull-cap seemed embarrassed.

'. . . So it is fifteen year, like,' he was saying in a sing-song voice to Jim (if it *was* Jim) 'since we, er, *found* you. It wass God's angels I wass seeking, yet yourself it wass found!' He laughed, high-pitched, nervous. 'No angel, Jim, you, eh? But *sent* by angels! Seen them both we have, eh? And hard you were to hide! For I am a public man who hath seen the Tower and near the block; my intercourse with hidden worlds doth scandalize fools who cry "demon" each time they take a shit, like! So. I must tell you, now . . .' – he turned to the magnificent man – '. . . why Milord Francis here and I put you out to common country grass where rumour could not stroke you with its poison . . . nor touch me with stake-bound rumour of you, it's true!'

'The good Doctor,' said the magnificent man, his voice energetic, his eyes hooded with an odd, sad humour, 'is a cunning man. Wise too. Now cunning and wisdom, though not the same, must not despise each other, for cunning is a raw beast that revives wisdom, while wisdom is the breath of the gods without which cunning remains bestial. So we must make ends meet as best we can.' And with a bow that came naturally out of the grace of his nature he turned to the young man. 'Now, young Jim, when you came to us, we concealed you safe, which is cunning, and taught you, which is wise. That is why we put you out at

Warwick with our friend Will. And now we can both see that Will has taught you well.'

But Jim – was it? – did not seem impressed. Striking the table with the heel of his hand he glared at the magnificent man.

'Oi do not see this, maister,' he cried hotly, his accent the thickest of all, 'Oi am no geck! Oi'd pash them as would bolter I wi' falsity.'

'Do not harrow yourself with that!' said the magnificent man, 'We are your friends. We speak no falsehoods.'

'. . . Jim, boy, we bring thee to London not slightly but since . . .'

'. . . the Doctor is counselled again by those that brought you . . .'

'. . . Indeed I am, Jim boy! And without mummery they tell me . . .'

'. . . that they desire ye, boy, to try the high door again . . .'

She saw Jim flinch; heard him cry as he drew angrily back:

'Oi'll not do that! It was sin and missed aim the first toim!'

'How speak thus of the Mystery?' the magnificent man chided him, 'What think you I am but another poor hidden one too! How can we greet our true family? Missed aim is opportunity to repair the poor shrunken heart of the soul that's lost in the miss! Do the cow-turds of Eden give ye such joy?'

'It is said,' she heard the country-boy cry, 'that when Christ cometh, *'e shall not find faith on the earth.* Why then ask Oi to return to that toim o' gallow'd folk where none lies easy? Why not thyself . . . Milord?'

That's telling the bastard! Jessica thought.

But the magnificent man was smooth.

'I born here, thou there,' he said easily. 'Master Bright, that which brought you among us now calls you forth again . . .'

'. . . At the Templar Round . . . at midnight . . . tonight, like!' the Doctor agreed, stammering anxiously; '. . . at the angel gate where the heads of mad saints grin and those who died on holy crusade are laid!' And at the young man's look he raised helpless arms. 'So my scryer saw! Why fear it?'

'An' if Oi doth not as thou sayst?' she hard that hot voice.

'It is not as *we* say,' said the magnificent man, 'but . . .'

'. . . those that brought you!' declared the unhappy Doctor . . . and Jessica hissed, suddenly aware that she saw the pool table through him. 'They that brought you now wish to return you whence you came!'

She saw Jim look for support to the magnificent man.

But he was fading. Jim was fading. The entire vision . . .

'Do not worry,' said another voice. 'Trust your visions. But be on guard against the Beast. You are chosen, and you must be tested, and soon you will go where you must and do as you must. Remember this, and all will be well. Forget it . . . and Jim will be sad. So will we all. Farewell.'

Jessica groaned. *I'm dreaming*, she assured herself, facing the unused pool table. For that was all she saw before her now. The emptiness of the Rock Inn. The rain still beating down. And nobody with her but the . . .

She turned, released from spell. But the stranger was gone.

The door – the door was still swinging.

'Asshole!' she cried angrily after him, 'Stringing me up with Jim-this, Jim-that, and . . . wait! Wait a minute, you crazy . . .'

But he was gone. Jim's belt-buckle lay on the bar-top.

She cursed, rounded the bar, ran for the still-swinging door, threw it open, rushed out after him onto the muddy rain-swept sidewalk.

He wasn't there.

Instantly soaked by the rain she peered up and down the empty street. The night was dark. Few lights lit the storefronts, the parked cars, the empty sidewalk. Sure, so tonight everyone was in, out of the dirty rain, plugged into their Reely-sets, now floating above Shasta's glare in the terrified company of Ron Byers, waiting for the big one to blow, wondering if maybe they should take off to somewhere safer than Asbill.

But he *was* here! she told herself. *He walked out only seconds ago.*

But she saw nobody. Nothing moved. And fear-chilled she stood, rain plastering her hair to her head, her sweatshirt and jeans to her body.

In disbelief she splashed round the corner to the parking-lot.

It was empty too. No cars. No stranger. Just rain.

'He can't just have . . . oh for . . .'

Shivering, she sloshed back past the door of the Rock Inn to peer down the weed-thick alley between the bar and the peeled white fence of the next property . . . and there . . . there amid rain-beat manzanita bushes for a moment she thought she saw a tiny violet will-o'-the-wisp that whirled and danced before her, making patterns that entranced and terrified her, for in them –

'*Jim!*' she screamed, not caring who heard, '*You're dead! You died fifteen years ago, and now you better stay dead, or . . .*'

Then the will-o'-the-wisp was gone too. She shut up. Nothing moved. Back to the Rock Inn she fled, confused and afraid, soaked and shivering.

You want pneumonia? she asked herself grimly. *So, Spook City tonight! So what? Go home!* And she turned off the lights. Then paused.

Trust your visions? San Francisco? London? The Beast?

Pocketing Jim's belt-buckle, she locked up and left. *You will never come back here,* whispered a voice. She turned. But nobody was there.

The rain had slackened. A rising north-easterly blew. Her hands shook so bad she couldn't get the key in the lock of her old yellow Datsun.

Cursing, she threw her head to the sky . . . and saw gaps in the cloud.

Through one gap low in the south east a brilliant star shone.

Then the gap closed and the star was gone.

She realized her hands had stopped shaking.

She got into the Datsun. It was manual, too old for the Grid, so she could only use it on back-roads, but she liked the old rattletrap anyway.

Slowly she drove out of town past the Chevron gas station, and was past the last streetlight before she realized her lights weren't on. With shaky care she followed the straight empty road south over the valley flats, past the Randolph Orchards to the Poh

Ranch. The wind like a big hand slapped and rocked the car; she was still so dazed that though doing barely thirty-five she missed her turn. Backing up, she nearly ditched before making the turn to bump uphill past dark tall pines twisting in the wind. Their weaving lower boughs, caught in her lights, confused her: she saw them as figures jumping onto the muddy, rutted track before her, waving their arms and trying to flag her down. 'Don't stop!' she cried in dreamy panic – then for one mad moment was sure she saw Jim's dead white eyeless face grinning at her. He was swinging upside down in the wind, legs hooked over a branch above the road. Teeth gritted, she put down her foot. The wheels spun in the mud, then gripped, and it was only as she bucked and roared under that branch that she saw – of course! – that Jim was just a tangled mass of creepers. Yet still she screamed, heart racing as she rocked round a final bend and past the woodshed to stall in the muddy yard by the porch of the run-down four-room tin-roof shingle-walled backwood house that she called home.

6.
Hot Water

Switching off the lights she stayed in the car, arms wrapped around her shoulders, teeth chattering, eyeing the dark house, *her* house, reluctant to enter it, for now, in the rising storm and after the madness of the last hour, it seemed no refuge at all; more like a lurking animal, watching her, waiting patiently. *Come in!* she seemed to hear it beg her, *Come in, light a fire, run a nice hot bath and have a little drinkie! Come on, Jessica! – pleaseprettyplease? Why be scared? You know me! Your home!*

'Yes,' she muttered, 'Why be scared? This is your home, Jessica! So stop this! Just get in there, run a bath and cool out!'

But when she opened the car door the wind instantly snatched it and blew it wide with a bang. She flinched, got out into the mud . . . and found herself staring at the sky. Thick cloud covered the hills to the north, but above the house and the pine-ridge to the south the sky was clear. Orion strode on high, and below and left of the Hunter, swimming in a clear field, that brilliant blue-white star she'd seen as she left the Rock Inn.

Sirius, she knew, obscurely troubled by the sight of it. Something she couldn't put a finger on. She set foot on her dark, creaking porch . . .

'Oh God!' she shrieked, jumping back. 'No!'

Then, shamefaced, she sighed and relaxed.

For a moment she'd been sure it was him again.

The stranger, sitting there in the old rocking-chair, eagle-feathered hat on his lap, just sitting waiting for her. Glowing.

And his voice in her mind, so clear with its funny accent:

'Yes, Jessica. Sirius. Where we have come from.'

But there was nothing and nobody. Of course not. And she was soaked and freezing. 'Bath,' she said fiercely, and ran out of the wind into the unswept living-room; turning on lights as she went. 'That's what I need.'

It didn't occur to her that she never took baths, only showers. Still shivering she poured a stiff shot of Old Crow. In the bathroom she ran hot water and soon, shrugging off wet clothes, stood naked in coiling steam, smiling now, for suddenly the house – *her house* – was her only friend. She yawned amid the warm, relaxing steam. *Thanks, house!* she thought, perching her drink by the tub, feeling a delicious weariness steal through her.

You're welcome, the house told her indulgently, *But won't you need the bottle too? That's a tiny shot there, and you need to relax.*

'Good idea!' Still smiling she skipped out for the bottle of Old Crow, ignoring a tiny voice that said: *Watch it, Jessica!* as she returned.

She shut the door behind her and set the bottle down on the tiles.

Draw the curtains too, suggested the house, *Don't you want to be cosy?*

'I do,' she agreed, and drew the print curtains tight shut, excluding the terrors of infinity. Then, yawning again, drawing the plastic shower-curtains tight behind her, she got into the bath, savouring the heat and stretching out with a moan of pleasure, settling ever deeper until her hair floated and only her nose and mouth and eyes were above water.

For a while she lay just listening to the wind rave through the trees, happy that it was outside and that she was snug so deep in the tub.

I'll drink to that! the house encouraged her.

'Good idea,' she murmured, reaching languidly for the glass. She took one sip, then another, and another, relaxing at last . . . but she couldn't forget what had happened. Or had it? A glowing stranger who'd read her mind and vanished . . . as mysteriously as Jim had vanished . . .? Oh God!

You just imagined it, the house suggested.

'Sure.' Eyes shut, she sipped again, and found the glass empty.

Have another! The whisper was so soft. *Go on! You need it!*

Dreamily she reached for the bottle. The chink of glass against glass failed to alert her. She put down the bottle but kept the glass.

'Yeah,' she said edgily, sipping bourbon, 'But he was there . . . he really was . . . and all that 'bout visions and going to San Francisco . . .!'

You imagined it, said the house. *The guy came in, but he was full of crap. The Coors sign behind him made him glow; he fed you a line and you bought it, and when he left you just didn't see him go. Right? Now relax!*

'Yes,' she slurred, numb now, floating in a clam warm sea, tendrils of steam forming twisting shapes before her as she sipped, the liquor burning down her throat. And now before her she saw Jim's ten-year-old face gazing at her through the steam. Tears ran down her cheeks into her open mouth.

Jim? she asked silently, *Did all that really happen? They took you?*

'That's right, Ma,' Jim told her, *'The Elohim zapped me.'*

She felt a choking sensation. *Ignore it,* soothed the house.

I couldn't stop it! she told him sadly, *I couldn't* . . .

'Don't worry about it,' said Jim. *'I'm fine now.'*

And your belt-buckle, she went on, a weight on her now, a smothering pain in her that she barely noticed. *Your belt-buckle, that was the worst of it. That's what I couldn't face. If only I'd been able to . . .*

'Go to sleep, Ma,' Jim soothed her, and she felt a tender pressure on her brow, stroking her, relaxing her into the warmth, *'Go to sssleep!'*

They said I killed you! she told him drowsily. The weight on her brow began to alarm her . . . but remotely: she was too relaxed to worry; too warm and heavy. *No body, you see, you just vanished, and Ben went crazy, and . . .*

'Go to sssleep, Ma . . .' Jim commanded, steam-face looming giant as the weight pushed her deeper, *'Jussst go to sssleep and everything'll be fine!'*

'Wha-ugh?' she bubbled. Terror seized her as the blackening face before her cracked into a triumphant grin that split its flesh. The weight increased; she heard mocking laughter; the empty glass fell from her hand and broke on the floor. *I'm drowning!* she realized, *GOD, I'm drowning!*

Then at last she began to fight; her hands groping from the water, her fingers scraping at tiles and shower-curtains, and still that cracking, peeling, fire-blasted face before her, and the pressure of giant slimy hands pushing her down as the voice boomed: '*Go to sssleep, Jessica! Give up! Let Go! No more trouble! No more pain! No more . . .*'

Your're not Jim! she screamed silently, *You're . . .*

'But be on guard against the Beast.'

Tricked! But he warned he! Where are . . .

Then before her she saw, pulsing in waves of light and dark that came and went to the violent beat of her heart, the stranger Pierre Belot.

'I was a shepherd,' he cried, reaching out to her with a crook. And even as she reached for it her fingers found the edge of the bath and held it; she pulled herself up against the weight; gagging and retching she got her head out of the depths as the voice of (*the house, the beast, her fake son*) roared: *'Give up! Shasta will blow! The Shift will shake this world and throw all you nasssty little creatures off it! See sensse! Give up!'*

But she was furious now. Heaving herself out of the bath, she ripped down the shower-curtains with a jerk as she rolled over the edge of the tub and fell gasping and sneezing onto the tiled bathroom floor.

For a while she lay, wind raving round the house which had just tried to talk her into suicide. *Of course,* she knew eventually, *It's not the house at all; but I'm not staying here any more!*

Then she was sick, retching again and again. In time, still sick and dizzy, she sat up. She crawled over, pulled the bathplug, watched water gurgle down the pipes, knowing she'd nearly gone down them too. 'How did I let that happen?' she asked wearily. But no answer came. She sensed only a faint, fading regret as, leaning against the wall, she stood. She pulled back the curtains and opened the window wide. Cold wind hit her, and with it the sudden strength of rage. 'I'm not going so easy!' she cried at the night. 'Do you hear me? You bastard! Whatever you are!'

But the wind just raved, and the stars just shone, remote and uncaring above the storm. Exhausted, she pulled on a bathrobe and shuffled to the kitchen with its week-old collection of unwashed dishes, mugs, and pans.

She stared at the banal domestic mess as if at a surrealist exhibit in a gallery. She saw it through a fog. Nothing to do with her. But . . .

'I mustn't go to sleep,' she told herself, very carefully.

Moving in slow motion, concentrating on every minor act, she started cleaning up. She played an old tape by Buffy St Marie. *'God is alive, magic is afoot,'* Buffy sang, as Jessica washed and scrubbed until at length the kitchen was sparkling clean. But outside the wind still blew, and the cold stars shone as weariness triumphed and she knew she had to sleep.

She fought it. The booze was still in her system. She had to throw up again. Then she began cleaning the living room.

You must sleep! Nervously she looked . . . and seemed to see Pierre Belot at ease on her settee. *Don't worry!* she heard him say, *It is all right now. No more danger tonight. Just sleep . . . and trust your visions!*

She yawned. She scowled. Then she grinned madly.

'I'm imagining you,' she said, and grew mournful. 'And I'm just a monkey going down . . . but maybe you're right . . .' – and so she went to her bed in the back room, walls bare but for a photo-collage of Jim; and nothing on the bedside table but a radio which, always turned to the all-night country station, was the only company she'd kept by night for more years than . . .

She sighed. *Poor girl!* cooed the house, *You're crazy with loneliness! Meeting strange men who don't exist, nearly drowning, acting like a . . .*

'Get lost!' she snapped, and the voice fell silent as automatically she reached for the Valium bottle – then saw it in her hand and grimly put it down.

'I sure as hell don't need that tonight,' she told herself grimly.

Dropping her robe over a chair, she shut the window, drew the curtains, turned on the radio, put the light off and slid between the sheets, and the tide of healing sleep came so fast that she heard no more than . . .

My mama's dead and my papa can't be found,
My mama's dead and my papa can't be found,
I an't got me nobody to throw my arms around.

Yon come the devil, gonna set this town on fire,
Yon come the devil, gonna set this town on fire,
'Low me a chance, come darkness, to bid this town goodbye.

. . . before the tide took her. Yet with the last flicker of wakefulness she wondered who the stranger really was, and seemed to see him, in the alley where she'd seen the will-o'-the-wisp. But he was no faint will-o'-the-wisp now, he was a pillar of blazing light, just like Jim that instant in Death Valley when the lightning struck. And now she saw Jim too, the older Jim, in the weird clothes. He stood in a dark place amid a circle of grotesque stone heads . . . and even as she watched he too was transformed into a blazing pillar – then he was gone, and she realized something, something about *Gates*, but . . . it was too late. The tide swept her away into sleep . . .

7.
Taikomol Returns

. . . until a spark stirs in that ocean, grows brighter, spirals up from primal depths up to realms of sensation; to needs, pains, fears and hopes all associated with . . . a form, a . . . body. Yet it remains latent until –

There's a *sound* – a yip, a wail, a bark – sudden and sharp. Groaning, head aching, Jessica opens her eyes – and at what she sees sits up with a gasp, a start.

I'm dreaming! I'm still asleep! But I'm awake too! She knows it. That's the first of many strange things.

She's in bed in her room. At night. No lights on. The window's open. The curtains too. *How that can be?* Stars shine bright through the window and there's no moon . . . but the room isn't dark, and, though a freezing wind tosses the curtains, though she's naked, she's not cold at all.

Because of the light!

The violet glow dances from every surface. Her body's alive with it! So too sheets, blankets, pillow; walls, carpet, ceiling; the oak bureau in the corner; the wicker chair and robe on it; the bedside table; switched-off lamp and switched-on radio on it. All shimmering and dancing! *'Mamas, don't let your babies grow up to be cowboys,'* Willie Nelson croons unheard as open-mouthed she gazes through the window at the brightest star.

Blue-white it blazes low in the south east between the dark silhouettes of two tall pines, their crowns ducking and whistling in the wind as . . .

Something moves at the foot of her bed.

Two bright red eyes, watching her.

Bright, red, knowing, intelligent eyes.

Her heart leaps. Her nostrils flare at the foetid smell. *'You let the Beast fool you!'* whispers a voice. She remembers terror. Drunk in a bath.

'Who are you?' she cries, 'What do you want?'

Then another movement lets her eyes grasp the shape to which those eyes belong . . . and seeing who it is she knows with sudden amazing joy that she's found the dreamtime of her vanished people, the Ukomno'm, the Yuki.

'Coyote!' She fears her heart might burst. 'Coyote!'

Coyote grins. He yawns, red tongue lolling, red eyes steady on her. He stretches, sits up on his haunches, yawns again . . . then turns and pads to the open window. There he stops, looking back . . . waiting . . . grinning . . .

'I'm dreaming,' she says, amazed, 'But I'm awake too, ain't I?'

Coyote says nothing. Coyote grins, and the bright star burns.

'You want me to follow you?' she asks, 'Where are we going?'

Coyote says nothing. Coyote grins, and the bright star burns.

'You *are* Coyote? Who walked with Taikomol in the beginning?'

Coyote says nothing. Coyote grins, and the bright star burns.

Fear returns. *Follow him and I'll never come back . . .*

Yet another voice says: *If you don't, you'll never find Jim.*

And though she never heard it consciously, it was then Willie Nelson was interrupted by a radio voice which, grave but shaky, said:

'All you guys under a hundred miles from Shasta who haven't got the hell out already are advised to run – *now*! She's gonna blow, an' it won't be no picnic! This applies in particular to those of you living south-west of Shasta – meaning Trinity, Humboldt, and Mendocino Counties! The wind's coming straight outa the north east at plus forty-five knots. Wanna get buried in hot ash? So move it! NOW! Y'heah? Just git the hell out!'

The desperation in the voice said it knew too well that its late-night constituents were not the sort to heed any warning from anyone or anywhere if it meant abandoning their land. Indeed, the item immediately after the warning was a live call from an irate listener in Eureka. 'Hey, if I want News, I tune into News. So drop that Shasta shit an' play the music! An' why doncha give us some Charlie Rich? I dig that good oldtime stuff.'

'Listen, friend,' the voice tried, 'if Shasta blows like they say she's gonna blow, tomorrow there won't *be* no more music from this station!'

The fan laughed. 'Tomorrow's a long time! Play the music – right?'

'Right,' the man on the radio wearily agreed, 'Charlie's comin' up – but first we got a track from Waylon already lined up . . .'

But Jessica's already following Coyote into the hills.

For even as she slid out of bed Coyote turned and padded through the solid wall under the open window, vanishing through it like grey smoke as on the radio Waylon Jennings started into 'T for Texas'. But she heard none of it. She was staring, amazed, at the spot where Coyote had vanished.

What's the big deal, Ma? a voice whispered. *In the subtle body we can all walk through walls. Your turn now . . . or are you chicken? Come on!*

So with Waylon fading behind she follows Coyote into the wall, her eyes fixed on the bright star . . . and finds the wall as thin as mist. And as she goes floating through it she knows she's leaving forever the daily routine of mail-order catalogues, Willie Nelson, late-night movies, cheeseburgers, income tax, mid-life crisis and Christian censure – leaving behind whatever the man on the radio's on about.

Exhilarated she enters the wailing, luminous, freezing night.

Free at last! Free of gravity, the pains of the flesh! Spirit-light! Yet, though subtle now, she still has a body, a personal form, for she feels chill wind against her skin, freezing mud under bare feet – though not as *cold* or *wet*, *hot* or *dry*, but as vital energy. She joins Coyote by the chicken-run where he grins as the hens in their shed all squawk in alarm. *Not chickens we're after tonight, eh, chicken?* – and she laughs as he turns and starts uphill into the windswept forest towards that star; laughs and follows Taikomol's agent into the shining night, past windy stands of pine, madrone, and black oak; all ablaze with inner fire; every bush and shrub and tree glowing as up, up, up they go. Behind, late lights shine in Asbill, miles away on the valley floor – but above! Glowing ridges, sharp against the stars! Stars blazing, shifting, dancing in her mind! And the planets: Jupiter, Mars and Saturn, humming in her too as she follows Coyote through the wild night, as strange voices whisper in her. *'Space is not empty!'* they sing, *'It's us who are lean!'* And she laughs, sure Coyote knows what he's doing and why as he leads her high above the valley, dim Coastal Range peaks rolling away to north and east as the forest fails and bare higher slopes beckon – but Coyote keeps on, and she knows he takes her to the rocky eagle-high seat where old Taikomol sits, white hair tossed by the storm-winds, speaking to a world that no longer listens. Now the world's naked and bare and mythic about them: now the familiar forms of things dissolve and shift as ahead Coyote pauses, looks back . . . and in his red eyes she sees not Coyote but that stranger who entered the Rock Inn unseen and unheard; who insists that Jim's alive and that she has to go to . . . and she sees her sorry self behind the bar, drowning in angry marguerita̧s, Pierre Belot telling her gently: *'For we who go through these fearful higher gates are wasted if we cannot alert you to the threat and promise of the Shift.'*

What did he mean? The stars press down with painful urgency. *Wake up!* And the brightest, Sirius, shines with greatest urgency; with a warning she can barely grasp, that she can picture only as chaos and terror.

(The world tumbling head over heels through space!)

'Taikomol!' she screams at the gale as Coyote reaches the rocky summit of the ridge where he flops and grins, red tongue lolling – and as he does his form shifts . . . she hears a river running; sees him turn into a huge dog with three heads and terrible serpent tongues; she hears desert wind wail; sees him change again, into a black jackal, tall ears like antennae at the stars, and she knows it's not Coyote but Egyptian Anubis (*But we're one and the same,* his red eyes tell her, *From Sirius we come, and deep in your old mind, woman, you know it . . . for I smell water in the desert where none else find it: I guard the gates that protect you from the depths that drive you mad if you cannot face them – but now you must face them: the Shift is due: you have no time left! Wake up now, or die!*) that she sees . . .

. . . and she sees . . . and hears . . . and feels . . .

. . . the shining eye of the bright star gazing at her . . ..

. . . a shaking, a shifting, a shivering that tears her apart as . . .

. . . the bright star (Coyote's eyes?) suddenly *jumps*!

Shimmering rivers of fire hiss over the heavens . . .

She sees a shining, transformed, but familiar fact that cries: *Ma! Ma! We're coming back, all of us who went through the Gates!*

And again Jessica sees the dark place where Jim blazed. He stood in a five-pointed star chalked on flagstones; the star was also ablaze; beyond it human shapes lay prone on the flagstones; all wore armour with shields and scabbarded swords strapped to their left sides. The feet of some lay on curled-up recumbent hounds. And beyond them (she moaned) a vast circle of grotesque heads leered and pulled obscene faces at her. It was only gradually she realized that they – men, hounds, heads – we all made of stone; that the forms on the ground were effigies; that the heads were set in head-height niches round the circular wall of the place. And in shadow to one side (she had to squint, the fire consuming Jim was so intense) she saw the two men she'd seen with him in her dream last night, and again by the pool table in the Rock Inn tonight when Pierre Belot had held Jim's belt-buckle. They stood under a rounded arch, the magnificent man in his rich velvet and the Doctor in his shabby black robe . . . and she remembered . . .

'. . . *At the Templar Round . . . at midnight . . . tonight, like!'*

But the blaze was so bright that she saw little else even as –

'Jeesuschristlookatthat!' Ron Byers cried to thousands of anxious folk in Northern Calfornia as Shasta at last broke loose, 'Aw *shit*, man, look – at – *that*!' – and those tuned in via Sensory Identification circuits knew his fear was no media fake; they felt it too. *'Jeezus get us outa here!'* he wailed at the pilot of the chopper in which he and Doctor O'Brien (his screams also audible) hovered too close to the rainbow fires bursting from Shasta's long-dormant summit – unfolding flowers which took at least ten seconds to reach the chopper, turning it and its human cargo into a ball of flame that hit the streets of Weed just twenty seconds later.

Ron Byers broadcast (though not intelligibly) all the way down . . .

All over the state people ran for their cars, suddenly realizing that it wasn't just a show; they had two or maybe three minutes before . . .

The north-east wind was blowing hard as millions of tons of red-hot ash erupted . . . as in her bed Jessica stirs in awe, for Taikomol has revealed his reawakened self in all his blazing glory . . . and Coyote grins at her from the mountain-top, sky blazing with sulphurous veils as the bright star dances, warning of the Shift . . . and then she sees a face in the sky, the face of an unknown woman . . . and she awoke muttering a name, and kept muttering it as she pulled on clothes, grabbed her bag and credit cards, checked she had Jim's belt-buckle, ran out to her car, and she drove and drove from Nome Valley beneath the lurid fire-raining sky.

'Diane!' she cried as she drove, the radio babbling disaster reports. 'You must find Jim. You must!' And she had no idea what she meant.

But 6,000 miles away, and two nights earlier . . .

8.
The Church of the Second Coming

. . . even as Met English police raided Radio Shangri-La, a grieving wild man in tartan rags stood raving a foot from his final leap off the crags of Arthur's Seat, the extinct volcano lurking bleak and raw a thousand feet above the wintry hard-walled Yuletide streets of Edinburgh in Scotland.

With his ugly black-bearded face and barrel-like body and roaring voice he looked like a Reely actor playing Rob Roy as he trembled at the very edge of the drop over Salisbury Craig, the loose end of his grimy old plaid whipping wild in the wind, one hand clutching a red bonnet to his head, the other shaking a claymore at the frost-sharp consumer nightlights of Princes Street a mile away. Sheepskins were tied round his legs; on his feet he wore rawhide brogues; from his back hung a round ox-hide targe; over his saffron shirt the plaid was gathered at the left shoulder by a big silver buckle . . . and over his right shoulder was slung his sole concession to twentieth-century gear – a bulky olive-green army-style kitbag. 'Fook aff!' he was roaring madly at the mocking voice he heard in the wind. *'Jump, Bobbie, Jump!'* it cried at him as amid the shining lights so far below he saw the flashing blue turret-lights of police cars . . . and through the wind he heard their sirens wail, at which his suicidal rage reached new heights. For it was two hours since word had reached him in his Duddingston hide-out that Calum (that bastard!) had shopped him; that the law was close. With crazy bravado he'd donned his battle-gear and got out by a back window into the close even as they surrounded the house and the megaphone bellowed: *'Robert Aird, we have you surrounded! It's no use! We know you're there! We know you did the Gruinard job, so come out now, nice and slow!'*

'It wisnae murder!' he'd wanted to roar, *'It wis mercy, tae put the puir bastards oot o' their agony! Hell, it wis my ane brither asked me!'*

But he was no fool, he'd run silent, keeping to the shadows, wind and rain and darkness helping, until up on the bare heath of Arthur's Seat he'd lost the pursuit . . . but with every higher step the deeper grew his grief and sense of injustice, for he knew they were bound to get him, meaning show-trial and the gallows, but worst of all meaning the bastard running-dog media damning him as a lunatic and crowing that the Knights of the Purple Heather were finished. Briefly he'd considered heading south and losing himself in the jungle of Metropolitan England – but with the word out and his build he'd not get far. Anyway, what man would hide in Satan's lair?

No. There was only one way out.

No way! No way are they taking me alive!

So with frozen heart he'd climbed these crags that tumbled in precipice to the west; and now he stood on the edge, vaguely aware he was out of his mind, shaking his sword and shouting at the wind, at the lights of polite, stuck-up hypocrite Edinburgh. *'Jump, ye murderin' shite!'* mocked the wind. Strangely, it had his own voice. *'That wis twenty human beings ye killed!'*

'Murderin'?' He laughed; but it was a painful laugh, full of trembling guilt. 'Nivver! I did whit the warrior does for mortally wounded comrades so they winnae fall intae enemy hands! Puir bastards! My brither begged me! Called me frae the clinic. *"I'm HIV Positive, an' they're no lettin' me oot, they're sendin' me tae fookin' Gruinard!"* he said. *'Bobbie, help me!'* So I did!' he cried with tears in his eyes, 'An' I'm no sorry! I ken ye, ye Lord o' Illusion an'

Despair, an' I'll fecht ye tae the end! For I hear the sound of a mighty wave,' he bellowed in his dismal rapture, 'I see a great fire comin frae heaven to sweep ye awa'!'

'But folk wi' AIDS have tae be put awa' safe!' the wind whined, amazed. *'Bobbie, ye cannae jist blaw 'em up an' hope tae get awa' wi' it!'*

'So stick 'em on an isle polluted wi' anthrax an' let 'em rot there, eh?' he shouted, brandishing his sword at floodlit Edinburgh Castle, up on its grim height the far end of Princes Street, 'An' ye say whit I did's nae mercy?' He spat at the Castle. 'Yer argument's fake! There's the proof of it! Keep yer fookin Tunes o' Glory! Tunes o' the Beast is whit they are! Kill for Christ! Kill for Money! My Country Right or Wrang – ye name it! It's a' the same. Ye're a fookin' plague on the human soul, an' ye think since folk dinnae believe in ye nae more ye've got us a' wrapped up! But I ken ye! I see yez! Ye bastard son o' the Nephilim! – oh, aye, I ken aboot that. It'a a' in Enoch, though ye got him took oot o' the Bible whan ye took o'er the Church in the name of Order! Or*dure*, more like!'

Yet as he raved at the night he was obscurely wondering if maybe it was just himself he was raving at, and he shuddered, his mind tumbling over the years which had brought him to this, standing here on the edge of the Big Drop, wailing at the wind, at the lights of a flint-hearted city ruled by lawyers, at the Beast he saw lurking in the sick hard heart of history.

Suddenly the wind changed and gusted violently, sending him staggering to the edge, the tears of rage flowing down his cheeks into his beard.

'Ye daftie!' cried the wind, cried the Beast, *'This is the only wurld there is, man, and it's MINE. Whit are ye wantin' onyway?'*

'Justice!' Bobbie panted, 'Nae more than simple justice!'

'Justice?' mocked the wind, *'So jump, Bobbie! Fooked up and now ye cannae find the guts to jump! So gie us justice. Do us a favour. Jump!'*

And his fury turned against himself.

'Oh, right enough, get on wi' it, Bobbie!' he cried derisively, heart constricting as he felt himself tense. 'Dae it now, ye stupid . . .'

It was then, through the wind from below, he heard the woman scream.

It was an hour or so earlier and two miles north-east of Arthur's Seat that the thin middle-aged woman had got off the bus by the stormy Portobello sea-front. Nondescript in an old brown coat over sweater, jeans, and black wellington boots, her face – pale, pinched, but set in a grimace of anxious determination – was framed by a faded brown woollen shawl from which, as she left the bus, the gale began tugging strands of tired grey hair.

Head bowed, she started up a long, potholed, badly-lit street ankle-deep in slush; its cracked uneven pavement unswept in weeks. No cars came by as she passed derelict factories, their rusted gates awry, their windows black broken eyes. It was years since they'd been functional, but at least they offered a windbreak . . . protection lost when at last she left the ruined estate to find herself at the seafront, on a wet concrete promenade against which wind-driven waves crashed in from a wild North Sea. Here the gale's full force hit her, making her gasp as it swept away over the Craigentinny Links the far side of the road. She paused by a streetlamp's tall stained iron stalk; with gloved, trembling hands gripped the promenade's cold metal rail. The lamp, like others up this road that bisected shoreline and golf course, was unlit. Only in the distance, near her destination, did a light gleam, so weak it barely showed the way. For with the recent foul weather and the huge demand for power the city council, at its wits end, had cut down street-lighting in all but the wealthy commercial areas of the city.

Frowning at that distant light, she looked doubtfully back the way she'd come, then up into the wild night sky, muttering – but what she said was inaudible even to her, for the gale snatched her words and threw them away over the links before losing them in its own whistling scream.

'. . . but it's months since I last . . . what if Gussie won't or . . .'

The freezing wind was exhausting her. She hadn't eaten well in weeks; every step was a trial. Yet on she struggled towards that dim light until in time she was near enough to make out the stone building on the sea-front beyond it. It was then the car, an old Ford Orion, came up behind her, but she remained unaware of it even when it stopped a few yards further up the road. All her attention was fixed on the building ahead as if sight of it alone might give her the strength her legs lacked. But as she passed the car the woman driving it rolled down the window and called out: 'Going to the Church, hen? Want a lift before you catch your death?'

Startled, she swung, nervously squinting, unable to see.

'The Church?' she stammered. 'Yes . . . thank you!'

I know her! the driver realized, puzzled – but only when the gaunt bent figure crossed the headlights on its way round to the passenger door did recognition strike. 'Diane?' she asked disbelievingly as the shivering woman got gratefully into the car. 'It's not you, is it? Diane Joyce?'

The woman sighed, and said in a thin, edgy voice:

'Well, if it's not me I don't know who it is.' Her brittle laugh made the other woman nervous as she asked: 'Is that you, Frances?'

'Who else?' Frances Ord laughed too as she drove on, but falsely.

Diane Joyce! she thought. *Well I never! Won't Gussie be glad!*

'Yes, it's me! But *you*, dear? Where have you been? It must be . . .

'Four months,' said Diane, still edgy. 'I last came in August.'

'But why stop away? And no word to anyone! We've been worried!'

'I had to keep it to myself.' Diane locked her gaze on the building ahead. Cars, none new, were parked under the lamp. 'Until now. Tonight.'

'Keep what? You've been poorly?' Frances, fair and freckled, eyed the woman beside her sharply. 'You don't look so . . .'

But Diane demanded: 'How's Gussie and her . . . husbands?'

'Oh!' Frances, shocked, tried to laugh. 'Still chattering away!'

Diane sighed. 'How was she when I stopped coming?'

Frances parked grimly. 'She called it betrayal. We got a lecture on loyalty from Iain when she found out you'd changed your number.'

'I had to.' Seized by coughing, Diane bent double. When it was over she added: 'She had my address. She could have visited. Any of you could.'

'Gussie's a little like the rest of us,' said Frances acidly. 'Maybe you hurt her. Listen . . . you're not exactly *persona grata*, and if . . .'

'Forget it.' And as Diane opened the door lamplight fell on her worn face and she turned with a look that took Frances utterly aback. For ever since Frances had first met this timid mouse of a woman and heard her weird tale of how years ago her husband and daughter had vanished, literally, into thin air, Diane's eyes had been veiled. No entry. But now Frances saw fire in those eyes – fire of a sort she'd met too often in spiritualist circles – the fire of obsession. 'The subtle world's shaking,' Diane said softly, 'The Shift's coming. Tonight Gussie must stop playing the fool.'

'What?' Frances groaned inside. 'What are you on about?'

'You'll know soon enough.' And Diane got out.

Frances locked the car and followed the thin, shabby woman through wind and slush to the wooden door of the two-storey grey stone building.

The door was shut, but chinks of light showed under it. Over it, dimly visible in the lamplight, was a hand-painted wooden sign, red on white:

CHURCH OF THE SECOND COMING

Come unto us, ye who are weary
and heavy-laden

EVERY TUESDAY AND THURSDAY AT 8 PM

'Yes,' Diane repeated, her smile too bright as Frances joined her, 'Soon enough. Tonight, Frances, those on the subtle planes will . . .'

She gasped and bent double, torn by violent coughing again. Wiping tears from her eyes she straightened up, opened the door and went in as – *as if to the stake*, thought Frances, abruptly seized by that ringing in her ears, by that sense of vertigo which infallibly (for in a former life, she was sure, she'd been one of the *taibhsearachd*, the seers) warned of dire events to come . . . and she wasn't surprised to find herself trembling as she followed Mrs Diane Joyce into the Church of the Second Coming.

And the first person Diane saw was Gussie Farquhar.

9.
The Seance

She entered that cheerless, cream-painted foyer with its cheap tinsel Christmas decorations and smell of paraffin from heaters which had never managed to live up to their name, and it all came back.

About a dozen folk, most elderly and badly dressed, milled about in the foyer, and as she came in she saw Gussie beyond them, in the corner by the coffee machine, talking to an old man in a blue serge suit that looked as if he'd bought it with coupons on Demob Day in 1945 and worn it ever since.

At first Gussie didn't see her, but others did, and she knew by their looks that there was trouble ahead. She breathed deep.

Once this building had belonged to the Closed Brethren, a puritanical fishermen's sect still big in north-east ports like Aberdeen and Peterhead. Their joylessness still clung to the place, though the Church of the Second Coming (Director: Mrs Augustine Farquhar) was unaffiliated to any religious body. A registered charity, it was part-funded by Lothian Regional Council as a refuge for the elderly disabled, twenty of whom lived in several cold rooms behind the cold hall used by the flock. Their conditions nourished fortitude: a year ago anonymous complaint (rumour said Mrs Joyce was behind it, which was why she'd stopped coming) had led to investigation of Gussie by Environmental Health and the Scottish Inland Revenue. Survival of the Church's funding was due, said rumour, to Gussie's third husband Mike, the Assemblyman for Portobello . . . who, though fiery in Assembly, was said to be putty in Gussie's hands; indeed was said to be going the same way as poor Iain (Name in the City) and poor George (Glasgow gynecologist) before him.

Such talk was banned in the Church. Cots in cold rooms beat cardboard under bridges. As for talk that Gussie preferred her husbands dead . . . well! Everyone knew Iain and George were happy Beyond, that Gussie was in loving communion with them. Every Tuesday and Thursday (except August, when she shot Iain's moor and fished George's Spey beat), prompt at 8.30 she set her large blindfold bulk down on the Chair. To Iain (Tuesdays) and George (Thursdays) she always turned as the lights dimmed and deep in trance she entered the shining worlds beyond mortal existence. Generous and loving in life, they were no less now in the Beyond. Through Gussie Iain advised the flock on matters of tax and inheritance; George consoled those seeking news of their own dear departed. Mike's role (when he went Beyond), gossip was sure, would be the urging of holy war against the English.

All this Diane resentfully recalled as she stood staring at this place where she'd spent so many Tuesday and Thursday evenings these last nine years since the death of Sam's father. She'd come north to Edinburgh to nurse him after Sam and Chrissa had 'gone'. Yes, it had been her refuge, a very present help in trouble . . . but as for Gussie Farquhar . . .

It was then (Frances, standing behind Diane, saw folk staring at Mrs Joyce as if at a ghost), that Gussie sensed the tension. She turned from the man in the blue serge suit . . . and her lips parted in shock.

A large rosy-cheeked woman, Gussie was made larger by her assumptive style (an orchid in her white bouffant hair) and by the flowing tent-like green silk robe that rippled about her as she started, eyes widening.

'My goodness!' she exclaimed, 'is that . . .?'

Diane felt her anger. Then Gussie Farquhar composed herself. She put on a smile and sailed forward . . . and Diane steeled herself as the Matriarch of the Church of the Second Coming, dark eyes gleaming, bore down and swept her up in an over-scented embrace much more possessive than welcoming.

'Diane! After all this time! We thought we'd lost you to the Outer Darkness! My dear, you don't look well! How can we help you . . . dear?'

Without compunction Diane twisted out of the embrace. A silence fell. Everyone stared. They saw Mrs Joyce hold Gussie's gaze until (Frances was as amazed as everyone else) Gussie stood back, looking confused.

'Help me?' Diane smiled thinly. 'It's the other way round.'

'Why are you here tonight?' Gussie demanded, breathing hard.

'Something has happened,' Diane murmured. 'Something . . . wonderful.'

'And we should credit your private fantasies?' Gussie barked.

'Tonight you will,' said Diane simply, and to Frances she seemed quite luminous as she looked about, meeting face after face in a steady way that was new to her. 'Because with me here They'll tell you.'

'Who's "They"?' insisted Gussie in a steely heretic-hunting voice.

'Those who'll help us if we help them.' With a wintry smile Diane said deliberately: 'I mean those who've left this world for the world of the Elohim, to prepare for this time of world crisis – this time of the Shift. They're ready to return now . . . my husband and my daughter among them.'

She's challenging Gussie on her own ground! thought Frances, as aghast as everyone else. Only later could she admit that she'd thought Diane up to no better than a power-game. Which is what Gussie tried to make out.

'You think you can just walk in here and take the Chair, eh?' Gussie was flushed. Only later Frances realized that *fear*, not fury, moved her.

'Not at all,' said Diane, and her look told Gussie: *I know what you fear. I've been there. Have you?* 'I'm sure they'll speak through you.'

Gussie's fixed smile hid her sudden doubt . . . for as she met Mrs Joyce's eyes she knew something – she couldn't tell *what*, but *something* – in the woman had changed, radically. Whatever it was, she could not, as she was accustomed to doing, beat it down by sheer force of bullying personality.

'Well! she said tightly, turning on her heel. 'Maybe so. But it's time! The Inner Planes call us. Come along, everyone! Come along!'

The wind was blowing harder as Diane followed Gussie into the hall.

About thirty people waited, seated on shabby blue canvas tube-frame chairs in rows facing the dais at the far end of the cold draughty hall. In her coat Diane sat alone at the back as Gussie's sparse flock – grey heads bowed, several noisily blowing noses or clearing throats – filled the front rows. A few were under fifty. Most were what years ago had been called pensioners. State welfare provision being a thing of the ignorant past, the old and incapable now had to rely on charities like the Church of the Second Coming, despite a majority on the Scottish Assembly of delegates belonging to what in Scotland still anachronistically called itself the Labour Party. It was the case everywhere else too. With seven billion people crowding the globe, human life came cheaper every day.

Yes. Diane told herself grimly, *It's time for a change.*

Ignoring her, Gussie flowed to the Chair on the dais. She nodded at stout Mrs Beattie the deaconess, who dimmed the lights. The hall seemed to grow colder still. Wind keened through creaking windows. The linen blinds rolled down over the windows flapped like mad birds; white candles in brass brackets on the dais and along the walls flickered wildly. Council grants, Gussie's pocket, or both, did not include double glazing or curtains. Some of the candles had blown out already. At least the draught dispersed the reek of paraffin fumes from the ineffective heaters.

Only Gussie ignored the cold. On the dais by the ornate Chair with its scrolled walnut arms, crested back and plush blue velvet seat she stood, her operatic bulk tented in flowing green, candles flickering round her as the storm raged . . . and Diane felt drawn back, as if to a rejected nursery.

Shocked, she realized how far she'd grown from all this.

She sighed as Gussie held up her hand for attention.

'We'll begin as usual . . .' – Gussie's boom shamed the storm – '. . . with a hymn. Let us fight this wild night with sacred song!' Her eyes bored to the back of the hall where Diane sat. 'Let us stand and sing *Rock of Ages* – as loud as the wind!' At which Diane stood. But she stayed silent. For as weak old voices fought the wind, Gussie's powerful contralto coming to the rescue, she felt caught in a Victorian poorhouse melodrama. *What on earth happened to us?* she wondered as the hymn ended, as throats cleared, chairs scraped, people sat. Some sneaked fearful looks at her. And as Mrs Beattie (red face gleaming) mounted the dais, she felt ashamed of what she knew was about to happen. *What do I know?* she asked herself as Mrs Beattie announced a fund-raising lottery on Logan Drive, Saturday night at 8, bake a cake and bring a bottle. *I get off a bus four months ago and hear Sam's voice; I sleep and dream of Chrissa like a haloed picture-book angel taking me on journeys to . . . Oh Diane! Really! Walking through walls to medieval France, and . . . that Beast, and . . . Sirius! It's insane! Isn't there enough daily horror to deal with without this?* – and as Gussie stared at her, she gazed back, wondering: *Why do I hate you, you bossy old fake? Where would I be without you? When I came here I was an utter mess! Here I began to live again. I met people, found I could still function! Now look at me! I cry in my sleep and wake up the house, I drink like a fish, I can't find work, I'm broke and I dream things that scare me so much I don't know who I am or what to do . . . and tonight because of a dream I come here acting as if I know what's going to happen and . . .*

An internal shock jolted her, making her heart leap. It coincided with a violent gust of wind that banged the windows, swept slates from the roof, billowed the blinds and put out candles from the back of the hall to the dais. People gasped; an old woman cried out in alarm as the lights dimmed further. Through her own scared daze Diane heard the old woman's neighbour comfort her – 'There, there, dear, Iain will have a nice message for you from Gussie and afterwards we'll have a nice cup of tea, and . . .'

Gussie fell into shadow and Diane, now unable to see her eyes, only her outline, looming on the dais, wanted to stand up and shout: *'No! Stop this! I warn you, it's too much to bear!'*

For now she felt *them* coming . . . and trembled, suddenly realizing deep in her gut that this business wasn't just her own dream, her private madness. It belonged to the world . . . and soon the whole world would know.

For the Shift was beginning . . . and *They* were coming . . .

But Gussie seemed unafraid. From the darkness came her voice: 'The world's on trial. Did you see the News tonight? War and lies and worse tomorrow as usual! The *paynim* at Istanbul's door; a madman blows up the Gruinard ferry; the Quota for Saharan Refertilization increases!' Her voice rose again the wind. 'Evil and disaster everywhere! What's the matter with us? God gave us heart, but we behave like burglars in our own house; like guilty intruders inside ourselves! It's no good!'

She shot a glance to the back of the hall.

'Tonight one of our flock who was lost is found! She returns with a message which, she says, will be given to us tonight! A message which – but we'll see! If it's true, our protectors on the Inner Planes will tell us! If not . . .' – she spread her arms – '. . . they'll warn us!'

Without more ado she sat on the Chair. Guiltily Diane realized: *She knows there's no option. She knows I've trapped her, but she won't back off! She's braver than I knew! Why did I have to confront her?* Yet she knew why. *I was always scared of her,* she knew miserably. *I didn't know how much I've learned. Now I've saddled her with my fear. Great, Diane!*

Now everyone got to their knees. Mrs Beattie tied a black silk scarf over Gussie's eyes. Dismayed at herself, Diane also sank down, covering her eyes . . . yet, peeping childlike through her fingers, she watched Gussie as Mrs Beattie left the dais and Gussie vibrantly intoned: 'Now do I descend into the Great Sea, whose waters rise and fall within my soul . . .'

And Diane shivered at those words, seeing that ocean where the Elohim glide in unending dance; that ocean-world circling the invisible third Sirian sun, the Emme Ya, where even now, she knew from her dreams, the Company of Those-who-pass-the-Gates prepared their return down the Sinking Ways to this Hidden World which Sam and Chrissa had left, and to which . . .

'Iain!' Through the wind came Gussie's voice. 'Are you there?' Iain, we have questions for you! Iain, are you . . . yes! Good evening, Iain!'

'Good evening, Iain!' echoed the congregation devoutly.

'Good evening!' came the voice from the Chair – a hearty, no-nonsense, man-about-town voice. 'I'm glad to be with you again. A wild night on the Outer Planes! Of course here we have no *physical* climate – but we have the climate of minds, bright or not so bright – and tonight I warn you that . . .'

Then Gussie, or Iain, was interrupted.

Diane felt it first. She felt the blazing light drench her again, and moaned, clenching her fists and throwing back her head, knowing she could do nothing but endure it, yet fearful for all the other folk in the hall, fearful for Gussie. Nightly for weeks this fire had flooded her sleep; painfully seizing her from her room on Rankeillor Street into the realms to which Chrissa and Sam had gone. Now she knew what must happen – at least, her dream-self knew. But her waking self! Until now she'd never really believed what went on in her dreams – yet now it was happening, a blinding silver blaze filling the hall as the wind blasted and the remaining candles blew out. Through her agony she heard shrieks: through half-shut eyes she saw Gussie now brilliantly limned by that blaze; saw Gussie half-stand for a moment, then fall back, writhing in the Chair, hands raised as if she fought an invisible assailant.

'No!' Gussie cried in a stentorian voice, 'You can't make me . . .'

The wind howled louder, drowning Gussie's voice as Mrs Beattie rose sternly to her feet. *Don't drive her mad!* Diane implored. *It's fine for the pair of you; you've been through it; you've forgotten how weak we are – and me too: I mean you nearly drove me to . . .*

'Who are you?' Gussie cried hoarsely as the light grew brighter still, twisting and coiling round her, a silver whirlpool shot through with violet flashes amid which two human forms were taking ghostly shape. Then: 'My name is Samuel Joyce!' declared a voice, apparently from Gussie's throat – and was followed immediately by another, different voice, also from Gussie: 'And my name is Chrissa Joyce. Thank you for inviting us!'

'But,' cried Gussie, and her fear was plain, 'I didn't in . . .'

'Don't be afraid!' croaked the first voice – and Diane, weeping now, saw Sam – *Yes, it's Sam!* – amid that blaze. 'Didn't Diane tell you?'

'Are you there, Diane?' cried the Chrissa-voice . . . and Diane, standing dazed, now saw forming, the other side of the Chair, a tall young golden-haired woman – and others also saw them, for there were cries of terror.

'Yes, I'm here!' Diane's voice broke. 'Please . . . be gentle!'

Gussie shrieked. 'Get out of me, whatever you are!'

'Listen!' cried the Chrissa-apparition as Gussie clawed desperately at the pair of them, 'Mrs Farquhar . . . we must speak through you! We have . . . no voices of our own yet! Let us speak – don't resist – we must tell you!'

'Tell us what?' moaned Gussie, writhing in the Chair.

'About . . . the . . . Shift!' The Sam-voice dragged as Gussie fought. 'This world . . . on the . . . edge. We who went . . . through the Gates can fight . . . this battle . . . with you. But . . . you must help us . . . before we can help you!'

'Listen!' Chrissa begged in a slowing-down croak, transparent hands flung out in appeal: 'Please! We're all trying. Everywhere in the world we're trying to reach you . . . tell you! The Shift is coming . . . fearful and final . . . unless you believe us . . . invite us . . . unless you *wake* up!'

'How can we?' Diane wailed. 'Oh, Chrissa, *how* can we . . .?'

Gussie's shoulders slumped in exhaustion, her eyes bulging in fear as Mrs Beattie, her burly red face set in grim no-more-nonsense determination, now simply marched through the phantoms and shook her fiercely.

'Now come on, Mrs Farquhar! Get a grip, or our funding will be . . .'

'Wait . . .' the Sam-voice croaked as the clamour increased. 'Wait . . . the Whirling Castle in the sky . . . then . . . phones all ring . . . on New Year's Eve . . .' – the voice was failing – '. . . signs and wonders for ye . . . of little faith!'

'Please!' the Chrissa-voice cried, 'It is . . .'

'Leave here!' Mrs Beattie roared, ablaze herself amid the fiery light as she shook Gussie, who flopped like a rag doll. *'Away, ye powers of the pit!'* Turning from Gussie she rushed back and forth through the phantoms, vainly beating at them, catching more fire with every charge even as Diane at last began pushing forward through the mass of terrified folk struggling for the exit. Mrs Beattie, abandoning her efforts, instead ran for the lights and turned them on . . . and this worked: the apparitions faded as the strip-lighting returned. Yet even as they did Diane, now standing helpless by the dais, saw Chrissa gaze at her, heard Chrissa's voice in her mind:

Diane! Mum! Go to London! But beware the Beast tonight!

And then, with the hall nearly empty, they were gone.

Gussie Farquhar sat in the Chair with a weak, silly look.

Diane stared, trembling. Mrs Beattie glared. 'What have you done, you stupid woman?' she demanded. Briefly Diane eyed her, and Gussie, before, wordless, she turned and ran after the rest of the petrified flock out into the night's merciful blackness, nerves still ablaze with the fire which had fallen from who knew where, filled with guilt and self-hate at the part she'd played in calling it down on Gussie Farquhar.

That wasn't Sam and Chrissa, she cried silently, *That was the Beast!*

10.
Arthur's Seat

Gasping, coughing, Diane fled from herself, from the Church, from the dim accusing glow of the lone streetlamp above her. Yet as she embraced the bitter darkness and crossed the road there was an angry roar. Twin beams of blinding light leaped at her. Dazzled, she jumped aside with a shriek – then realized that it was one of the cars which had been parked outside the Church. *But they all hate you now!* her self-loathing hissed, *You'd better get off the road before someone tries to run you down!*

In a panic she straddled an iron fence and ran over a dark wasteland, skidding through mud,. barking her shins against abandoned junk, a stitch now gripping her side, but she did not stop; she came to another road and crossed onto the links, breathing in hysterical gulps, rushing past unseen trees until she met a ditch that tripped her and sent her sprawling. Icy water sloshed into her boots as she scrambled clear onto wet turf.

Bewildered she stood, the storm at her back, soaked feet already numb. She stared at the night. Distant lights shone; orange-bellied cloud raced over the sky. *I'm on the golf course*, she realized dully, the pain in her side sickening. In her anguish she didn't feel it. What had happened? She knew only she couldn't go back to Portobello and the bus-stop. Once and for all she knew she was beyond waiting for buses or flagging taxis.

It's my fault! she scolded herself, shivering with self-contempt. *I shouldn't have gone! Poor Gussie! I'm no good! I'm poison! From now on I stay clear of people and don't curse them with the Beast in me. Because that wasn't Sam and Chrissa. They'd never behave like that. That was the Beast! He tricked me, same as he tricked Sam into attacking Chrissa, and I fell for it, because I'm rotted by booze and loneliness and . . .*

Frenzied, remembering too much, remembering things she couldn't face, she reached into her coat pocket for the half-bottle of Bells. She drank raw spirit. It brought her brief warmth but didn't reduce her confusion. She turned to the gale roaring off the sea. 'Do your worst, you Beast!' she screamed. 'You can't do worse than you've made me do already! And why go to London? What for? I'm going home!'

She stumbled on towards Restalrig. Beyond lay Holyroodhouse, shadowy under the bulk of Arthur's Seat. Something made her lift her eyes to it. She could just make the hill out against the orange urban night-glow.

I'll take the path up Salisbury Craig, she thought feverishly – for Rankeillor Street where she lived lay under Arthur's Seat: in her present mood she longed for the wildest, least urban route home; the route furthest from streets and people, closest to the storm in her soul. She didn't like taking the bus anyway, especially not since that night eighteen months ago when, changing at Waverley amid the crowds, she'd been knocked flying by a young thug – one of those terrorist fools calling themselves 'Knights of the Purple Heather' – really! – who seconds later had been shot dead by the police as he tried to escape through Princes Street traffic. And of course it had also been while getting off a bus at Waverley last August that she'd first heard Sam's ghost-voice in her ear.

'Diane!' it had whispered, terrifying her, 'Diane!'

Look what's happened since! she told herself, sloshing through a muddy shallow burn at the edge of the golf course. *Look at tonight! I've gone mad! That's all there is to say about it! You're bad news, Diane!*

She left the links for the shabby prim rectitude of Restalrig's high-walled streets, teeth chattering as she paused wearily at a corner to empty water from her boots. Sure she was mad she laughed aloud: two leather kids coming out of a Chinese takeaway across the road eyed her uneasily, then shrugged before kicking their Korean bikes into life and roaring away to whatever designer-dope action the cold unwelcome night might offer.

She didn't see them. On she went, so cold and tired she could barely lift her feet. Through empty streets she approached the Meadowbank Sports Centre, which once had known sporting glory, hosting a Commonwealth Games famed for a boycott by black nations who'd felt the Commonwealth not common enough. Passing this white elephant, she crossed the busy London Road, so consumed by self-loathing that she never saw or heard the traffic swerving to avoid her, including a police van too busy to stop. It was speeding to the scene of an arson attack on a Newtown nightclub – one of several recent Tartan Army attacks on clubs so stupid as to employ Reely-Show or holoshelf acts sponsored by heathen Metropolitan English money.

She crossed the London Road without disaster, aware only of her self-hate and the freezing wind as obscure instinct led her to a curving walk through high-hedged gardens past the dour facade of Holyroodhouse.

She'd been round this palace often, fascinated by its grim history of lust and murder; by the bloodstained floor at the door to the rooms of Mary Queen of Scots, where Mary's secretary Riccio had been murdered. Now tears wet her eyes, for as she walked the icy palace gardens, she was seized by the mad conviction that she herself was Mary; poor Mary, her husband dead, her lover murdered. 'Davie,' she cried, 'if I had thee back alive I'd kiss Auld Clootie's arse!' And even as she cried this the wind gusted wilder, leaves whirled – and she stopped dead, eyes wide, joy and terror invading her – for standing before her she saw the spectre of a sly dark man.

'Davie!' she cried, 'Davie Riccio! Is it thee? But . . .'

The ghost said nothing. It could not. Blood bubbled from its slashed throat, staining its ruff of Dutch lace as it bowed low. A voice cried in her: *'Mum, don't be fooled! It's the Beast!'* But she ignored the voice.

'Sweet Davie!' she cried in horror, 'You welter wi' blood!'

With a smile of dreadful invitation the ghost turned away, starting up the path to the heights of Salisbury Craig. Gathering up imaginary skirts, she pursued it unthinkingly. But the higher she went the fainter it grew, so that she ran ever faster amid the gale. Then new confusion seized her.

She heard a voice cry '*No*!' and seemed to see a golden-haired young woman, oddly familiar. *'Diane!'* whispered this fresh ghost, '*Please! We can't save you from too many stupid mistakes! Walk by the streets, go to London where you'll meet friends who know what to do! Please, Diane!*'

She stopped. *Diane? Who's Diane?* Shivering, she stared about. The narrow path had steepened, a rock wall to her left, a vertical drop to her right. The Princes Street lights shone a mile away. At the sight of them terror seized her. *I'm mad!* she realized, swaying in the wind on the path which, she knew vaguely, was dangerous, with sudden corners round which on wild days the wind could gust hard enough to spin you right off the edge if you weren't careful, and yet now here she was . . . capering in total delirium.

I'm Diane! she told herself, suddenly terrified, *I'm . . .*

The ghost of Riccio, glimmering faintly blue, reappeared – or did she imagine it? Her heart hammered. It grinned at her, blood gouting from its neck. It bowed. Its pallid hand gestured her on up the path. Then it was gone, and maybe it was just the wind and her scrambled wit after all. In a daze again she eyed the lights of Princes Street. Even at this hour hordes were out after last-minute Christmas bargains. She could see them hurrying under the festive lights. She sighed in contempt and regret. All that was so far away and meaningless now to Diane Emily Joyce, her husband and child kidnapped by the Elohim; herself now alone and terrified as the winter gale blasted her, as ghosts fought for her soul. *I must get home!* she decided giddily . . . and on up the path she went, an odd, cold blue light like a will-o'-the-wisp dancing before her now, the gale's contrary voices howling in her until at last, with only half-a-mile to Rankeillor Street and her room, the path rounded a corner . . . and as it did she was shocked and caught off-balance by the sound of a man crying out in agony, apparently just above her. And it was then the wind gusted so hard and sudden that, taken by surprise, she was snatched by it – snatched and spun to the edge of the darkness below. And in the teeth of the wind that blue light flared.

'Gotcha!' she heard the ghost crow as, too late, teetering on the edge, she knew how, ever since leaving Portobello, the Beast had exploited her guilt to bring her here. To her death. Calmly she eyed the darkness.

An instant later that calm was replaced by terror.

'Chrissa!' she screamed. 'Sam! Help me!'

That was the scream which Bobbie Aird heard as he himself was about to jump . . . and the terror of that cry on the wind checked him. He dropped to his knees and peered over the edge. And what he saw and what happened next later had him swearing to God that he'd never give up hope again.

For maybe ten feet below (even amid his shock he laughed, for looking down he saw he'd forgotten about the path – had he jumped he'd have broken a leg, maybe, but no worse) he saw what at first made no sense.

Apart from the throb and glow of Princes Street's distant commerce it was a pitch-black, starless night. Up here on the bare heights of Arthur's Seat there should have been no light worth the mention. But there was. It was a blue, whirling, writhing light he looked down into; a cold cloud that set his teeth on edge and made him think he wasn't really awake, for, as he saw the thin grey-haired woman who'd screamed, her wide-eyed face terrified as she swayed on the edge of the fatal fall he'd meant for himself, he also saw (and a groan froze in his throat) how, shadowed in the cold blue light of the wind that beat at her, was the wavering apparition of a man kitted out as outlandishly as himself, in Elizabethan fancy dress, complete with lace ruff, doublet, baggy hose, sheathed sword and pheasant-feathered hat.

The spectre also had two mouths.

One, where mouths ought to be, gaped wide with that evil grin.

The other, below the first, gaped wider, splitting the throat – and from it Bobbie saw, as the ghost tried to wrestle her over the edge, blue blood gouting in spasms, soaking ruff and doublet and her terrified face –

It was nightmarish. He couldn't move.

Then amid her despairing fight she looked up.

Her eyes met his . . . and widened in redoubled horror.

For above her crouched a ghost as fearful as the one she fought. She saw glaring down at her a wild blackbearded highlandman, tattered tartan plaid whipping in the wind. His face looked as if it had been crushed by a sledgehammer. In his huge hand he held a broadsword. She screamed at the sight of him. And what moved Bobbie then was not compassion but self-pity and wounded pride at the horror on her face; the horror that said that he, Bobbie Aird, was as frightful as the ghost at her throat.

But at least her horror unfroze him.

'No!' he roared furiously and (without realizing until he'd done it) down he jumped into that foul blue light, 'I'm nae like that!'

He seized her arm and pulled her back. The apparition gibbered in fury, and as the shock of that blue fire ran through him he decided maybe he was already dead; that he'd jumped and died and that this (what else?) was the Pit itself . . . but he bellowed with laughter, knowing he had nothing to lose as he fought for her life, the lights of the careless city shining below.

'So here ye are, ye Beast, ye Lord of Illusion, ye bastard Watcher!' he raved. 'Ye hae two gobs already, now here's a third!' – and yanking the woman behind him he swung the great sword in a flat arc that went straight through the ghost's neck. To little effect. The blue light flared; for a moment the ghost dissolved, but then it was back; mockingly puffing out its cheeks: a fresh blast struck so hard that they both went spinning back to the edge of the fatal fall. 'Can you nae do something?' Bobbie cried at the terrified woman, still gripping her arm as, frantic now, he managed to stab the sword down into the thin stony soil on the edge of the path. It was just enough to hold them firm for a moment. 'Fer fook's sake, I'm nae in the habit o' fechting ghosts – I'm flesh an' blud too!'

Then unexpectedly Diane began laughing. 'You don't fight ghosts?' she shrieked, clinging to him as he clung to the sword, 'I do – all the time!'

Bobbie's mouth fell open. They were almost over the edge. His cap blew off and whirled away into the night. 'I dinnae get the joke,' he bellowed, fighting for dear life as the Beast-wind buffeted and slapped them, but she only laughed more loudly.

Then she saw the fury on the spectre's face.

'The Beast doesn't like being laughed at!' she cried.

She stopped laughing. She cocked her head, as if listening.

Chrissa? Is that . . .? What are you trying to . . .?

For like a distant echo she heard Chrissa's voice (not the new Chrissa, but the 12-year-old who'd vanished) cry a sound which –

'AEIOU!' Diane screamed, not knowing what it meant, 'AEIOU!'

Then Bobbie was further amazed. A fire exploded so fierce yet pure it filled him with ecstatic pain. The wind abruptly changed direction even as the sick light failed amid the brighter light that now embraced them.

Still holding the woman he was thrown back on the path and out of the wind. There they lay. *Aye,* he agreed with himself, *I'm deid fer sure.*

Then he knew deeper astonishment.

Amid the blazing light a man and a woman stood watching them.

The man had a thin dark face and a shock of grey hair. And the woman! Her blue eyes shone in a tanned face crowned by a cascade of golden hair. A real stunner, and Bobbie's mouth gaped wide. But not just at her looks.

For they stood on thin air. A good six feet off the path. Impossible. But there they were. He stared. They stared back. He had to look down. Their gaze was too clear. He couldn't face them. *You fool, Bobbie,* he seemed to hear the young woman say – but there was no rancour: in fact he felt she was . . . laughing at him? *But maybe you can redeem yourself by* . . .

Redeem? He didn't like words like 'redeem'. But . . .

It was all he could take in. *It's nae real,* he told himself, head roaring as he stole a look at the woman who'd . . . called them?

He saw her eyes fixed on them. He saw her lips moving. She seemed surprised, even shocked. But not scared. Apparently she knew them. But before he could think straight, suddenly they were gone. Just like that.

Darkness returned. This time it was total. The Beast-light was gone too. The wind was falling. They both lay stunned. For a time they lay there, silent on the bare path below Arthur's Seat. Far below glowed the lights of the city. Distant traffic roared. Sirens wailed. Then:

'You saved my life, Bobbie,' she said out of the darkness.

His jaw dropped. 'Ye ken my name?' he heard himself ask.

'They told me.' Her voice trembled. 'I know you. Gruinard Isle.'

Bobbie's shaking grew worse. 'I came up here tae . . . tae jump . . .'

'I know,' said Diane Joyce. 'At least, that's what *you* thought.'

The police sirens were closer, wailing along Dalkeith Road below.

'Fine,' he whispered, lowering his head. 'Them sirens is fer me. I'll bide here an' nae hairm ye. Ye can tell the polis. But,' he said angrily, 'I did what I thocht right. My wee brither . . . though now I ken fine how . . .'

He stopped. She'd laid a hand on his head. To his horror he began to weep. 'Stop it,' she said sharply, 'I'm not telling anyone. An hour ago I'd have gladly . . .' Catching herself, reluctantly she added: 'It's quite different now. *They* said so. We're going south. Together. To London.'

'What . . .?' He was floundering. '. . . I'm nae asking ony favours . . .'

'I'll explain later,' she said, exhausted. 'You'll have to hide in my room until we go. Is that clown's costume all you've got to wear?'

'It isnae clown's . . .' – Bobbie stopped himself. 'My regular gear's in the kitbag,' he croaked. 'But . . . whit in hell is this aboot?'

'You'll know soon enough,' she said, 'We all will.'

That was how Bobbie Aird met Diane Joyce.

11.
Knights of the Purple Heather

'Aye,' Bobbie grumbled an hour later, sitting on her floor nursing the last of her whisky, 'There was polis there at the jetty as thick as flies under the lights, tommyguns pointed at the puir sods getting' oot o' the bus. They wisnae watchin' the boat, an' it wis a black night, so I put on the wetsuit an' swum oot frae the rocks, climbed on the far side, stuck the charge in the engine room, an' swum back again. I thocht: *Hey, Bobbie, you sure about this?* Then (I wis in the trees by the water) I saw Ronnie – ma brither – an' I told masel', *Man, if I wis in his sheen I'd want it quick; so . . .*' – he shrugged – '. . . when the boat (folk call it "Charon's Ferry") wis halfway over I pressed the button an' . . .' – his ugly face showed no joy – '. . . that was it. Boom. I trekked back o'er the hills tae the car, an' I wis almost back in toon when I heard on the radio they wis lookin' fer me. That bastard Calum shopped me so's they wouldnae stick him in Peterheid fer a job he did at Fort George. An' that's it.' He sighed and drank. 'I ken fine them spooks telt ye a' this a'ready, eh?' And he drained the bottle.

Diane eyed him remotely, horrified, fascinated too. Not often a madman casually told her he'd just blown up twenty people out of charity. Not to mention the rest of the tale he'd just told her.

She stared at him. She felt an unbridgeable gulf between them. *This must be a dream*, she thought. But he'd saved her life on Salisbury Craig. And she'd managed to call Sam and Chrissa . . . as she'd often done in her dreams. Yet it was no dream now. She had to admit she knew it. But she didn't like their advice. How could she? She thought back. Sprawling on the path with Sam and Chrissa shining before her, both scolding her for getting in such a mess. 'Mum, that was really stupid!' Chrissa's voice like a bell. *And me her mother*! But was she? Who knew what the pair of them were now? Nothing on earth, that was sure. Yet what could she do but take their advice? Even so! For after ticking her off they'd told her just who and what the shivering man beside her was. And told her not only to *trust* the hairy murderous brute, but to go to London with him? 'But he's a . . .' she'd started protesting silently.

'At least he's not a lawyer,' Sam had cut in, a remark so typically, cynically Sam that it was suddenly plain to her that translation to aeonic realms hadn't changed him much. Or maybe he was just angry with her.

'Christ walked with thieves and sinners, Mum,' Chrissa added. 'Come on, you'd be dead by now, and at least he's streetwise, and . . .'

'You'll need muscle in London,' Sam had said, adding mordantly, 'Diane, we don't have spare energy for this sort of intervention. There's a lot going on, a lot of opposition, and we don't have the substance – yet.'

'But what's going on?' she'd cried.

'Go to London and you'll find out,' said Chrissa patiently. 'Don't you remember? We took you and showed you! Just go to London – we'll be in touch; and you'll know the what and when and who when you meet it.'

'But this man . . . you say he's the one who . . .'

Sam shrugged. 'He's an overgrown version of the kids I used to deal with at GRYP. Keep him in line, tell him what to do, and you'll find he's more like a St Bernard than a pit bull.'

'But it's a criminal offence to harbour a . . .'

'We've got to go now, Mum. Just watch your dreams.'

And they'd gone. And she took their advice, though hating it. Taking this mad thug home? A St Bernard? But look how the big bold man had wept when those sirens came wailing and she'd patted him on the head! And he was biddable. He'd grumbled, but she'd got him to chuck his ludicrous Rob Roy gear. 'Over the edge with the lot of it!' she'd insisted. 'That big sword too.' And he'd done it! Maybe he meant to sneak back and get them while she slept. Anyway, now he was less than romantic in work boots and jeans, tatty teeshirt riding over his beergut, leather jacket with burst seams even more tatty. He wouldn't have got far as Rob Roy! Luckily it was no great distance from the crags to Rankeillor Street, and it had been late, pubs shut, few people about. Even so, on St Leonard's Street a patrol car had passed . . . but Bobbie, following some way behind her, had faded into shadow as she hurried alone along the poorly-lit pavement.

'What's up, missus,' a cop in the patrol car had asked.

'I'm just going home.' She'd been frightened. Her fear had showed. 'Only a few more yards.' She'd pointed. 'Rankeillor Street.'

'Aye, well, you need to take care. There's loonies about.'

'Loonies?' Her mouth so dry. 'What do you mean?'

'The bastard who blew up the ferry, missus.' They'd seen her safe back to Number 13. Inside all was dark. When they were gone she'd slipped out to call Bobbie in (half-hoping he'd be gone), and up creaking stairs they'd tiptoed in unison to make it sound that there was only one pair of feet.

So she'd got him here safe, locking the door and drawing the curtains before turning on light, kettle and fire with hands that trembled.

'My neighbours moan a lot,' she told him, 'I've been shouting in my sleep, and the walls are as thin as paper. So keep quiet, because . . .'

'Dinnae worry.' He'd touched her arm; she'd flinched. He'd eyed the tv. 'Can we see the News? Wouldnae have a drink here, would ye?'

She'd given him her half-bottle and turned on the tv. The

midnight News did nothing for her. The same as usual. More wild storms across the world; the Mahdi's armies rampant; weirdoes trying to colonize Queen Maud Land in Antarctica to 'get away from it all'; Andrew Lloyd Webber's new smash hit, *One-way Ticket to Auckland* – then local stuff. Power cuts, frozen sheep, frozen people. Nothing about Bobbie. Nothing at all. She eyed him covertly, but he showed no emotion. *Here goes*, she'd thought.

'I must know more about you,' she said.

He just shrugged, not meeting her eyes.

'You're a Knight of the Purple Heather, aren't you?' Shakily she went on before he could answer: 'I saw one of you killed last year at Waverley. I was getting off a bus. He came running out with the police after him; he knocked me over. They shot him as he tried to get through the traffic. He was dressed like you; the News said he'd been trying to break into a . . .'

He'd laughed flatly. 'Ian Sproat. Silly sod! Wisnae ane o' us.' He shrugged. 'Well, so he wis – before the Split when we played at sodgers. Doin' battles, ye ken. But that Ian wis always an idjit. We kicked him oot when it got serious, but the idjit held ontae his card, so when . . .'

'What do you mean – playing at soldiers?'

Hunkering on her floor, he'd begun to explain – or confess. He was full of anger, but as he told his tale she remembered how up on the path he'd wept. Like a little boy never tenderly touched. And the more he said the more she'd felt a maternal urge, hard to deny, for it was soon clear that, just as she'd been deprived – by huge mischance – of the pleasures (dubious often, but far better than the vacuum of these years on her own) of life with her husband and daughter; so this fierce-looking man was, whatever he'd done, at heart little more than a scared boy trying to sort out why he was alive. Sam had been right about that.

'I wis born in Greenock,' he told her after much prompting. 'Family o' nine. I'm fifth. When I wis ten my da got laid off. Nivver got a job again. I left school an' signed on. Nivver wurked neither. There wis the YTS an' that, but I skipped it. Jist used tae watch videos, an' sleep a lot, an' drink a lot, an' get intae bother. It wis the probation officer that found me a "creative outlet" – the Knights o' the Purple Heather.

'It wisnae serious at furst. Jist a way tae pass the time. It wis guys like me an' our burds wi' nothing else tae do. We'd get together on a Saiturday afternoon wi' targe an' blunted swords, an' whack it out face tae face fer a coupla hours then get intae the nearest pub an' get wrecked.

'We nivver thocht aboot politics. Jist liked tae dream we wis bold braw hielandmen back when there wis nae modern shite. I ken fine now the same bastards wis always on top, but I wis jist a kid then.

'But efter a time we got serious. We stairted wurking wi' companies frae Kent an' York an' you name it, puttin' on proper battles o' British history, like . . .' he reeled off a string of names and dates without pause – '. . . Hastings 1066, Bannockburn 1314, Mortimer's Cross 1461, Flodden 1513, Marston Moor 1644, Culloden 1746 and so on. They wis on the battlefields, wi' the right period gear, an' spectators behind ropes so they wouldnae get hurt in the melées, an' it wis no jist guid fun, we wis makin' a livin' at it efter twa years.' He grinned so boyishly she had to fight not to smile back, reminding herself of what he was. 'Because we wis ane o' the best companies in the whole bludy country; invited tae a' the best battles, an' as fer masel', I winnae brag, but twa times before I wis twenty I won the single combat outright. No many can handle the claymore – the wurd's frae the Gaelic *claigh mhor*, meaning *big sword*,' he'd explained, as pedantic as any professor – then added, brow darkening, 'an' I wish tae hell I hadnae let ye make me chuck it away. That's my soul ye made me chuck away!'

'You won't get far carrying a big sword.' Though pale and alarmed she kept her voice steady. 'But . . . why a Scots company at English battles . . .?'

'Why d'ye think! Mercenaries! Micks an' Jocks couldnae get wurk at home ony mair then than now, so they signed up wi' English armies as shock-troops who had tae fight harder 'n anyone else. If they wis on the losing side, even if they escaped slaughter they wis still as guid as deid, stuck in England far frae hame wi' naebody tae say a guid wurd for them! Onyway, we made a fine living out of it . . . till things got hairy wi' the North-South Split. Companies frae different regions began really goin' fer each other; blokes stairted getting hurt – bludgeoned, stabbed, shot by airchers who "fergot" tae tip their arrows wi' rubber. Then in '94, doin' the Battle o' Lewes 1264 a guy got his head cut off by a bloke frae a Scots company – stupid bastard got sent down fer life. Questions wis asked in Parliament. But it wis '95 it got totally hairy. We got southern companies up tae Stirling tae do Bannockburn 1314, where Robert the Bruce beat King Edward. It went fine at furst, but in the heat o' battle a troop o' Yorkie horse cheated. They wis meant tae flee before the Scots, but they cheated. It wis on tv like a sairt o' Reely-Show – an' mibbe it gave the Metropolitans the notion fer Reely-Show wars wi' the Pseudodeath technology. They jist turned and chairged – an' six o' us got trampled tae death! I wis there!' he told her grimly, and Diane agreed that, though for years she'd ignored the outside world, she recalled it. 'The shites! It wisnae the old guard, it wisnae oor Yorkie mates, it wisnae because o' what happened at Lewes, though the English media made that their excuse – revenge, ye ken – it wis undercover SAS set up by Tories wha didnae like Scotland votin' against 'em an' thocht we needed a lesson. I see 'em now, riding us down, howlin' "Get the fuckin' Jocks!" An' they did! I wis lucky – jist a bust rib. Aifter that we knew it wis real war. So we stopped playin' an' stairted learnin' about explosives and Kalashnikovs.' He shrugged. 'Then the Split came an' we found the Assembly here's near as bad as Whitehall. But mibbe no quite as bad . . . as ye'll find when we go down South – mark my wurds!'

That was the first indication she'd had from him that he was seriously thinking about taking her up on the business of going to London.

'Aye,' he went on broodingly, 'Aifter that it went crazy.' He eyed her, face strained. 'Ye wantae ken aboot Gruinard?' He raised a hand. 'But shut yer gob till I'm done! It's no easy . . . an' I still say it was a mercy. Ye ken aboot it? Back in 1940 MoD scientists frae Porton Down sowed the soil wi' anthrax spores – germ warfare test, ye ken. The dirt's still poisoned. They say it's safe these ten years, but everyone kens it isnae. It went up fer sale, an' I dinnae ken the history, save that three year ago our fine Scottish Assembly decided in its wusdom that it wis jist the place tae put miserable sinners wi' AIDS, oot o' the way o' decent folk, an' let 'em die slow. So they bought it, and . . . Ye'll hear me out?'

She'd nodded, but her face was white as in a flat voice he told his tale, dark eyes fixed on her, and he was sweating by the time he was done.

'And that's it,' he finished, and sighed, and drank. 'I ken fine them spooks telt ye a' this a'ready, eh?' And he drained the bottle. 'So I'm crap, but I did it fer Ronnie an' the ither puir sods – that's the truth!'

Still she said nothing. She was somewhere else. He dropped his eyes, grieving the loss of his gear. *But mibbe that's nothing,* he told himself morosely. *Not aifter a' that. If it happened.* And he stared at the weird books this daft old bitch had scattered over her floor – titles like *The Powers of Evil* and *Forbidden Mysteries of Enoch* – as he tried to grasp what had happened on Salisbury Craig and why he was here now. Sure, he'd been about to jump when it went crazy, with the ghost of a bloke with a slit throat, and that other guy and that gorgeous wee hen standing on thin air.

Now here he was with this faded auld wifie that had him spilling the beans as if she was his mother. Who wanted him to go to London with her . . .

'Truth is,' he muttered, 'I'm scared shiteless. I'm nae ane fer the spooks, an' if I hadnae been there I'd say ye wis a total nutter.'

'*I'm* the nutter?' She was flabbergasted. 'After what *you* did?'

'Spare me the sairmon, hen!' he snapped, 'I'd dae it again!'

'But it wasn't just the AIDS people! The policemen! The boatman!'

'Murderin' collaborators!' His face darkened; he waved at the phone. 'So call the polis an' turn me in,' he offered again, 'I'll nae hairm ye!'

Diane sighed. 'No,' she muttered, 'I won't. I need your help.'

'Aye. Fine.' He grinned sourly. 'So drop the moralizin' and get doon tae brass tacks.' His gaze, not drunk at all, pierced her. 'So ye wantae go tae London wi' a gorilla like me tae fecht fer ye – but efter whit I seen I dinnae ken how ye're feart o' anything in *this* wurld!' He laughed, too loud, for she shushed him; he went on in an exaggerated whisper: 'Why are ye feart? Ye command the spirits o' the vasty deep, ye beat the de'il himsel'! And ye fibbed tae the polis when they asked if ye'd seen me!'

Diane signed. 'So I did,' she admitted.

'Okay! So I'm nae complainin'. But why?'

'Because Sam and Chrissa told me to.'

'Sam and . . . wha're they, if ye dinnae mind me askin'?'

'Those two you saw standing on thin air,' she said, light-headed with weariness and disorientation, 'My husband. And my daughter.'

'Oh aye,' he said sceptically, 'Sure. Yer auld man an' yer wee gurl. I thocht as much. Come frae Mars tae pay the maintenance, wis he?'

'Shut up!' she flared, forgetting herself – then she froze. Bobbie stared at her. When no angry thumps beat the walls, she sighed, relaxed, and said: 'Sorry. Now just listen, and I'll tell you.'

She did. She told what had happened fourteen years ago; how Sam had rediscovered the ring his grandfather had given him and found the place the ring liked – the gate amid the stone circle near Gairloch; of Chrissa's dreams of a burning man and how Sam's dreams too had been invaded until at length, obsessed and lost, he'd plunged through the gate; how Chrissa had followed, trying to stop him . . . and how she, Diane, had watched helplessly as Chrissa too was consumed by that writhing, horrible fire . . .

'Aye,' said Bobbie, awed. He eyed her with new respect. 'I remember. I was jist sixteen. It wis in the Daily Record and the News o' the Wurld.'

She stared at him. 'So you don't think I'm totally crazy?'

'Oh aye, ye're as barmy as naebody's business,' said Bobbie easily, 'But that's no surprisin'. So whit happened next?'

Flatly she told him of her pain after they'd vanished. The press and police investigation. Madness seizing her. Giving up teaching in London, moving to Edinburgh to look after Sam's invalid father. Working as a VDU operator after the old man died in 1990, moving here . . . and her discovery of Gussie's Church. 'In all that time,' she said, low-voiced, 'I was a zombie – just a breathing and eating and sleeping machine. It only changed four months ago. I got off a bus at Waverley and . . . heard Sam . . . speak my name! That's all, and of course there was nobody there – in the flesh – but I knew it *was* him! Then the dreams began.' She paused. Bobbie seemed awed. 'Chrissa started visiting me,' she went on, 'She looked just as you saw her tonight. I didn't know it was her at first; I mean, I last saw her when she was twelve – a pale kid in glasses. So when she came again . . .' – Diane smiled faintly – '. . . I was scared silly. But she started taking me where she'd gone . . . through the gate . . . back to the thirteenth century where her burning man lives. In southern France.' She nudged a book on the floor, called *The Cathars and Reincarnation.* 'She was with the people this book talks about. Heretics, wiped out by the Roman Church seven hundred years ago . . .'

Bobbie shuddered. He felt a cold wind blow through him. *Jump, Bobbie!* it howled, and in that moment he saw more clearly than he'd ever seen.

'The Beast wha got 'em damn near got us,' he heard himself hiss, 'The Beast frae the earth wi' lamb's horns wha marks the heids o' the buyers an' sellers wi' his number, the name o' a man, 666. Oh,' he went on, eyes wide on her amazed face, and he was amazed at himself too, 'I ken fine it's nae jist the Roman Church. It's in a' folk wha think they're a' right an' the neebor's wrang. It's folk thinkin' Evil's jist an, an . . . *abstraction*,' he said, struggling for the word, clapping hand to heart. 'It's aye in here.' He heaved a savage sigh. 'But . . . ferget that! So whit aboot . . . *Sam*, is it?'

He knows that? she wondered, uneasily impressed, shutting her eyes as into her mind swam a vision of that awful day a month ago: out temping at a Lothian Road office when suddenly on her green screen she'd seen not the sales forecasts but Chrissa, the new

Chrissa, fighting a writhing mist from which hydra-faces glared, and one of them had been Sam's, Beast-possessed.

That was the last day she'd worked, the last day she'd dared go out.

But two nights ago Sam and Chrissa and Chrissa's Cathar friend, Pierre Belot, had come from the bright star to tell her they'd beaten the Beast, at least in his form as Azazel the Watcher – but not forever, for: '. . . *he still owns the Earth* . . .' Sam had said as they showed her the aeonic ocean world of the Elohim; showed her this lovely earth lost in gravity's abyss, the ever-shifting images of the Beast squatting on it, drowning the minds of people in amnesia, division, greed, envy, suicidal despair, plotting the Shift and the extinction of life on earth which alone could guarantee him his death and the end of his aeons-old imprisonment. '*Trigger the shift!*' she'd heard him whispering in the world-mind, '*Who gives a damn? Here today and gone tomorrow, so who cares about tomorrow? Who told you suckers you had a right to live anyway? Haven't you had enough? So vote death – now!*' And they'd told her: '*That's what we're up against*,' even as a huge force had torn her back to sweat-soaked wakefulness in her cold dawn sheets here, as the shining voice cried: '*Wait! Wait! Be ready! Soon!*'

And last night Sam and Chrissa – Pierre had not been with them – had come again and told her what to do, so tonight she'd gone to Portobello . . .

'Lost yer tongue?' prompted Bobbie uneasily, for there was a freezing remoteness on her face. But when he spoke she snapped back to the present.

'It's hard to tell,' she whispered. 'It's in the apocryphal books of the Bible. The Beast was . . . is one of the fallen angels. Long ago . . .'

'Oh, the Watchers,' said Bobbie. 'Aye. "*There were giants in those days* . . .".' He nodded. 'There's a rock band called the Watchers. "*Aw ma mind's bin murdered by Mars*," 'he sang in a cracked whisper, "'*But I don't put no faith in them stars* . . ." Number One right now.' And at her look he said: 'Diane, I'm nae a bludy *materialist*; I'd nae blaw up twenty folk if I thocht *this* fuckin' wurld's the only game in toon – eh? An' I seen yer Sam and Chrissa, right? So skip the heavy stuff an' jist tell me whit's up.'

So she told him. About the Elohim. About the ocean world in orbit round the invisible third Sirian sun. About the Shift approaching and . . .

'Aye.' Bobbie yawned. He didn't know why, but none of it seemed odd. It was as if he'd known it for years. 'Nostradamus, Mother Shipton, the Brahan Seer an' a' them folk telt us, right? The Beast tries tae kill us wi' oor ane fear, right? Storms an' Star Wars an' folk mad wi' Reelies an' fake religion.' He yawned again, his open mouth cavernous. 'Diane, yer no exactly wide awake, ye need yer kip, and me too. But furst . . . why London?'

'I don't know.' Diane yawned too. 'They say I'll meet people who'll know what to do. They . . . can't help us unless we can . . . materialize them. Before it's too late. How, I don't know. Not yet. Maybe in London . . .'

'Gettin' tae London's no easy since the Split,' said Bobbie, 'Ye need a return ticket fer a start – and that's even if they let you in.' He rubbed his scalp. 'I'm on the run . . . an' I'm nae exactly invisible . . .'

'No,' Diane agreed grimly. 'You're not.' And suddenly it all seemed hopeless, stupid, a waste of time. 'We could shave your beard, and if I had any money I could go out tomorrow and buy you a suit, but . . .'

'Oh, the cash is easy,' said Bobbie, casually upending his kitbag on the floor, 'though I'm nae sure I wantae lose my whuskers.' Rooting about in a mess of clothes he found an envelope from which he tipped of wad of Royal Bank of Scotland £50 notes. 'Winnae buy us a bean in London, an' I dinnae hae nae plastic,' he said, giving it to her, 'but it's a' yours.'

She stared at it, at him. She opened her mouth.

'Haud yer tongue,' said Bobbie. 'It's cash. But that's the least o' it. Even if naebody spots me an' we get on the train and *still* naebody spots me, it's my bet you don't have Metropolitan ID any mair'n I do.'

'But,' said Diane cautiously, 'they don't acknowledge the Split.

They don't recognize the Assembly or the Union; they pretend we're all still – you know – equal British citizens. So why do we need Metropolitan ID?'

'Whit they say and whit they do are twa different things,' he said. 'Listen. Ye get on the train, an' doon at Peterborough the train stops fer a "ticket inspection". That really means Customs and Immigration. If ye dinnae have Metropolitan ID or credit like American Express Gold Card they pull yae aff and put ye through it. If ye havnae a return ticket they put ye back on the furst train north. If ye have a ticket an' cash an' guid reason tae visit their luvly land, then maybe they'll let ye in. But furst they change yer cash fer Met plastic. The exchange rate is lousy. Wurse, they mak ye sign a No Claims agreement – an' that means signin' awa' yer rights not only as a "British citizen", but as a human being. It turns ye intae trash; means yer free game once ye hit the streets – an' since ye have nae credit but whit they let ye have, the only streets ye can afford are in the Closed Areas. Ye ken aboot them?' He grinned fiercely at her tentative look. 'Ye havnae bin keeping abreast o' the News, eh?'

Diane was forced to admit she hadn't.

'I thocht not. That's why yer Sam an' Chrissa telt ye tae tak up wi' a villain like me – right?' His grin faded. 'Okay. Closed Areas means areas whaur onything goes – all part o' the Reely-Show. Cop snatch squads patrol the streets when the pubs close. They pick ye up, that's it. Magistrate sees ye in batches o' fufty – they ken fine ye've signed the No Claims – and aff ye go tae a Reely-Show battle fer a Pseudodeath implant – ken whit I mean? – or mibbe ye wake up three days later tae find yersel' in the Sahara wi' a pick in yer hand and a born-again Ayrab wi' a Kalashnikov an' whip on yer back.' He grinned mirthlessly. 'Ye ken the Maghreb Motorway?'

She was having difficult breathing.

'If you mean the Saharan Refertilization Pro . . .'

'Aye, "refertilization". Like "final solution".' His face was savage. 'Diane, the Mets say there's too many useless folk alive. So whit tae do wi' 'em? Why, export 'em, sell 'em off fer dinars tae prop up a "service economy" that has nae real base o' production!'

Diane shivered. 'It sounds like hell on earth.'

'Aye,' said Bobbie, 'since that wicked woman . . . but hush!' He raised a warning hand. 'We nivver speak her name! Why invite the Beast in?'

'But then how can we . . .?'

'Oh,' said Bobbie, 'There's ways. I ken a guy in Finsbury Park. If he's still there. He used tae mak armour fer the . . .'

'I used to live just over the hill from Finsbury Park!'

'That wis then, Diane,' said Bobbie ominously. 'It's a Closed Area now. Ye'll see. If we get there. Now fer God's sake let's kip.'

And without embarrassment or more ado he laid himself down on the carpet and, even as she watched, his eyes closed and he began to snore.

Fully dressed she went to bed. And slept. And dreamed. Of a volcano erupting; of screaming faces and fiery rain; of the Beast's hydra heads all howling with laughter; of a black-haired woman driving desperately through a lurid night-land, and as she met the black-haired woman's terrified eyes she heard her cry: 'Diane! You must find Jim. You must!' – and somehow knew her name was *Jessica*, and that soon . . . but then Jessica's face turned into the Riccio-Beast, covered in blood, gaping mouths grinning as Bobbie Aird flung himself on her, grunting furiously, claymore raised . . .

She awoke with a gasp. It was dawn, cold and grey. And Bobbie Aird was there on her floor, snoring, as large as life and twice as ugly.

She pinched herself. Awake. And knew again: *This is no dream.*

12.
Leaving Home

She lay in her bath feeling suffocated by the dream of eruption. As for Bobbie . . . nothing round her seemed real. This feeling increased as the day wore on: in fact it would take her some days to learn that her growing sense of existential dislocation was not peculiar to herself alone; that the Madness didn't discriminate on grounds of race, class, age or religion.

London, she told herself, *We must get to London.*

Bobbie seemed bemused as she woke him, took his measurements, and told him to lie low while she went out shopping. Half-an-hour she waited in the chill windy street for a Princes Street bus, Bobbie's cash (more than she'd seen in years, and no, she didn't want to know how he'd got it) carefully folded in a zipped pocket inside her tightly-buttoned coat. The next three hours she spent fighting Christmas crowds in Princes Street stores. She bought so much she needed a taxi. The cabbie went on about: 'that bastard who blew up the Gruinard ferry', and how, when he was caught, the law would see to it he never got to trial alive. Taking her silence as licence, he told her how in Portobello last night: 'Some Spuritualists went crazy and saw ghosts. Folk shouldna meddle wi' the occult. It isn't Christian!'

With relief she got home . . . but while struggling upstairs with her load she ran into Mr Oswald, the crabbed old widower in the room above. He was among the tenants kept awake by her nightmares these past weeks. Now she cannoned into him as he emerged from the bathroom by her door (why was he in it, with one on the floor above?). Her parcels went flying. Normally he'd have grunted at her to watch where she was going, and stamped away up to his room without looking back. But today he managed a pale smile, and bent to help her. 'Christmas shopping, eh, Mrs Joyce?' he asked eyes and voice both saying: *Where would you get the cash for Christmas shopping*?

'Yes!' Smiling too bright, she improvised hastily, 'My sister – she's asked me south for Christmas with her and her family, it's the first time in years we've seen each other, so I just had to go out and . . .'

'How nice.' Obviously he didn't believe it. He piled the parcels in her arms. 'Now let me open your door – you'll never manage with all that.'

'I can manage,' she said, thinking: *Oh God he knows something, Bobbie made a noise, or maybe he had to . . . go, and he pulled the chain, or didn't pull the chain, and* . . . She flushed, standing with a stupid smile, waiting for the old bastard to bugger off. 'Really,' she repeated, 'I can manage.'

'Of course you can't,' he said, amazed, prising her room-key from the hand in which she'd been holding it since coming in. 'I insist!'

She prayed silently . . . and as he opened the door she let a parcel fall. As she grabbed for it she stumbled into him, pushing him back. 'Oh sorry,' she babbled, plunging past him, faint with relief, for Bobbie was nowhere in sight. 'And I'm so sorry I've made it hard for you to sleep lately but I've been having the most awful nightmares – you know I lost my husband and daughter years ago but it still seems like yesterday and . . .' – there in her door she stood babbling, blocking him. Retreating at last, he worked his liver-spotted ruin of a face into another fake smile. 'I do understand,' he said in that awful silky voice, 'So before you go you must join me in my rooms for a glass of sherry? 6.30 this evening? I'd be *most* honoured!'

'Yes, yes, 6.30,' she babbled, 'I'll see you then! Goodbye!'

And shutting the door in his face she dropped the parcels and sank onto her bed with a groan, feeling old and tired and harassed as the door of her wall cupboard opened and out came Bobbie, grinning like a lunatic.

'What are you laughing at?' she hissed in a whisper.

'Ye nivver telt me ye wis ane fer the lads!' he hissed back.

'Get *lost*, you . . .'

'Shhh!' His eyes widened in mock-alarm. 'He might be there yet!'

'What were you doing? He's suspicious. You must have . . .'

'I've been sitting here reading yer books, Diane. Not a sound have I made. Not a step have I taken outside yer door! Yer paranoid!'

'You haven't used the toilet? You haven't . . . ?'

'No.' He shrugged. 'Someone rang the bell. I let it ring, but I peeked out the windae. It wis a wifie, aboot yer age – fair hair. She went aff.' He shrugged, and Diane thought with a guilty shiver: *That was Frances*! 'As fer the toilet,' he admitted, 'if I don't go I'll bust!'

So her nerves suffered worse. She kept watch until he was safe back. Then she opened the parcels. There were clothes, accessories, scissors, hair-dye. 'Right,' she said grimly. 'Soon your mother won't know you!'

'She nivver kent me onyway,' said Bobbie glumly.

'. . . And when I'm done we'll go. Tonight.'

'No way,' said Bobbie promptly.

Her face fell. 'What do you mean?'

'My ID! Ye dinnae think they'll let Robert Scott Aird ontae the train, eh? There's a guy jist doon the road. You gie him a call an' go roond. Five hundert'll fix it. Do it now an' mibbe it'll be ready in the morn.'

Her sense of nightmare grew. But she did it. Leaving him watching old Roadrunner cartoons without the sound she went out again. The short winter day was already over; snow was falling as she came to a blackened Victorian stair off Clerk Street where, feeling like a gutter hag out of Robert Louis Stevenson, she knocked on a door, endured spyhole inspection, explained her mission, handed over cash and ID, and agreed to return at noon next day.

Back home it was time to undergo trial by sherry in Mr Oswald's rooms. The old goat *fancied* her! Two hours of evading his pawing papery hands left her exhausted. Out she went again, up the road for fish and chips. The snow was swirling thicker as she returned to her room. Bobbie grinned to hear of her ordeal as she made sure the curtains were drawn.

'Just get this stuff onto a couple of plates,' she snapped.

She turned the tv volume high as they ate. It was an import of the Carmody Cee Show. The famous chat-show host wore the face-fitting mask of a beautiful youth which, he told his guests (Paul Arouet, the 'Valentino of the Reelies'; Ibn Khalid the fashionable Egyptian poet; Philip Agutter the Metropolitan Home Secretary), represented Narcissus – 'Just a comment on the love we all feel for ourselves in London here and now as the millennium approaches,' he said with the outspoken cynicism for which he was famous.

But neither Diane, brand-new barber's scissors in her nervous hand, nor Bobbie were listening. 'Now,' she said with a strained laugh, 'I'm going to wipe that smile off your ugly mug! Come here! Sit down!'

The door-bell rang. They froze.

Again and again it rang. At length it stopped.

Diane dared a peek through the thick curtains and saw a slim female figure walking hunched down the street to the parked Ford Orion.

She felt faint with guilt. *I don't ever want to know what happened to Gussie*, she realized, and turned to see Bobbie staring at her. He didn't need to say anything. His look was enough. *On the run, eh*? it said.

She sighed, nodding him to the makeshift barber's chair.

Two hours later Bobbie Aird had been transformed.

At last she stepped back to view her creation, and she was smiling, for the hideous truth was that for the first time in years she was happy as she eyed the shaven blond-dyed man sitting uncomfortably in velvet three-piece suit, high-collared shirt, tartan cravat and bright black brogue shoes.

'Perfect!' She clapped her hands. 'Like a rugby-playing solicitor!' – for he sat there as sprucely glum as a little boy (*the son she'd never had*?) forced into poofy Lord Fauntleroy fancy-dress for a party.

'Aye,' he muttered, biting his shaven lip, 'I wis feart o' that.' He eyed her ferociously. 'I'm nae yer kiddie,' he warned, and the good humour left her. 'Stairt thinkin' it's a game, the game'll screw ye – get me?'

She did. That night, fully dressed, she lay in bed, Bobbie curled up at the foot of it, polar wind rattling the window and her nerves until at last she fell into confused sleep full of sad cries that had her weeping in the dark, unable to tell who cried, or where, or why. Frightened, she awoke at dawn . . . and instantly sat up to ensure Bobbie was there. Which, to her vast guilty relief he was. *But he's a killer*! Yet already she knew she'd let him into her starved heart . . . and knew he knew it. They were joined – by Salisbury Craig, by some deeper bond, as yet unknown, but part of whatever Chrissa and Sam wanted her to do. Her main confusion, that grey dawn, was moral. *How*, she asked herself, still appalled by him, *can I justify this*?

At which a voice whispered in her:

Diane, the War of the Light is fought for sinners, not saints! So call the cops. He won't hurt you. But can you face him when they come for him?

She knew she couldn't. She felt bad enough about the fun she'd had the night before; dyeing and dressing and clipping and cutting as if he were a doll of her middle-aged girlhood. Now he awoke to find her frying him bacon and eggs and black pudding. 'Don't get it over your suit!' she cried as, half-awake, he started eating, greasy plate over the neatly-folded clothes she'd bought him. He raised bleary eyes from his new-shaven face and told her to piss off. She bridled . . . but there were more important things. She went out for his altered ID. It turned out his number had been revised by a single digit, his name by one letter. 'That's worth five hundred?' she asked, tossing it at him when she came back. He grinned. 'Diane, a miss is as good as a mile. They use computers. Computers is stupid. Baird isnae Aird, right? 9 isnae 8. It's stupid tae change it more'n ye have tae. Onyway there's a molecular code in the plastic he'll have altered.'

That night, after hours of tense, silent waiting in the darkened room (twice more the door-bell rang: on neither occasion did either of them even peer past the curtains to see who it was) they tested his theory. When he was dressed to her satisfaction – (Yes, a muscular solicitor or man of the cloth, or maybe a financier) – she called a cab to pick them up at a corner three streets away. She left her room with the sense and the hope that she'd never see it again. Down the creaking stairs she went, case in hand, and hushed him out after her. Onto the slushy street with nobody to see them go. *Doctor Jekyll and Mrs Joyce*, she thought giddily, unable to believe what she was doing, detached and watching herself from a distance as they waited for the cab. Then at last they were clear away through the wet streets, over the Bridges to Waverley Station, to the ticket office, to the security gate that stood between them and the Aberdeen-London King's Cross train even as it pulled in. It was then she began to shiver.

'I don't know,' she said, 'I don't know if I can . . .'

'I'll take care of it,' Bobbie told her calmly, impeccable in brand-new suit and double-breasted wool overcoat, evening paper under his arm with the slimline computerized briefcase she'd bought him. He didn't look anything like mad Bobbie Aird! Or did he? Her shivering got worse.

'No,' she muttered, 'I can't go through with it.'

'Dinnae gie me that, Diane!' he told her brusquely, and took her elbow solicitously as they came to the cop at the gate.

'Good evening,' he said, amazingly accentless and to the middle-class manner born as he proffered their papers and tickets.

'London, eh?' said the cop, feeding their IDs into the scanner, eyeing them both. Diane tried but couldn't stop shaking. 'Travelling together?'

'Yes,' said Bobbie, and leaning to the cop's ear as the IDs came out, green light beeping, he said: 'She has to see a specialist at a woman's hospital down there. I'm her nephew. I don't want her worrying, it's serious, but there's just a hope that . . . know what I mean?'

The cop – smooth and young – eyed her dubiously. She hadn't heard a word Bobbie said. Her teeth were chattering now. Oddly this seemed to convince him. 'Good luck,' he said tightly and, handing them their IDs, waved them through as if he couldn't see the back of them fast enough.

'I gave him the idea yer dyin' o' the Big C or mibbe something worse,' Bobbie said casually once they were safely through, and chuckled. 'Ye wis shakin' sae bad I couldnae think o' nuthin' else. Didnae even look at me!'

'You're a bastard, Bobbie Aird,' she said wearily as they got into a half-empty carriage near the back of the train.

'Aye. But nae by birth. Talent I learnt in the school o' life!'

I really am awake, she told herself dully some minutes later, heart thumping as the aged 125 pulled out past the black bulk of Arthur's Seat and into the darkness east of Edinburgh's suburban sprawl, Bobbie's knees politely crossed on the seat opposite her, his face buried behind the evening paper. *Assembly Votes Scottish entry to NEC*, said the front-page headline; and on the back, *Hearts 6-Goal Thriller at Ibrox. It's really happening! We've got away with it . . . so far . . .* then she realized how she'd put it. *We've got away with it.* Not *I. We.*

Just me and Bobbie McGee, she thought, trying not to laugh, for it was too crazy, herself and this now-neat, shaven, three-piece-suited 15-stone lunatic so meek and mild behind his paper, on their way down to London, down to . . . what? *Diane! You must find Jim!* Jessica had cried in her dream. But who was Jim? Who was Jessica? She sighed, avoiding the curious eyes of a couple across the aisle, adrenalin still flooding in her. The way that cop had stared . . . *I'm not sure how much I can take*, she told herself.

'Jist relax,' Bobbie muttered through the paper, 'It's okay.'

She hoped he was right. She tried to settle with a book she'd brought along at random. Opening it, she stared unseeingly at the first page as her mind ran wild and Bobbie fell asleep. And the train ran clickety-clack clickety-clack through the windy night towards Berwick and the south.

13.
Sitting Ducks

Agutter never got to bed that night. One madness led to another. The CSU call – Diane Joyce and the Five-Oh-One-Alpha-Zero-Five – meant coded Ghost Project calls, and nobody happy to be woken up. Then back to what John Robinson's crackly voice claimed came word-for-word from the man who'd ordered the Great Pyramid. Back to the Khufu Tape. And yet again as the wind beat at his curtained window the Home Secretary listened, fascinated, fearful too. '. . . *and on that day,*' he heard, '*when the Whirling Castle appears again in the sky you will know that the Shift is near. There will be a ringing of bells all over the world, and that is the sign of the . . .*'

The Whirling Castle? What the hell's that! The man's nuts. But . . .

Then another override. News of the Shasta eruption, followed by a new rush of ISO updates, each to be assessed media-wise. *Now.* By himself in person. Agutter delegated nothing. With a sad look at Gillian smiling at him from the holo he poured another scotch, emptying the bottle, and said:

'STOP playback. START File *MEDIAWISE* 23-12-99. RECORD status of following stories.' Rapidly he dealt with each. 'Shasta – FULL RELEASE, NO RESTRICTION. Wotan rally riots in Hamburg and Dresden – LOW PROFILE, Code "LEFT-WING ELEMENTS RESPONSIBLE". Writing on the Wailing Wall – FULL RESTRICT. Unexplained powercuts – LOW PROFILE. NORAD computer malfunction retargeting US MIRVs on US cities – FULL RESTRICT. Loch Ness Mon . . .'

He shut his eyes. The wind had dropped. Dawn was near. *Mad*, he knew, kneading his brow. *Trying to censor the collective unconscious? What when the ghosts really begin to fly*? Draining his glass he coded the last item:

'. . . President Taurac's breakdown due to visit by Joan of Arc – FULL RESTRICT. CLOSE and SEND File *Mediawise* as appropriate.'

That was it. He got up, wearily drew back a curtain, and looked east, over the Weald, past the paddock where Gillian had kept her pony. When she was a girl. . . . He shut his eyes to the foggy dawn. Upstairs Carol would be awake already, grieving. *I can't face her*, he thought, *I've had enough* . . .

The printer began chattering again. He stared in disbelief, then tore off the print-out. It was the monthly breakdown of significant Met social indices. His eyes widened. A doubling in one month of traffic accidents, suicides, mental breakdowns and illegal abortions? 'RESTRICT TOP SECRET the lot of it,' he rasped, turning to the window again. 'I think I'll . . .'

The printer began chattering again. In a frozen calm he stared at it.

'Madness would be preferable,' he muttered through clenched teeth.

But reluctantly he ripped out the new sheet and read:

ISO

INITIAL REPORT

GLOBAL SOCIAL RESPONSE TO FACTOR X

'Okay,' he said, suddenly absorbed. Scanning the page he

reached for the whisky bottle, found it empty, and switched on the coffee instead.

It took him two cups of black Colombian to find his concentration.

Slowly he focused, and on page 2 began to read:

. . . that the 'singing' reported by 75 per cent of respondents frequently carries 'information' in redundant languages: i.e. Latin, Greek, Hebrew, Egyptian and Sumerian. Ninety per cent of these respondents claim understanding at the time of contact. Eighty three per cent of this latter group indicate however that understanding (or memory) fails when 'Factor X' withdraws.

Asked: 'WHAT IS "GLOSSOLALIA"? 93 per cent of respondents did not know. The rest gave replies including: 'Visitation of tongues by the Holy Spirit'; 'Telepathically hearing and knowing other languages'; 'It's what happens when you understand what a foreigner says without knowing how you do.'

All 7 per cent who gave positive responses to this question were members of the remaining 17 per cent group claiming to 'remember' what they had been 'told'.

This 17 per cent we break down into four main psychotypes: (1) the Apocalyptic; (2) the Optimistic; (3) the Stoic; (4) the Catatonic.

(PSYCHOSOCIAL OUTLINES OF EACH TYPE IN SECTION 3A BELOW.)

Variations from these psychotypes were statistically unimportant or cannot be quantified within existing parameters. However:

(1) All 17 per cent express desire to 'commune' (common-denominator term used as closest to the norm) with FACTOR X again: 'as soon as I can'; 'as Allah wills'; 'right now'. NOTE: Region-by-region global breakdown of this percentage provides no usefully significant variations. Such statistical uniformity on a global scale may in itself be seen as significant.

*(2) Asked if their intention would alter upon introduction by law of criminalization of 'communing' on threat of death or other major default of personal liberty, over 99 per cent of the 'Communers' (or 'Chancers': SEE *7 BELOW) indicated that it would not. (Some*

respondents laughed openly when asked this question, and claimed the very idea of such denial to be 'absurd'.)

(3) NOTE that 'Communers' (representing, we indicate, 1-in-20 of world population), CONSCIOUSLY reject existing political/devotional orthodoxies. Manichaean/Dualist influence on their worldview cannot be underestimated. Over 65 per cent of the sample explicitly define the 'State' or 'status quo' as the 'BEAST', the 'GREAT SATAN', 'AHRIMAN' (et. seq., as appropriate).

(4) This CONSCIOUS recalcitrance is buttressed by a . . .

But there he stopped reading. *Dualists.* He stared at Gillian's holo. 'Your lot were Dualists, weren't they?' he whispered. 'Those Cathars you went down to research,' Then he drew sharp breath. His lips tightened.

'Gillian,' he whispered, 'if you just vanished to join the Chancers then you've caused your mother and myself a lot of . . .'

He laughed at himself in disgust. *So what if she did*? he told himself, *It's our fault to start with. Original Sin? Great! I've had enough*!

Which was true, even if nothing else was.

Sinking down in his chair again with head in hands and elbows on his desk before the flickering screens he thought: *Agutter, you're a fink.*

And staring at those screens his memory unreeled the last decade, and found nothing in it to comfort him.

He'd been a radical once, yes. A Tory radical, a wet come home to port when She-Who-Must-Be-Obeyed had at last foundered amid a public chaos not seen in Britain since the Chartists; chaos reflected throughout Europe, throughout the world. Credit had collapsed. Debt both private and public had grown so great that nobody could even pretend to pay. The immediate crisis had passed – but with it the United Kingdom had also passed – into history. 1996 had divorced 1707. The Union was over. So too NATO and the EEC. There had been riots and starvation. But after the Split wide boys had emerged from holes to invent new games and find new suckers. Now in the new Met the old party went on. The poor were criminal *per se.* Those able to afford it buried their conscience in Reely-Show sand. And Agutter?

He'd accepted a post in Harry Fisher's 'reformed' Tory government. '*We pledge to resist big business wherever it acts against the interests of the community and of the environment as a whole.*' So he'd claimed on a party political broadcast in 1996 immediately after the first Met 'election'.

A lie from the start. He'd known fine that no western government could resist the sharks of banking and the deregulated media. It had been clear right away that Fisher's administration was end-game misgovernment – an *eat-drink-and-be-merry-for-tomorrow-we-die* fraud pretending democracy while in practice helplessly waving its hands and pocketing the pay-offs.

Yet after three years of it here he was still, Home Secretary, publicly mouthing the platitudes, privately bemoaning his conscience.

The symbol of his conscience (though not his department; nothing to do with him) was the Maghreb Motorway, alias the 'Refertilization Project'.

This multi-lane motorway was being built from Oran to Accra by British navvies transported on a lend-lease agreement. Some called it a new wonder of the world. Others saw it as a crime against humanity on a par with Pol Pot's efforts in Cambodia, or Hitler's in Belsen. Agutter was among them.

In October, after Gillian's disappearance, he'd guested on the Carmody Cee Show – (the re-run of which Diane and Bobbie ignored during their last night in Edinburgh). Carmody (in his Narcissus mask) had quizzed the Home Secretary on the morality of an agreement by which dinars flowed into the Met and down-and-outs out. He'd driven Agutter into such a hole that next day (the show taped but not yet broadcast) the Attorney-General (advised by Police Commissioner Rae) had tried to quash it. However the Law Lords had thrown out the injunction on the grounds that Met citizens had the right to question a policy that brought in revenue by selling the poor into the hands of a foreign power with, as Carmody put it, 'cash but no compassion'.

The show had gone out. Agutter knew Carmody had won because he had dirt on the private lives of three of the five Law Lords. That was how the Met worked; why Carmody was so hated and feared in certain quarters. He was a pragmatist: he knew that, in the Met, moral crusades succeeded only by arm-twisting and blackmail. And though that broadcast had begun his Cabinet decline, Agutter was glad now that Carmody Cee the Masked Marauder had forced him to admit publicly that Met policy was, essentially, Nazi.

Now this dawn with his head in his hands he was still glad. It was strange, but Gillian's disappearance had changed him – radically.

Oh well, he thought as at last he got up from his desk, *Delilah fooled Samson, but he pulled down the temple of the Philistines before he fell.*

Leaving the room he felt suddenly calm, at peace with himself. 'Bee!' he called at the dog-basket in the corner of the high dark hall. With the black labrador drowsy at his heels he went through to the parlour, where he pulled on wellies and Barbour jacket. 'Come on, girl. Walkies.'

Outside, fog obscured the dawn. Not even the fountain at the end of the lawn by the wood was visible. Bee eyed him mournfully. *You're crazy,* said her mournful eyes. He stared into the cold winter murk and abruptly hated that shrouded English sky. He shivered, not hearing what sang in him.

Diane Emily Joyce, he wondered uneasily, *Who are you*?

Behind him, a discreet cough. He didn't turn round. He knew he was a prisoner too as he leaned down and patted the dog. 'Come on, Bee,' he said, restraining his anger. 'Let's see if we can find a bunny or two.'

His MI6 minder followed dog and master into the wet December woods.

Clickety-clack. Clickety-clack. A long ride on the longest night, storm-winds rushing the train south to the Scottish border and on through the Union cities of Newcastle and Darlington down to York where last May Jack Ayrton, who in '96 led northern revolt against London, was murdered in the Minster as the rebel Archbishop anointed his forehead in a ceremony not seen in a thousand years – and not likely to be repeated. Shots had rung out, and the cathedral, only a decade earlier struck by lightning, was now struck by assassination. After the chaos, crowds surging into the rainy night, a dazed man was arrested. But like many other political killings, recent and ancient, it was soon clear that the killer was a pawn – of *what* wasn't so clear. Easy to blame the Met, or the CIA – but the facts didn't add up. A scared boy with a gun killed Black Jack. *A quiet lad all his life,* declared his flummoxed family. *Kept to himself. We never knew him. No girlfriends. He read a lot. Something turned him into a beast.*

Some were glad Black Jack was dead. As for the killer, he never came to trial. He was found hanging by his braces from the window-bars of his cell, face purple, tongue stuck out. Why was he left with his braces? Who cared? He was dead. Good riddance. Case closed.

So the train rocked south. Bobbie slept like a babe. Diane dozed, and nobody got on or off during the half-hour 4 am stop at York. It was a trip through an endless normal hell. Occasionally she opened her eyes to see other folk in the carriage – dim shadows slumped in semi-sleep like corpses in the ugly blue light. Only Bobbie, stretched out opposite her, evening paper still over his face, feet up on the seat beside her as he snored, struck her as having any real essence. *Ten years since I last came south,* she realized faintly as the train went CLICKETY-CLACK through darkness lit only by Pottery flares in the distance, *I used to live here. England*?

But the name meant nothing at all to her. Not any more.

She considered prodding Bobbie, waking him up . . . then sadly smiled to herself. *Chrissa*? she asked, *Are you here*?

But there was only the lonely clickety-clack, clickety-clack.

And with that sound hypnotizing her she fell asleep without knowing it; she slipped into dreams of endless corridors of shut doors that couldn't be opened, masked faces receding before her, and she didn't even wake up when, two hours later, the train stopped at Peterborough and the Met inspectors – brisk, tight, uniformed young men – boarded.

'Madam? Sir? Your ID and tickets please?'

Bobbie awoke instantly. He smiled as pleasantly as one can smile at 5 am on the longest night of the year. Diane was still asleep, her face careworn and tired. Out of his breast pocket he shovelled tickets and ID. 'She's with me,' he said, not brightly. 'She's nae well. We've got return tickets and cash, right? Do us a favour and don't wake her up.'

The inspector had the gaunt pure face of one who went for a three-mile run through the Fens every weekday morning after this pre-dawn routine. He eyed Diane coldly as he slipped their ID cards into the scanner at his hip.

'She's nae well,' Bobbie repeated, 'Now come on!'

The inspector pulled their cards out of his scanner and shrugged.

'Afraid you'll both have to get off,' he said, keeping their ID cards, neither a smile nor a frown on his face. 'Routine check. Wake her up.'

'Thanks,' said Bobbie sarcastically, 'You're a real pal!'

The inspector shrugged again. 'Now!' he said.

'Welcome tae civilization,' Bobbie grumbled as with a dozen others they were herded off the train through bitter wind into Peterborough Station's 'Transients' Lounge'. 'It's like a waiting room in a magistrate's court,' he went on as they entered the shabby, depressing, bare little room. 'Jist designed tae make ye feel bad. Whit's the bet we're here fer hours?'

Though on her feet, Diane was still asleep as the door shut behind them. She dreamed she stood as heavy as lead on a stained grey carpet facing bare walls shining dirty yellow under naked striplighting. High, tightly-shut windows gaped vacuously black above rows of moulded green plastic chairs so grubby she doubted she could make herself sit on any of them. The stink of urine was faint but persistent. The naked heat-pipes along one wall kept coughing like a terminal nicotine junkie. A broken coffee-machine stood by a few battered old video-game machines. On a scratched table were piled stained, dog-eared copies of the *Reader's Digest, True Confessions, Reely-Go-Round*, and Metropolitan Tourist Board pamphlets (*London: Gateway to a Million Dreams*). Feeling lost, she let Bobbie steer her to one of the less filthy chairs. Other derailed travellers also sat. Nobody spoke or looked at each other. Time passed. She stared at the black walls. Over half-an-hour went by before the door opened. A tall young black Met copper came in, glanced at her clipboard. 'John Anthony Dodd?' A pale young man in lurex jeans, shaven scalp sprayglowed purple, reluctantly followed her out. The door shut again. Still nobody spoke. Only windows creaking in the wind and the heat-pipes made any sound until Diane, unable to hold it back any longer, released a harsh, hacking cough. It woke her up abruptly. She saw faces staring, a few with sympathy, most blankly. 'That's the first time in . . .' she started, automatically apologizing, then stopped.

Since Portobello, she realized, *Since I met* . . .

Bobbie nudged her. 'Hey. Diane. Everyane coughs.'

She realized his accent was back, and of public volume. A new tickle in her throat abruptly froze. She stared at him.

But you spoke perfect English at Waverley, said her betrayed look.

Bobbie beamed. 'Are ye better the noo, auntie?'

She glared. *Why draw attention*? He shrugged. But when everyone had returned to their stupor he leaned over and added privately:

'Don't play games when they call ye. Jist show yer cash, say it's a sentimental journey tae see auld friends an' that. If they ask aboot me, I'm jist . . .' – he aped a face – '. . . an idjit that's seein' ye doon tae . . .'

'. . . Tae the pit, eh?' she giggled, feeling lightheadedly unreal.

Oh God, she thought at his baleful stare, *I've taken the piss*!

'Pick yer time fer the funnies, Diane,' he whispered fiercely, 'Jist try tae relax. An' if they try the clever crack on ye, shut yer gob.'

She said in a rising voice, not noticing as the door opened:

'Bobbie, it's your charm that drives me so . . .'

'Diane Emily Joyce,' said a flat voice behind the door. She flinched, hesitated. 'Move it,' said the flat voice, its owner still hidden.

'Ye dinnae have tae talk to her like that!' said Bobbie.

'Want to be on the next train north, Jock?' asked the flat voice.

'Aw, tae hell,' Bobbie muttered at her, 'Jist *go*! Afore I . . .'

'I'm coming,' she said quickly, fearing mayhem or, worse, Mr Baird's self-betrayal. Patting her hair grimly she stood and rounded the door.

And was shocked. *But he's just a boy! I've taught them older than him*! she thought, and said sternly: 'You don't talk to people like that!'

The sandy-haired boy-cop's face stayed utterly blank. Shrugging with his clipboard he motioned her before him into a bland yellow corridor. The sight of it took her aback. It was the corridor she'd just dreamed of on the train. The corridor that goes forever past shut doors. Now in a daze, her feet echoing, she was passing those shabby doors. They'd been painted off-white years ago. One by one their scratched black plastic name-plates blurred past her. At last the young man stopped. 'Here, ma'am.' His voice not unfriendly, he unlocked and opened a door to 'Passenger Counselling.'

'But I don't need any coun . . .'

'Sorry, ma'am.' He was blank again. 'Please.'

Unhappily she entered the windowless cubicle. The youth switched on an overhead bulb to reveal two ergonomically-moulded puce plastic chairs either side of a chipped desk that bore an unlit anglepoise.

'Inspector'll be here soon,' he said, 'Best sit down.'

'You're going to lock me in?' She stood half-in half-out.

'Might be a minute or two. Want a cuppa while you wait?'

'I could kill for a cup of tea,' she said, and wondered why.

'All you have to do, ma'am, is sit down. I'll be back.'

He gave her a nod then shut the door on her. It took a moment to sink in. She shivered and laughed shakily. 'Is it Darkness At Noon?' she asked 'Passenger Counselling' aloud, 'Just to visit London? What *is* going on?'

Claustrophobia twinged. So did panic. Gingerly she sat, crossing her arms, clenching her body against the shivering. *Come on Diane*, she begged herself . . . and when the cop returned with a mug of tea she seemed composed.

'Careful,' he said, standing over her. 'It's very hot.'

It was very sweet too. Yet she sipped with gratitude.

Don't buy it! she told herself fiercely, and looked up.

'Why is all this necessary?' she demanded in her severest voice.

'I don't make the rules.' He shrugged. 'Rather be home. In bed.'

'You live with your parents?' she asked artlessly, sipping again.

He scowled at her. 'I'm married. Three kids. Boy and two girls.'

My God, she thought wearily, wishing she hadn't succeeded in getting a rise out of him, for in his face she saw more than she wanted to see.

'How does your wife feel about all this?' she asked, sipping.

'All what?' He swam blank before her. 'She's got what she wants.'

'Sorry.' She felt hugely tired. 'Will this take long?'

'Inspector's a busy man, ma'am.' He seemed taller; his voice rang huge and hollow in her head. 'Don't worry. Got a return ticket?'

'Yes, I . . .' She yawned wide. 'Yes, but I still don't . . .'

Waves swept over her. The mug was enormously heavy. She tried to reach the desk to put it down, but the desk had retreated beyond reach.

'It's all right, ma'am. I've got it.'

Hands took something she was dropping.

'I have to . . .' – she yawned herself inside out – '. . . sleep . . .'

'Do it, ma'am,' the flat voice boomed. 'I'll wake you when he comes.'

And she dreamed she was on a stretcher with an unknown wound, carried through serpent corridors to an ambulance that raced wailing through empty streets. Through a window of the ambulance she saw a bright star shining, and in its light saw Chrissa and Sam . . . but their backs were turned. The fear began. On a trolley she was wheeled into a shining room where masked faces were backlit so that she couldn't see them or what they did. 'Alpha-Five-Zero order here,' boomed a voice, 'Code 76-E-678-DEJ.' Light flashed. There was fiery pain. Something writhed in her head. She fell to a stony plain where nothing was left but voices booming above her where she lay . . .

'Ma'am?' Hands shaking her, lifting her. 'Wake up!'

Very slowly she found herself slumped in the chair. Light blazed in her eyes and her head ached abominably. It was worst in her left ear. With a feeble gesture she tried to ward off the glare. It diminished.

'Ma'am? Wake up. The Inspector's here now.'

'What . . . happened . . . to . . . me?' she asked, clutching her skull.

'You fell off the chair when I wasn't looking, ma'am.' A concerned face. 'Cracked your head. Must have been a bad dream. Any better now?'

'I'll be all right,' she said listlessly.

'Sorry about the delay, Mrs Joyce,' said a second, older voice. Brisk and unsympathetic, it sounded not sorry at all. Vaguely beyond the light she made out a glint of rimless spectacles. 'Now. Your situation . . .'

'I had an awful dream,' she said through pain-clenched teeth.

'Well, that's public transport for you,' the Inspector said crisply. 'Can't expect an easy night if you will insist on not having a car, eh?'

She started to say: 'But I can't afford to . . .'

'If you can't, then why come here?' asked the face, a blur behind the light. 'You must realize that in the Met we don't cut corners any more. We all have to pay our way. Your lot hasn't bought that yet – eh?' To which she had no answer as the voice went on: 'Now. Your ID and ticket are in order, but we require appropriate credit references.'

Dully, trying to remember her dream, she dug in her bag.

'I've got . . . about five hundred . . . in my purse here . . . but what about my friend . . . Mr Baird . . . he's looking after me . . . my health, and . . .'

'Mr Baird has signed the N97 and may proceed,' said the face, ducking forward as a hairless white hand reached over the desk for her purse.

'I checked it, sir,' said the young cop. 'Royal Bank. In order.'

'Good,' the Inspector said. 'Issue credit exchange and a seven-day pass after she's signed the N97.'

'You . . . went through my purse?' she asked the youth in disbelief.

The spectacles glinted impatiently behind the light.

'Lived in Crouch End, eh, Mrs Joyce? What street was that?'

'Ber . . . Berkeley Road,' she said weakly, remembering Bobbie's advice. 'Round the corner from the Inland Revenue offices . . . look, you see, I've been sick, and before . . . if anything happens . . . I mean, I only . . .'

'Yes.' The spectacles smiled. 'There's no problem. Just sign the N97 No-Claims absolving Metropolitan authorities of any responsibility in the event of accident, illness, destitution or Act of Man or God befalling you or yours while on Metropolitan territory,' the Inspector rattled off in a brisk let's-get-this-finished-and-we-can-all-go-home voice. 'Officer?'

From the clipboard came a form and a biro. 'Sign here, Mrs Joyce.'

'Shouldn't I read it first?' she asked uncertainly. The ear-ache was intense. That dream? Or was she still dreaming? She wished she knew.

The biro was in her hand, the clipboard on her knee.

'Standard form, Mrs Joyce.' The Inspector stood. 'Ensures that Met taxpayers' benefits aren't abused by . . .' – he shrugged – '. . . aliens.'

'But . . .' – she struggled to think – '. . . what if I'm mugged, or . . .'

'There are trains north every hour, Mrs Joyce. It's been a long night, and I'm sure you want to end your journey. And I'd like to get home.'

'Come on,' said the copper wearily. 'Just sign it, and we'll fix you up with an Anadin and get you on the next train with your boyfriend.'

What do I do? she asked herself – then signed.

Five minutes later her cash had been changed for a plastic card she fumbled into her bag unexamined. The cup got her two Anadin then led her back to the waiting-room. It was empty but for Bobbie. He stood, eyeing her with concern. Very slowly he shook his head at the constable.

'You can both go,' the cop said flatly, 'Welcome to the Met.'

'Aye, and a Happy Christmas,' Bobbie growled.

He said no more till they were on their own on the platform. It was full winter daylight, a cold grey harl of wind-wracked cloud skeltering above. He took her by the arm. He still looked concerned.

'Jesus Christ,' he said, 'Ye wis hours. It's efternoon! I've been waiting fer hours and they wouldnae say a wurd. What did they do?'

The train was coming in. She shook her head, fighting tears as they found seats and pulled out on the last leg to London. Avoiding his eye she stared out at the flat Cambridgeshire fields. The Anadin was useless.

'Whit did they do?' he repeated, 'Ye look terrible!'

She tried to smile. 'I don't know,' she whispered, fighting the tears. She bit her lip. 'I was in a room and they gave me a cup of tea while I was waiting but I fell asleep and an awful dream, and I woke up with a foul headache.' She clapped her left ear. 'He said I fell off my chair while I was asleep and banged my head. They were so rude, and . . . I don't know!'

'Sounds fishy tae me.' He stared at her. 'Whit did ye dream?'

'I don't know.' She stared back, her face white. 'I can't remember.'

He sighed. 'Well. Mibbe that's whit happened. Why would they bother ye?' He grinned sourly. 'They didnae give me nae trouble. Jist straight through. Signed the no-claims an' Bobbie's yer uncle, as ye might say.'

She sighed. The ear-ache was fractionally easier now, but she still felt like death warmed up as London's grey suburban sprawl began and they came rocking through Wood Green and past Alexandra Palace, until at last, not far short of four o'clock in the afternoon, another night not far away, they slid through a dark tunnel to a final halt in King's Cross Station.

Only one thing she was sure about. *They did something to me*, she thought groggily as they left the train, *I don't know what, but they did.*

14.
Taking Chances

Yet once off the train into the Metropolitan hustle her weariness and headache vanished so fast it felt like magic. It didn't even strike her as odd how she left the platform with a new spring in her step. It was like passing a gate from one world to another which, though feared in advance as alien, was, now they'd arrived in it, both exhilarating and familiar.

I'm home! she realized with a shock as it came back to her how fourteen years ago in the wake of Sam and Chrissa's disappearance she'd rejected not only lost youth but London and the South too, fleeing north to hide with an incontinent old man. And since he'd died she'd stayed in hiding. Now she realized: *They weren't the only ones who vanished. I did too*!

For King's Cross, though face-lifted since, still felt and looked much as she remembered, and as they weaved onto the high-canopied concourse past uniformed police and whirring robot baggage-trolleys Bobbie saw her smiling like a starstruck kid at the crowds, at the smooth hustlers round the fast food joints and tobacco kiosks, at the babel of voices and tongues – Anglo, Greek, Rasta, Urdu, Bengali, Filipino, Arabic . . . and at the giant overhead Reely-screens, holo images dancing above electronic message-boards relaying the latest world headlines . . . and she read:

. . . 10,000 Feared Dead in California Eruption . . .

She gasped and stopped dead. The new colour drained from her cheeks.

'Whit is it?' Bobbie demanded. But she didn't answer, for –

. . . as 'Holy Mountain' Shasta Explodes 0600 Hours GMT . . .

– abruptly she was back in her dream three nights ago:

The volcano erupting; the screaming faces and fiery rain; the black-haired woman driving desperately through a lurid night-land – a woman whose name, she knows, is Jessica – and Jessica meets her eyes . . .

'Diane!' Jessica cries, 'You must find Jim. You must!'

But someone's shaking her. Hands lifting her onto a . . . a trolley; she's wheeled into a bright room where masked figures hover. 'Alpha-Five-Zero order here.' Light flashes; then . . .

'Oh God!' Clapping both hands to her head she moaned and swayed, for suddenly the ear-ache was back and the world about her wavered as . . .

'Diane!' It was Bobbie shaking her. 'Snap out of it.'

She did. But she was shivering as she stared at him.

'Whit is it, fer godsakes?' he demanded.

She breathed deep. Looked up at the electronic message-board.

. . . Al-Khash Delegate Ibrahim Sid' Ahmed in London Talks with PM Fisher Denounces Amerislav Papal Orbiting Platform (POP) Proposal and Warns of New Hezbollah Military Initiatives if the . . .

'I don't know.' Wildly she looked for a news kiosk and, spotting one, without explanation dropped her case and left him standing. 'Fer heaven's sake,' he muttered as she vanished into the crowd. 'Whit am I doin' here wi' this mad auld biddie?' And it occurred to him for the first time, but not the last: *Mibbe it's the price I have tae pay . . .*

At the stall Diane picked up the Standard. KRAKATOA 1999! screamed the blood-red headline. She felt in her bag for her cash, then realized she had no cash, not here, only a piece of Tory-blue plastic, the holopic of Winston Churchill etched in it over a set of silver numerals. 'In 'ere, lady,' said a glum Pak youth in the kiosk (the concourse was warm, yet he was swathed head to toe in a Maghreb-style striped wool djellabah), 'In the credit point 'ere.' She fumbled her card into the slot, wrong way round at first, then she got it right: a green light glowed, and the plastic which, when she'd put it in, carried the numerals 425.57, emerged reading 424.82.

Carnage in California! ran the sub-head of the Standard, also in blood-red. She stood staring at it, Bobbie forgotten. The bottom half of the front page consisted of a full-colour holopic. It showed a helicopter tumbling apparently right into the radiant orange-and-scarlet maw of the erupting volcano. Under the holo-pic was a black blob, slightly luminous, next to the advice: *Scratch here for Reely-sim then turn to centre pages for more great holopics of 1999's worst calamity*! And as Bobbie saw her and pushed through the crowd, she scratched the blob, then flinched, for the holopic came to crawling life right on the page: she saw the chopper plunge, rotors whirring, into the inferno; saw plumes of orange-and-scarlet earth-fire soar up to meet and consume it – then it faded and turned black.

The effect had lasted two, maybe three seconds. 'Whit're ye up tae?' Bobbie demanded, reaching her, putting his hand on her arm, but she shook it off and turned to the centre pages, where more holopics were offered.

'No!' she snapped, scratcing page 16's holopic blob. 'Get away!' And *Panic in Redding*! came to life: howling faces against a backdrop of fallen buildings and burning sky; then that holopic too was spent.

'Don't waste time wi' shite, Diane!' Bobbie roared as she scratched the page 17 holopic blob – *1,000-Year-Old Giants Destroyed For 200 Miles About*! – and saw a redwood forest rage with flames, deer and other dimly-glimpsed animals fleeing. 'But I saw it in my dream!' she hissed as again he tried to grab the Standard, 'There was a woman, Jessica somebody, I don't know, and get away from me, *just get away*!' She glared at him: he stood back, folding his arms, for two coppers a dozen yards away were watching them.

'Diane,' he said carefully, 'this shite belongs tae the Beast. Dinnae let it get tae ye, or ye winnae last long. Now let's get out o' here!'

'But I dreamed it before it happened,' she said dully.

He shrugged. 'I'm no sayin' ye didnae.'

'Then what are you saying, Bobbie Aird?' she demanded.

'Whit I'm sayin',' he said patiently, 'is that, dreams or nae dreams – don't turn round – there's two cops watching us. Now,' he went on as she froze, 'furst we cool down, then we eat, then we get up tae Finsbury Park tae find if my mate can gie us a bed. We do that soon, because if he isnae there, or if he cannae put us up, then we'll need tae find a hotel before the snatch cops is out an' lookin' fer folks like you an' me – Get me?'

'You make it sound like an inhuman jungle,' she said resentfully.

'That's the truth o' it. Now. I'm famished.' Plucking the Standard from her he waved it through the crowds at the bright neon of a Casey Jones joint. 'How about a Deluxe half-pound cheeseburger wi' all the trimmings?'

She shrugged. He tossed the Standard into a bin and picked up their cases. The cops had lost interest. Dully she followed him to the Casey Jones, where a skimpy tunafish sandwich and mocha coffee put her back from 424.07 to 418.14, VAT included. Amid the plastic and neon she sat in her headaching dream again, watching him polish off his coronary meal.

'So now we take the tube to Finsbury Park,' she said, disgusted as with a satisfied belch he wiped the plate clean with his last crinkly fry.

'No,' he said, picking his teeth, 'We take a cab.'

'We can't afford it! What's wrong with the tube?'

'I can handle the muggers an' glowboys an' pseudodeath zombies,' he told her with no smile at all, 'but I cannae handle walkin' fer miles.'

'But it's only a few hundred yards from Finsbury Park to . . .'

'The tube disnae stop at Finsbury Park, Diane. Closed Area! No public services.' He stood up. 'Okay? Or are ye stickin' back in 1985?'

'Think you know it all, don't you?' she muttered.

'I wis here last year. Let's go.'

So again she followed him over the concourse (. . . *Chancellor Wood Claims Record Met GNP* . . . relayed one message-board; . . . *Chinese Population now at 1,500,000,000: Infanticide Official* . . . another informed; and a third asked: . . . *Vagabond Bonnie King Charlie Incognito in Met Closed Area?: Buy News on Sunday this Sunday!!!*) past Underground escalators through automatic doors to the cold windy outside world of Euston Road and a curving cab-rank pier.

It was getting dark. Shivering they queued behind other travellers – but as the big black London cabs wheeled in off Pancras Road and they edged forward it was Shasta she had on her mind. *Jessica*, she wondered, *Who are you? And Jim? Something to do with the Company? With Sam and . . .*

Bobbie turned and nudged her: 'Look at that!'

'At what?' she muttered angrily, but then she saw, and her mouth fell open. Around them some people gasped in horrified disbelief.

For approaching along the crowded pavement of the busy Euston Road was a chanting column of hundreds of people – men, women, children too.

Many were naked from the waist up. The rest wore rags. They carried placards daubed with slogans she couldn't make out any more than at first she could hear what they were chanting against the roar of the traffic.

All that was odd enough. But it wasn't what shocked her.

It was the whips and sticks that shocked her.

For they were beating each other like medieval flagellants in terror of the Plague, the mounted police escort making no effort to stop them as they staggered closer, half-naked in the vicious cold wind, chanting in ragged unison. Still it was hard to hear them, but now the message on the front placard, borne by a scrawny old man, was plain enough. *Take a Chance!* it read, and the one behind, carried by a lank young woman with thyroid eyes, exhorted: '*Try to Dance!*. And as they beat each other past Diane realized that this was what they were chanting – '*Take a Chance! Try to Dance!*' – and a cold thrill seized her as she also realized that the placards, read one after the other, delivered this simple rhyming message:

Take a Chance!
Try to Dance!
The Shift is Nigh!
Through Pain We Fly!
Forget Your Name!
Forget the Game!
Leave Your Home!
Seek the Stone!
Time is Short!
The World's Been Bought!
But the Shining Light!
Is Coming Bright!
To Beat the Beast!
And Heat the Yeast!
So Take a Chance!
And Try to Dance!
Before it's Too Late!
To Open up the Gate!
So Take a Chance!
Take a Chance!

She stood frozen as the lunatics passed not twenty yards away. The Shift! The Beast! The Gate! Now their chant – *Take a Take a Take a Chance! Try to Try to Try to Dance!* – lost all verbal meaning for her. It beat in her brain like drums. A bursting inner pressure surged in her, and the blood rushed to her face even as Bobbie turned, grinning.

'Ever hear o' the Chancers?' he demanded loudly, himself so taken aback that he didn't notice her glazed look, 'That's them. Stupid idjits. Think the end o' the wurld's nigh in eight nights, on Hogmanay, 31st o' December 1999 – end o' the millenium, and a' that shite.' He gave them two fingers. 'Dinnae worry about them, Diane – they're total nutters.'

'How *dare* you, young man!' demanded an old woman in tweeds in front of him, and she stopped him seeing what was happening to Diane, for even as he turned to face her, Diane gasped, shutting her eyes. '*Take a Take a Take a Chance!*' For her brain, beating to the chant, suddenly seemed to rupture.

Appalling pain flared in her: she was swept away from King's Cross on wings of mad rhythm; she was consumed by raging fire amid a crushing void; her heart beating to a pulse so enormous she feared it must burst even as she saw faces watching her. Faces familiar from her dreams of the war Sam and Chrissa had fought against the Watchers. She saw the mocking masked face of a raven-haired woman and knew it was She who'd seized Sam. She saw the Beast squatting on the clouded breast of the Hidden World, throat slit, mad eyes gloating . . . and the Beast saw her and laughed as his cloacal breath smothered her. Now she couldn't breathe. She was drowning. Yet even as the black wing of panic roared over her she sensed the others about her.

Later she said they'd resembled Doré's angels – beings, light and free and rhythmic; shifting clouds of light that swam into her mind and relieved it. Briefly in her mind's-eye they seemed to take individual human form; she thought she saw Sam and Chrissa among them and heard, in the pulse of her heart and beat of her brain – 'Take a Take a Take a Chance!' – then they coalesced into a blinding river of light plunging into this blazing (yet dark thick heavy) void from a gate, or door, so high and radiant she could not face it. Yet they were in and of her and she knew they were helping her to fight the death-guilt bred in her by the Beast!

'*We are the company of those who return to time for the Shift!*' she heard them chant, '*But we can't return if you won't help. The gate is as wide as courage, as narrow as fear! So take a take a take a chance!'*

She felt petrified, elated, and doomed all at once. Strangest of all was that amid this violent vision she remained aware of King's Cross. From her pain-height she saw, as if watching a puppet-play, her tired old body standing at the cab-rank, knowing that the TAKE A TAKE A TAKE A CHANCE rhythm of the flagellants had somehow triggered this vision.

She saw how Bobbie, his back to her, faced an outraged old woman.

'How DARE you!' she heard the old woman cry, and saw Bobbie glowering as the Barbour-jacketed old gent with the old woman said sharply:

'Lily, be careful! We're not in Leominster now!'

But Lily ignored him, bashing her walking-stick at Bobbie's feet.

'How DARE you!' she repeated, glaring at Bobbie. Before he could speak she rushed on: 'Don't you see that evil rules this world? I have lived a long time, young man, and . . .'

'Lily, please!' the old bloke tried again, eyeing Bobbie uneasily.

'It's okay,' Bobbie seemed not only amused, but impressed.

'. . . you should be ASHAMED of yourself! Those people may be deluded in many respects," Lily continued as the Chancers went on towards Islington, their chant diminishing, 'BUT they are NOT – what did you call them . . .'

'Total nutters,' agreed Bobbie, nodding engagingly.

'Yes. Exactly. At least they recognise that . . .'

'. . . We live in Satan's wurld,' he said, stealing her words, and Diane saw her smile as Bobbie spread brawny hands wide in appeal. 'Lady, don't get me wrong! I laugh because life's bad enough, but they make it wurse! They parade pain as a big deal! But we a' ken that!' His voice had risen. Other people had turned to listen. 'They say the wurld's tae end soon! But that's because they're full o'shite. They're a' fookin' wankers!'

'What do you mean?' Lily demanded, the slight smile on her face.

'I mean . . .' – Bobbie laughed – '. . . folk that whip themsels is fooked! They've fallen tae the Beast! They're doin' his job fer 'im!'

Lily's smile broadened. 'So you're not just a thug.' she said, as from her painful-height Diane heard herself say loudly:

'But Bobbie, that's just what you did . . . isn't it?'

He still hadn't noticed her weird condition. 'Aye,' he said, turning, 'so I ken why it's fooked, right?'

Then he saw the bright glazed light in her eyes. 'Whit's the matter?' he asked, suddenly concerned.

She eyed him down a long tunnel. 'Take a chance' she whispered, 'and maybe you'll find out.'

'Aw, Diane!' Waving a hand he turned away. 'That's shite!'

The queue had shortened despite the fact that flagellant parade cabs had been pulling in every few seconds. Eyeing Diane, Lily said: 'My dear woman, if you're with this brute I pity you!' But as her husband pulled her away Bobbie forgot her. Because he was scared now; scared by Diane's look.

'You're wrong.' She felt remote, cauterized by the fire amid which – what? Already it was hard to recall. 'If they're mad, I am too. You saw their placards? You don't remember? I just met them again.'

'Whit are ye on about,' he asked uneasily, eyeing her flushed face even as Lily flagged the next cab with an angry walking stick.

But she said no more. She wasn't sure herself. The pain in her was like a fire, burning up all she knew of herself . . .

15.
Worms

. . . And she had no idea how, in the CSU labs barely two miles away on the fifth floor of a dilapidated 1960s highrise eyesore in Holborn, a young technician in charge of gear he didn't understand (demand for chemotronic trackers had outstripped trained supply) cursed in a sweat as, too late, he interpreted incoming data, saw what was happening, and cut the strength of signal in the unique Code Blue Five-Oh-One-Alpha-Zero-Five installation, *Diane Emily Joyce*, (76-E-678-DEJ), presently at King's Cross Station.

His name was Mike Goss, he was eighteen: he'd learned the theory but this was his first day at CSU, and it was his bad luck to be standing by console 77 when the operator, Joe O'Brien, a married man involved in a complex love triangle, received a hysterical phone call from his mistress Claudine.

'I am going now to the top of the Monument,' she shrieked down the line at Joe, 'and if you are not with me in thirty minutes I will know you love your wife and not me – and when I am dead, my lawyer opens an envelope!'

Joe had never run out on the job before. Normally, he'd have laughed at her – dared the silly bitch to do it. But just lately . . .

Joe had joined CSU after five years on developing tracking techniques for Pseudodeath brainstem implantees. He was an artist at tracking without the sucker suspecting, so that the awful moment of Pseudodeath shock always came as a surprise as much to 'actor' as to 'audience'. He'd programmed for Hitler, Goebbels and the rest in *Berlin Bunker*, following that hit with acclaimed work on ever gorier Reelies (*Hiroshima Now; Gilles de Retz*, and *Ayatoliah's Agony* among the best-known) that catered to the growing market for Sensory identification with sadistic death. His expertise had won him a five-room apartment in Chelsea, plus homes in LA, Nice and Kiev.

A good life . . . but . . . hell! There had to be more. Even the punters who gobbled it despised him. Everyone trading in Pseudodeath despised everyone else. For a time he'd tried justifying it on therapeutic grounds.

'Listen, you liberal jerk,' he'd shouted at Carmody Cee during one of Carmody's more contentious broadcasts, 'we can't afford more major wars on this planet. We all know it! And everyone but bleeding hearts like you also knows we're still semi-evolved primates with murder in our hearts. So isn't it better to tie up the lower neural circuits of dominant primates in vicarious fantasy death than letting them loose to create the *real* havoc that turns history into a charnel-house? Listen! My clients looped into Pseudodeath shows get rid of that bloody tension – in us all – which in the past always led to wars in which millions were *really* slaughtered! Right?'

'Wrong,' Carmody had sighed. 'Met crime rate's up 50 per cent this year. There are twenty *minor* – non-nuclear – wars currently in play round the globe. Amnesty International estimates real-war deaths last year at ten million – not to mention those driven to death by imposed economic, race, or class situations of a sort not usually described as war *per se* . . .'

'But it would be even worse if . . .' – Joe had tried to interrupt – but Carmody (in his Wilberforce mask) knew how to deal with people like Joe.

'But,' he'd gone on, 'you ignore the evidence that your suckers who contract Psuedodeath – what's your slogan? – *Pseudodeath Times Three Buys Prosperity?* – end up total zombies. The shock destroys the central nervous system, right? So, three 'deaths' and they get an inflation-linked pension – but what's that worth to zombies? They're so traumatized they're useless to themselves and deadly dangerous to everyone else. Can you deny it?'

Ben *had* tried. But (maybe it was Eve's persuasion; or maybe something called conscience) barely a month later he'd jacked it in and joined the CSU for a derisory wage. This made the News. 'It's time I did something useful,' he'd mumbled, ducking the camera's eye. 'If we want to stay free then we have to fight the retards who want to wreck our prosperity.'

So for a year he'd been tracking suspected anti-Met subversives who'd been bugged by devious means that meant most of them never knew it.

The bio-plastic radio-sensitive bugs used by the CSU were known in the trade as 'worms.' Indetectible by X-ray or electroscan, visible only to an electron microscope, the worm was fed into the brain by way of the parietal lesion, optic chiasm, or by one or another of the aural passages. Surgery was minimal: there was no external evidence of interference. Once in the brain, the worm, utilizing its augmented virus properties, would rapidly reproduce itself, feeding on brain-cells to strike out along the ganglia much as a fungal parasite takes over and kills the branches of a tree.

The tracker radio-controlled the speed, extent, and direction of this reproductive spread, sending worm-filaments throughout the left cerebral hemisphere and limbic system, and especially to the amygdalae which, being connected to cortex and hypothalamus, received input from every sensory mode. Worm-nets infiltrating this organ were employed, via signals radioed from the tracker's console, to elicit specific mood-changes in the bugged subject. They also operated as the main transmitter, sending out impulses which, amplified on tracking screens, could be read by skilled trackers to reveal exactly what was happening in the subject's immediate environment.

It took real skill . . . and for some hours Joe O'Brien had been directing worm-spread through the new implantee (76-E-678-DEJ), also fine-tuning the amygdaloid net to pick up any response by the subject to Chancer neurogenic activity in the vicinity – the worm being pre-coded to stimulate and signal subject response to a known range of Chancer profiling. So when the ragged crew came by King's Cross as Diane waited for a cab, she heard the chant, her amygdala picked up the incoming data, the worm recognized the data ('*Take a Take a Take a Chance*') as a profiled Chancer hypno-rhythm – and promptly triggered her hypothalamus and pituitary into violent activity, saturating her brain with hormones and sugars commonly associated with the hallucinogenic experience . . . and up, up and away she went.

And all because Mike Goss didn't know to interpret the data.

Had Joe been there he'd have picked up warnings from the incoming data; he'd have damped down amygdaloid stimulus and avoided a hallucinatory flare of the sort that often alerted individuals who knew the technology to the fact that the CSU had bugged them. All would have been well.

But Joe wasn't there. Lately he'd been under stress. Since joining the CSU (giving up his homes in LA, Nice and Kiev) his relations with Eve (they had no family: kids cost too much) had disimproved dramatically. And six months ago, during a 3 am boozing session with French ISO colleagues on the Rue Réaumur in Paris, he'd met Claudine. Maybe it was then he'd begun to snap, for at the sight and scent of her his hypothalamus had flooded his blood with a dizzy array of chemicals that caused instant reaction. As for Claudine, she knew a promising situation when she saw it. Joe was English, thus probably about as passionate as a flounder, but his Gold Card spoke volumes. Thus after one night he'd promised her the earth . . . and a week later found her a Camden Town flat. Idiot! He knew it, and didn't blame her . . . but lately he hadn't slept more than three hours a night;' he'd kept going on coffee, coke, sex, scotch, and increasingly flimsy lies to Eve, who now impatiently spoke of *finding herself on her own*. And Claudine . . .

But the signs of his crisis – daily hangover, wild talk, criticism of authority – had been ignored by Chief Super Macdonald who, himself under mounting stress, refused to reprimand and risk losing his top tracker.

So when Claudine called threatening suicide, he slammed down the phone, spun round in his chair, spotted Mike Goss, and called him over.

'Hey, kid! Yeah, I mean you. Sit in here for me for two hours and it's worth 500 U's. You know what to do? Nothing's on Red – all routine – cover me and I'll see you right when I get back.'

He was out of the door before Mike Goss knew what had happened.

'Excuse me,' Mike asked the next-door console cautiously, 'But . . .'

'Don't worry, kid,' the Console 78 operative assured him, 'Joe's been having a hard time. Just watch what's coming in and keep it balanced.'

Which he did, no problem. He was even getting confident, when Contact 76-E-678-DEJ erupted without any warning that *he*'d been able to foresee.

'Jesus!' he yelped as the telemetry went wild, but even as the Console 78 operator turned to him he remembered his training and cut the amygdaloid stimulation level which had run over into the red.

It flowed back down to a pacific green. He began to relax.

No harm done, he assured himself, but he was still shaking.

Leaning over him, the Console 78 operator had a look. He sighed and said: 'Not your fault. Joe shouldn't have done it. But we can cover up.'

'Cover up what?' asked Mike Goss.

Console 78 laughed. 'That's what we're here for. Covering up. But just – for now – damp her right down. Okay?'

Joe returned an hour later, eyes wild but otherwise okay: it had taken him forty minutes from Holborn to the top of the Monument. Of course the bitch hadn't jumped. He'd been suckered – again. He could live with it.

'Okay, kid?' he asked, 'No problems?'

Mike Goss eyed Console 78. A nod and a wink. Anxiously he said: 'No. Subject's now in Closed Area N4. Stroud Green Road, Finsbury Park.'

'Good on you.' Joe clapped him on the back. 'Thanks a lot. Gimme your plastic and I'll see it uprun 500 U's. Okay?'

'Sure,' said Mike Goss, and that was that. Nothing was said. Not then. Not by anybody. Because no problems admitted meant – no problems.

But at a Cabinet meeting Philip Agutter was having problems.

'Harry!' he said angrily, on his feet facing a silent Prime Minister and sober Cabinet colleagues, 'if we don't discuss it now we'll get into a situation we not only can't predict but have no hope of controlling.'

He waved the file of ISO reports in his left hand. He knew the PM was bothered by Sid' Ahmed's demand for a steep increase in the Refertilization Labour Quota, but he was determined to get this on the Cabinet minutes.

'I know it sounds crazy! It *is* crazy! But it's not just in the Met! It's everywhere! In the last three hours I have ISO updates from New York, Seoul, Sydney, Moscow, Rome, Bucharest – you name it – and whatever it is, it's on the increase. The curve's exponential, and if we don't . . .'

'What events, Philip?' Joy Hoeller, the Foreign Minister, gave Harry Fisher a look that said: *He's cracking. It's his daughter.* 'What are you on about?' She shrugged at him. 'Unreliable rumour, that's all.'

'That must be true, Philip,' said Chancellor Peter Wood, his smile more engaging than usual, 'Let's face it; we're nine days from the end of the century – the end of the millennium, if you like – and inevitably we face a rash of madcap apocalyptic rumours that . . .'

'It's not the end of the century for Muslems, Jews, Chinese, or the rest of the global population that doesn't use the Christian calendar,' Agutter said tersely, hooking thumbs in his belt and standing his ground. 'Please explain the reports I've had in the last hour. In Riyadh: mass riots following collective vision of Al-Khash as Son of the Prophet! In Jerusalem: riot after the appearance on the Wailing Wall of writing in dripping red letters that appeared with nobody to . . .'

'What did the writing say, Philip?' Even in deepest winter Transport Secretary Tom Fanthorpe wore an MCC tie, '*Mene Mene Tekel Upharsin*, and all that?' – and his fat face looked round for a laugh, which he got from Joy Hoeller and Bernard Dick the Trade and Industry Secretary.

The PM's face showed nothing at all. It never did, these days.

'Yes,' said Agutter wearily. 'Exactly what it did say.' From his file he plucked a holo and spun it over the table to Dick. 'Reuters. An hour ago. The Knesset's meeting now. The writing won't scrub. Do you get me? Do you want more examples? I've got about fifty or sixty right here. From every part of the world. People saw dragons in the sky over Beijing two nights ago. In California a few hours ago, of course, they *did* see the dragons – volcanic dragons. At least ten thousand dead – so far.'

'What's this to do with us?' asked Bernard Dick. Pushing the holo away he started doing the Times crossword. Annoyed, Agutter rushed on:

'Here! A report that President Taurac's under sedation. Seems Joan of Arc called on him last night.' He eyed the PM fiercely. 'That's why you couldn't get him about the Havre reactor leak this morning, Harry.'

The PM only tightened his already tight lips.

'These are isolated events,' Agutter went on wearily, 'the visible tip of the iceberg. So far here in the Met we're relatively unaffected. Or so it seems. But I have other figures. Met admissions to mental hospitals doubled last month. Likewise suicides, violent crime, traffic and domestic accidents, abortions.' He breathed deep and stared round the table. Weak light fell through the veiled windows onto locked faces. 'These increases are paralleled in Russia, the States, Africa, the Middle East . . .

everywhere.' He went on, 'Religious vision, paranoid dementia, or the mass eruption of the collective unconscious – call it whatever you like, but don't deny it! We *can't* deny it. The evidence is plain.' He eyed them each in turn and grew depressed. 'It's happening even if we can't define it or decide yet who's behind it,' he said dully. *Why bother?* he wondered, then privately knew: *Yes, I have to.* Briefly he met Joy Hoeller's eye. 'Something nobody knows about!' he insisted, trying to rouse them, slapping the ISO file. 'Nothing in this fits any parameters of normality. But – it *is* happening! And we must at least try to find a strategy to deal with this . . .' – his voice rose – '. . . *crisis* in the affairs not just of the Met, but of humankind!'

Nobody said a word.

Sixteen pairs of eyes stared at him, collectively so blank that as he sat again he felt his good intentions switched off like a power cut.

What's the use? he wondered. *We can't see anything we're not used to seeing, and if we do see it, the rest call us mad. Even when the house is burning down we're still lynched if we say it's happening.*

Maybe that's what the Chancers are saying, he thought – a thought that horrified and divided him. *What am I thinking?* He laughed silently. *Now, come on, Philip! You're trying to crush and discredit them. They're just the same old idealistic troublemakers – mystic gnostic anarchists – aren't they? Eh, Philip? What practical goal or policy have they got?*

He sighed. The Khufu tape. He'd heard it over and over again in the last forty-eight hours. *What if it's true?* he asked himself almost absent-mindedly.

'Philip,' said Harry Fisher, 'what are you talking about?'

Agutter raised his eyes to the ceiling. 'Must I say it all again?'

'No, Philip,' the PM said heavily. 'We hear you. But what are we to do about it? Shouldn't people run their own lives?'

There was a time, Agutter remembered as he met Harry Fisher's old grey eyes, after the last election, the party safely back with Met economy on an upswing again, when he'd got on well with the PM. But that time was gone – and it was gone, Agutter now grimly knew, because Harry, Peter, and Uncle Tom Fanthorpe and all just couldn't cope with whatever didn't fit their preconceptions. Quite apart from the fact that most of them, Harry included, were now firmly slotted in Commissioner Rae's capacious pocket.

Of course it fitted the masked nature of the Met nowadays that the real power, the power behind the throne as it were, wasn't at this meeting of the inner council of government. He didn't have to be.

Agutter met Joy Hoeller's eye again and looked away.

They'll live and die in fear and fantasy, he thought. *Me too.*

'Harry,' he said sadly, 'People govern themselves by electing people like us to govern them. That's why we're here.' He smiled sarcastically. 'We're meant to be the cream of a once-great nation, Harry. We're meant to be more than babies, Harry,' – his voice was rising – 'we're meant to be wise men and women with the moral, emotional, and intellectual capacity to rule the destiny of millions of other people who put their trust in us!'

'All right, Philip!' Harry Fisher slapped the table, his eyes alive at last, and Agutter thought: *Well now! We're getting somewhere!* 'You're overstating the case!' the PM went on, to nods and mutters of agreement round the Cabinet table. 'Philip, we know you've been working hard. And of course your poor daughter! We sympathize. Naturally you're concerned. But we cannot let private worries influence our public duty!'

'Harry, my daughter has nothing to do with it!' Agutter cried. 'What I have to get across to you is that . . .'

'So,' – the PM waved his objection aside – 'there's a problem. I see that. But we have more immediate problems. Clause Five of the Maghreb Agreement, for example. I have to answer to Sid' Ahmed by 9 am tomorrow. Thanks for your contribution, Philip, but I believe in letting sleeping dogs lie – until they bite! Now! Can we get on with *real* issues? The Quota . . .'

Amid a chorus of 'hear-hear' Agutter cried out:

'But Harry, the dogs aren't asleep any more.'

But he was ignored . . . and in that moment he knew what to do.

16.
Closed Areas

'Stroud Green Road, mister.'

Bending to the smoked-glass grille of the cab Bobbie peered past the steel armour plate to the vaguely-visible driver, a grizzled black guy who promptly shook his head, his voice echoing tinnily back.

'Sorry, mate. Closed Area. Against regulations. Junction of Hornsey and Seven Sisters Road is as far as we go. So what's it to be?'

'Hornsey Road then, if it disnae paralyse ye,' Bobbie grumbled.

'Listen, Jock!' the cabbie snapped back, 'We don't need whingers like you here. If you can't hack it, go back where you came from – right?'

'Back where *I* came from?' Bobbie howled, 'That's rich, you bl . . .'

Diane, exhausted, freezing too, jerked his sleeve hard.

'Okay,' he muttered, breathing hard, 'If I didnae have a lady here. . . . So make it Hornsey Road, *Winston*!'

'Just slot it!' said the cabbie, making it an insult.

'Here, Bobbie!' Hurriedly Diane gave him her card. 'Cool down!'

With a thunderous face he slotted it. It went in at 418.14 and came out at 403.02. 'Fifteen bludy quid!' he moaned as the cab door opened.

I'm in London, Diane reminded herself. *This is it. Where I lived.*

They entered a sealed velveteen interior. 'Nae a cab, it's a fookin' cathouse,' Bobbie said loudly as they sat, 'an' whit in hell is this?'

For before them, in place of the traditional sliding glass between them and the cabbie, was a 48-inch holoscreen that came to dazzling life as soon as the door locked behind them and the windows automatically opaqued.

The cab took off into the traffic, presumably to Caledonian Road.

And there on the screen was their driver in full living 3D.

'Hi,' he said, softly grinning from his living-room with its Ashanti deco, 'Marcus St John Christie your driver welcomes you to a world of entertainment provided for your travelling pleasure. You'll find channel and volume control on the panels by you; also a Reely preview option and Sensory Identification input for clips from a great new Civil War battle – show out soon, starring Jon Bones as Oliver Cromwell, and Steven Graves – remember him as Lord Byron in *Don Juan's Last Trip?* as Prince Rupert, gallant Royalist loser in *The Battle of Marston Moor?* So just slot it, dial your choice, slip in the SI bug, lean back, identify, and enjoy!'

The cab lurched into traffic. Diane eyed Bobbie in amazement. He made a face at her as Marcus St John Christie's face and voice were replaced by the channel tuned in, presumably, by the cab's last fare.

'. . . taking us now to Northern California for a further update on the catastrophic eruption of Mount Shasta,' a brunette in dazzling purple lurex announced at ear-shaking volume from a glittering newsdesk, 'so stay tuned during this message from our Channel Three sponsors – Rotley's, the brewers of Rotley's Famous Special Bitter – the Brew that Gets your Rocks off like a Rocket . . . and Gives your Hair that Special Sparkle!'

The volume! Diane couldn't believe it.

'Turn it off, Bobbie!' she howled, 'This is mad!'

'Ye cannae turn it aff, Diane!' he roared back at her, 'All ye can do is change channels!' Which he did, so that next they were hit by an ad for pantyliners which amazed even Bobbie. 'Christ, that's gross!' he bellowed, switching again. They saw soccer fans going for each other with flails and spiked boots. 'By popular demand!' screamed the voiceover, 'Channel Eight presents *Great Soccer Riots of the Eighties!* And today we kick off this great new series with the Heysel Stadium riot of . . .'

'Then turn it down!' she shrieked.

Bobbie twisted the volume control – then shrugged helplessly.

'It *is* down! As low as it goes!'

She clapped her hands over her ears and shut her eyes.

'The make him stop and let us out!' she demanded.

'How? Diane, there's nae communication. We cannae reach him.'

'But how on earth . . . how do people put up with this?'

'Nae choice,' he bellowed back. 'Like us.' He shrugged. 'I might as well tune intae this Marston Moor number tae see whit a hash they made of it. It'll at least save ye frae the racket.' He tapped his head. 'The soundtrack's internal. Sensory Identification. I guess I'll go fer Prince Rupert. Don't get upset if I shout a wee bit. Folk can dae that on SI.'

'Wait!' she cried, 'I need to know what happened back there!'

'Back where?' he bellowed, his face reluctant.

'You know a lot. Maybe you can tell me!'

'Tell ye whit, Diane?' He looked bored.

'Bobbie, I don't understand what happened!'

'Okay, okay,' he grinned. 'Jist tell yer Uncle Bobbie!'

'Piss off!' she cried, and his grin widened. 'Bobbie, listen. When those people came along chanting their "take a chance take a chance," I was okay to start with, but then I was, well, torn out of my head! I think it was the rhythm of their chant. But who are they? What are they?'

'I telt ye! Jist stupid shites that cannae face this wurld.'

She eyed him in aggrieved silence. He felt diminished, as if he should have had something sharper to say. 'The law wouldnae let 'em parade like that if they meant onything,' he grumbled uneasily. 'They're jist nutters!'

Abruptly turning from her, he slotted plastic, dialled up the Reely clip, and stuck the cabled SI bug in his right ear. Abandoning her.

The holoscreen went blank. Silence fell. It was complete save for the dim distant sound of traffic filtering through the opaque windows of this lunatic mobile padded cell. He leaned back. She stared miserably at him. The nightmare grew worse. First his eyes glazed, then his body stiffened. Then his face changed alarmingly: she had the crawling feeling that it was no longer Bobbie Aird beside her, but someone else entirely.

. . . as Bobbie finds himself riding into bloody chaos. All day he let Newcastle and Eythin dissuade him from attacking Cromwell's unready army, then, worse, he thought it safe to let his men break ranks to eat. Night's falling. Christians don't fight at night! So Cromwell, godless bastard, seizes his chance. Now Ironsides charge out of the setting sun; already over the ditch; the musketeers can't fire with their own cavalry in the way, and Prince Rupert Aird, too late coming up from the rear, finds his men in disarray. 'Swounds, do ye flee?' he roars, 'Follow me!' But no good. Total confusion, the Scot Leslie hitting the flank hard, horses screaming, men running in terror, the stench of spilled guts, the flash of demi-culverins, his fury as he realizes: *It's lost! It's all lost! It . . .*

Abruptly the SI circuit cut out and Bobbie came back to find Diane eyeing him anxiously as the cab came to a jolting halt and the holoscreen flickered. 'Thanks for travelling in my cab,' said jovial Marcus St John Christie, 'Enjoy your stay.' His face faded: a mechanical audio said: 'In the event of proximity to a Closed Area this cab's doors are programmed to remain open for a maximum of twenty seconds as required by law. Fares are asked to exit as soon as the door is opened. The door opens in ten seconds – nine – eight – seven – six – five – four – three . . .'

'Are you all right, Bobbie?' Diane demanded. 'You were shrieking . . .'

'Nae a bad Reely,' he grumbled as the door opened and the cab spilled them out, 'Historically correct, ye ken. Now let's get movin'.

Night was falling. They stood on the cracked pavement by a Safeway supermarket near the junction of Hornsey and Seven Sisters Roads.

'Half a mile,' said Bobbie, hefting their cases, 'Nae bother.'

And he started walking, not waiting to see if she was with him.

At first she paid no heed to what was around her. Dazed, she followed him over Hornsey Road's traffic lights and up Seven Sisters Road, using his bulk as a shield against the weave of humanity. The hum in her head didn't seem natural, but then nothing the last few days, let alone weeks, seemed natural. *I have nothing to go by*, she realized, remotely eyeing the motley street-scene. *I don't even know what's going on here any more! Except that* – she felt a flicker of distant 1970s-style social indignation – *people look even more shit-poor than they did when I was round here with . . . with Sam and Chrissa and we lived over the hill where . . .*

"Aw, Diane, come on!' Bobbie snapped, 'Why're ye greetin'?'

'You're scared of emotion, aren't you?' she snapped back at him as the tears rolled down her cheeks, making no effort to wipe them away.

'I dinnae ken about that!' he said, aggrieved, but he couldn't meet her in the eye, and she felt a brief unworthy sense of triumph.

'I lived here!' she cried, pushing past a gang of sprayheads without noticing, 'I had my husband and my daughter and my life! It was destroyed, and you ask why I'm crying! Because I'm sad, you silly sod!'

'Aye, well, whit about the present?' he muttered uncomfortably.

'That too! It was bad then!' she shouted, 'It looks worse now!'

'Aw, Diane,' he grinned, 'ye mustae bin a Guardian reader!'

'Bugger off!' she cried at him, amazed and afraid, 'You're a cynic, Bobbie Aird! And worse! As I know! So don't get too sharp, or . . .!'

Bobbie stopped too. 'Or whit?' he said carefully, his black eyes fixed on her, 'Ye brought me here tae help ye! All right?'

'Yes, all right!' she snapped. 'Just give me respect!'

'Come on, now! Gie yersel some respect! Don't blame me!'

She subsided, too cold to stand arguing. 'Where are we going?'

'Stroud Green Road,' he said curtly, 'It isnae far.'

'I know where it is!' She pointed out a vast old dampstained highrise housing estate. 'Sam used to score dope there. Silly sod. If he hadn't been so out of it maybe none of this would have . . .'

'Do I hiv tae hear this whingin' a' the time?' he asked. 'I mean, when is it: "Bobbie, how're ye feelin'? Bobbie, how're ye doin'?" Diane, I'm nae interested in yer past! Right?' He glared at her. 'Can we get on?'

'But where?' she demanded again, arms about her like armour.

'Tae this guy I ken! I telt ye! Lionel! The armourer!'

'That's the first time I heard his name,' she said angrily.

'Diane, yer gey fashed, an' me too! Let's jist get there!'

He turned and stamped away along the broken trash-strewn pavement and she followed, brooding as the darkness and decay grew and the Closed Area deepened round them. *Who but myself am I kidding?* she wondered miserably as the ugly black railway bridge over Seven Sisters Road into Finsbury Park station loomed ahead. *It's a Beast-joke; the Beast saved me from the Beast; now he's leading me straight to hell. Chrissa, why did you . . .?* But then she felt street-corner eyes on them; on Bobbie's loud new three-piece suit – but Bobbie was big and twice already an armoured police van had cruised by: nobody accosted them save a ragged kid with rotten teeth in a scarred grinning face who ran up as they entered deeper dark under the bridge.

'Ash halak!' he cried, hands out, and Bobbie bellowed: 'Bugger aff, ye wee turd!' – at which the kid retreated, throwing two fingers and a sneer.

'Why treat him like that?' Diane demanded, half-angry, half-scared, for drab shadows lounged round a coal brazier at the entrance to the pedestrian tunnel that curved under the station, 'What did he say, anyway?'

Bobbie smiled mirthlessly. 'Ash halak,' he said, 'It's Arab. Means, How ya doin'? Diane, most folks here cannae speak the King's English.'

He turned to the tunnel, roughly pushing past a firelit group of men no smaller than himself. 'Bobbie, wait!' she called. One of the men spoke to him. He jerked a thumb at her and made a remark that apparently they found riotously funny. He laughed with them then shouted back: 'Come on, ye daft auld woman – these boys willnae touch ye!'

With ears burning she scuttled past them, vowing revenge on him as he paused at the tunnel-mouth. 'Stay with me an' watch yer pockets,' he told her curtly, looking back. Then, without waiting for a reply, he plunged into the tunnel's dark, smoky, stinking clamour; into a realm so instantly nightmarish that she followed with a sense of leaping off a cliff.

But I used to use this tunnel whenever I caught the tube, she realized, instantly revolted in the narrow darkness, struck by a stench compounded of human offal, smoke, and paraffin fumes. Choking, with tears streaming from her eyes, she ran into an unseen balk of wood a foot off the ground. Agony flared in her shins: she fell full-length onto a ragged heap of bones that hoarsely cawed at her to fuck off. *Bobbie*! she cried silently, but a grim angry pride wouldn't let her implore him aloud. In amazed disgust she got wincing to her feet, limping on after his shadowy bulk. The creature she'd trodden on went on screaming amid the echoing blare of radios as voices muttered and mocked her from dim half-seen shelves above. *But there were buskers down here once, and people going to work, or coming home*, she told herself dully, close to tears, trying to stay close to Bobbie Aird as he led her down that long descending curve, a murderous unmusical Orpheus who wouldn't look back, who didn't care, who was probably laughing at her as he ploughed on through the chaos. For until at last her smarting eyes adapted to the darkness (here and there briefly thrown back by some dim poor local flicker of candles, oil-lamps, or coal-fires burning in drums), again and again she ran into hard obstacles or stepped on feebly cursing bodies. It was only when deep into this stinking, freezing, smokily hellish urban wormhole, surrounded by the rat-like scrabblings and whisperings of unseen *people* whose means of existence was unimaginable to her, that her sight began to adapt to the gloom, and she saw they were passing a continuous front of pathetic private shelters, each of which housed entire families.

Shakily erected against the tunnel wall, these shelters were cobbled together from cardboard, old curtains, rusted sheets of corrugated metal – anything their occupants had been able to scavenge – and though they were tiny, allowing each family only a few square feet of private space, they took up most of the available room in the tunnel, leaving against the other wall to her right only a few feet of open, communal passageway on which many people with no other shelter at all just lay on the hard naked floor.

'Careful,' Bobbie warned again as, for once, he paused and turned to help her over a new obstacle – three prone old men, the glint of Carlsberg Special cans in their arthritic blue-veined hands; hands that pawed at her even as a gang of tattered children tore into them, poking and hissing like trainee Morlocks. Bobbie, a confident predator in this jungle, scattered them with a roar and a few well-placed kicks; she shuddered and gritted her teeth, and on they went, slipping and skidding through stinking stuff she was happy not to see, on and on until at last they were ascending the final curve of this awful place, and she saw before them the mouth of the tunnel.

She felt unutterable relief as he led her out to the windy chill of Wells Terrace where once the Crouch End buses had pulled in.

Gasping for breath, smoke-thick tears still pouring down her cheeks, she faced the wind that came roaring under the high metal canopy beneath which the buses had docked. Now there were no buses, only crude shantytown shelters and several roaring fires round which dozens of people crouched, the wind whirling sparks away into the urban night as Bobbie, firelit face like a devil-mask, stopped with a bearded grin and turned to her.

'Now do ye get the picture,' he asked grimly. 'This is a Closed Area, Diane. Nothing fine about it. Jist mad starvin' dogs pantin' an' howlin' round the dinner tables o' the West End!' He gestured round at the misery. 'There's people here will die tonight. There's others'll get snatched an' end up on the Motorway. That's how it is.'

'Bobbie, you're no humanitarian, are you!' she muttered.

'Yer jokin'!' he told her in disbelief. 'You auld hippies!'

'Don't people get organized any more? Common interest alone . . .'

'Organized?' His eyes glowed like coals. 'How d'ye organize against the Beast when the Beast is inside ye?' And he laughed. He had the nerve to laugh, striking a spark of anger in her. He swept his arm about as if he owned the place and all its misery. 'There's nae organization here!' he exclaimed, 'Remember the Loony Left? They killed any chance the socialists had. Now it's jist survival entreprenoors. These folk are as bad as the evil shites that bite 'em, so dinnae try yer mystic crap on them, Diane!'

She had no clear answer to this. She was cold, tired, hungry, and utterly revolted. She simply stared at his firelit devil face, angry but speechless . . . yet as she stared it was not him she saw, but Chrissa, the *new* Chrissa, face redeemed and refined by suffering, by the experience of the fiery death of her Cathar friends . . . and in that moment she no longer saw Bobbie and herself and all that lay about with fear, but with huge pity.

'Now can we get on?' he muttered uncomfortably, for in her gaze was a sudden luminosity he found hard to face. It cast too much light on the dark divisions in his own lost heart. He'd hoped the experience of the tunnel would crush her into admitting there was nothing in London (or the world) now but poverty and mad self-interest – but here she was, eyeing him in a way that hurt him in a way he didn't understand and didn't like.

'Oh, Bobbie!' she cried as that fierce tender fire poured through her, 'You've let the Beast fool you into fake belief! Do you know what the word *sin* means? It means: *missing the mark!* Which is what you're doing . . . but don't think you'll be happier if you get others to join you.'

'No more of this shite, Diane!' he muttered, looking aside.

'Exactly!' she cried, suddenly joyous. 'Just so! No more of it!'

He shifted on his feet like a diffident boy.

'Whit the fook are ye on about?'

'I mean this left-right crap of community versus self!' Elated, she seized his shoulders, made him look at her. 'Bobbie, it's narrow-minded nonsense! There are other ways. The Gnostics and Cathars knew it, which is why the Church killed them and drove them underground, because they woke people up to the simple fact that material poverty doesn't mean you have to be a spiritual pauper too! Bobbie,' she appealed, 'expediency is rotten because rot is all it breeds! We – my *hippie* generation that you despise so much – knew it, but most of us forgot it because we were weak, we had it too easy. When things got bad in the 1980s we bowed like reeds in the wind! But at least we saw it! Your lot's had nothing to feed on but envy and official greed telling you you're nothing unless you've got money.' And she laughed, plucking plastic from her pocket and waving it in his face. 'Is this what you want, you silly sod? I know it isn't! So why tell me people must be rotten because their situation's rotten? It doesn't have to be true – unless you make it so! You're just trying to excuse your own bad conscience! Do you really want me to join you in your hell? If not, wake up and beat the Beast in you, Bobbie! – or you're nothing at all!'

For a long, long moment he stared at her. Then, dourly, he said: 'Yer soundin' good, Diane. Now can we get on before we freeze tae death?'

'Not before we've had this out,' she declared. She was shivering with passion but her voice was firm; she felt a strength in her that must have been asleep for a long time, maybe all her life. 'If all you can say is that everything's rotten, then I'm not staying with you or your friends; I'll just walk off in my own direction and take what comes.'

'Aw, Diane!' he bellowed, 'Ye can see whit it's like!'

'That's the world and the Beast,' she cried, 'We have to do better. We must remember where we come from and where we're going. So stop telling me it's all shit. *Religio*, Bobbie, *religion*, means: *to reconnect.* So let the world be rotten if it will, but we don't have to buy it. Okay?'

Bobbie Aird sighed and cast his eyes up, and after a moment said:

'Diane, it's true, I thocht ye'd be sae feart by whit's in there,' – he indicated the tunnel – 'that ye'd jist fold up.' He shrugged. 'So mibbe I'm wrong. Mibbe it's the easy way out, bowin' down tae the rotten shite an' turnin' rotten yersel'. I hear ye. But now can we get on!'

'Yes,' she said, the passion leaving her. With a grunt of relief he turned and marched on past the blazing fires to Stroud Green Road. *Why did you send me here?* she implored Sam and Chrissa as she followed him. *Are you testing me? Don't you trust me?* But no answer came. Only the bitter wind and the bare pot-holed road, unlit save whenever some clapped-out old car rattled past. She began coughing again, shivering in the cold; and knew she couldn't go on much longer; she was longing for a nip of scotch round a nice warm fire as he led her past closed store-front soup kitchens (*Reel Meet Broth Only 3 Units a Bowel*! read the scrawled sign outside one), drab pubs and boarded-up windows to a flaked green door by a halal butcher, the steel plate down over its windows for the night.

'Here,' he said grimly, surprising her as he stopped, for she'd begun to believe they'd never get wherever it was he'd said they were going.

Ringing the bell, he stood back, stamping his freezing feet. 'Now do me a favour,' he said dourly, 'Dinnae say a wurd tae Lionel about Gruinard. Jist keep yer mouth shut till we learn whit's up.'

Angrily, patting back wind-blown hair, she faced him.

'You didn't hear a word I told you, eh?'

'I'm nae a saint, Diane,' he muttered uncomfortably, avoiding her eyes as he rang the bell again, 'An' I'm the furst tae admit it. But I'm doin' my best by ye, that I swear – even though I dinnae ken why.'

'Well, Bobbie, you can't hide from yourself,' she said.

'Aye.' He rang again. 'Where the hell is that bugger?'

And they waited and waited and waited.

'Awww . . . *shite!*' he roared after a minute.

'Are you sure he still lives here?' she asked.

'I'm nae sure o' nuthin', Diane, but that he isnae here now!'

'Can we go to a pub for a while, then come back and try again?'

'That's the furst sensible thing ye've said!' he told her, nodding furiously. 'That's *exactly* whit we'll do!'

17.
In the Cumberland

It was barely six, but the night was dark and the wind was rising outside the Duke of Cumberland when Bobbie and Diane came shivering in to find the vast barn-like public bar already crammed, steaming and jumping with its Closed Area clientele. 'Ye ken I dinnae like tae drink in a pub wi' the name o' a bastard like Cumberland!' Bobbie told her, gallantly steering her in off the street into the full-speed holo-blare and babble of hundreds of folk just glad to be warm, 'But Lionel likes this joint – mibbe he's here.'

She saw, smelled, heard what lay before her and balked at the door.

'What do you mean, Cumberland?' she asked nervously, the brief fiery confidence which had illuminated her at Wells Terrace quite gone now.

'*Cumberland!*' he roared, 'George the Second's brother! The bastard wha did us at Culloden! The English named a flower efter 'im – *Sweet William.* We Scots know whit he wis. We named a weed efter 'im – *Stinkin' Willie!*'

Edgily she eyed first him then the raunchy crowd.

'You won't cause any trouble, will you?' she insisted.

'Aw, Diane! Me cause trouble? Come on!'

He eased her in, using the cases and his bulk to push through the wall-to-wall crowd of Closed Area survivalists who stood shouting at each other as they smoked and drank or nursed their pints of piss-water beer . . . and as the thick fug caught her throat and started her coughing again she winced and held her ears, deafened by the holo-hustler yammering from a shelf high up one peeled brown wall: '*Sick of being a nowhere man? Think it's time you set the world to rights? Okay! Here's how Mythmakers will help you do it . . .*' – and she gasped as she looked up. For capering up on that shelf it was a three-foot dwarf she saw roaring down at them.

'Half-size holo!' Bobbie bellowed in her ear, pushing her on to the bar as he looked around for familiar faces, 'They triple the volume tae make up for it. Now let's get a drink.'

Blinking smoke from her eyes, dizzy and scared, she let him press her to the bar, apology on her face as she prised her way through the ill-clad roaring mob of men and women who, their gabble only partly drowning the holo hustle, were as usual on about anything and everything under the sun:

'. . . that prat couldn't find his arse with a flashlight and a . . .'

'. . . psychoenergetic phelomenon . . . I mean . . .'

'. . . *because we at Mythmakers guarantee your heroic reality*!'

'. . . Hey, you stick your fuckin' finger in my face again and I'll . . .'

'. . . blowing every circuit in the city's power-system! Yeah, and . . .'

'. . . *in the privacy of your very own universe! and every* . . .'

'. . . shot off, but not for those pricks. So I told them to . . .'

'. . . psycho . . . ener . . . geticphen . . . oliminal . . . oh hell, I mean . . .'

'. . . *Mythmakers reely is guaranteed trauma-free! Total* . . .'

'. . . into the pineal, then they turn on the juice. *Whooomph*!'

'. . . *sensory identification and electrohit optional, so* . . .'

'. . . upping the quota again, the bastards, send us all to the . . .'

'. . . so long as they dunno it's in yer mouth, see . . .?'

'. . . *just wire us your unit-code and birthchart, and* . . .'

'. . . Sphinx on the Virgo-Leo cusp of the world zodiac, and . . .'

'. . . faked an implant and told the bloody death-freaks about . . .'

'. . . psycho . . . ener . . . getic philaminon! Yes! No . . .'

'. . . *a prefrontal scan and for only 998 Units we at Mythmakers guarantee that you will save the world that dreadful day when the evil watchers come crawling out of the pit to project their paranoia onto us!*' shrieked the capering holo-hustler as Bobbie, Diane struggling behind him, at last got his elbow on the shiny beer-puddled bartop even as a shivering man with bloodshot eyes next to him suddenly slammed down his glass and shrieked:

'*For the Love of Jesus turn that death-clown off!*'

Then he turned and hurled his glass in a long, high, accurate arc, up and up, spilling beer as it went . . . and it crashed through the holo-dwarf, who yammered heedlessly on: '. . . *yes, the shining ones choose you to save the world in this brand-new millennium Christmas special from Mythmakers!*' as beer-soaked drinkers cursed, shouted, and began an angry jostle.

The punter who'd snapped was a bald man in a drab suit and very frayed clerical collar. For a moment he tremorously faced the crowd, then buried his face in his arms and began to weep. Bobbie met the eyes of the nearest barman, a slim jet-black man with a gold scarab set in his left cheek.

'Free round if I sling 'im?' Bobbie bellowed.

The barman shrugged. Bobbie dropped the cases. 'Sit on 'em,' he told Diane, grabbing the weeping punter by the scruff of the neck and seat of the pants. 'Back in a minute,' he bellowed, 'It's okay! Don't worry!'

She shrugged helplessly as Bobbie vanished into the shouting crowd, using the reverend head as a battering-ram. *I don't know what's going on*, she told herself, sitting carefully on the cases, *but there's nothing I can do about it now.* And suddenly, oddly, she felt at peace as she eyed the seething human mass. *Nobody here can hurt me*, she told herself. *They're as ignorant as I am. In fact, I know more about the real. . .*

It was then she sensed it . . . and without thought turned so fast that she caught the eye of the black-haired, high-cheekboned young man who sat on a stool further down the bar. The young man who'd been watching her through the shift of bodies between them. He had no time to look away or pretend he wasn't looking . . . and for an instant their eyes locked.

It was no casual gaze. In that instant the bar and everyone in it melted and ceased to exist for her. Her heart pounded and her blood sang; that power which had infused her outside the tunnel now infused her again. Breathing deep, she rose to her feet without realizing it as back and forth between them the dizzy energy spiralled, surging up to heights of . . .

What's this? she cried silently at him, volcanoes erupting in her as she held his gaze, and briefly it was no black-haired young man whose eyes she met, but a woman, a woman called Jessica, calling desperately:

'*Diane! Diane! You must find Jim!*'

But even as inner doors opened, from the door of the Cumberland there came a bellow of triumph, the bestial roar of a familiar voice. Distracted she flinched and looked aside through the shifting crowd, breaking the gaze and the spell even as that same voice bellowed again, this time in delight:

'Lionel! Ye auld arsehole! Am I glad tae see ye!'

Fooled again, you idiot! she thought, exasperated at herself, and immediately turned back to seek out the young man again. But now, though only seconds had passed, he was hidden by new drinkers come to the bar.

Now or never! she thought. *Take your Chance, Diane*!

She took a deep breath, steeling herself, skin prickling with nervous excitement, knowing herself to be on the edge of a crucial encounter as she started pushing through the crowd towards . . .

'Where ye goin', Diane?' Bobbie shouted.

She stopped. *Oh hell*! she thought as he reappeared before her, beaming happily, arm round the boilersuited shoulders of the resigned-looking bloke he'd dragged in from the door as selfishly as he'd slung the other man out.

'Diane! Here's Lionel! My Man!' Bobbie bellowed, clapping Lionel on the back. 'Say hullo! He'll nae see us wrong! Will ye? Eh?'

'Hullo,' Diane said heavily, knowing the moment was past.

Lionel's mutter said he was no happier than she was. He seemed dazed, or maybe just winded by the exuberance of Bobbie's greeting. Tall, thin, fiftyish, with drooping moustache and lank long flaxen hair tied back in a ponytail, he looked like an old hippie who probably still owned a mouldy stack of early Grateful Dead albums – not a Bobbie Aird type at all.

'His monicker's Lionel Blair,' Bobbie roared happily, 'His mum named him after some dancer or musical writer way back when . . .'

'Yes, I remember!' she said sharply, flicking her eyes along the bar. But the scrum of the drinking bodies still blocked her view.

'Talk tae her, man!' cried Bobbie, turning to the barman as Lionel and Diane eyed each other warily. 'Twa pints and double scotch on the hoose,' he bawled and Diane, suddenly tired, said: 'So you're Bobbie's friend.'

'You could say that,' said Lionel, with no enthusiasm.

'He wants you to put us up,' she said, just as flatly.

'He told me already,' said Lionel, 'With his usual charm.' Relaxing a bit he scratched his head, grey eyes studying her. He seemed puzzled, as if he thought he knew her but couldn't place her. 'It's okay by me. I'm easy for a night or two. But I have to think about Ruth and the kids.'

'Ruth? Your wife?' Again she flicked a look along the bar.

'Yeah. Bobbie and Ruth don't get on so well.'

'That doesn't surprise me,' Diane said, and he smiled, a little.

'Yeah. Let's leave it for now. But you . . .?'

'Let's leave that too,' she said, 'for now.' She turned. Bobbie was still waiting, and the press of bodies still hid the young man. *Maybe I imagined it.* But she knew she hadn't . . . she knew an important opportunity (*for what?*) had just been missed. She shook her head. 'We don't know each other,' she told Lionel, 'but can you tell me what's going on in here?'

She explained about the punter chucking his pint through the holo-hustler, then weeping like a lost soul before Bobbie bounced him.

'The guy broke the rule.' Lionel shrugged. 'You don't do anything in here that brings the law down. Deal dope, kill someone – they don't give a damn . . . but screw with the advertising and woe betide us all.' Again he shrugged. 'Poor bastard knows he's dead. The word goes round. No shelter here or anywhere else. From now on he's fair game . . . which means dead.'

'But why did Bobbie . . .?'

'Credit for bouncing him. Bobbie got there first.' Lionel grinned humourlessly. 'With him on your side, you're okay. I don't know why you're here, and I won't ask – but at least you've got good protection.'

With Bobbie still waiting for drinks she mulled this over.

'Why do *you* live here?' she asked. 'Do you have to?'

'The evil here isn't hidden,' Lionel said sharply. 'Somewhere else I might start forgetting what the world's like, might start fooling myself things are better than they are.' Again that humourless grin. 'But don't get the wrong idea. I sold out – I work for the Reelies too.'

And without knowing why she asked it she asked:

'So you know anything about the Chan . . .?'

Lionel was fast. He didn't let her get it out. He clapped his hand over her mouth, tight, and only slowly withdrew it.

'Don't say it! Not here. Someone hears you speak that name, you're fair game – and so's anyone with you. You'd be dead or shopped in an hour. Ask me later. Just remember that.' Then he looked up. 'Oh hell!'

For even as Bobbie brought their free drinks a new ad came up on the holoshelf. Apparently it was a favourite, or maybe too strident to ignore, for as Bobbie gave her a double scotch the bar-babble died appreciably.

She looked up . . . and saw three gory-robed half-sized druids sitting on a rock, sarsens and trilithons of Stonehenge outlined against sunset behind them. Wearily, bloody sickles in their hands, they wipe woad-stained brows and eye the bits and pieces of hacked-up bodies all about.

'*I never knew folk had so much blood in them!*' sings the first in a hugely amplified fake-Welsh cadence, '*It's utterly whacked I am, like!*'

'*Mucky work!*' booms the second in vaudeville Yorkshire accent, '*But where's blood there's brass – more brass for t'Union!*'

'*But it gives you a really bad thirst!*' whines the third in Scouse.

'*True that iss, now!*' sings the first, '*But if Rotley liketh not our sacrifice the Met will continue to beat us . . .*' There was a huge partisan cheer from the watching drinkers at this, '*. . . And our thirst will kill us! So let us sacrifice another dozen of the Met bastards to be sure, like!*'

This line brought on loud booing . . . but then thunder rolls, the black sky flashes, lightning sears (at which, unseen by Diane or anyone else, the black-haired man at the bar flinched) and the druids jump amazed to their feet as a golden grail, brimming with amber nectar, materalizes before them, followed by a huge voice from the roiling heavens:

'*I, Rotley, smell the stench of your offering and am well pleased! Drink now from this my holy grail, and I shall cure your suffering!*'

So they drink, and from the holoshelf came shimmering special effects, and again a cheer from the punters as the happily stoned druids float from Stonehenge through magical dimensions to a pink-hued astral paradise where a choir of voluptuously naked druidesses swing their hips and sing:

'*Rotley's Holy Special Bitter, only five units a litre!*'

'Crap!' Bobbie muttered to Diane, 'Anti-Union propaganda. Whit else can ye expect in a dump wi' a name like the Cumberland?'

She ignored him, staring amazed as the druids strip off their bloody robes, grab the priestesses, and leap with them into a huge gem-studded bath of Rotley's, where they thrash about in erotic ecstasy before leaping out all shining and clean with hair that really shines. '*Rotley's!*' they sing in stoned post-coital full-frontal chorus, '*The brew that gets your rocks off like a rocket . . . and gives your hair that special sparkle!*'

There was a burst of spontaneous cheering, clapping and

laughter as the holo-image faded and temporary silence fell from the shelf.

'That's it, Diane,' Bobbie told her. 'Crap. Total crap.'

Lionel, who hadn't been watching the ad, said casually: 'Bobbie, don't turn round. There's a bloke watching us.'

Diane started. Neither of them noticed. She didn't dare look.

'Whit kinda bloke?' growled Bobbie, 'D'ye ken him?'

'Never saw him before.' Lionel shrugged. 'He's turned away now. Asiatic type. Black hair. Mongol cheekbones. Wearing denims."

'You sure he wis staring?' said Bobbie, 'Ye wisnae imagining it?'

'Just got that feel.' Lionel gestured with a shivering hand.

No, thought Diane, suddenly aware that any confrontation now might wreck more than she could begin to imagine. *Not yet. Not here.*

'Let's go!' she begged them, 'I don't want trouble. Anyway I'm starving. Isn't there somewhere we can go to eat and relax?'

'Aye,' agreed Bobbie, 'We've had a hard day and a wurse night.'

'Ruth and the kids are at her mother's tonight,' Lionel said, by way of agreement. 'We can pick up a takeaway and a bottle down the road.'

So they drained their drinks and left, Diane making a huge effort not to look back, though once outside and a few yards down the street Bobbie and Lionel hung about, watching the door to check that nobody followed.

But the black-haired man just stayed where he was, eyes dreaming deep in the pint which had sat untouched before him for over an hour, listening to the talk, speaking to nobody, noticed by nobody save the three who'd left, looking up again only when holoscreen News came on with pics of Shasta still erupting, spewing ash all over Mendocino and Humboldt and Trinity counties. '. . . *Fears that the death-toll may rise once the full extent of the disaster is known* . . .' tolled the newscaster, '. . . *communities up to two hundred miles south-west of Shasta are submerged in many feet of mud and ash. Amid Scenes of horror roads remain choked by the cars of thousands who tried to flee too late. Messages of condolence have poured into the state capital at Sacramento not only from the rest of the United States but from all over the world. Meanwhile predictions of further catastrophic eruption around the so-called 'Ring of Fire' appear to be confirmed by reports from New Zealand, Hawaii and Alaska that . . .'*

He nodded slowly as he slid off the stool. As he did a man with a face half-eaten by disease caught him by his denim sleeve. 'Friend,' the human horror whined, 'You want your drink?' The black-haired man eyed him without expression. ''ave it,' he said, his accent broad, possibly West Country.

'Let me shake you by the hand, mate! What's your name?'

'Jim Bright,' said the black-haired man in his odd, curiously old-fashioned accent, briefly taking the cracked, scabbed, claw-like hand.

The hand held onto his. 'Where are you from, mate?'

'California.' Jim Bright smiled without humour. 'And the year 1590.' Then, disengaging his hand, he left the pub for the freezing Closed Area winter night. The sick man glared after him. 'Clever sod,' he cried, and stood to follow, 'Think you can take the piss out of . . .' But something made him shiver violently. Cursing, he stayed put and drank the free pint.

18.
Fire from Heaven

. . . and Jessica drove, radio babbling crisis zone reports and biblical texts as she left Nome Valley, twisting and turning up through the pines, the night sky behind bloodier every minute as she headed along 162 towards Dos Rios where the road crossed the flooding Eel, many others also escaping Nome Valley with her, all desperately fleeing what an hour ago seemed only another media fantasy (*The Shasta Story!*) but now the evidence that it was *real* glowed brighter every minute, beautiful deadly veils of fire expanding and catching up behind them, luridly edging ridges above the river as cars streamed along the narrow mountain road to Bloody Run Creek where once the Yuki were slaughtered as they fled the white man; where now, tonight, the descendents of white and red alike fled in their saloons and pick-ups, juggling and jostling and overtaking without any regard for safety.

Yet amid that chaos in her old manual Datsun she remained caught in the vision in which she'd gone up the mountain with Coyote; she was laughing as some madman (*Man Serves: God Preserves* reads the luminous sticker in his back window) overtook her, almost forcing her off the road as deliriously she rocked round the bend . . . for in that moment before her she saw Jim.

Not the ten-year-old Jim she recalled, but – the *new* Jim, adult face adrift in the night like a magic lantern.

Ma! she seemed to hear him whisper in that weird accent she understood without knowing how, *Just keep stroight on an' thee'll meet me.*

'But where am I going?' she cried over the blare of the radio she didn't even know was on, 'And why? What the hell's going on?'

To San Francisco, Ma. Then London. To meet me. And Diane.

'Who's Diane?' she demanded, braking hard as she met the tailback of traffic at the mouth of the Eel valley where 162 met Highway 101 south towards San Francisco.

She's loik thee, Ma, Jim told her confidentially. *'Er kid got tyken too. We's all the Never-Never kids, Ma, and we's all comin' back. But she's to foynd me' and thee's to foynd 'er – meaning first foynd thyzelf.*

Then, with the sky pulsing ruddier every minute and no forward motion possible, she cried, not knowing why: 'Diane! You must find Jim!' – and briefly saw Jim replaced by a faded, grey-haired woman who was watching her, as surprised as she was. Yet even as this vision failed she found herself changing channels on the radio . . . and heard an old bluesman sing:

I've got ramblin', I've got ramblin' on my mind,
I've got ramblin', I've got ramblin' on my mind . . .

So grimly, yard by yard, with Robert Johnson's voice (*But he's been dead sixty years*) to soothe her, she inched over the Eel and round the last bend to the 101 junction, to see cars ahead (still on manual; 162 not yet on-Grid) gaining southbound lanes only by forcing their way into the locked Grid-flow. It seemed half Northern California was trying to get out, the wind wailing, the blazing sky booming like a choir of giants. She couldn't hear herself think, far less hear the softer sound, the sound of – she now realized as the temperature grew – hot ash which had begun falling as she inched so slowly up to the junction. *We could all die here,* she realized, switching off the radio, mesmerized by the fiery grey flakes whirling ever more densely through the lights, blistering the paint of the cars, turning to mud on the rain-slick road . . . and as she sat revving her engine for every additional inch, Death Valley paraded before her . . . *the lightning marching at them, Ben making out it's nothing even as Jim leaps away from the picnic table and starts prancing like a clown the instant before . . .*

'Hey! Lady!'

She started with shock as the face loomed through her windscreen.

'Hey! For the love of Christ will you gimme a ride! C'mon now!'

Slowly she realized she was staring at a real person: at a terrified young man, his hair and once-neat suit visibly singed by the falling ash, his face smudged and desperate. 'C'mon!' he cried, 'Lemme in . . . please!'

She hesitated . . . then leaned over and unlocked the passenger door.

'Jeeesus!' he cried as he scrambled in, terrified eyes fixed on her as he brushed ash from his hair: 'Lady, my car got taken away from me – my name's Dan Brown, and – you on automatic?'

'No,' she said, staring at him, 'I'm not.'

'Thank God!' he gabbled, 'Then we've got a chance. Go north six miles, then head for the coast road, and maybe we'll beat it.'

'What are you talking about?' she demanded, 'Who are you?'

'Listen!' he cried. 'The southbound Grid's locked! Nobody on auto can get off.' He gestured at the chaos ahead. 'None of these fools can make it! They're locked in Grid! Don't you see? I *ran* from Laytonville, I got here before folk in cars! The southbound Grid's jammed, but lanes north are free, because nobody's heading north. So get to Laytonville, and onto the coast road, and we have a chance, because the coast road's off-Grid!'

'But,' she managed, 'If that's the case, then everyone else will . . .'

'They *can't*!' he yelled, 'They're on auto; they can't leave Grid except on foot – but you've got this old wreck; you have manual *choice*!'

The ash was falling thicker now: she was sweating in heat natural to July, not December . . . and the tyres were losing their grip.

'Okay,' she said, seeing what lay before her. She knew 101 and she knew the coast road: she accepted the argument. 'But how?'

'The Grid gives twenty feet between each vehicle. That's enough!'

'I hear you.' She was thirty yards from the junction; cars ahead were edging into the southbound flow which was moving at no more than walking-pace. It made sense. She breathed deep. *Did you send him, Jim?*

'Sit tight,' she said more calmly than she felt. 'What's your name?'

'Dan.' He eyed her imploringly. 'Dan B-Brown. Now . . . please . . .'

'Okay. I like it. But don't hassle me. Stay cool.'

'Right.' Dan slumped, folded his arms, and shut his eyes with a sigh. He was exhausted. The last few hours had been nightmarish. The vanishing hitcher, his arrest, Laytonville jail . . . then, not two hours ago, a deputy – an old wild-eyed guy – had let him out. 'Okay, boy. God's Judgement's heading our way. So get outa town and good luck.' And he'd gasped: 'What do you mean?' The deputy had shrugged. 'Shasta,' he'd said, 'and I don't hold with the Grid. There's people will die because of it tonight.'

'You *ran* from Laytonville?' Jessica asked, the sky glowing fiercer as she jerked and crawled to within twenty yards of the 101 junction.

'No big deal,' Dan mumbled, 'I jog every day. Now lady . . . *please . . .*'

'Don't pressure me!' she snapped. For now ash was steaming on the wet road; it was like driving on mud; and beyond the stream of headlights she saw trees glowing as the ash loading their branches began to ignite . . . then she'd reached 101 as the car ahead steered manually into the Grid, only for its driver to lose control as the Grid locked it automatically into the long, helpless queue of vehicles moving so slow towards Willits, Ukiah, Santa

Rosa and San Francisco that none of them, she realized, would . . .

'*Now*!' screeched Dan, bolt upright as a new gap emerged, 'Go for it!'

She did. Bursting through the gap she slithered into the empty north-bound lane, straight into the blinding glare of southbound lights; straight into Shasta's terrible ashen rain. It whirled so thick out of the north that she nearly lost the road before, squinting tensely over the wheel past screenspray and wipers on double-time, she could see where the road went.

'Good,' Dan muttered, 'At Laytonville there's a road on the . . .'

'*Shuddup*!' she screamed, 'I know where the goddamn road goes!'

'You've got enough gas?' he demanded anxiously, fidgeting.

'Listen, fool, I've done martial arts, I can turn you out here!'

'Okay, *okay*! I just wanna *live*! That's *all*!'

'Why bother? I mean *why* bother? For *what*?'

'I don't know,' Dan admitted, in the flaring sky seeing that hitcher he'd picked up who didn't show up on police videos, 'I just wanna *live*!'

'You're suckered on biological imperatives,' Jessica muttered as she drove on at a crawl through the falling ash, 'But so what? So am I.'

She fell silent. Mercifully Dan did too. On she drove, her sense of unreality growing with every mile. The conditions got worse. The stink of burning paint made her gag. But so far no burning rubber. The rain on the road still absorbed the heat of the ash. *If the tyres blow we're dead,* she knew, crouched over the wheel, dazzled by oncoming lights as she slithered north, forests either side blooming with fire whipped up by the wind until – her watch said it was only twenty minutes – she reached Laytonville.

The town's power had failed, but there was no need of it. The glare of burning sky and woods and houses plus the lights of the jammed southbound flow lit up Laytonville like a devil's kitchen. She breathed hard, and . . .

'There! There!' Dan screeched, 'The turn! Take the turn!'

'I know!' she yelled, 'Stop bugging me!' Angrily, wheels sliding. she swung left . . . and too late saw the wooden barrier across the road. It was flanked by dim figures, bulky in asbestos suits, bringing up guns as . . .

'Go for it!' Dan roared, 'Or we're dead!'

She did. Gearing down, for a moment she felt the rear wheels skid in the sodden ash. Then the tyres bit: the Datsun leapt forward as the guns came up and they struck the barrier; the left headlight shattering as they ploughed through, slewing almost out of control. Fire bloomed from a gun; Dan cried out as the rear left window imploded and let in a gust of burning air; Jessica bit her lip and put her foot down as a bullet caroomed along the Datsun's flank . . . then they were away round a bend, the ash-fall already hiding them from the vigilantes as they rocked up the snaky road between flaming trees, the heat intolerable as Dan, wrenching off his jacket, yelped: 'Jesus, why shoot at us? I mean why block the fucking road?'

'Christian justice,' Jessica snapped, sweat-soaked, not daring to stop to remove her coat, 'Making sure as hell the last won't be first.'

'Crazy!' Dan muttered as she rocked on round burning bends, the wipers squeaking through ash, 'I mean totally! Ever since I picked that guy up. Hey! I dropped him where I met you and . . .' – he almost said: '. . . *and then he vanished*,' – but he had a block about the hitcher called Pierre Belot, so instead he shut up, realizing dully: *That guy saved my life. If I'd gone to Garberville like I'd planned . . . And . . . and he was going to Asbill.*

He eyed Jessica nervously, but she didn't respond. Her gaze was fixed as she slewed into the gorge carrying the Eel's South Fork. Ahead through the fire miasmic steam-clouds rose where the red-hot ash plunged into the swollen river. It was almost impossible to see; like driving in a bubbling cauldron, and she had no time to listen to this gibbering fool beside her. The stench of burning paint (and now rubber) was worse every mile; scarier too. *The tires can't last*, she knew, *If we don't get out of this soon . . .*

Also as Dan gabbled she was thinking about Pierre Belot

who'd come into the Rock Inn only hours ago, who'd told her she'd drive to San Francisco tonight . . . and then vanished into thin air. No, all too much, and even though now, with the waters of the Eel hissing alongside them, it seemed that visibility was improving, the woods both sides burning less fiercely, the ash-fall less thick, still she felt that she and this creep with her had entered a crazy halfworld where all normal laws of nature were suspended . . .

'I think it's getting better.' Dan eyed her cautiously. 'Maybe we're far enough west, or the ash is too heavy for the wind to carry this far.'

'Maybe,' gibed Jessica, sliding round a bend, 'Maybe maybe maybe, but don't speak too soon and don't break my concentration, because . . .'

Then, '*Him* again!' she shrieked, jamming on the brake as Dan saw the two figures standing only yards away in the middle of the road, highlit by fire and the single headlight, one with a blanket over its head, the other (hand up saying *Stop!*) wearing a poncho and . . . a battered cowboy hat with a feather in it. *Him again? She met him too?* Dan wondered in terror as the two jumped aside, as the car stopped inches from them, Jessica so outraged that she nearly took off again and left them to die. Then she realized: *No, it's not him!* For through the ash-caked window she saw only a young man and woman, clothes smoking, faces ghastly as he – beard smouldering – bent and stuttered through the inch of window she unwound:

'Ma'am, puh-puh-please, give us a ride!'

'So get in,' Jessica cried furiously, 'God, you took a chance!'

'J-j-just that!' the man cried, pushing the woman into the back before him. Tears channelled her filthy cheeks, but he laughed as he scrambled in. 'Tonight's the n-nuh-night!' he cried in Dan's shocked face, slamming the door as Jessica took off at speed. 'This is the su-sign we've been waiting for! The su-sign that Gaia's puh-pissed with us and the Shift's coming!'

Jessica shuddered so violently at that – '*For we who go through these fearful higher gates are lost if we cannot alert you to the threat and the promise of the Shift,*' she heard Pierre Belot say – and she nearly lost control, while Dan's mouth fell wide open. *The Shift?* he wondered, and heard his hitcher say: '*Soon the Whirling Castle is seen again. Soon the telephones all ring at once. The Shift approaches, my friend.*'

'What do you mean, the Shift?' Jessica heard Dan ask the stranger.

'The pu-pole-shift!' The guy grinned, teeth chattering, eyes bright in his ash-masked face. He hugged the woman weeping beside him. 'Don't you know it? Ha-happened before; it's cu-coming again. We're a cancer, eating up the biosphere, killing our Mu-Mother, and she's had enough! L-l-listen! G-get to Point Reyes and we'll see the whales d-d-dancing. *They* know!'

'But that's what he said!' Dan cried, amazed. 'He said he'd just come from Point Reyes! He said he'd been talking to the goddamned whales!'

'*Who* said?' Jessica demanded, so tired now that (though the ash-fall had stopped) she was having a hard time concentrating. 'What do you mean?'

'The guy I picked up I just told you about!' he said angrily. 'The guy I picked up at Willits and dropped at the Asbill turn-off this afternoon!'

Jessica's heart froze. She managed to stop the car.

'What guy?' She eyed him fiercely. 'Describe him!'

'Some old hippie,' Dan said, tightlipped, waving into the back, 'Wore a hat like this guy here, a hat with two beat-up old eagle feathers, and . . .'

'Did he tell you his name?' Jessica whispered.

'Yeah.' Dan stared. 'French. Pierre something. Below, I think.'

She shut her eyes. 'Did he say where he was going?' she asked faintly.

'I *told* you! Asbill. But . . .' – he stopped, unable to say it.

'He came to see me,' she said dully. 'You dropped him at the turn-off, he came to see me, and . . . well, forget that . . . then I pick *you* up, and . . .' she eyed him sharply, 'did you notice anything *weird* about the guy?'

'Yeah.' Dan's flesh crawled. 'After I dropped him I looked in the rear-view mirror and . . .'

'He'd vanished?' Jessica's voice cracked.

Dan stared at her, his mouth wide open.

'Well . . . *had he*?' she demanded.

'Yeah,' said Dan, 'But I . . .'

Her face a mask in the lurid half-light, she turned to the two they'd just picked up. 'Do you know about this?' she asked in a dragging voice.

The woman was still weeping, more softly now. The man said, in a voice as soft as the weeping: 'You du-don't call it an a-accident, do you?'

'*You* tell *me* what *you* think,' said Jessica.

'I think you should keep on duh-driving,' he said. 'We have things to do, but we can't duh-do them if we . . . duh-die here.'

What things? she wanted to know, but asked instead: 'You can drive?'

'Sure I can.' He managed a grin. 'Sure. I'm Walt.'

'Then take over,' she said, 'I've just done fifty miles of pure hell.'

'Okay.' And from the back he said. 'This is Julie. She's . . . it's ju-just we've had a hard time. But I can drive. Take my m-mind off . . .'

'I can drive too . . .' Dan started to say, but Jessica ignored him. She got out. Only an inch of scummy ash on the road here. The night above was black shot with red above the trees. *I made it, Jim*, she thought. 'Okay, guy,' she said, passing Walt – then weariness swept her as she slumped in the back and Walt took over. 'How you doin' honey?' she asked Julie tenderly, but Julie went on weeping. *Jeeze!* she thought.

'Hey,' said Walt. 'This is all manual, right?'

'Yep,' said Jessica, 'Can you . . .'

'Sure.' Walt took off smoothly. Relieved, Jessica smiled faintly at Dan's glare. 'Relax,' she told him, and, with a sense of aquittal, she hugged the girl beside her and asked again: 'How you doin', honey?'

19.
At Point Reyes

Walt drove for the next half-hour, and nobody said a word, though from time to time someone sneezed out the hot ash-thick air swirling through the bullet-shattered rear window. Jessica relaxed as best she could, arm round Julie, who'd fallen into an exhausted sleep. It was still hotter than hell or July, but she felt as cold as an iceberg. *So what's going on*? she asked the burning night. *Who was that guy? Pierre Whatever. How come he knew everything? He almost touched me and it felt like a million volts. And . . .*

She eyed Dan. He'd been sulking since Walt had taken over.

So this creep's involved, she thought. *And these two. Walt speaks of the Shift and whales dancing, triggering Idiot Dan to make known connection between us that neither of us chose or knew about. And Walt acts like he knew we were coming. But how? And if I hadn't stopped? It's organized? Who's got that kinda control*? And silently she cried: *What is this, Jim*?

She wasn't answered. They passed through the tiny burgh of Branscomb. Its single street was clear of ash. Lights still shone . . . but the town was deserted. The population had fled. On they went, radio drowned by static. Leaving the Eel they switchbacked through dense redwood, the Datsun doing stomach-churning rhumbas even in second, then cascaded down slippery bends until at last they reached the sea to join the coast road, Highway 1. The sky behind was still red-shot and lurid, but where it met the Pacific there was a break in the cloud: over the ocean a few stars shone through a high grey wrack. Before them as Walt pulled in they saw a steady stream of manual traffic heading north to Eureka; a lesser flow moving south.

'That's weird,' said Walt dreamily, 'Them going north.'

'Try the radio again,' Jessica said from the back.

Dan stirred from his sulk, switched on the radio, and ran up and down the FM and AM bands. After some seconds of nothing but static he picked up a faint, crackly voice edged with hysteria. 'Fort Bragg,' he said, tuning in . . . and straining their ears they heard how Shasta fall-out was hitting the coast in a hundred-mile band from Fort Bragg down to Drake's Bay just north of San Francisco. 'Route 1 still open to manual,' the voice gabbled, fading in and out, 'but the going's real . . . ash is lighter now . . . but you people out there *do not* repeat *do not* try 101; it's blocked from Santa Rosa to . . . and reports we . . . trapped on automatic . . . folks, if you're clear of it just stay put, don't go nowhere . . . glad you're alive, and . . .'

'Turn it off,' said Jessica.

With a shrug Dan did that. 'Now what?' he asked.

'The flashlight. In the pocket,' Jessica said. When she had it she let the still-sleeping Julie carefully back and got out. Walt was already out. 'Check the tyres,' she told him, playing the flashlight over the ash-caked, blistered Datsun as Dan got out too, standing apart, sneezing in the thick hot air as Walt got down to examine the tyres. 'Tread's burned off,' he said, running a finger round the bald rubber. 'Thought so. Felt like skating, coming down those switchbacks.' Plucking ash from his beard he shrugged at Jessica. 'But I knew we'd make it.'

'Yeah, and the whales told you we were coming round the bend just when you were standing there,' Dan muttered sarcastically.

'That's right, friend.' Walt grinned up without malice.

'You're goddamn Chancers, aren't you?' Dan demanded heatedly.

Looking mildly distressed, Walt stood up.

'I'm not *goddamn* anything, friend,' he said quietly.

'But you're Chancers – right?' Dan demanded, very worked up, his fists clenched. 'All that stuff when we picked you up about Gaia and the pole-shift . . . I knew a woman in Berkeley who was on about it all the time, how the Earth's got a nervous system and thinks for itself, and we're just a big-brained bio spin-off that has to be pruned – she was always on about it, and she was a Chancer, she admitted it, and . . .'

'Cool down, Torquemada!' Walt seemed amused, but his voice had a hard edge and Jessica decided not to intervene. Maybe she'd learn more if she kept quiet. 'So,' he went on, 'you think Julie and me's *Chancers*, whatever that means to you – but does that give you the right to rant?'

'Well,' Dan demanded, 'why're you on about whales dancing and Gaia deciding we're just a cancer, and chucking us out with . . . with all this . . .!'

He gestured mutely at the blazing north-eastern horizon.

'You think I made Shasta blow?' Walt asked, still quietly.

'Aw, *shit*, no!' Dan cried, 'But you don't have to take so much *pleasure* in it, do you? You're as bad as the Twice-Born who . . .'

'Pleasure in it?' Walt eyed Jessica. She shrugged. 'Listen,' he went on, 'if this good lady hadn't come by, Julie and me'd be dead by now . . . and you too, I guess – she picked you up too, right?'

'What's that got to do with it?' Dan cried.

'Just attitude,' said Walt evenly, 'None of us count so much, we all go sooner or later . . . so why get angry just because you're scared?'

'You're not scared? You were scared when we picked you!'

'I thought you said I was taking pleasure in it,' Walt said.

'Clever asshole!' Dan cried, stalking away. 'Full of fucking words, is all!' And pounding a fist into his palm he vanished beyond the light.

'So what's up?' Walt asked Jessica, still quietly.

Her laugh was brittle. '*Are* you Chancers?'

'It matters?' He eyed her curiously.

'Depends,' she said, meeting his stare.

'On what?' he asked.

'Attitude?' When Walt didn't laugh she went on: 'I mean, I don't see Chancers like the media does, as a bunch of mystic commies out to wreck our great society. I think maybe it's about,' her eyes narrowed, 'vision?'

Walt shrugged. 'You heed your dreams?'

'I have to,' She breathed deep. 'They *make* me.'

Walt eyed the fiery sky and said remotely: 'We were up on the ridge in a place we use for retreat. No phone, radio, or tv. Just us, woods, sky, a dirt-track, and a truck that won't start. We'd have fried, but' – he glanced into the car where Julie still slept – 'Julie dreamed we were running through burning woods down to a road. And she saw you stopping.' He eyed Jessica. 'She woke and said we *go, now*! I didn't argue. We went. Only, we weren't sure which road she'd dreamed. I said Willits-Fort Bragg. She said Laytonville. She was right. So here we are.'

'And the whales?' Jessica asked, staring at the darkened sea.

'Cousins of the Elohim. They've been dancing down at Point Reyes for a week. They should be up north, but they know it's coming.'

'Who do you mean – the Elohim?' she asked disbelievingly.

'You know!' he said urgently. 'You said it. You met a Messenger. Of the Shining Ones. Pierre Whoever-he-is. He told you. So drop the verbal cortical crap!' He pointed excitedly over the ocean. 'Sirius opens in the midbrain, not the cortex. Via pituitary and hypothalamus in fact.'

Sirius! The bright star! She saw it hanging low over the ocean; it flashed in her . . . and then she heard herself telling him all of it, from Jim's disappearance to what Pierre Belot had told her only hours ago.

'It was crazy,' she said breathlessly, giddy again as the starlight swam into her mind, 'he said he'd gone through a gate to . . . to another world, him and a lot of others, and that we have to bring them back in time for . . . this *Shift*, and . . . he said Jim had gone through a gate too, and . . .'

Walt shrugged. 'So it's crazy. We go crazy too if we deny it. So now we go see whales dance, and you get more evidence it's not you that's crazy – it's the Shift beginning, like your man said. We have work to do.'

'Just like that?' She felt desperately tired. 'People dying tonight, and you explain it away as some kinda goddamn pagan Rapture?'

'Aw, Jeeze!' Walt was upset. 'It's our fate to meet!' He eyed the sky in frustration; his voice rose. 'Maybe we're the bu-buddies your guy foresaw! So why start yelling "Ra-Rapture" and "heresy" like Dan there . . .'

'Yeah! Okay!' she yelled, 'So I'm sorry. So what are we doing?'

Walt sighed. Then he grinned. 'We go see whales dance,' he said.

'We need new tires first,' said Jessica. 'And gas. And a bite.'

So they came to Fort Bragg. Ash fell lightly: nothing to what they'd been through. Gas and tyres were something else. Fort Bragg was doing a roaring trade, charging Buy-Or-Die prices to frantic refugees. It took a mad hour – amid sirens wailing, engines revving, people wailing, bullhorn preachers ranting – to find a full tank and four new tyres, fitting on the spot, for just six hundred bucks. Hamburgers and cokes cost another fifty.

'Bastards!' Jessica snapped as Walt drove them out of the madhouse, 'Sometimes I'd like to see a punishing God hit bastards like that!'

'That's just what they believe in.' Julie, awake at last, had cleaned herself up in a restroom. Tangle-haired with mischievous eyes, she pulled a face. 'A vengeful God who sent Shasta's fire so they can make a profit!'

'So what's wrong with profit?' Dan grumbled.

Walt laughed. 'So why did you pick Pierre up?'

Dan scowled. Reaching forward, Julie mussed his hair. He flinched but kept quiet. Julie grinned at Jessica, who didn't smile back. 'C'mon!' she teased, 'You're in on the Big Event! Praise the

Lord, man!' Walt laughed, and though Dan only grunted, he relaxed after that as Walt negotiated the winding ash-slick coastal road to arty Mendocino where the same Buy-or-Die hype was going on . . . and on through the night, traffic and ash thick enough to make every bend a trial, until with dawn near Walt swung inland through Bodega and Tomales, and back to the coast by the long inlet of Tomales Bay. There, turning west onto the Point Reyes peninsula through Inverness (the ash here still inches thick) he drove over a windy coastal plain of grassy dunes, past sullen breakers crashing onto the long northwestern strand, to the car-park at the end of the road. Here, on its rocky promontory, a dark lighthouse jutted out into the huge swell of the surging, ash-grey Pacific.

And here at last he stopped and cut the engine.

'Right,' he said, getting out, 'Now we walk.'

Yawning, stretching, they emerged to a fresh offshore wind, to a sombre overcast dawn. Only a faint interplay of muted fire in the dark northeast testified to the calamity they'd escaped.

'Gotta be a brand-new day,' muttered Dan, shivering as Jessica tossed him a blanket . . . and in silence along the railed catwalk cut into the cliff-face they made their way to the lighthouse, and from its base they stood staring over the grey expanse of the vast wide western ocean . . . until . . .

'See,' said Walt meditatively, pointing. And Jessica sighed as she saw them. Dan saw them too . . . and he gaped.

For there they were. A mile offshore. There they were. The great blue-grey denizens of the deep dancing; dancing in such a way that none could deny the purposeful intelligence of their dance. For at one moment nothing was visible above the waves at all: at the next, in a precise co-ordination of timing and distance, an entire school of up to twenty adults appeared, huge backs gliding in smooth curves, and in a pattern which . . .

'What are they doing?' Dan asked, forgetting himself in fascination at what he saw, 'I mean, what the hell?'

'They dance the Fibonacci Series,' said Walt, 'The Golden Mean.'

'What are you telling me?' Dan cried excitedly.

'Their periodicity.' And seeing Walt's delighted smile Jessica knew she could trust him. 'The exact distances between them. See the ratio? – 1:1:2:3:5:8:13:21 – that's their dance; the spiral of creativity. That's what they do, and what we do at our best – echo *true* science!' And though Dan scowled he went on steadily, with no stammer, meeting Dan in the eyes. 'Remember this and we won't go down under the negative dream the Beast sells us!' He eyed Dan sharply. 'So drop your cynicism. Take a Chance!'

Dan stared from Walt to the whales, wordless for quite a time before he said: 'I think I need a new name. A Chancer name.'

'No, Dan,' said Julie, 'Your own name is all you need.'

Jessica said nothing. For as she watched the whaledance she'd seen for an instant a man with two eagle feathers in his hat, walking on the face of the ocean amid the great grey ones. And Jim's voice in her said:

He measures the patterns of the Shift, Jessica.

And when she turned she knew, with a shiver: *Nobody else saw him!*

20.
Gaia's Daughters

So they drove on, Jessica as awed by her sense of essential connection as Diane in the Cumberland 6,000 miles and many time-zones away. *This is all real*, she knew in amazement as Walt drove them south past Stinson Beach where giant breakers fell on empty grey sands. The wind had turned north-west: fine misty rain began drifting in from the sea, and from her distance she heard Walt mutter as the car slid up the wet, ash-slick road through a cutting high above the strand's long curve. Yet as she looked down it was not dreariness she saw, but Stinson Beach on a bright golden day long ago, *breakers creaming, the jewelled foam blinding as it races in round her and round Jim's chest as he fights her grip to run out further to Ben who's coming in on his board. 'Okay, little man,' she laughs, tousling his hair, 'let's go!' – and they run deeper into the . . . heaving and tossing of . . .*

In the back of the car nausea seized her. Her heart constricted; she groaned audibly. 'Hey!' said Julie beside her, 'You okay?'

'It's nothing.' And Jessica forced a smile.

But Julie saw her agony as Walt slid on through the slippery, swooping blind bends, laughing as he got the hang of it. 'Hey!' he sang, Dan beside him terrified, 'After *this* I'll *waltz* black ice! – geddit? *Waltz*, man!'

'You egotistical sonuvabitch! Just stick to the road!' Julie screeched at him, annoyed, and with quick loud sympathy told Jessica:

'Relax. He knows what he's doing. He's just showing off.'

'It's not his driving,' Jessica muttered, staring ahead.

Julie eyed her again . . . and this time felt her pain.

'Okay,' she said, muting her voice, 'I hear you.'

The day grew dark. Jessica fought her memories as Walt slid them past the mother grove of Muir Woods round Mount Tam and through Mill Valley, the remaining headlight full on as the storm beat harder and the road filled up. Approaching the junction with 101 at Richardson Bay Walt turned on the radio and tuned through a babble to the 101 Grid Patrol report:

'. . . *All up the line*,' a rapid impersonal male voice was saying, '*Grid has failed between Santa Rosa and Eureka. Traffic north of Santa Rosa has stalled. Santa Rosa to San Francisco open only to southbound manual. No northbound traffic north of San Francisco. Golden Gate open with no toll but no accommodation available in San Francisco or Bay Area at this time. Average 101 speed south 12 mph. Road conditions worsening. Northwesterly gale rising. Shasta eruption is over with no immediate danger of further eruption but stay at home! Do not travel unless life or death emergency*.'

'Join the mud-dance special, folks!' Walt said sharply, turning off the radio as they caught up with tailbacked traffic pulling into 101 southbound manual flow. The stop lights had failed: through stormy semi-darkness they saw chaos ahead; headlights jousting like energy-swords under a black sky. Jessica saw a holoboard's cheery message pulsating: '. . . *It was granted to take peace from the earth, and that men should slay one another . . .': REV.6:4 (NASB)*, it told her. Digging nails into her palms she sat bolt upright in the back of her Datsun and wondered: *How can we bear this?*

It took Walt half an hour to get into the four southbound lanes of ash-caked cars. Feet at a time they floundered past Sausalito's houseboats and precarious hillside condos into a tunnel and through a cutting . . . and then at last before them, spread on its peninsular hills beyond the Golden Gate Bridge,

Jessica saw San Francisco. Even in this poor wet light it gleamed like the City of Dreams itself. She scowled to hide her feelings as they crawled onto the hump of the bridge. Julie, gazing with wrinkled nose past Alcatraz to the blur of Treasure Island and the distant double span of the Bay Bridge, saw her face and misunderstood. 'It's a real crime,' she said sadly. 'It was a great city before those LA creeps won Prop 13.'

'Right!' Dan swung round, eyes gleaming. 'Take me. I live in Redwood City. When the wind's off the Bay it's like a sewer.'

Jessica wondered what they were on about. Thousands had died. Ghosts were running amok. Whales were behaving strangely.

'The south has the votes.' Walt shrugged. 'The north gets the shit. It's one reason we moved out. This is no place to live.'

'Yeah, Money out, Mex-power in!' Dan cried fervently, 'Show your white face on the Mission or in City Hall?' He made a face. 'Forget it!'

'Aw, c'mon!' Julie was disgusted. 'That's racist!'

'It's fact!' Dan eyed her gloomily. 'The Bay's third world now. I don't blame them. They smell it the same as anyone but they can't afford to move. They can only vote – meaning Alvarez and her Mex-Cath cronies, meaning anyone else gets screwed for wrong sex, race, or religion.'

'You gay?' Walt asked, tuning in on what he guessed was the real reason for Dan's disgruntlement. They were half way over the bridge.

Dan shrugged. 'Yeah. But I like living. So I'm celibate, I don't eat fish, and I don't walk downtown alone.' He grinned with no humour. 'Macho never liked my kind, so now' – he shrugged again – 'I take care. A knife in the gut kills faster than AIDS or Bay bacteria . . . or Shasta.'

'What are you on about?' Jessica asked wearily, eyes fixed through the drifting rain on the distant pyramid of the Transamerica Tower.

Julie realized Jessica was sometime somewhere else.

'The *Bay*, lady!' she exclaimed. 'Can't you *smell* it?'

Jessica could, now it was mentioned. The wind through the car's broken window carried the distinctively unsubtle scent of an old latrine.

'I thought that's why you were looking sick,' Julie said.

Jessica remembered now. Back in '94 the California electorate had been persuaded that water should be piped south so that agribusiness could grow giant mutant fruits in the Mohave Desert, so (the argument went) avoiding state-wide recession, the defence industry having collapsed. This scheme, rejected throughout the 1970s and 1980s, had led to the construction of the Peripheral Canal . . . to the diversion of water from the Sacramento and other rivers which for millennia had flushed out the San Francisco Bay . . . to silt, eutrophication, and the stench hitting her now as amid nose-to-tail lunacy Walt geared off the Golden Gate Bridge past open toll-booths and on through the groves of the Presidio military reservation into the over-ripe city.

'What do Chancers say about it,' she asked in an acid-rain voice.

Walt laughed jaggedly. 'You asking me?'

'Well, right now I don't have anyone else to ask.'

Walt sighed. 'You know what *anarchy* means, Jessica?'

'Come on!' she snapped in a sort of terror, 'don't shit me!'

'Greek,' he said, crawling past the Palace of Fine Arts to stop lights at Lombard Street. '*An-archos – without a ruler.* Means you answer your own questions. Good western tradition.' He laughed. 'You know more than I do! The Messenger came to you, not me, so don't ask *me* silly questions.' The lights went green, but he turned, bright eyes fixing her. 'I wouldn't answer your questions if I could. Why? Because Gaia won't hit positive Shift if we waste time asking each other what to do!' With horns behind him blaring he grinned. 'I'll drive for you, but don't ask me stupid questions when you know the answers – Oh foolish wise Daughter of Gaia!'

With that he took off into the city, swinging hard right onto Van Ness. It was raining harder, so dark that the streetlights were on, the Christmas windows of auto showrooms and big stores gleaming, pedestrians hurrying on the sidewalks, umbrellas up over nervous faces. Walt pulled in by a yellow Chronicle vending machine and flipped Dan two quarters. Dan was soon back with the paper. Its front page was naked but for, in huge red letters:

SHASTASTROPHE!

That summed it up. Deeper into the city they crawled past the snarl-ups, Dan agog at holopics of what they'd survived, Jessica not knowing what to think, Julie quiet too as Walt brought them to Church Street and steeply up 24th to a three-storey wooden Victorian right under Twin Peaks.

'Here we are.' Through her daze she heard him. He parked, got out, stretched, and without waiting turned through a wrought-iron gate carrying a painted plate declaring, 3690 24th. Up concrete steps through a garden of palms, firs and dancing stone fawns he climbed to the porch of a strange house. Perched on the verdant apex of this, one of the city's innumerable minor hills, it was plastered and half-timbered with little gables, and sat on its knoll like a watching, waiting gnome. Jessica hesitated.

'Mo and Samma.' Julie assured her. 'Good folks.'

Jessica shrugged. Walt above rang a bell. She was halfway up to the porch when the door was opened by an owlish man who reminded her of Woody Allen. She'd always liked Woody Allen. 'Hi, Mo,' she heard Walt say.

Mo's eyes widened; he turned and cried into the house, 'Samma! It's Walt and Julie! They're okay!' then turned back, his gaze flicking over Jessica and Dan behind. He wore jeans and a teeshirt that announced, in three columns: *10^{10} Humans on Earth* = *10^{10} Neurons in Brain* = *Gaia mind!* 'Hey,' he cried at them, 'You guys just walk outa the goddamn caldera!'

'Something like that,' said Walt.

Seconds later a buxom woman in a rainbow-striped poncho was at the door too. 'My *god!*' she said, eyes widening, brushing back ringlets of lustrous brown hair, 'You poor people! Come on in!'

So they were welcomed in, yet as they entered past a jungle of plants Jessica and Dan met each other's eyes with looks that agreed in doubt.

Who are these people? she was wondering. *Who are the Chancers*?

Then Mo shut the door behind her, locking out the storm.

Six thousand miles further east Diane was also walking through a door.

From the pub with Lionel and Bobbie she walked down Stroud Green Road past armour-plated shop fronts, hunched against the freezing wind and the Met patrol that cruised by just seconds before Lionel got his key into the Yale lock of his flaking green door next to the halal butcher. And in her waking dream Diane – *Jim*! she kept telling herself, *That was Jim Bright, whoever he is*! – looked over her shoulder at those flashing blue lights.

Bobbie raised despairing eyes to the stormy dark sky.

'Dinnae pay 'em nae heed!' he groaned as if at a child, 'Why d'ye think they've got them flashin' lights but tae hypnotize losers?'

'Ah, shuddup, Bobbie!' Lionel said. Opening the door, he drew them into a narrow dark stairwell. 'Give her a break.'

'It's her health I'm lookin' tae!' Bobbie bellowed over her head, then bellowed at her: 'Is that nae right, Diane?'

Before she could speak a phone rang upstairs. Lionel cursed. Diane flinched. The shrilling sound split her head. She remembered that Sam-voice croaking from Gussie: '*. . . phones all ring . . . on New Year's Eve . . .*'

Bobbie slammed the door shut even as Lionel, bounding upstairs, got to the phone. The shrilling stopped . . . but not in her head where, unknown to her, the CSU worm-net crawled . . . broadcasting from her mid-brain. *Eight days*? she wondered, slowly climbing the stairs, *Can I wait that long*?

Interlude:
Act of Faith

It was the eruption of Shasta that brought Sam, Chrissa and the rest of the Company the hope and energy which by then they so desperately needed.

It came in the nick of time. From their vague, perilous orbit above the world they'd dived time and again into the Beast-ridden chaos, fighting to reach their contacts . . . exhausting themselves by doing so. Returning to the Hidden World was a bloody, divisive business. Sam and Chrissa knew it well by now. Getting through to Gussie Farquhar had been hard enough, like trying to dictate to an idiot secretary through asylum walls. Dealing with Jim Bright, the Californian kid blasted back 400 years by one of Doctor John Dee's Enochian rituals, had been harder still. Organising his trip through the Temple Gate to London 1999 had almost finished them. As for the fight to help Diane and Bobbie on Arthur's Seat . . . they'd returned to orbit above the Scream in despair, Sam crying angrily: *We can't help them if they can't help themselves!* Chrissa had agreed sadly, wearily saying: *If she calls us again we have to ignore her.* So when Diane did call again, in her drugged dream en route from Peterborough station to the CSU operating theatre, they could only turn their backs and hope. Worse still, they knew that the CSU worm was necessary to their plan, despite the pain it caused Diane . . . and them too. For her pain was theirs: coping with pain cost valuable energy. And not only pain. Anger, jealousy, pessimism and other negative emotions ruling the Beast-realm increasingly divided them. Chrissa had been angry with Pierre since he'd declared himself eager to contact Jessica Bright. And he'd done it. He'd not only contacted Dan and Jessica, he'd come back hearty, unhurt, trailing images of Jessica as base as Chrissa's reaction.

I thought it was ME you wanted! she'd snapped, her projections growing dark. And ignoring Pierre, she'd turned to Gillian Agutter, who so far seemed unable to contact her father, claiming she'd never loved him.

He messed up my mother! Gillian insisted angrily. *He thought buying me ponies meant I'd love him. How can I reach him when I hate him!*

Similar conflicts were spreading throughout the Company. Exhaustion and disillusion were setting in. Maybe the Elohim had rightly abandoned the Hidden World. It seemed to corrupt and corrode whatever it touched. Despite their best efforts they sensed the Beast feeding off them, draining them, laughing at them. The open mouth gaped ever wider.

Didn't you realise? Thisss is MY world!

Then Mount Shasta erupted.

Like a Beast-belch the eruption seared through the clouds. On Earth it was a catastrophe. But to the Company it was – unexpectedly – a feast. The charged ions of Gaia's vomit flooded them so potently that instantly they flared from exhaustion to alertness. Of a sudden their dance was bright again. And before guilt at this feast had a chance to set in Khufu seized his chance. Of a sudden Sam and the rest of them saw that little red-brown man seated on the cedar-wood podium, the flat hat on his head.

Khufu raised his hand to quiet them. Light poured from him.

'Listen,' he cried. 'So now we know how weak we are! We have let the Beast affect and divide us. Yet this eruption proves that death-energy is life-energy too! In every world this happens!

The contradiction of life! The fire that kills also fills us with the power we need to draw folk up to the level of vision that'll banish the fear on which Azazel feeds. For he does not own this fire! Such processes were set in motion long before he came to this world. It is fire of cosmos, fire of creation, fire of death, fire that takes no sides, fire that warms, burns, kills – and creates!

'Yes, it's hard! But we were warned. Now here above the mad world we linger. From here we descend into it and expose ourselves to the Beast's traps. Who finds it easy! We're still human; we fall prey to fear that our fight is futile and that the world inevitably belongs to darkness. Yet this is a lie! Gaia belongs to Gaia; now by feeding us directly She denies the Beast's false dominion over Her. For Azazel preys on weakness. Faced by love and true communication he's lost. He is not the true lord of the world! Living in darkness, he shrinks from the light we bring! And now Gaia Herself makes Her energy available to us in the first stirrings of the Shift . . . and we have our friends on Earth, ready to act.

Yes! thought Sam, elated; *Yes!* realised Chrissa. *It's true!*

'So let us eat and drink from Her cup!' the Great One went on. 'Let us take heart! The Lady of the World prepares Shift-birth, and we are here as midwives. Who is Her husband? Why, those on the Earth, those born of Her, who fight to see their Child born despite every effort by the Beast to kill it! Their Child, our Child, Her Child, the New Way – Horus, we called him in my time on Earth; Horus, born of Isis and Osiris despite all Beast-Set's efforts to destroy him and prevent his birth. A New Way, not to be denied, for it is affirmation. And now? Now we see how, despite all the pain of their descent into and birth in the world, many Last Days folk still fight Azazel's delusions! They still refuse to be dominated by Azazel's false philosophy! If Azazel cannot crush *their spirit, how can he crush us?*'

Yes, yes! cried many voices, yet others were still muttering dubiously, darkly. And Khufu knew it. The Great One changed his tune.

'Yet caution is needed,' he went on. 'This energy that's delight to us is terror to many on Earth. We may feel weak and ordinary, but we must see the shock our appearance causes in those whose help we need. For now *we* are the Shining Ones! Remember how the Elohim once appeared to us as gods or demons – inexplicable beings exciting fright and denial? We must remember the weakness of others, we must remember our own fight to reach the Elohim world, and how slowly we learned that what on Earth seemed like god-forces beyond human control are no more nor less than our own unknown strengths!

'Remember this and Azazel can never win! What can he offer but the finality of death! But there IS no finality! Belief in finality, like belief in barriers of time and space, is sinful because false. The truth is: *there is no end of the sort the Beast seeks!* Worlds destroyed are worlds reborn! The truth is: we will win this war! Yes,' he cried, 'we will! Why else would She now bring us the fire we need? Gaia wants us to return. She wants that Beast off Her back! She wants us to throw him off – and we do that by returning, both in flesh and spirit, which is what we came to do. Now we can do it! Now! Now! Take the fire that bursts in us! Take it, feed on it, all of us as one! Take it, and let us manifest the Whirling Castle so that all on Earth may see it and find the faith to burst through the blindness that Azazel imposes . . . and call us back!

'LET US DO IT NOW!' cried Khufu.

And they did . . .

And . . .

between, but we must see the [illegible] our [illegible] others [illegible] those whose help we need. For now we are the [illegible] Ones. Remember how the Elohim once [illegible] of us [illegible] a [illegible] — [illegible], [illegible] fools and [illegible]. We must remember the weakness of others as we must remember our own [illegible] to [illegible] the [illegible] world, and how swiftly we learned that what we then [illegible] a god-[illegible] human could [illegible] no more [illegible] than our own unknown strength.

Remember [illegible] asked [illegible] What can we take for the [illegible] that [illegible] Shining [illegible] in [illegible] [illegible] of time and space [illegible] the [illegible]. [illegible] [illegible] of [illegible] the [illegible] World [illegible] worlds [illegible]? [illegible] we will [illegible] What [illegible] Why [illegible] now [illegible] the [illegible] we [illegible] [illegible] the [illegible] of [illegible] as [illegible] — [illegible] we [illegible] the [illegible] which is what we [illegible] to [illegible] How we can [illegible] we [illegible] the [illegible] Take [illegible] Shining Ones [illegible] [illegible] and find the faith to [illegible] through the [illegible] [illegible] and [illegible] us back.

LET US [illegible] SHOW [illegible]

And they [illegible]

And

Part Two
Arianrhod

Knowest thou what thou art in the hour of sleep –
A mere body, a mere soul – or a secret retreat of light? . . .
I marvel that in their books they know not with certainty
The properties of the soul, or what form are its members;
Into what part, and when, it takes up its abode,
Or by what wind or stream it is supplied.

Welsh, *The Book of Taliesin*, thirteenth century collection of older oral material, origin possibly sixth century AD

21.
The Whirling Castle

. . . so it was precisely at 5.02 pm GMT on Christmas Day 1999, Arianrhod the Whirling Castle reappeared above the Hidden World.

One moment it wasn't there – or wasn't detectable. The next, there it was, brighter than any star, planet or satellite, blazing from the ecliptic between the Pleiades and Aldebaran in the constellation Taurus, which had, in Britain, just risen above the horizon in the wake of the setting sun.

It was a cold, clear night. Few were out. Even derelicts in London's Closed Areas were in halls leased by the Salvation Army or St Vincent de Paul, slivers of turkey and soggy Brussels sprouts on tin plates before them. Millions more fortunate were inside their houses round the Christmas tree, guts stuffed, watching holoshows . . . and it was from the News that most people first heard of the marvel . . . and rushed outside to stare at it.

So the Madness began. During the following hours most of the world's population was swept by the singing flood that invaded the mind on the very first exposure to the mystery; a flood of sensations so awful and strange to many that immediately they fled indoors and hid, hearts hammering.

But some stayed out in the bone-chilling night, staring with naked eye or through binoculars at the dancing, shining sphere, blood pulsing to the visions they saw and singing they heard, standing mesmerized, mouths agape, until implored or dragged inside to brandy and familiar fires. Numb, they told their siren tales. 'I saw the Truth!' they'd cry, 'But here I forget! Let me go! Get out of my way!' So fights broke out in kitchens and halls; wild-eyed ones strugglig to get outside, fearful ones reproving or trying to stop them. 'You won't go out!' wives shrieked at husbands, children at parents. Yet quickly all over Europe crowds gathered in streets, parks and squares, instinctively self-herding, restlessly gazing upwards as Chancers moved among them and the police (dazed like everyone else) awaited orders.

Philip Agutter, flying to an emergency Cabinet meeting, tried to stop staring at the star . . . but looking down from the chopper past silent crowds lining Westminster Bridge he saw it still, reflected in the Thames . . . and again he felt that dizzy singing. Only tinnitus? He knew better. It was strongest at the back of the skull . . . and he could hardly forget what he'd heard over and over again on the Khufu tape, or read in the ISO report.

'You all right, sir?' Ted Grant his M16 pilot-minder asked.

'Right as rain,' he said. 'How about yourself?'

One more chance, Harry he decided grimly when minutes later he entered Number 10. He found chaos. Ministers all babbling at once, acting like over-excited kids, not drunk, but. . . *They're stoned on the Star*, he realized with an odd pleasure, fingertips on fire and head ringing as he tried to reach the PM. 'Now do you see it, Harry?' he urged when at last he made it. Again he tried to tell the PM about the Khufu tape, about the Shift approaching and what this thing in the sky meant – but the confused old man, Police Commissioner Rae glowering beside him, could talk only of the immediate arrest of all Chancers and their sympathizers. Agutter avoided Rae's hard eye and for safety's sake nodded agreement. But he thought:

Maybe we should be listening to them, not arresting them.

We're not ready yet, a voice in him sang, *Be careful.*

He was. But he worked as lies were broadcast over the world, as 1999 ticked away and *it* sailed the sky in awful serenity, visible to all who dared look; brighter some nights, fainter others, but definitely *there* – a rotating sphere, diameter seven kilometers, in elliptical Earth orbit, perigee nine thousand kilometers, apogee thirty-five thousand, nature and purpose unknown . . . for it spoke, sang, or thundered direct in every mind, making official denials laughable as full churches rang to Old Testament fulminations, as streetcorner end-of-worlders did well amid riot and fear.

Hourly Agutter scanned ISO updates. Chaos everywhere. Earth changes and aberrations. Even the Mahdi's rampant army stopped before Istanbul to pray; in the Holy Land rival Soldiers of God landed their F19s and stood, blind Sauls on the Damascus road, before returning to business as usual.

In San Francisco, after escaping a riot on Market Street on the 27th, Walt showed Jessica the Examiner editorial. Blood from a knife-cut he'd got in the riot smeared the paper. They were both exhausted. 'Hey,' he laughed, 'Even old Hearst's gone radical! Now *that's* a miracle!' And she read:

> *Not even the crassest Reely fan buys the administration line that IT is a new SDI device defending us against evil Islamic terrorism. In the last forty-eight hours we've been fed lies that deny our intelligence, common sense, and – most of all – our direct experience. Whatever IT truly is, we all know that no nation on* this *Earth put it there. Thus in the Name of Humanity we call upon the leaders of the international community to come clean and say what they do or don't know abut this phenomenon. Is it truly the Star of Megiddo, a sign of the Antichrist's birth? We doubt this crude populism! We demand a rational explanation.* Will our leaders please give it!

Next night from St Mark's Cathedral New York, in the so-called 'Hellgate Sermon', Abe Lincoln Daley's globally-screened address to the US Senate made it clear he, for one, thought the Star of Megiddo a sufficient cause:

'Christ said,' roared Twice-Born Abe, Archbishop Marcinkus by him, '*For then there will be great tribulation such has not been from the beginning of the world until now, no, and never will be*. Also it's said,' he went on, full of the strength of the Lord who had blessed him with power and dominion, 'that Israel is the fuse to light that fire which at its great, holy climax shall witness His Return! Will America take this great event sitting on its butt? *No Sir! Israel, America will not spurn thee!*'

At 3690 24th Mo and Samma groaned; Jessica eyed Walt, who shrugged.

'If that mobster creep met Christ on the Cross' – Dan gave Abe his finger – 'he'd sell him painkillers then turn him in as a junkie.'

But Abe's rant was for the US public only. The world was in shock. For days media rave drowned everything else. The West feasted on space invasion movies, dire speculation, and bizarre scandals like the *Twinkle Twinkle Little Star* number. For in the first forty-eight hours after IT appeared. *Twinkle Twinkle Little Star* was recorded by over a thousand bands world-wide. On the 28th a KPFA Berkeley DJ, Dick Albemuth, filled twenty-four hours with these new recordings, not one repeated. This involved some four hundred plays, few exceeding three minutes. He made the full twenty-four hours only thanks to an unscheduled live set by mystery hit band The Watchers, who filled the final hour with fiery heavy metal over occult Twinkle-Twinkle vocals.

Next day in LA their lead singer was killed by a hit-and-run driver.

Within hours the US was ablaze with rumour: the CIA did it. And then Abe admited it openly. 'He was a Chancer,' he laconically told the press. 'Thou shalt not suffer a witch to live. This battle is for God, not man.'

Amid the confusion and fear a new threat emerged: everyone, even those who hid behind curtains and refused to look, had begun to dream.

And such dreams. Such shining, terrible dreams.

And such crimes and confusions they led to.

Hourly Agutter's ISO workload swelled as the general tumult and fear of mental plague grew; the sense that the world had gone mad and might even end. Violent blood rituals designed to ward off the hideous eye in the sky were reported increasingly. Police leave was cancelled. Met army reserves were called up and put under the direct command of Commissioner Rae. On the 29th Dreamer crowds in London, Coventry, Maidstone, Exeter and a dozen other cities were broken up. Violently, with live rounds.

It was then, four nights after IT's first appearance, that Agutter knew Harry Fisher could never handle this. It was now or never. 'We must stop Rae,' he told his Ghost Project colleagues at a hastily-called meeting in a secure house somewhere in the south-east. 'Harry's paralysed. Rae'll have us all doing the goose-step to the gallows if we don't move now.'

The Ghost Project, as its name implied, occultly employed public funds which had never been voted in Commons, Cabinet, or Special Committee. In short, a conspiracy. How secret had yet to be tested. And how to act? An interim strategy was decided. And near midnight, as the meeting broke up and they left the house, two bright flashes were seen in the sky near IT.

'The *Gogol*,' Agutter said grimly, 'and the *Jefferson*.'

Everywhere in the world those flashes were seen. Nowhere did the media report them. Everywhere it was assumed that THEY had responded to the – menace? salvation? – in standard fashion: by trying to blow it out of the sky.

If so, no government on Earth admitted it, though some publicly accused others of what Carmody Cee caustically called, on his international hook-up crisis holoshow of 30 December, 'premature ejaculation'.

'The truth is,' Carmody told satellite viewers, a vast image of the new star onscreen behind him, his unknown face masked tonight by the fierce, stern, white-bearded image of the prophet Jeremiah, 'that nobody knows what it is, so with our usual primate anxiety our response is to piss on it and try to drown it. Looks like some bold military men have tried doing just that. But it's still there.

And if our guv'nors won't give us a line on this, we have to find our own. So now . . .'

He introduced the man about to become famous as the man who named *it* and thus made it more familiar, even if no less terribly strange.

In London N4 Diane and Bobbie, with Lionel and Ruth and their three adopted kids, were among the millions tuned in.

So was Philip Agutter, down in Sussex.

John Lloyd, minister to souls in a parish by Trawsfynydd nuclear power plant over the Union border in Wales, was an unlikely hero. Tall, silver-haired and in his sixties, his intense eyes rather than his clerical collar spoke of a missionary's zeal. He was a fervent Celt with a great store of learning in him, as Carmody had learned on Boxing Day, the night after *it* appeared. Carmody had used his special pass to cross the border and visit his favourite ex-wife, Esther, a potter who lived and worked in the parish. But Esther wasn't his sole purpose for visiting. He had notions for one of the scandalous exposés for which his show was famous; for in this poor and remote parish the hill-farmers still suffered the after-effects of fall-out from the Chernobyl nuclear disaster in Russia thirteen years earlier, being unable to sell their sheep in any market anywhere ever since. As for the effects of Trawsfynydd itself, no official figures were available, though local folk spoke darkly of levels of leukaemia twenty times the national average. Carmody thought he could do something with this.

As it turned out, what he came up with was very different.

For with Esther, on that night after *it* first appeared in the sky, he'd gone to a party (more like a wake) in the house of Dafydd Evans, a renowned local ex-poacher who'd given up his hobby not because of bailiff pressure but because, as he never tired of telling:

'You tell me: why take fish when they're all blotched and bloated with cancer, and when you put them on the scales they bloody glow!'

At this uproarious party (the Welsh, being Celts, felt affirmed rather than denied by celestial threats of disaster) John told

Carmody how the new light in the sky fitted myth in the *Mabinogion* and other Welsh tradition.

Carmody heard the man out then, thinking fast, he asked:

'Will you appear on my show on the 30th?'

John thought Carmody in the flesh a cut above his media personality.

'Why would you want me to do something like that?'

Carmody looked through the frosty window. Snow had fallen. The new star shone too bright. The night slopes shone too bright. The mystery for which John had a *name* rode the sky above, amazing and unknown.

'Because we need ministry,' Carmody said. 'London's full of armageddon rubbish. Babylon's about to break out – unless we inject some sense.'

'But Ken,' – Carmody's real name was Ken Cave – 'what about a visa?'

'I'll sort it,' Carmody said. 'And I'll want you to say what you just told me. This thing needs a *name* – or we'll start looking for scapegoats.'

'You want a new romantic paganism?' John asked suspiciously.

'No. Just tell 'em straight what you just told me.'

John agreed . . . and later regretted it, not for what he said, but for the trouble it brought him. On the 30th, believing some good might result, he took the train to London. At Bristol, he found the ticket inspection less bother than Diane had done at Peterborough a week earlier; Carmody's media pass did the trick. A Welshman who didn't even have to leave the train!

At Paddington a Channel 3 car took him to the studios in Camden, where Carmody (Media-man now: face blank though no mythmask yet hid it) met and steered him past lunatics who wanted to dress, design, and make him up.

At last, after an hour of waiting in the wings, an idiot in a loud red suit pushed him through a curtain to rapturous applause.

Blinded by the light, he sat in the indicated chair.

It took him time to be clear what Kenneth alias Carmody – if it was Carmody behind that fierce Old Testament mask – was asking him:

'John, you administer not only to people's physical needs but to their spiritual requirements. Tell us: what are we are really looking for?'

Vaguely John Lloyd recalled: *He said he'd ask me this.*

'Hope!' he said, forgetting everything he'd prepared.

'That all?' Through the mask Carmody's eyes fixed him. 'That all?'

John Lloyd's will surged. He remembered all the times he'd walked up Snowdon through the mist and rain. He leaned forward, facing the camera.

'I don't know what there is without hope,' he declared, hitching a thumb through the narrow belt holding up his grey flannel trousers.

'And is that how you see this . . . new star?' Carmody prompted, under his breath hissing:'*Come on, John, just say it like you said it to me!*'

'New star?' Before millions John fought for his wits. He breathed in, he gasped . . . then he sat back, crossed his legs, knitted his fingers and said quietly: 'It's not a *new* star. It's nothing like that at all.'

'Oh?' Carmody's Jeremiah mask scowled. 'Then what is it? Do you say there are *traditions* to explain this terrible phenomonon to us?

Again John fought off the fear he felt at being here, in this heat, under these lights and examination. Breathing deep, the studio audience murmuring restlessly at his Welsh cadences, he leaned forward and said:

'Indeed there are! I'm no doctrinaire, believing every literalism of texts purged and translated many times by politically-motivated scribes, but folk-memory has its integrity. The signs attending Our Lord's Birth weren't accident! The shepherds and wise men both saw this Star we see . . .'

Carmody, sensing imminent uproar, leaped in:

'But what of the older messages? The . . . Whirling . . . Wheel?'

'The Whirling Castle.' And John launched himself into material from a deeper source than the Judaeo-Roman message he represented. Maybe the New Star had caught him more potently than he knew. What he was about to say not only made him famous but got him in trouble with his bishop, his flock, and the law . . . for what came out of him came not from two centuries of head but from six millennia of heart. 'Among the Children of Don of Welsh myth,' he started, 'was a goddess, Arianrhod, meaning "Silver Wheel". Her name, and the fact that of old the Corona Borealis or Northern Lights were named after her, places her firmly in the sky.' He smiled, jabbed a finger up, not seeing Carmody discreetly wave back his producer, 'So in *Arianrhod* you may, if you like, see no more than a poetic description of the Northern Lights. Yet in an old Welsh poem, the *Hanes Taliesin, Taliesin's Tale*, we find it was in Arianrhod's "prison" that the hero-child Gwion-Taliesin – whose "original country is in the region of the summer stars" and who "was instructor to Eli and Enoch" spent "three periods". Now, on one level, to be in Arianrhod's "castle" or "prison" is to be in Purgatory, awaiting resurrection, and indeed . . .'

'How does this affect us now?' Carmody urged uneasily.

'Patience!' John, glaring at the unsure audience, waved this aside. 'In this ancient poem the riddles whereby little Gwion-Taliesin tells of his identity and origin were already' – his dramatic gesture made the producer groan – 'many more times ancient to the chronicler than he or she is to us. We refer to a tale written in the form we find it maybe only twelve hundred years ago. Now listen!' and his impressive brow wrinkled, the cameras closed in as he shut his eyes and chanted:

Primary chief bard am I to Elphin,
And my original country is the region of the summer stars;
I know the names of the stars from north to south;
I have been on the Galaxy at the throne of the Distributor;
I have been three periods in the prison of Arianrhod;
I have been fostered in the land of the Deity,

I have been teacher to all intelligences,
I am able to instruct the whole universe,
I shall be until the day of doom on the face of the earth;
And it is not know whether my body is flesh or fish.

He opened his eyes slowly. His voice had resounded impressively. The audience was silent. 'These,' he went on, 'are among the riddling answers that Gwion-Taliesin gave King Maelgwyn – riddles which, I believe, derive from a mystery originating in a much more ancient time.'

'Like what?' demanded Carmody, 'How much more ancient?'

'Six thousand years?' John had forgotten the cameras. 'Three hundred years ago Archbishop Ussher claimed the birth of the world for – I quote from memory: "*the entrance of the night preceding the twenty-third day of* Octob. *in the year of the Julian Calandar, 710 . . . 4,004 before Christ*". Now we laugh at that – but I say that date refers to something specific; to an event marking a radical change in the fate of this planet.'

'Go on,' Carmody urged, Jeremiah-sober, narrowing the man down.

'This year 4,004 BC,' John Lloyd went on, bony fingers steepled, 'marks the start of the age of Taurus – against which constellation the artefact or satellite that I call *Arianrhod*, the Whirling Castle, chooses to manifest itself to us again. I say that the myth of Arianrhod is more than poetic description of charged-particle activity in the Van Allen belt. And I betray nothing not already public if I add that to Masons past and present this year of 4,004 BC is known as the *Anno Lucis*, the Year of Light . . .'

'Do you belong to a masonic order?' Carmody interrupted.

'. . . in which year,' John Lloyd went on, his shrug imperceptible, 'came the Flood.' He smiled, raised a hand to forestall the sceptical muttering that began in the audience. 'Now. Certain sources attribute the Flood to the effects on the world of a supernova – Vela X – the explosion of which reached the world in that year. Can we prove this? Listen. Just thirty years ago a man called Michanowsky deciphered a Sumerian cuneiform clay tablet which' – he glanced at a scrap of paper – 'is catalogued as #BM-86378 in the British Museum. This describes the explosion of a giant star in a specific area of the southern hemisphere – within a triangle formed by the stars Zeta Puppis, Gamma Velorum, and Lambda Velorum. The tablet also says this star will again be seen by men . . . in six thousand years!'

There were gasps. 'You mean . . .?' Carmody began.

'No. Not Arianrhod. Let me finish. At the same time as Michanowsky, and unknown to him, an English astronomer, Antony Hewish, tracking a pulsar – known, by the way, as PSR 0833-45 – determined by its pulse-rate that the original star went nova circa 4,000 BC.' Again his chill smile. He paused. 'The position of this pulsar, this collapsed star Vela X, coincides exactly with the position of the supernova as given by the Sumerians. So, just as they predicted, we have indeed 'seen' it again – by radio telescope.'

'But that doesn't prove the . . . the Flood,' said Carmody numbly.

'No,' John agreed kindly. 'But it suggests the objective reality of the Anno Lucis. It suggests that James Ussher wasn't the utter idiot we now assume. And it's not unreasonable to assume – indeed, there's further evidence I'll leave for now – that this gigantic explosion had a cataclysmic effect on the world and on humanity. The human world did indeed end – and begin again – in 4,004 BC. The event was so terrifying that, as in cases of individual shock, it induced in mankind what one can only call a collective amnesia. Yet it wasn't altogether forgotten. To make sure we'd remember, the builders of that time began a work which still stands, which many now see as prophetic encyclopedia, a book of number, measure, and history writ in stone.' Slowly he smiled again. 'All but one of the ancient Seven Wonders of the World have perished – the Statue of Zeus, the Pharos of Alexandria, the Temple of Diana and the rest . . . but the oldest remains!'

'You mean . . .?' Carmody prompted . . . as at home in Sussex

Philip Agutter, watching Carmody's show with his wife Carol, who was deep into a bottle of Stolichnaya, suddenly realized: *This man's a Chancer1 And . . . Carmody?*

Staring at the closed, sky-hiding curtains of the room he also knew, with a sudden certainty: *That bloody thing up there communicates directly. It's already too late. All we can do is try to respond.*

The ISO phone rang. He ignored it. His chill increased as he realized he wasn't going to answer . . . the singing voice told him not to.

Carol tore her appalled face from the screen.

'Aren't you going to answer it?'

'I want to hear this,' he said, wondering: *Should I tell her now?*

But still he said nothing. Despite his plans he was in turmoil.

'Yes!' John Lloyd nodded. 'That great monument built by Khufu when Arianrhod was last seen in the night sky; when those who put it above our poor world decided, after the Flood, to draw back from their mission.'

'You mean the Great Pyramid? But,' Carmody objected, true feelings hid behind his Jeremiah mask, 'surely it's dated to *circa* 2,600 BC, not 4,000 BC?'

'I say it was built,' John went calmly on, 'to ensure survival of the wisdom brought by those who were "instructor to Eli and Enoch." *As Above: So Below!* the ancient hermetic formula! For after the Elohim left, their knowledge – and memory of the Anno Lucis – lived on in riddle and poem, but only once in six millenia since has Arianrhod been seen again . . . and then as a light Herod could not see yet which he feared, with good cause, for Rome then – as now – had nothing to teach humanity but greed and degradation.'

'But this . . .' Carmody prompted again, ignoring his now-frantic producer who was gesticulating at him to *Get this nut off!*, 'is surely a . . .'

John Lloyd unhooked his hands, drew back, and with fire from his Welsh preaching ancestors he waved down the rising audience response: he had more to say as through his mask Carmody grinned at his appalled producer.

Scared? his grin demanded, and the producer shrugged and fell back –

'. . . Because for centuries,' John cried, 'we've been trapped in Wars of the Blind, Wars of Left Versus Right – false diversion from our real need! Poets and Gnostics know better, but they're killed or corrupted. This *new* light in the sky, Arianrhod returned, is the station where those sent by the Elohim to enlighten this Hidden World were – literally – imprisoned in human bodies! Some never escape! Insider trading with a vengeance! We're fools,' he cried, 'persuaded by fools to fight each other for temporary gain that fails the moment our heart or our lungs or our bought beliefs fail under the weight of evidence that we worship false gods! What whirls above us now but the halfway house between life and death; royal purgatory of our collective fate! Why are we amazed by its appearance in "our" sky? Because we know what it is! It was here long ago, introducing us to our fate – now it says it's time we did what we've feared to do since it last came – time to take responsibility for this world, now that the Shift approaches!'

And then he finished and sat.

There was a long, long silence.

In Closed Area N4 Lionel did something that proved unfortunate.

All . . . *right!*' he cried, 'That guy has – Taken – a – Chance!'

Beside him, Diane cried out at the splitting pain in her head.

Above London, above the world, the Whirling Castle whirled as, in San Francisco, Jessica Bright bought a ticket to London.

But that was not all, not by any means.

22.
Khufu's Message

For even as John Lloyd spoke Sergei Ivanovich Bilibin was undergoing an ordeal that the world didn't hear about until, two days later, a broadcast was made that no power on Earth could jam. This broadcast confirmed the worst, so far as millions were concerned. It was also the first that the Metropolitan English government officially knew of the Euro-Russian flight which had taken off three nights earlier from a space centre in Yakutsk.

Mission: to examine the Whirling Castle.

The Mets were in the dark, since a decade earlier the then UK government had opted out of Euro space research. When on 28 December the *Gogol* took off (crewed by Russian pilot, co-pilot and navigator, German exobiologist and French semanticist), the Soviet and Northern European Community departments involved kept quiet. Time to talk would be when a triumph could be claimed.

Of course the launch was tracked, as was another from Edwards Air Force Base in California, but, lacking statements, nothing was said in public – though diplomatic notes and hot-line calls flew fast and furious.

Sergei Bilibin, the *Gogol's* pilot, was great-grand-nephew of the artist Ivan Yakovlevich Bilibin (1876-1942), whose mythic, colourful, heroic work had lately enjoyed renaissance in Moscow and the west. Later he said this heritage had helped him survive what killed all but one of the rest of the *Gogol's* crew. They died not of physical wounds, but of fright and heart failure. 'Or perhaps,' Bilibin said, 'of failure of the imagination.'

The launch and early part of the mission were routine. The Russians – Bilibin; co-pilot Mikhail Derebin; navigator Igor Kuchinikov – had been topside often. Klaus Micus a year ago had spent a month on the *Lermontov* platform, conducting experiments on the behaviour of viral organisms in a vacuum: he could handle freefall but spoke worse Russian than the Russians (save Bilibin) spoke German; his reputation from the *Lermontov* as a Neo-Wotanist puritan had preceded him. Both Bilibin and Derebin had protested his inclusion, but to no effect. As for Marie Nelli, nothing was known about her save her reputation in her field – one which had lifted her off-Earth only far enough to fly to third world lands to study the linguistics of vanishing Amazonian or Papuan tribes: her inclusion seemed a political sop to the French; at the pre-launch briefing she too seemed mystified by her inclusion, as Bilibin, who spoke French well, found out for himself. She was thirtyish, unmarried, dark-complexioned, from Limoux in the Aude, and though as cropped, clipped and efficient as the rest of them she exuded – maybe because she was a woman among four men, but other women had been up on shuttles and on the *Lermontov* platform; there were always problems, it was more than that, Bilibin soon decided – a sense of *otherness* as definite in its effect on his nervous system as the *otherness* of this mystery they were being sent to investigate. Almost as if she came not from . . .

Yet she was the least of his pre-launch worries, no more important than his fear of death. Space technology remained relatively as primitive as that which, just eighty years earlier, had carried pioneers like Alcock and Brown or Lindbergh over the Atlantic. Statistically, coal mining, deep-sea diving, or prostitution in an AIDS-ridden city remained safer. Space was an edge-game, and part of the reason why (Bilibin had privately decided) the USSR had stolen a march over the USA's much-and-long-vaunted technical supremacy lay in the Russian respect for and love of poetry and imagination – not just as accessories to the civilized life, but as essentials to the art and act of survival. When it came down to it, what made him a good pilot – some said, the best – was not his *reason* when faced by real-time problems of a hundred displays offering different data simultaneously; but the right-brain power to override left-brain logic circuits by intuition.

Maybe it was this power that got all five on board the *Gogol* into the Whirling Castle alive as, almost at the same moment, the US crew on board the *Jefferson*, impacting with the energy-fence around the intruder, were psychically as well as physically vaporized.

The *Gogol* too was physically vaporized.

These were the flashes that many eyes down on Earth saw four nights after the Whirling Castle first appeared; the flashes that led many to assume that their leaders, as usual, were trying to blow mystery out of the skies. So the common sense of learned cynicism told many.

But for once the common cynicism was wrong.

But not *so* wrong.

Both the *Jefferson* and the *Gogol* carried weaponry.

The crews of both shuttles had been briefed by elderly grey-haired generals whose world-view was essentially, realistically, paranoid.

Bilibin, who'd inherited the dark, refined, handsome features and high-domed head of his great-grand-uncle, was a neo-Lamarckian, no Darwinian. He believed one generation could transmit positive social characteristics to the next. His belief was temperamental, not scientific, though he knew that the new breed of gene-splicing bio-engineers said much the same. He thought Darwinism a pessimistic curse foisted on the human race by cynical self-seekers wishing to maintain their own self-defined

Top Monkey status in their self-defining jungle. 'Survival of the fittest' he thought a mad tautology: a meaningless phrase that guaranteed only the meaninglessness it embraced, defining only the truism that monkeys running the biggest trees in the jungle don't like change they can't control. So when elderly grey-haired generals briefed him (just as, in California, similar elderly grey-haired generals briefed his opposite number on the *Jefferson*) to blast the bastard out of *our* sky if there was any attack or if he got the chance, he nodded and agreed, but mentally gave them the finger.

Soon Khufu was to tell him that this was why the *Gogol's* crew was given a chance while the *Jefferson's* crew was not.

'*One of the basic laws of cause and effect*,' the spectral pharaoh was to tell him, '*is that curses rebound on those who curse.*'

For when the moment came and the bright expanding plasmoid ball surged at them from the shining sphere, Bilibin refused to fire even as the pilot of the *Jefferson* (Col. Bill Dodd of Louisville, Kentucky; a rangy six-foot Twice-Born believer whose moment of Rapture was not at all rapturous) did as he'd been told and reached for the button.

On the way up the *Gogol* and the *Jefferson* had remained in radio contact which, if not quite friendly, was not unfriendly either. Bilibin and Bill Dodd had often met. Under various exchange and co-operation deals each had piloted the other – Bilibin taking Dodd up to the *Lermontov*, Dodd lifting Bilibin up to the US platform, the *Eisenhower*. They had little in common, save in that both belonged to the most exclusive club in (or rather, off) the world. They shared mutual respect and a guarded sense of brotherhood. Much separated them, for reasons private as well as political. Bilibin thought Dodd's Christian fundamentalism lunatic: Dodd prayed for Bilibin's Commie soul, though Bilibin *was* in fact a Christian churchgoer, at least when visiting family in Leningrad. Even so, their professional expertise and the way it isolated them from others required them to acknowledge an uneasy camaraderie which, in years past, had brought each of them as guests to the home of the other – Dodd to Bilibin's bachelor dacha near Yakutsk, Sergei to the luxury Palm Springs home where Bill spent as much time as he could with his wife Belinda (an Adventist elder) and their two kids, Jane and Bill Junior. It was a half-friendship that caused in each of them an odd frustration – one which Sergei, perhaps, understood best. 'We are not unlike,' he'd said in his improving English one hot night on Bill's porch, the crickets in full cry as Dodd basted spare ribs at the Rotissomat. 'By different ways we come by nature to the same. We believe different things that turn out the same. But our history don't let us speak the same – not even when the words are the same. I speak some American, you speak some Russian – but not you nor me know what . . . emotional-historical weight hides behind these words that we use to each other.'

To which Bill had just grunted. Now, on the way up to match orbit with the intruder, Bilibin, thinking back to that sweet warm Californian night as he made routine diplomatic contact with the *Jefferson*, sighed to hear Bill's computer-enhanced mid-west twang sounding in his ears.

'Guess we'll get there about the same time, Sergei, huh?'

'I hear you, Bill,' he replied in English, resisting the urge to look over his shoulder back at where Nelli lay strapped onto the vacuum-couch. Since entering freefall she had been continually sick, and, what made it worse, apologizing. Derebin had been cleaning up, scrambling about with a plastic scoop and a bag while Kuchinikov, ignoring the globules of vomit, continued punching revised co-ordinates into the *Gogol's* computer as Micus, his scowling brow outraged, kept muttering in fury, squirming on his couch away from the floating contents of Nelli's stomach. 'The way he goes on you'd think puke'll kill him!' Derebin muttered in Bilibin's ear as Bilibin sighed and told the American: 'I guess we will.'

'Merde!' Marie Nelli was groaning, 'Oh, maman, oh . . . *bleaugh* . . .'

Maybe it's why she's here, Bilibin told himself, strangely wanting to laugh. *Us poor apes in space! She's an expert, she knows all about the problems of language . . . about the emotional weight of words.*

Yet now as the brightness grew before them he felt an ecstatic dread consuming him, as if his secret soul knew what lay ahead; knew it, feared it, yet welcomed it. *I've been here before,* he told himself, clinically observing his own confused emotions, the acceleration of his heart-beat, the sensation of siren-voices in his mind, sounding like . . . immortals from the mythical lands old Ivan Yakovlevich had painted; painted in the bright fairy-tale images which had greeted his childhood and stayed with him ever since. He saw *Ruslan and the Head* in that light before him; he saw . . .

'Everything cool your end, Sergei?' Bill asked.

'Just the usual problems, Bill,' Bilibin replied, calmly enough.

'Know what you're looking for, kid?' Bill demanded harshly.

Not the same as you, my friend, he thought, gazing at the ever-brighter light, now only a thousand kilometers distant against the infinite darkness beyond. *Not the same as you at all.* 'No,' he replied over the radio-link to the *Jefferson*, which showed visually to port as a bright spark . . . but not nearly as bright as the mysterious sphere they both approached, 'Do you?'

There was a brief pause. Light blazed in the blackness. Then: 'Sergei, I ask you to remember,' came Bill Dodd's voice, sonorous and formal, '"*Then I saw a beast coming up out of the sea*" . . .'

The orb ahead was dazzling now, hypnotic, and the singing . . .

'Bill, have you orders to start shooting?' Bilibin whispered.

A laugh crackled over the distance between them.

'Hey! "*Whoever is meant to be captured will surely be captured!*"'

'I hear you.' But in his heart Bilibin groaned. *A great pilot,* he thought, *But his beliefs? God save us!* 'I remember,' he said wearily, his head pounding. 'You told me. But what of Revelation 13:9. "*Whoever is meant to be killed by the sword will surely be killed by the sword*" – eh?'

'You're learning, you Slav bastard!' Bill Dodd cackled.

'You teach me, Bill. But have you learned it yourself?'

'The Word of the Lord is not to be despised,' came the answer.

'And the words of generals?' With his crew in uproar behind him, Bilibin shrugged, light-headed, no longer sure of his name, race, or creed as he heard himself cry: 'Up here are we not beyond the sphere of Earth's madness? Bill, my friend, must we obey old criminals and lunatics?'

Bill Dodd laughed angrily. 'Fear God and praise His greatness!'

Dazzled by the light, by his fear and ecstasy, Bilibin laughed too.

'I thought it was: "Praise God and pass the ammunition!"'

'You asshole! "*Use your sickle and reap the harvest, because the time has come; the earth is ripe for the harvest!*"' Bill Dodd laughed again.

'Did you ever such such Light, Bill?' Bilibin wanted to weep, for now he saw, floating towards them through the singing radiance, a multitude of shining beings, terrible and beautiful too. 'Did they tell you to shoot?'

'Sergei, I guess my boys told me what your boys told you.'

Bilibin laughed again too. 'That's right, Bill!' he cried as Derebin, still scooping up vomit, stared past him. Nelli raised herself up, shading her eyes. Even Klaus Micus seemed overawed. Distantly Bilibin heard him mutter the lines from Schiller's *Ode to Joy* with which Beethoven had opened the great chorale at the end of his final symphony – *Oh Freunde, nicht dise Töne!* – and again, understanding the German, Bilibin laughed. 'Oh friends, not this tone!' he sang as the light grew brighter still. 'How here can we do what the mad generals tell us that goes against God – eh, Bill?'

That light flared like a sun going nova and Klaus Micus screamed: '*Freude! Freude! Freude, schôner Gôtterfunken.*'

'Sergei,' Bill rasped, 'Can't talk to you any . . .'

'Joy! Joy!' Sergei sang along, 'Oh joy, thou lovely spark of God!'

'. . . *Tochter aus Elysium, wir betreten feuer-trunken . . .*'

'. . . daughter of Elysium, we enter, drunk with fire . . .'

The radio link was lost as the plasmoid ball leaped out of the shining sphere to envelop both the *Gogol* and the *Jefferson*, super-heated electrons invading both shuttles and their crews . . .

'. . . *Himmlische, dein Heiligtum!*' Klaus Micus wailed.

'. . . Immortal Goddess, thy holy shrine!' Bilibin echoed, laughing – and there was an instant in which one last decision was possible.

Bill Dodd went for it. Bilibin did not. And . . .

23.
Gloria in Excelsis

Philip Agutter knew nothing about that, not even a night later when, lying low at home in Sussex and after Carmody's show, he told his wife: 'Dear, there's something we must discuss.' Unhappily he mounded his hands over his belly. 'About this thing in the sky. I've been . . .'

But Carol regarded him with such suspicion that he stopped. Like two mutually-battered boxers in their corners between rounds they sat facing each other either side of the blazing Yuletide fire that lit up the high-ceilinged, Christmas-card-hung, Adam-designed, Chippendale-furnished blue room of the Georgian country home that his success had brought them. Deep red velvet curtains, hung from ceiling to floor, were closed so tight that not a chink of the night was let in. Against the wall opposite the fire, incongruous under the gilt-framed Turner he'd bought from a Texas magnate bankrupted by the last Crash, the holoset flickered silently. For as soon as John Lloyd had finished Carol had pointedly turned off the sound, in her drunken state aiming the remote control at the screen like a gun, creamy sleeves sweeping her nearly-empty glass of vodka to the Bokhara carpet.

He'd seen that. He'd said nothing. He never did, these days.

Now she stared at him as if he'd said something obscene, her eyes under the powdered, piled-high Regency hair-do as cold as ice.

'Why be like this?' he asked sorrowfully, sipping his Clynelish – then he started in shock as her man Biggs – a classic English servant smoothly outfitted in the silks and powdered periwig that she herself had designed – glided in past him to repair the fire. His entry had been utterly silent, visible only to Carol, who hadn't let on. Upset, Agutter demanded:

'Biggs, can't you at least cough when you creep in behind me?'

Biggs bowed. He had narrow, mean, expressionless features.

'Milady's orders, sire. Silence is golden, I'm told.'

'I'm not bloody *sire*, Biggs,' Agutter exploded, 'I'm . . .'

'Quite right, Biggs!' Carol slurred, with a vodka-wave indicating her glass on the carpet. 'Thank you. The same again. Ignore this arsehole.'

Biggs replaced and refilled her glass from the almost-empty bottle of Stolichnaya occupying a silver tray on the table by her elbow.

'Carol,' Agutter said cautiously, 'don't you think you've . . .'

'For a man who can knock off two bottles of whisky in an evening you're remarkably puritanical about others enjoying themselves!' she said acidly, 'Another half-inch, Biggs. That'll do. And a splash of whatever.'

'Biggs,' he said, grinning, 'What do you think about the star?'

'What star . . . *sir?* Biggs' face was utterly blank . . . as blank, Agutter realized, as Nelson's must have been at Trafalgar when he put his blind eye to the telescope. '*Star*, sir?' Biggs asked again, brows creasing.

'That's all, Biggs,' said Agutter wearily, 'Don't come back tonight.'

Biggs flicked a quick look at Carol, who waved an imperious hand.

'Do what the master says, Biggs,' she said sarcastically.

'Very good, Madame. Good night Madame. *Sir.*'

And Biggs, bowing, backed out.

'Jesus *Christ*, Carol!' Agutter shouted as soon as the man had shut the door, 'When will you grow out of this idiocy? Can't you face what's going on? I know you hate it, but will you please *listen* to me for once?'

Carol pouted. She was a handsome woman; an ex-English Rose, once vital and outgoing, energetically aiding his ambitions. But since Gillian had gone she'd buried herself in reclusive drunken fantasy, surrounding herself with tarted-up flunkeys like Biggs, turning herself and the entire house into an eighteen-century dream. *All she wants*, he thought furiously, Star-crossed himself, *is for everything to stay in the past forever!*

'Are you sure I should hear it?' she demanded petulantly. 'Isn't this thing in the sky a matter of national security?'

Agutter laughed. *We're all mad*, he thought, and explained, as if to a child: 'National security can't cloak the *sky*, Carol! We can't stop folk using the eyes and wits God gave them – though God knows we've been trying to do just that for the last ten years!'

'Well, I don't want to hear about it!'

'Carol, *listen!* These last two weeks . . . Christ, the only way *not* to go mad is to face it! If you won't hear me, you'll never recover from this!'

'I can't stop you talking,' she said sulkily, 'But why should I *recover* from it? Will it bring Gillian back? Will it makes things any better?'

'Whatever happened to her has to do with what I must tell you, Carol,' he said savagely. 'You're not the only one who can't face it. Frankly, I'm the only one in the entire bloody Cabinet willing to look at it, and soon Harry'll give me the push, because that bastard Rae . . .'

'Phil, you still think you should have been PM . . .'

'Right now I'd rather be the Man in the Moon! Carol, the ISO reports I was getting even before this damn thing appeared in the sky . . .'

'I don't want to know!' she snapped. 'And why didn't you answer that call? Anyway it's *treason* to tell me! Official secrets.

You could go to jail for just telling me. So could I, for just hearing!'

'Oh, Carol, *please!*' he shouted, half-rising, angered yet oddly excited by her fearful lack of the sympathy he sought. 'Listen! Don't you realize what I'm going through? Do you think I'm not coming to bed because I don't want to sleep with you? God Almighty!' He laughed aloud as he refilled his glass. 'Carol, you have no idea what I'm dealing with!' He shook his head in wonderment. She scowled blankly back. 'Carol, the world's gone mad.' He gestured helplessly. 'Old gods and promised redeemers sprouting everywhere. Tibetans are rioting against the Chinese due to reports of the birth of Maitreya the new Buddha. In South Africa millions of blacks have abandoned the cities these last few days to join the 'Abakulu-Bantu', the 'Perfect Men'. Mexico's in chaos because everyone's seeing Quetzalcoatl, the Plumed Serpent! Look, Carol, don't you want to find out what happened to Gillian? Listen! Wotanism in West Germany. Appearances of Fatima throughout the Muslim world, the Virgin Mary through the Catholic world, and' – he laughed in her angry face – 'ten separate sightings of the Loch Ness Monster in the last week alone, five of them confirmed by Sunday Times observers from Fort Augustus. Plus endless reports of people meeting angels, elves, trolls, dakinis, fairies, nature-spirits, and about ninety-nine different varieties of 'space being'. Plus five military coups in South America in the last fortnight alone. And the Shasta blow-up, and other eruptions and earthquakes all over the place, plus reports of the polar wobble; the Chandler Wobble, it's called; on the increase – and bloody Chancers everywhere. I could go on for hours! And all this before this . . . *Whirling Castle*, or whatever it is, appeared.' He gestured wildly. The voices in his head were singing again. *Don't trust her!* they sang in no language that he remembered learning, *The Beast has her.* He ignored them. 'And it's getting worse. For you, me, and everyone. Carol' – he knew she wasn't listening – 'did you ever hear of "glossolalia"?'

She stared distantly past him . . . then shrugged, sipping vodka.

'Glossolalia,' he went on, in agony now, begging her to listen, afraid of what he'd already done that Carol knew nothing about, 'means "speaking in tongues". It's what happens when people hear voices speaking foreign languages in their head, but they know what the words mean. You get it in the Bible, in the Acts of Apostles, at Pentecost, when the Apostles went out and spoke to the masses in their own . . .'

He paused. In a slow grand drunken sweep she had risen. Without once looking at him she went to the music centre; with great concentration she selected a holotape. He wanted to weep as she rammed the tape into the player; as a miniature Italian orchestra and choir in eighteenth-century period costume appeared on the holoshelf above the Constable and launched into the first effervescent, triumphal trumpet bars of Vivaldi's *Gloria.*

'People have been hearing foreign languages and voices in their heads all over the world these last few nights since that thing appeared in the sky!' he cried, as Carol, ignoring him, waltzed over the blue room round the Chippendale furniture, starting drunkenly to sing as the choir broke in.

'*Gloria! Gloria!*' Trumpets gleaming. '*Gloria! Gloria!*'

'Yes, Carol!' he bawled furiously, 'that's right! Gloria in bloody excelsis! But it's going on *now* – not 1750 or whenever you think you are!'

'*In Excelsis Deo!*' the choir sang, she sang: '*In Excelsis Deo!*'

'Who the hell knows if it's God or what it is!' he snapped, getting to his feet, a sudden panicky ugliness in him, for still she ignored him as she swept round the blue room, daintily lifting her skirts, bowing and nodding as if to some long-dead powdered foppish beau partnering her –

'Gloria! Gloria! Gloria! Gloria!' she screamed, laughing at him, her face a private English agony, *in extremis.* 'In Excelsis Deo!'

He ran to the windows and wrenched the curtains wide open . . . and there, high above them in the night sky, what John Lloyd called Arianrhod whirled.

'See it?' he cried savagely as a different song began to sing in him, 'Do you see that, Carol? Do you hear that? It's *now,* Carol!'

'Gloria! Gloria in Excel-el-el-sis Deo!' she cried in his face as she whirled about the room, and she was weeping now, the tears drawing ugly tracks down her over-powdered cheeks, the otherworldly light shining in on her as suddenly she turned and ran to the music centre; turned the volume up full. '*Gloria in Excelsis! Gloria in Excelsis!*' roared the choir, shaking the walls, and Agutter didn't even hear himself bellow back as in his fury he seized a sawn length of ash from the pile in the wicker basket by the fire – '*Gloria in Excelsis Deo!*'

The room vibrated to the volume of the music. 'You're just too spoiled to face the facts,' he shouted, running past her, 'You won't listen to me because you won't hear what you can't face! Well, that's too bad!'

'. . . *in Excel-el-elsis* . . . –'

'No!' she screamed, suddenly realizing what he was up to as he raised the log above the music centre and –

'. . . *Gloria* . . . *in* . . . *Excelsis* . . . *De* . . . *o!*'

'And let's have some glory for us poor suffering bastards down here on the Earth as well!' Philip Agutter howled as he brought down the log on the $55,000-worth of music centre; once, twice, three times –

The music failed. The holoshelf flickered and went out.

'Now,' he panted amid the sudden silence, 'Will you listen!'

'Wonderful!' she snapped, swaying. 'I suppose it's all *my* fault! All this happened because *I* wasn't a good mother, or because you . . .'

'Carol!' he roared, raising the log, 'Carol!'

But her stare set him back. With a crash he threw the log onto the fire and turned to the naked window.

I never belonged here, he thought, gazing fondly out at the fearful night; at the . . . the Whirling Castle, Arianrhod.

'I am going to bed now!' she announced with drunken precision.

'You really won't listen›' he asked, maudlin with sudden sadness.

'Listen?' Behind him she laughed. 'All I ever hear from you is how I don't understand the . . . whatever they are. The stupid damn . . . under people! I say let 'em rot!' Her voice rose. 'Too many of 'em anyway. AIDS-ridden shits! Send 'em to the Maghreb and save honest taxpayers like us money!'

'Go away!' He swung round, shaking, furious not so much with her but with himself; for wasting his life on false gods. 'Go on!' he cried, 'Go to bed and drug yourself and sleep forever . . . you idiot!' And then buried his head in his hands – (*poor head; so full of muttering voices and strange sights; so full of conspiracy that as yet had no clear outline or goal*).

'This is the end, Philip,' she said from the door, 'I'll be . . .'

'. . . talking to your lawyer in the morning!' he cried derisively. 'You stupid . . . human being! Nobody'll be around tomorrow, Carol! It's not just New Year or New Century, it's New *Millennium!* Even if the bloody lawyers were in their offices, do you think they'd care? Don't you see it's all changed? It's nothing to do with *us* any more! What *we* want doesn't *matter* any more! We'are all under . . . under *God!* So go and sleep it off!'

'I suppose you'll be working all night again,' she said, vengefully timid . . . and even as she said it, the ISO phone rang again.

'Yes.' He sighed at the squalling instrument. 'Probably.'

'If only so you won't have to sleep with me!' she cried. 'And tomorrow you're going to that party? At Brenda Bruce's.'

He was amazed at the implication. *I'm trying to make sense of madness and she thinks I want to sleep with an overrated actress?*

'Yes,' he said wearily, 'I've been trying to tell you. I have to see somebody about all this. To let them know. It has to be unofficial.'

'Be careful, Philip! Things don't change that fast!'

She slammed the door and left him to answer the phone.

He let it ring ten . . . eleven . . . twelve times. He was crying. He was laughing too. He could no longer tell the difference.

'So monsters surface,' he muttered, considering the Khufu tape and John Lloyd as he stared at the blazing fire. In it he saw Gillian's face lifted up to the sky: eyes wide, mouth open. He couldn't tell if she laughed or screamed . . . but he knew what she saw. Through the window he eyed Arianrhod as – sirens singing madly in him – he lifted the phone and said wearily:

'Agutter here.' And heard that a Five-Oh-One-Alpha-Zero-Five implantee (76-E-678-DEJ) was broadcasting Chancer connection from Closed Area N4.

He quashed the raid and that night slept on the couch in his study.

And he dreamed a dream. A strange dream.

24.
In Lionel's Den

Meanwhile Lionel strode furiously along a dirty deserted N4 pavement, head singing madly with Arianrhod's song from above. He didn't know a raid had been quashed but he was sure one had been set up. Diane's reaction to his incredibly silly remark at the end of John Lloyd's tv rant couldn't have been caused by anything but a CSU worm migraine. 'All . . . *right!*' he'd cried, 'That guy has Taken a Chance!' – and she'd clutched her head, screaming in that sudden violent agony that invariably meant worm-response to a trigger-phrase. Final proof – was it needed? – that she'd been bugged since arriving with Bobbie a week ago. Yes, he'd feared it from the start, taking care to say nothing that would trigger her . . . until tonight, a moment of damn carelessness, and instantly he'd known that, with all pretence of secrecy now blown, the cops would arrive any minute, meaning that not just Diane, Bobbie, Ruth and the kids would get nicked, but himself too. Which he couldn't allow. Not with the Hour so near. He didn't know much, but he knew enough, and if they got it out of him (they always did) . . . well, a CSU bust now would certainly mess things up. He'd acted fast. 'Explain later,' he'd snapped, bundling Ruth and the kids to folk across the road, sending Bobbie and Diane to the pub, telling them to lay low until he got back.

He groaned, wanting to kick himself, in his guilt still seeing Diane's pain-twisted look. As if he'd betrayed her! *But what else could I do?* he demanded angrily, head swimming, *I've got to warn the Old Man. I need advice. In person. Can't risk the phone.* And uneasily he decided: *She's okay in the pub. It's common ground. To get her the bastards'd have to grab everyone. They won't try that. She's okay with people round her.*

As for Bobbie . . . Clenching his fists he knew: *All that idiot wants is to die gloriously.* God knew why (he deliberately hadn't asked) but clearly in Scotland Bobbie had got into trouble he couldn't handle. Mind-boggling! Trouble Bobbie Aird couldn't handle? Bobbie's second name was Trouble! Always had been. He'd been born with T for Trouble stamped invisibly on his brow, like the Mark of the Beast. And Trouble was what Lionel had smelled the moment Bobbie had grabbed him at the door of the Cumberland a week ago. But just how much trouble he hadn't begun to guess . . . until the Big Gorilla had barrelled him through the crowd to meet a thin grey-haired woman who'd looked exhausted, fed-up, and lost.

That had been his first impression of Diane Joyce.

Then he'd looked again . . . and seen more. Nothing he could finger, save maybe in her eyes . . . but what he'd seen there had set his nerves on full red alert. *Watch it,* he'd thought, *something's wrong here.*

Sure. He'd suspected it rightaway. He knew CSU methods; he'd seen too many people go down due to a brief lapse in concentration. A word in the wrong ear was enough. So what had he done? He'd asked them home! Like a mouse asking the cat in for supper. Asked them home, despite the way Diane had begun babbling aloud about Chancing in the pub – despite the way that black-haired Asiatic guy had been watching them. A CSU agent? Probably.

You fool, he thought dizzily. *For all you know Bobbie's part of the set-up too. So it was a bright idea, eh? Take her home! Find out who and what she is. If she's important, get onto the Old Man and show you're on the ball. It'll be okay if I'm careful – my record's clean, eh? Lionel the Armourer. Honest John, the Man with a Trade. Never met her before, M'Lud. She needed a room. Couldn't deny Christian charity at Christmas, could I? Chancers? Dunno what you mean, M'Lud. If you ask me, they're a bunch of wankers. Send 'em all to the Maghreb, I would.*

Now he wondered: *Would I have risked it if I'd known what I know now?* And again he seemed to see that Asiatic guy who'd watched them in the pub that night. For just a moment he'd met those eyes. CSU eyes. Laughing angrily, he kicked a can, sent it clattering down the street. *You fool!* he scolded himself again, staring up at Arianrhod, *You'd have done it whatever the risk. You knew it all along. You saw it in her eyes, and you guessed, but she fascinated you, and you wanted to act big, so you stuck your head in the noose, and when that thing appeared you went and asked "Who is she?" and the Old Man told you – but still you can't keep your trap shut!*

He sighed. *So I took a chance. That's what it's all about, right?*

Right! And derisively he saluted the night, saluted the empty road, gazed up and saluted the whirling light that sang in him, confusing his sense of time and space. 'I'm a prat!' he cried at Arianrhod.

For he'd taken them home. To find the phone ringing. That had been the next bad hint. For behind him as he ran up the stairs he'd felt her flinch at the sound. *Just nervous reaction,* he'd told himself, and then – it was coming back now like a bad dream – he'd had to deal with nervous reaction himself. It had been Ruth on the phone. Down at her mother's in Ealing with the kids. Ruth didn't know (or let herself know) about the Old Man. No cheating involved; it was just safer for everyone if she stayed in the dark about his . . . activities. He suspected she knew it too.

But he couldn't hide the arrival of the Big Gorilla from her.

Ruth had loathed Bobbie Aird ever since ten years ago they'd all first met at the Battle of Mortimer's Cross (1461). She'd been with the Shire Company; he with the Knights of Albion; they'd been getting on fine when this hairy Scotch prat had invaded the pre-battle beer-tent and tried it on with her. But Lionel, so far from standing up for her, had just laughed.

'You just sat and let that big gorilla paw me!' she'd cried.

He'd shrugged it off. 'Relax! He's only fooling.'

That had nearly finished them. But not quite. She'd moved in with him. Yet ever since she'd made it an annual issue that Bobbie shouldn't be let through their door. And ever since then Lionel had said: 'Look, I like him. He's just another guy stuck in the wrong time. He's doing the best he can – and he's great with a sword, a real poet. So he grabs at you, but he's not serious. If he was,' he usually added, 'I'd . . .'

'Do what? Beat his brains out? *You* – Lionel?'

'I'm going out,' he'd say.

'To the pub again?'

'That's right.'

And if often enough she'd sought him in the pub and not found him (he knew she had), she'd never said anything about it. Never accused him of running around with . . . whoever or whatever. Maybe because he'd never given her the edge to do it. No blonde hairs, crucifixes, or guilty looks.

But – Bobbie was Trouble. Trouble a decade ago, trouble now.

'. . . You're not letting him *stay*, are you?' she'd exploded on the phone as Bobbie brought Diane up to the landing. 'I must,' he'd muttered, 'For tonight anyway . . .' But as he'd turned, grinning apologetically, covering the mouthpiece, still her outrage had sounded loud and clear.

'You know how much I hate that Scotch prick!'

Diane's mouth had fallen open. Not, Lionel soon realized, because of Ruth's anger. She was staring at his phone-stand; at how the phone sat on the gauntleted left hand of a suit of armour which, burnished and finished in riveted cold steel, shone under a spotlight. Helm, cuirass, cuisse, polaine, greaves and sabatons were strapped round a tailor's dummy, pinkly visible here and there through the joints. One rigid extended hand held a jousting lance, heel on shabby floor, its point almost touching the peeling ceiling. The other supported the phone, its squawking receiver in Lionel's hand as Diane stared from the armour to him. A difficult moment.

'Come on,' Bobbie had grunted, guiding her to the kitchen. With Ruth still raving on he'd watched Diane stand in the doorway, nervously eyeing dirty pans, dirty window and all the rest of it while Bobbie (filling the kettle) boomed in what he'd no doubt thought a confidential whisper:

'Dinnae worry. They'd alwiz rowin', but Ruth's okay, an' the kids – all adopted: there's two is black, one's Chinese, the ither's Irish – ye'll like 'em. Good folk in a bad age, an' nae straitlaced, they jist . . .'

'*Bloody hell!*' Ruth had screamed through the phone.

'. . . shout a bit,' Bobbie went on, unconcerned. 'Now where the teabags?'

When at last he'd rung off Diane had made a rueful face. 'Sorry about this,' she'd said, 'Are you sure we're not . . . you know . . .?'

The strange thing was, Lionel liked her. But then upstairs in his workshop she'd started asking questions. And not about his work as an armourer.

'Watch your head,' he'd told her, showing her into the crammed attic, full of swords, shields and armour, Bobbie licking his lips at the wicked-looking morning stars and maces that hung from poles running horizontally at head-height, both making sure that she ducked these on her way to the fireplace past his work-benches, lathes and kilns. He'd lit the fire, laced her tea with whisky, and set her down in the best chair to relax while he and Bobbie swapped news. Of course he'd known it was going to be difficult. The Hour was near, and if Diane was important, or if the law had already got at her, then the less said the better. As to what Bobbie was up to, why he was with this woman and dressed up like a City ponce, God only knew. Which was fine. As far as Lionel was concerned, other people's business was usually best left in God's doubtless world-weary hands.

'Let's keep it light,' he warned Bobbie, 'No serious shit, right?'

But as they'd talked Diane's face had got glummer and glummer. She'd kept giving Bobbie sad looks as if he wasn't saying something he should.

And Bobbie – he looked more nervous and itchy than Lionel had ever seen him. Like a man with a bad conscience. Lionel's lips had tightened.

'Whit's the matter?' Bobbie had growled at Diane. 'You okay?'

'I'm fine,' she'd said, but her firelit face hadn't agreed.

'Sorry,' Lionel had said, 'Bobbie and me go back a long way.'

'Oh, forget about me.' But then she seemed to reach a decision. She eyed Bobbie again. 'Don't you think we should start talking straight?'

And at her look Bobbie, tensing up, had cried: 'Dinnae look at me like that! I'll fecht fer ye – but speak fer yersel'!'

Hesitantly she'd turned her gaze on Lionel. 'Can we . . .' she'd asked (massaging her brow as if she had a headache) 'talk now abut the Cha . . .?'

But as in the pub he'd interrupted her before she could say it;

'Sorry luv, dunno about them. Bunch of crazies, is all I know.'

'But . . . those people we saw at King's Cross?' she'd faltered.

Grimacing, Bobbie had told him what had happened at the station.

'Proves it.' Lionel, hiding his feelings, had cut him off too. 'If Old Bill was with them how could they be up to anything? I'd drop it.'

'But I felt so . . .,' her face had been so white, 'I mean . . . I'm here to meet someone . . . something . . . and . . . on the train . . . when they stopped us . . .'

'Where did you stop?' he'd asked. 'Where did they check you?'

'Peterborough,' started Bobbie, 'They gave her a . . .'

'They said I bashed my head when I fell asleep,' she'd said, 'I . . .'

Now, striding along, he told himself: *That made it clear enough.* And so it had. 'Okay,' he'd said, 'That's enough.' He'd locked eyes with her.

Listen! his gaze had said, *We survive in silence. So keep quiet!*

For a long moment they'd held that gaze, Bobbie not getting it, until, to his great relief, Lionel had seen realization spread over her face.

'Oh!' she'd said – but so faint, and she'd looked so dizzy that he'd half-stood in case she . . . 'I'm sorry. I'm tired. Can I . . .?'

'Sure. There's a spare room. And hot water, if you want a bath.' But he'd felt super-tense, trapped by his own rashness, and as she'd left the room he'd wondered: *Can I handle this? Can she? If she's . . .*

But he hadn't even let himself think it. That was the trick. 'Listen, Bobbie,' he'd said once she was safely out of hearing, 'There's stuff going on that neither of us need to talk about. It's best that way, right?'

Then, staring into Bobbie's dark eyes, he'd seen something there he'd never seen or expected to see. Terror. Holy terror. 'So if you have anything to say, tell me when she's not around,' he'd finished lamely.

'I reckon they bugged her,' Bobbie had said.

'You know any reason why they should?

'Oh aye!' said Bobbie, his terror now naked, 'She's nae jist . . .'

'Don't tell me!' He'd spoken sharply. Deep waters getting deeper. 'It's safer all round. But . . . where do you stand if things get to . . .?'

And Bobbie, with real grief in his eyes, had said something that had struck Lionel hard, that stuck with him now.

'My life's forfeit onyway,' he'd said.

Oh yes, he remembered now, he'd been troubled by that, and by all of it, including his own willingness to stick his neck out. And Ruth? Next day she was back with the kids. There were rows. She demanded that Bobbie and Diane move over the road to a bloke who owed Lionel a favour. Bobbie and Diane lay low; Bobbie in the attic and Diane in the spare room which Ruth reluctantly conceded. The row went on for over twenty-four hours.

Before it was resolved, the first sign of the coming Hour appeared.

For suddenly blazing from the sky above was the Whirling Castle.

Lionel thought he knew what it was. He'd heard the Khufu tape round at the Old Man's. He saw it through the kitchen window, and his heart leaped in mingled joy and awe as the singing began in him and he heard himself cry: 'Something weird's in the sky. I'm going out to take a look.'

But first he'd knocked at Diane's door, got her off the bed where for a day and a night she'd lain. 'Something you ought to see,' he'd whispered. 'But take it easy. Say or think nothing you'd not want an enemy to hear.'

Pale, she'd followed him out. One by one Ruth and the kids and last of all Bobbie emerged too. All up and down the road people stood and stared. Traffic had stopped. A police van was stalled in the middle of the road, the cops staring like everyone else. Nobody paid them any attention.

Everyone was seized by the terrible wonder of that shining light . . .

And on Diane's face as she stared Lionel saw . . . recognition.

'They're coming back!' she cried, tears in her eyes. Then she met his gaze and shut her mouth. Yet even as she did he gasped, for like a ringing bell he heard her cry in his mind. *But we have to call them!* she cried, *And I'm one of those who has to do it. But how? And who are the others?*

Then in his mind's-eye flashed the face of the Asiatic guy who'd been watching them in the bar. And the face of a black-haired woman who . . .

That's enough! he'd told himself, shocked. *If the CSU . . .*

'Bloody Yanks!' he'd yelled, sticking two fingers up at the sky as he turned away from *it*, from Diane too. 'So it's bloody Song Wars now.'

'Hey, Diane!' Bobbie cried, sounding drunk, 'Are ye okay?'

Lionel went back inside before Diane could speak. Sharply Ruth pulled the kids in after him. Grace and the two youngest were crying. Justin, the oldest, didn't want to go back in. 'Do as your mother says!' Lionel said angrily – then ran upstairs, and from a window saw Bobbie out on the street, eyeing Diane where she stood staring up, starlost. Bobbie looked scared. Like a diffident boy he tugged at her elbow. 'Come on,' said his lips, 'Ye'll freeze tae death!' Numb, she let him lead her back inside.

Lionel turned from the window even as Ruth raged in. 'I want every curtain in this house closed tight!' she snapped. *As closed as your mind?* he'd wondered . . . but when in the kitchen Diane tried to meet his eyes he'd avoided her gaze. The tension was acute. 'I've got to go out,' he told nobody in particular. 'Be back later.' Which he was. Very much later. It was after 3 am when he came in and Ruth met him on the landing.

'Where were you?' She'd been crying. 'The kids are having nightmares. What's going on? Why aren't you ever around when you're needed?'

'The dreaming'll get worse,' he'd said curtly, rounding her on his way to bed, 'So we might as well get used to it.'

'You bastard, don't you dismiss me like that!'

But he'd scarcely heard her. He was in shock. He'd just been bawled out by the Old Man – in a whisper. Those ice-blue eyes had pierced him.

'*Not very clever! Why didn't you tell us before? We've been looking for her. Now you've got her, you'd better keep her with you, worm or not. It's not long now. Take the Chance – but take care too!*'

Now, striding feverishly along, he thought:

He's right. I did it out of pride. Clever Lionel! But . . .

That first night of Arianrhod had been wild. The children all wailing at once. Next day the adults were all wailing too. Displacing their fear. Ruth on about unwashed dishes. Diane in a frenzy about her hair. Bobbie bellowing he was sick of being shut up and 'I'll need the *claigh mhor* when it comes tae it, Lionel!' Him snapping at all of them to shut up while the kids whispered fearfully, making no attempt to play with their Christmas toys. Ruth made it plain that 'that thing' was taboo, not to be mentioned. Yet she'd stopped demanding that Bobbie and Diane go at once. She seemed dazed. On the second night the nightmares came again. Next morning Diane, looking desperate, tried to corner Lionel privately. 'Just help Ruth,' he told her grimly. 'Don't ask questions. Don't even think.' And again he vanished for hours. On the days that followed, as the crisis spread, he saw Diane grimly try to help Ruth with the sweeping, cleaning, cooking. But Ruth gave not an inch, accepting her efforts with cold condescension. And as the days passed Diane got more confused and exhausted, often trying to meet his eyes with a look that plainly said: *I can't stand much more of this.* He sympathized. He felt the same. It was hard, finding excuses for what couldn't even be admitted. Hard pretending nothing was wrong. Hard to bear the way Bobbie lumbered about being extra polite to Ruth, ignoring her insults as to his breath, dress, and physical appearance. Amazed by this self-control, Lionel suspected Bobbie managed it only for Diane's sake. A weird relationship. His paranoia grew. For Bobbie was clearly afraid of . . . what? He kept eyeing Diane as if she might betray him. Their story about how they'd met and why they were together was so banal that – no matter. 'My life's forfeit onyway,' Bobbie had said. What did he mean? And that demand for a big sword. Plainly he'd done something awful. The Gruinard Ferry business? Was the law blackmailing him? Lionel didn't ask . . . and Bobbie didn't say. So fear grew all round – but everything had to stay under wraps – until – until what the Old Man had called: '*the day of the great ringing of bells . . .*'

Until then, the less said the better, but he'd hoped that day wouldn't be long. For Diane's sake especially. *Poor woman!* he thought now, passing a basement from which the Watchers roared: '*Aw ma mind's bin murdered by Mars.*' Suspecting but not knowing what had been done to her. Even talk of a worm was enough to trigger the bastards. He'd had to stonewall her. And until now there'd been only one crisis. Two nights ago she'd started on about her husband and daughter and about . . . phones ringing. *Phones? Bells?* He'd cut her off. 'Relax,' he'd snapped, telling her with his eyes: *Just wait! Wait for the hour!* 'Cool down, okay? I've got kids to feed, and right now I've got to go and talk to Channel 3 about armour for a Bosworth 1485 production. Y'know? "*A horse, a horse, my kingdom for a horse*"?'

So they'd got along like misery personified, pretending that the kids didn't cry in their sleep every night as *it* whirled above. And the worm had remained latent until, an hour ago, they'd been watching the Carmody Cee Show . . . and in his joy at John Lloyd's rant he'd at last dropped his guard. 'All . . . *right!*' he'd cried, 'That guy has Taken a Chance!'

And Diane had clutched her head and screamed. Now here he was, turning into Hornsey Road. Soon he came to a door, right by the police station. That was the Old Man's sense of humour. Looking both ways, he knocked six times, carefully spaced, then waited, hoping he'd hadn't blown it entirely.

The door opened. There was a face. He gave his name. The door shut behind him, leaving him in a dark hall. Then an inner door opened. He was beckoned into a dim room. Eyes fixed on him, the Old Man's included. But when his mouth fell open it wasn't because of the Old Man's amused look.

For he found himself facing the black-haired Asiatic guy from the Cumberland. The Old Man chuckled hoarsely.

'Meet Jim, Lionel,' he whispered, 'Jim, – meet Lionel. Lionel's been looking after one of your contacts . . . . haven't you, Lionel?'

And Jim Bright asked, in his ancient accent: 'Doth he knaow my Ma?'

25.
The Twice-Born Airline

Jessica had found it totally bizarre. On meeting her and after Walt had casually told Mo, '*They're okay*,' Mo and Samma, alternating like some over-excited double act as they guided her and Dan through the Amazonian fantasy of their porch at 3690 24th, had taken all of two minutes to tell her not only their life histories but how they'd embraced Chancing (via a Gnostic group in San Anselmo where Van Morrison lived); what Chancing was (basically an updated Manichaean-dualist position freely adapting elements of Cabala, Gnosis and alchemical marriage with a modern scientific Marxist phenomenologically guerrilla approach to Gaia's crisis); what Chancing was for (to regain that dynamic fusion of pragmatic materialism with spiritual insight permitting global collective action through enlightened individual responsibility); and what they thought they could achieve.

'Nothing less than the reinvigoration of the world!' cried Mo.

'Heaven in a grain of sand,' Samma supplied.

'And Eternity in an hour,' Mo backed up.

'You see,' said Samma, steering Jessica past a budding manzanita, 'the synergetic consequence of Einstein, Jung, Teilhard's *noosphere*, Heisenberg, Bucky Fuller, Paolo Soleri,

McLuhan's global village, Chomsky, plus fifth-generation computing and late-sensate culture leads us inevitably to . . .'

'*Don't let the motherfuckers get you down!*' a harsh voice screeched from the mazanita, and Jessica flinched in shock and pain as claws dug into her shoulder. '*Take a Chance! Take a Chance!*'

She shuddered, Dan behind her screeched, and even Walt looked taken aback as the cockatoo flapped back into the bush.

'That's Plato,' said Mo proudly, 'We call this Plato's Cave.'

'You guys must have been at Berkeley,' Jessica said, breathing hard. She felt depressed and exhausted. Walt eyed her, then told Mo and Sammy sharply.

'Hey. You got to drop this crap. I know you pull it as a blind, but Jessica's okay. And the time's here.' In case they didn't get it he showed them his scorched sleeves. 'Julie and me'd have burned to death last night if this lady hadn't . . . happened by.' He shook his head wearily. 'So drop the crap.'

'That's right,' Julie agreed, 'Give us a break.'

And Mo and Samma had instantly changed.

'I'll make the coffee,' Mo said.

'You'll want baths,' said Samma, 'I'll run 'em. Just come on in and sit down.' She smiled at Jessica. 'Sorry about that, honey. Fact is, as Walt knows, everyone we never met we snow like this. No offence. But the best way to smuggle donkeys is to disguise them as donkeys. You get me?'

And she weaved gracefully away through a living-room drowned in more plants to run the baths. Mo was already in the kitchen.

'What the hell are they on about?' Dan asked faintly.

But Mo and Samma weren't as crazy as they first appeared.

Before Arianrhod appeared Jessica learned a lot from them. During the next week, as Arianrhod sailed the sky and the world began to go mad, she learned more – maybe more than she wanted to know. She heard the so-called Khufu Tape, several times. Most important, Jim spoke to her in her dreams.

Thus on the 30th she bought a ticket to London. That night

Walt and Mo drove her out to San Francisco International. But it was 3 am before, after hours of delay, her TWA flight took off. The problem was caused not only by air traffic control chaos (which since Arianrhod's first appearance had plagued every major airport in the world), but by a weird tragedy just as she was about to board.

A Seattle flight coming in over the San Mateo Bridge made a perfect touchdown – three hundred yards short of the runway, in the Bay.

The water was not deep at that point, but impact tipped the nose of the aging 727 and broke its back: so far seventy passengers and crew were known to be dead. It looked like inexplicable pilot error: there had been no alert or Mayday; until the black box was recovered it would remain unclear what had happened . . . but Walt and Mo were in no doubt. 'The guy was zonked on the goddamn sky,' said Walt as they waited with her in the departure lounge amid hundreds of anxious travellers, every one of them wondering exactly the same thing, though few dared say it aloud.

'Yeah.' Jessica laughed shakily.

She didn't say it either.

'It'll be fine,' Mo reassured her. He stabbed a significant thumb skyward. '*They* want you in London – that means you'll get there.'

'Does that mean *they* wanted the Seattle flight to crash?' she muttered.

'Nope.' Mo shrugged. 'The guy just fucked up.'

'I'm glad you're so sure,' she said drily.

'I'm sure,' said Mo. 'So when you get to London you call this Lionel fellow, y'hear? Just stick to the story and stay cool. Nothing about us, right? No trigger-stuff. They don't have free speech there no more.'

'Didn't realize we had it here,' she said.

'Well,' said Mo. 'Comparatively speaking, we do . . . but they don't. So watch your step. You should be okay with a US passport . . . so long as . . .'

'You told me all this a hundred times already!' she snapped.

Behind her back Walt gave Mo a warning look.

'Sure,' said Mo, 'Sorry.'

'I'm just wound up,' said Jessica. 'I don't like flying, and what with Shasta, and the whales, and the Khufu stuff, and now this, and you telling me the goddamned Elohim are looking out for me personally – c'mon!'

Mo sighed; made a helpless Woody Allen-type gesture. 'What does it take to persuade you to get on line?' he asked. 'So it still sounds crazy to you, but you've a real important role to play, and if you fuck up, then too bad for all of us. Why did the messenger come to you? Why did he tell you the whole deal if you don't believe it? How come your boy's talking to you in your sleep? *Come to London*, he keeps saying, *I'm here, Ma, waiting for you!* Don't you believe it? You're gonna form part of the core group, and we can't do nothing if you and this Diane and whoever else don't get it together. So get on that plane to London, Jessica, and Walt and Julie and Samma and me – and Dan, if he wants to come – we'll head down to Arizona, and maybe in a month if it all goes . . .'

'Okay, *okay!*' Jessica glared at him, then eyed Walt in despair. 'Mo, you're a good man, I like you a lot, but did anyone ever tell you that you don't know when to shut up? I mean, I know all this: you've told me maybe a hundred, maybe two hundred times – right?'

'I guess I'm wound up myself,' Mo admitted, and lapsed into a gloomy silence for a moment before nervously springing to his feet.

'What's up now?' Walt asked him with a scowl.

'Need another coffee,' Mo jittered.

But it was then, to Jessica's mingled relief and terror, that her flight was at last announced.

'. . . *TWA Flight 755 to London now boarding Gate 23* . . .'

'Right, boys,' Jessica stood shakily. 'Here we go.'

An hour later she was eating grilled trout and sipping Chablis from a plastic cup at 30,000 feet over the Rockies heading east towards the dawn of the Old World, towards London. She had a window seat; if she'd chosen she could have rolled up the blind to peer out at the shining, threatening mystery that whirled so high above in the black star-studded night.

But that would have been drawing undue attention to herself. Walt and Mo had warned against it. 'We sail on a Song that scares most folk silly,' she'd heard Walt say. 'They're regressing centuries every day that thing's still up there. Soon we'll have witch-paranoia, all of it . . . so when you're out there duck your head, shut your eyes, and keep the blinds drawn like everyone else.' Which sounded like good advice. She was following it. Yet even with head ducked and blind over the window like everyone else in the old 747, she could feel *it*. She could feel *it* in her bones, in her blood, in her mind. *You*, Jessica, *it* was saying. She felt taut yet light, scared yet hopeful, and knew now (no matter what she'd told Mo) that she was rushing down rapids. Only a dream? *No*, she knew, forking the last of the trout, *more than that. But because none of it fits what I feel happy with I keep trying to dismiss it like that.*

'Excuse me, ma'am,' the soft voice of one of her friendly in-flight hosts interrupted, 'Sure you won't hook into the Reely?'

The Economy Lounge's Reelyshow, she knew from the friendly in-flight holo which had done the safety routines at takeoff, was the new remake of *King of Kings*, with Saul St Paul as Christ. Twice-Born okayed, it had grossed $60 million the first week. But when the host (human, no holo) had asked if she wanted it she'd been back in last night's dream, hearing Jim tell her what to do. *Come to London, Ma. I'm waiting for you.* Speaking that weird brogue, like Ollie Reed in some Thomas Hardy hayrick saga. *Tess of the UFOs*, or *Jude the Shining One*, or something. Easy to joke? Hardly. She'd found it scary, that voice. And what she'd seen in the dream. Jim spinning out of the fire in that place where those ragged weirdoes all . . .

She'd forgotten all about *King of Kings* until now.

'Sensory identification with Simon Peter, the Virgin Mary, or Judas Iscariot,' the pedantically insistent voice informed her.

'How about Jesus?' she said without thinking.

'Ma'am, that's sacrilege!'

Amazed, she looked up into the genuinely, righteously shocked young blond face that hovered above the TWA company uniform.

Gathering her wits she recalled the scandal a year ago about a radical Italian Reely – *Yeshua, King of the Jews.* It hadn't only had put out an SI circuit for Christ, but portrayed Him as a worldly revolutionary, a leader of the Zealots against Rome – a warts-and-all human being, his tale twisted by base men for base ends. Amid uproar it had been banned throughout the USA, Twice-Born pressure damning it as blasphemy sponsored by the Chancers, Communists, and Muhammad Al-Khash. No Hollywood studio would now dare risk portraying The Lord with anything but the respect that Twice-Born morality (and money) demanded. Now, with the Star of Megiddo whirling through the sky above, Jessica suddenly realized, as she looked about, that she was the only passenger in the entire Economy Lounge who wasn't devoutly hooked in.

Jeeze, she thought in wonder, eyeing the tyrannically devout face of her in-flight host, *By these Reelies ye shall be saved, is that it?*

'What's the problem?' she asked.

'Ma'am.' His voice was frozen, his gaze fixed midway between her neck and sternum. 'The Reely. *King of Kings.* Are you sure you won't . . .'

'But it's optional, isn't it?' said Jessica, not thinking.

'Of course, ma'am.' He breathed in deep. 'But we ask you to remember: this is a *Christian* company, and while we do appreciate every right of the individual conscience, we do also request that our passengers extend the courtesy of proper respect for our company's faith.'

'Oh.' Recalling Walt's advice, she said, 'Sure. Hook me up.'

'Thank you, ma'am.' He was flushed. 'You want SI too?'

'Yeah.' She grinned. 'How 'bout Mary Magdalene?'

'Sorry, ma'am.' The kid looked ready to groan. 'But the Virgin Mary is an option. The Angelic Visitation is considered really rap.'

Screw the Virgin Mary! It almost burst out of her. Her mouth opened: but on seeing his face she realized, *Say that and he'll probably chuck me out of the emergency exit, even if it means Rapture for everyone on board.*

'Fine,' she said, smiling sweetly, 'so tie me in.'

And she was tied in.

It was hard to go on thinking straight with her neural pathways syruped by the sickly sweet emotions with which Hollywood had flavoured the Virgin. That no doubt was the purpose. *Drown in sugar, honey.* Glumly she endured it for five uplifting hours; weeping at the Crucifixion along with everyone else in the 747, including the masochists who'd hooked into Judas Iscariot, and roaring righteously when that miserable bastard hanged himself in shame and remorse. Only after the Reely, dazedly recovering amid a grey Atlantic dawn, did she recall Mo, yesterday, going on about Judas Iscariot meaning Judas the Sicarius – the sicarius being the small curved dagger favoured by the Zealots for political assassination. 'Sure, Christ set him up, so to fulfil the prophecy,' she heard Mo say as coffee and croissants came round.

There was a general in-flight air of relief and self-congratulation: *it* had ducked under the western horizon without anyone noticing; The Lord had won and soon they'd all land safe in good old London town. People began talking but still she heard Mo's voice. 'It says that in Matthew, in black and white, okay? Someone had to betray him to get him crucified, and Judas drew the short straw . . . or rather, the piece of bread dipped in the dish. So Judas gets to be hated all through history.' And after a sip at his tea he'd gone on: 'Funny how they arranged the euphony – the first syllable of *Judas* – *Jew* – hateful, treacherous *Jew*das who sells his master for thirty pieces, right? Those bastards knew what they were up to. Real PR pros.'

'Of course,' he'd added, 'Judas had to be hated. Part of the deal. He knew it. That's why he's a bigger hero than dumb Simon the Tough Guy, who when Last Days didn't turn up fast enough bought Paulianity instead. But Judas understood. The guy who gets to play the Beast always does. Some guys who get to play

Saint do too. Simon Peter didn't. He got to be the foundation of the Church of Rome instead.'

'The Beast guarantees Christ,' Samma said, 'Dark guarantees Light.'

Jessica could hear herself laughing at them.

'Like I said,' she cried, 'You guys must have been at Berkeley. You talk like you're still at college. I mean, who cares about this?'

Now, high above the Atlantic, flying a Twice-Born airline that had her marked as a subversive for not wanting to hook into *Kings of Kings*, and *then* for wanting to identify with raunchy Mary Magdalene instead of a soporific male-invented Virgin who had her kid by hygienic divine intervention and none of that nasty messy biological sex-stuff (You know it gives you AIDS) – now Jessica heard the echo of her own voice and groaned.

Come to London, Ma, she heard, *I'm waiting for you.*

Standing in that place with the fire blazing around him!

But who are you? she wondered fearfully, *You can't really be Jim any more. Not the kid I knew. That's impossible. I'd be a sucker to think it. So what are you? What am I seeing when I dream? Is that really you in that place? The . . . Temple? Mo's right?*

That place. That place with stone heads grimacing round the wall, the effigies of dead knights on the flagstoned floor. That round place with the five-point star on that flagstones and Jim (or whatever *claimed* to be Jim: she couldn't get that out of her head) amid it, consumed by fire . . .

Forget it! she told herself as the 747 began bucking into a low off Iceland and the *Fasten Seat-Belts* light came on. *You can't fit it into a known frame of reference – it won't fit! You're just getting scared.*

Well, it was hard not to be. Mo, Walt and Samma had all told her that yesterday while analysing what Samma had called – seriously – 'Jessica's Symbolic Dream of Initiatory Transformation.'

To which Mo had said, with a fond sneer:

'Bullshit! Why be symbolic when you've got the real thing?'

'Yeah,' Samma had argued, 'but she uses symbols to see it because its parameters go beyond her existing reference system.

It's an event she can't understand, right? So until she *lives* it she has to transform it symbolically into myth-play – or she goes crazy. Dreaming's like laughing – a psychological way of dealing with shit that'll break us otherwise!'

'Thanks!' said Jessica, but they'd been too busy arguing.

'Come on!' Walt cried. 'She dreams she sees her kid – sorry, Jessica, I mean Jim – go into this round-type church in a medieval city that may be London, right? He goes in there dressed medieval with two guys she dreamed about before and that this messenger Pierre showed her by the pool-table in her bar . . . and one of them chalks a pentagram on the floor and . . .'

'. . . Sounds to me like John Dee,' said Mo lugubriously, but Walt ignored him, Samma too, though Jessica wondered: *Who's that?*

'. . . Then he just kinda . . . burns up.' Walt had nodded fiercely at Samma, not Jessica. 'That's your transformation fugue, Samma. Right? But it's real. This is all real. He's really coming through time. Through . . .'

'. . . The Templars built circular churches,' Mo said tersely. 'They were eastern dualists, Gnostics, not Rome Christers at all, and that's why . . .'

'. . . One of the Gates,' Walt went on, 'that the Elohim . . .'

'. . . Rome and Philip the Fair of France jumped them in 1308 or 1309, accusing them of kissing the ass of this idol called Baphomet – which ties up with the Gnostic Sophia – but also because they had a lot of loot . . .'

'Will you shut up and let Walt speak, Mo!' Samma cried.

I thought it was my dream, Jessica thought now. *Obviously not.*

'. . . The point is,' Mo had insisted, 'they got persecuted in Europe, but they found refuge in England, and built one of their typical round churches in London – the Temple – and Jessica, I think that's what your dream's of!' He'd grinned at her. 'The Temple in London! Look. Here's a picture.'

Triumphant, he'd produced a book on English churches; and there in the picture she'd seen the flagstoned floor, the effigies . . . and that circle of mocking stone grotesques . . . and where she'd seen the two men standing . . .

She'd felt sick. She felt sick now. The 747 was yawing through the sky like a berserk beast. She wondered if the pilot heard singing voices.

'Recognize it? Is that it?' Mo had demanded like a bloodhound.

'It's just a dream!' she'd muttered, terrified.

'Dream, yes, but not *just!*' He'd snapped the book shut.

'Mo, sit down and stop hassling her!' Samma had demanded.

'So then?' Walt had eagerly gone on, 'Suddenly it all – *Shifts!* Right, Jessica? One moment you're looking down on Olde Englande rooftops; the next it's hitek hirise London 1999. Big City towers, right?'

And Jessica groaned. *Right, guys! You got it right! You know all about it – right? Wrong! Because you don't! It's happening to* me!

The storm was getting worse. First the plane plunged hundreds of feet, then careened violently up as if punched by a giant fist. She gritted her teeth as passengers began shrieking, praying, and bending to the sick-bags.

Just getting scared? she asked. *Damn right!*

For the fate of the Seattle flight was one thing. What lay ahead was another . . . even assuming Mo was right and *they* – or the pilot – got this old wreck safely down. As for the Khufu stuff on *guys, on UFOs of fiery chariots or from Roanoke or the Marie Celeste or* – approaching – easy now to believe it with the elements shrieking round this frail flying sardine can. Peering past the blind she saw the wings bend and twist; saw bright sparks flare . . . she shut her eyes. Nausea rose again. *Jim*, she thought wildly, seeing him spin dazed from Gate-fire into waiting hands, *You went out like all those guys, on UFOs or fiery chariots or from Roanoke or the Marie Celeste or – Christ could have been one of you! Now you're back because of the . . . that pharaoh stuff, right? Pole-shift, Velikovsky Day, and just five months to get it together before our ugly collective thought-forms blow it entirely!* She laughed, not happy. *But I thought we'd blown it anyway. You really mean there's hope? Jim? Are you there? Are you really there?*

But she heard only the storm and the engines roaring as the 747 lurched down the Irish coast. *Is this the Madness beginning?* she wondered, and to distract herself began looking through the glossy info-pack provided to tell US visitors to Metropolitan England what awaited them. It was written in a turgid official style, full of words like 'marginalize' and 'viable', but with the 747 bucking so madly she made herself focus on how, since the reform of the USSR and the collapse of NATO and the EEC, the reunification of Germany had led not only to the birth of the Northern European Community but (via a series of events too arcane for her to comprehend) to the Split – the division of the UK into Metropolitan England, (now the USA's last European ally), and the NEC-affiliated federation called the British Union.

Since the Split, she read, US–London flights could no longer overfly the British mainland, the Union being anti-US, but instead had to approach from the south-west, down the coast of Eire and up the Bristol Channel. The blurb went on:

> *NEC signatories welcome overflights or landings from Canada, Mexico, and elsewhere in the Americas. The NEC attitude to the USA (the Bonn Assembly lately denounced the US government as a 'fascist theocracy', indicating the degree to which NEC signatories have fallen sway to the siren song of the so-called 'Russian Renaissance') has been protested in the UN as elsewhere. To date however, the ban on US overflight persists. Hopefully these states, from which so many of our ancestors (it seems with good reason!) emigrated, will soon review their prejudice, and reopen trade and diplomatic links with their great neighbour across the Atlantic.*

This 'prejudice,' she read on, was also extended by NEC signatories, especially those in the British Union, to Metropolitan England – which, regarded as a 'stooge' of the Maghreb and of the USA, was held by the NEC to have 'rejected civilized values', due to its '*controversial policy of encouraging its unemployed to take up "migrant consultancies" abroad, especially in the construction of the much-needed new Saharan road link.*'

Ho-hum she thought, grimly clutching her stomach as the jumbo turned east past the south of Eire. With an increasing stony face she flipped through the rest of the pack, through glowing descriptions of the Reely-Show Industry and other pleasures awaiting the open-minded tourist, pausing only at a sheet outlining '*Current Met Style – the Mask Craze*'. She read:

> *London society is justly famed for its ironic wit, directed mostly at itself. Recently this wit has found expression in a number of forms of which you should be aware. The current craze (seemingly initiated by chat-show host Carmody Cee) involves the adoption by guests at social and public functions of biomasks and full dress disguise in the personae of historical figures epitomising past British glories. The Victorian Age is especially viable at this time. Thus, if invited to a Top Persons' social function in London you should first visit a 'Mask Shop' (most prestigious are those found in Bond Street), and avoid social humiliation by equipping yourself with an appropriate persona. For US visitors the following personae (choose according to taste) are recommended . . .*

There followed a list of US greats including Jefferson, Walt Whitman, Ulysses S. Grant, General Custer, Harriet Beecher Stowe, Scott Joplin . . .

But then (to her vast relief) the instruction to fasten seat-belts came on. There was no need to ask people to extinguish cigarettes. Smoking was banned on international flights. It was, Jessica recalled as the captain's voice broke in, considered not only unhealthy but unchristian and immoral.

'This is your Captain speaking. We'll be landing at London Heathrow in just ten minutes, at twenty-thirty-six local time.' The voice coughed, and added soberly. 'Sorry about the rough journey, but it's just part of the Tribulation, so let us praise Him "whose goings forth have been from old, from everlasting". For surely it is the Lord who has brought us safely over the vast deep on this, the last night of His second millennium.'

The friendly in-flight hosts led the Economy Lounge in fervent prayer as the 747 bucked ever lower through the gale . . .

as lights below appeared.

'The Lord is my shepherd, I shall not want . . .'

Jessica groaned. She sensed ordeal in those burning lights.

Come to London, Ma. I'm waiting for you.

26.
Disraeli Gear

'*Gnosce teipsum*, Know thyself,' Philip Agutter kept muttering under his breath to himself an hour later when, under a lurid sky, he came by hansom from Hyde Park's heliport to La Bruce's party in an exclusive new Victorian development behind Harrods. He had worries. Behind his urbane Disraeli mask – as the carriage came bumping over the cobbles under the sputtering gas-lamps – he was angry, nervous, and unsure how he'd react tonight. From the chopper he'd seen the fires burning out of control south of the river. But they were the least of his problems. The last twenty-four hours had been hell.

He knew he'd told Carol too much last night. Then that foul nightmare. Someone trying to kill him. And the row over Carmody Cee. Denying that bastard Rae a warrant for Carmody's arrest (on security grounds) and an injunction against further Carmody Gee broadcasts. Sticking his neck out by blocking a CSU raid on Closed Area N4 last night when implantee 76-E-678-DEJ's worm began wailing Chancer connection. All pure folly, he knew. 'Death' Rae was getting more dangerous by the hour. Rae had the PM sewn up; was rumoured to have had secret talks with the heads of M15 and M16; he was thriving on the chaos, and though Agutter as Home Secretary was the nominal police boss he knew that, when push came to shove, Old Bill on the beat would follow Rae, not 'some jumped-up old prat like him' (he'd winced at this description in one of his CSU spook reports). *Spooks!* Not funny! Not after what happened while dressing at home for this thing. And the Ghost Project, leaking like a sieve. Support falling away. Someone was talking. He hated to think who . . . but coming up from Sussex, the chopper yawing wild through a ruddy starless sky above the fires raging out of control in South Circular Closed Areas below, he'd found himself eyeing the silhouette of his M16 pilot. Sergeant Ted Grant had flown him for three years. *What if he's working for Rae?* He'd rejected this as paranoia, but when they'd landed in the VIP Hyde Park heliport, (even as he made angry calls to PM Fisher, Scotland Yard, the ISO in Paris and the CSU in Holborn) it was to find Rae's armed police everywhere. Not encouraging.

They were outside the hansom at this moment, disguised as peelers.

But all this was secondary to the shock he'd had at home this evening while donning his Disraeli gear. With Arianrhod under the horizon.

He'd been struggling with the huge, floppy black Disraeli tie when that siren song began ringing in his skull again. And this time the ringing had briefly the tone of a human voice – one that was all too familiar.

You'll never come home again, it had sung, so high-pitched, seemingly from the night outside. *Poor Dad. You'll never see Mum again* . . .

'Gillian?' he'd cried in disbelief, tears in his eyes as he turned to stare through the uncurtained window at the cloudy sky.

And he'd seen her! His lost daughter! Yes! He really had! So faint and spectral against the rain-streaked window, mouthing . . . warning him?

Then she was gone, and the singing too.

He'd nearly changed his mind about tonight's operation.

But he had no option. And it was too late to back out now, he knew as the cab reached La Bruce's. Yet as he stepped out of the hansom amid the many others parked along the cobbled street, he seemed the very epitome of fin-de-siècle elegance and gentlemanly self-confidence. Slim and faintly sinister in top hat, white gloves, starched collar, black frock-coat and ankle-length black cape, he gestured with his ivory-handled cane at Ted Grant, up on the high-seat, and told him to wait. His voice was firm, though suitably affected: his designer-grown Disraeli mask (authentic down to the elegant kiss-curl on the high, pale, Byronic forehead) hid his anxious face as he checked in at security and took the lift to the seventh floor where, leaving hat, gloves, and cape at the cloakroom, he gave his card to the grave, balding Jeeves at the gilded entrance to the main saloon.

'My Lord the First Earl of . . .' the Jeeves began announcing loudly above the babble from the crowded salon.

I'm still in shock, he thought remotely, *I need a minute.*

'One moment.' He raised a hand. The other, in a pocket of his frock coat, lay on the object he'd brought. If this was a trap he was ruined. He felt dizzy and unreal. Here he was. At La Bruce's utterly bizarre self-praise and Eve-of-New-Millennium party. From Sikorski chopper to a horse-drawn cab; from halogen floodlights to cobbled gas-lit streets! He shook his head. *I shouldn't be here*, he told himself angrily as he saw La Bruce alias Victoria Regina. The Oscar-winning *Widow of Windsor*, sailing about amid the self-acclaiming cream of Met society. Fantastically masked and made up they mingled, confidently concealed, languid over their exotic cocktails, ignoring the chaos outside. Amazing! It made him want to gag. In a daze he searched the mass of masks for a sign of the man he'd come to meet. In a candlelit alcove nearby a pale young pianist played Schumann's *Trâumerei*, high-bosomed young women in long pale Empire gowns sighing in transport about him. *Pathetic Neroes!* he scolded them silently. *You've all seen it. You've all been dreaming. Don't pretend you haven't. You all watched Carmody last night. Gilded dinosaurs!*

The cough of the Jeeves hinted impatience. 'My Lord . . .?'

'Yes, yes,' he muttered, wondering, *What if he's not here?* and then, *Don't get paranoid, Philip.*

But was it paranoia? That implied unreal suspicion. *Who here knows what's real or unreal?* he wondered acidly. And his hallucination of Gillian was explicable. He'd hardly slept since Arianrhod's appearance. He'd kept going on scotch, coffee, and cream crackers. No wonder he was seeing ghosts. Anyway, the whole damned Met had been lost to dreams long before *it* appeared. Everyone was haunted. So he'd seen her. So what?

Yet behind his mask he felt sick, scared, and very weary.

'My Lord,' the Jeeves tried again, 'Is something the matter?'

'A faintness,' Disraeli replied in arch irritation. 'A moment.'

No, though Agutter, *I've nothing in common with this. I never did. But I never did much to resist it either. I tried . . . sort of . . .*

Sort of. In the last days of the Pre-Split crisis, sure, as Social Services Secretary he'd gone against the government, arguing for the NHS. Very quixotic. He'd told reporters how sometimes he still dreamed of his mother crying 'Unforgivable!' at the NHS surgeon who'd authorized the blood transfusion that saved him after a crash when he was ten. 'I am convinced that people require more than solely material answers to crisis!' he'd told the media. *Fine words, Philip!* he thought now. *And what happened as soon as it all collapsed and Harry offered you a place? The ostriches buried their heads in Reely-Show sand . . . and you rushed to join them!*

Now Arianrhod circled the Hidden World . . . and he knew he had to follow the singing, the vision. A chance, at least, to regain his self-respect. But he was fearful as he sought his man amid the mad dream of La Bruce's party. Reely mad, and surely he was mad too. He recognized not only most of the roles people were playing, but he knew many well enough to guess who lived under each mask and disguise. The Queen herself (easy, that was La Bruce) talking with Palmerston (seemed familiar: couldn't quite place him) and Wellington (he feared he recognized Wellington's brawny rugby player's shoulders. *What's he doing here?* he wondered with a chill). Mrs Florence Nightingale – that voice sounded like Marie Hudson the soprano: his sworn enemy ever since he'd banned Met productions of Wagner and Richard Strauss) – was in animated conversation with Mr John Ruskin, whose excited, birdlike gestures suggested Canon Richard Gadd, the muscular Christian who sided with Commissioner Rae in demanding death for crimes against property. The frontage of Lola Montez swooning over the pale young pianist looked not unlike that of Lulu La Liberté the porno star and AIDS campaigner; the pop eyes of Oscar Wilde next to her, one arm ostentatious round Bosie's slim shoulders as he wittily entertained Mr Beardsley and Mr Yeats, betrayed, even through his mask, the libidinous zeal of Ibn Khalid, the hyperactive Egyptian poet. Agutter had tried to deport him a year ago on a morals rap; a word in his ear from Sid' Ahmed the Maghreb ambassador (via Harry Fisher) had put a stop to that. Money, of course. And they had their backs to a foppish Prince Kropotkin who, under a sparkling chandelier, was loudly trying to persuade Lord Salisbury and Mr Randolph Churchill (he couldn't place either of them) of the moral virtues of anarchism. But Kropotkin?

He stared at Kropotkin, then knew he wasn't his man. too stocky.

Why did I agree to this? he wondered, in a sweat under his mask. He eyed Wellington discreetly. *I wouldn't put it past Carol to . . .*

'My Lord,' the Jeeves complained. 'There *are* others to announce . . .'

He turned. Robert Browning bowed. Elizabeth Barrett Browning made a dainty curtsey. He gave them a languid, mournful eye.

'Very well.' Disraeli nodded. 'Get on with it.'

In plummy orotund tones the Jeeves did his bit.

'My Lords, Ladies, and Gentlemen . . . your indulgence for . . . My Lord the First Earl of Beaconsfield, Viscount Hughenden of Hughenden, the Right Honourable Leader of Her Majesty's loyal opposition . . .'

Massed ranks of masked faces politely turned to bow.

His own mask hid his hatred of them all as he bowed back.

'Mr Disraeli!' It was La Bruce herself. Breaking off her conversation with Palmerston and Wellington, the Widow of Windsor swept dowdily, plumply out of the dense crowd to greet him. She was, as ever, in black, still mourning Albert. 'We wondered at your absence, sir.'

Reluctantly he bowed. The Duke of Wellington, magnificently togged out in scarlet tunic with a chestful of medals from the Peninsular Campaign, eyed him with haughty, disdainful suspicion.

'Ceb broke a wheel on the turnpike, Me'em.'

He spoke in an affected lah-di-dah accent which, he fervently hoped, concealed his true identity. He didn't like the way that Wellington . . .

'And . . . where is your good lady wife, Mr Disraeli?'

'Taken poorly, Me'em. She asks me to convey her apologies.'

'Indeed?' The Empress of half the known world clasped white powdered hands. Her eyes narrowed. 'We do hope it is nothing . . . serious?'

'The flux, Me'em,' he replied, 'and aggravated by a chill caught while riding to hounds on Thursday last.'

'You will of course convey our hopes for her swift recovery?'

'I will indeed, Me'em, and thenk you for your interest.'

Victoria Regina smiled graciously. At her shoulder Wellington still glared. 'And yourself, Mr Disraeli?' she fluted, 'Time is not idle on your hands? I trust you burn midnight oil in compiling the fine edifice of yet another of your social romances that the public finds so . . . educational?'

'I hold the pen mightier than the sword, Me'em,' he replied, nodding at Wellington who, he was now chillingly sure, had precisely the front-row forward's build of Police Commissioner Hector Rae. And the stony eyes. He added in a measured tone: 'Though some present might disagree.'

'Quite. Quite.' And with a wave of one plump hand she swept away to engage a minor duke of Schleswig-Holstein and his wife in talk.

But for a long moment Wellington continued glaring at him, before turning contemptuously away, taking Palmerston by the shoulder.

'Pon my soul,' the Iron Duke loudly drawled, 'The man's not

only a demmed cad, but a demmed Jew to boot – if you take my meaning, sah!'

'Yes, indeed, haw-haw,' Palmerston guffawed, turning with a poisonous look that nonetheless had in it not a little of Chancellor Peter Wood's bland charm, 'Boot the poxy Jews, I seh, what? Bad as the Irish, what?'

'Absoluteleh,' nodded the Iron Duke, 'Jews and Paddies – boot 'em.'

Accepting a pink gin fizz from a servant's gloved hand Agutter faded to a corner, assumed an attitude discouraging approach, and gathered his wits.

They know. He was sure of it. But it was too late to back out now.

He scanned the mob, fearing he'd made a terrible mistake.

Not just the Khufu message was on the cassette in his pocket, but the ISO Report on the Chancers . . . and how to neutralize them.

'Mr D, you don't look happy,' said a high, piping voice, 'In fact you look as if you'd like to see this place burned to the ground.'

Agutter flinched. He turned and met the pale blue eyes, the precise face, the new-fangled all-wool suit of the man he'd come to meet.

Is that you? he asked the masked face silently. *If not . . .*

With a freezing heart he committed himself.

'"*Arson, after all,*"' he quoted cautiously, '"*is an artificial crime.*"'

'"*A large number of houses deserve to be burnt*,"' was the response.

Agutter didn't dare look at Wellington. 'Mr Polly, I presume?'

Herbert George Wells shrugged. 'Carmodacious, Mr D.'

Agutter leaned against the wall. 'The War To End War, Mr W.' He felt faint and heavy, as if all his blood had drained into his feet. With an effort he looked away from the man he hoped was Carmody Cee.

Across the room he saw Wellington watching them.

A gaze that made him feel like an insect pinned to a board.

What's the matter? he asked himself. *Losing your nerve?*

H.G. followed his gaze. Hooking inky thumbs into well-worn

pockets he said, with sarcastic emphasis: '"*Notice the smug suppressions of his face. In his mouth are Lies in the shape of false teeth.*"'

Agutter managed to laugh. His senses were swirling. In the background the sensitive pianist was playing a Chopin *étude.*

'Lies as evil as the death-Raes of your famous Martians, Mr Wells,' he muttered. 'I fear we're rumbled. The question is: what to do?'

'Be bold,' said Mr Wells, his eyes veiled. 'You have a cigar for me?'

Agutter tensed. Then, casually, he fished in his pocket.

'Hate to insult your taste, sir, but I have a Hamlet or two. Don't smoke 'em myself. A Christmas Tree gift. Have 'em if you want 'em.'

'Don't mind if I do.' And Carmody rapidly palmed into his pocket the Khufu tape under the Hamlet five-pack that Agutter handed him. Flicking a cigar from the pack, he peeled the cellophane, lit up with a Swan Vestas, and blew out smoke. 'And how is your good lady wife, Mr D?'

'I fear,' Agutter admitted, 'that she may be taken by the Beast.'

'I fear,' said Carmody Cee, smiling through his Wells mask with eyes that were suddenly blank, 'that many have been taken by the Beast, Mr D – But we can't cry over spilt brimstone, eh?' He clapped Agutter's frock-coated shoulder. 'I must away, to prepare an address . . . to all the *damned* fools of this world, eh? Take care, old friend – the tribe of Levi bears more fruit than the Beast kens – so don't let the fools get you down.'

And he was gone. Agutter watched him weave through the crowd, greeting Browning, Haggard, Lang, Kipling, and other literary luminaries as he left.

Also he saw Wellington's steely gaze follow Wells's departure.

Why is he here? Agutter wondered, leaning by a window . . . and as he eyed the street far below his attention was caught by a glimmer of fire. By the far kerb he saw a shadowy man standing by a horse-drawn barrow. The fire glowed from a brazier in the barrow; coachmen were queueing up for . . . what? Hot chestnuts? Maybe. All very Victorian. *Too* bloody Victorian.

Turning back, he saw Wellington alias Hector Rae leaving the room, and under the Byronic melancholy of the Disraeli mask his expression grew depressed. He felt exhausted. He'd arranged to meet Carmody here because it seemed safer than anywhere else. But . . . now his head was singing and ringing again. He thought of Ulysses, ears stopped, strapped to the mast as he sailed past the Isle of the Sirens . . . struggling to escape, to dive overboard and swim towards the deadly singing and ringing . . . the singing and ringing . . . he felt his heart buzzing and fibrillating . . .

At last he realized that the ringing he heard was the shrill call of a fake antique telephone, upright and bakelite black, that stood on a coffee table nearby. He realized this only when La Bruce alias Queen Victoria herself answered it, swooping from the crowd and snatching it up.

'What is it?' she cried in an irritated, most un-Victorian voice, 'I thought I told you people to hold my calls tonight until . . . oh . . . what . . .?

Even as her mouth fell open and speechlessness seized her at whatever she heard, it slowly began to strike Agutter and many others in the room that something incomprehensible was happening. For of course as La Bruce answered her phone it stopped ringing. But as soon as it did, the buzzing or ringing tones of other phones became audible. The pocket phones of the guests, concealed about their Victorian persons. All ringing at once, in perfect co-ordination. At first the minor tones of the pocket phones had been drowned not only by the chatter but by the major tones of La Bruce's table phone. With a chill Agutter realized that the apparent fibrillation of his heart was in fact the muted buzz of his own pocket phone, tucked into his waistcoat pocket over his heart next to a fob watch (which – a nice touch, this – had apparently really belonged to Disraeli, being inscribed: *B.D. – M.A.W-L., 27.8.1839* – referring, the antiquary from whom he'd bought it had assured him, to Disraeli's marriage to Mary Anne Wyndham-Lewis).

A sense of dreamlike terror swept him. His hair stood on end. *This is it!* he knew instinctively. For a long moment he was unable to answer his own call. Nor did anyone else answer theirs. Masked faces gazed uneasily at each other and La Bruce. For as she listened she was visibly shaking. Slowly, like a sleepwalker, she pulled off her Queen Victoria mask, dropped it to the floor, and shook loose her severely back-combed hair if to say: *The games are all over.* And as she listened she began to weep. Her eyes glistened, tears ran down her cheeks . . . until at last, with trembling and parted lips, and the holy, innocent awe of a child on her white face, she turned to the man beside her, the man with the Disraeli mask.

'Mr Agutter,' she whispered, the room now utterly silent save for the muted buzzing of maybe forty unanswered pocket phones, and in her eyes he saw no trace of plot, plan or design, 'They – they want to talk to you. You must . . . you must answer your call!'

Her tearful gaze swept the room, touching on all of her guests one-by-one, Sarah Bernhardt and Oscar Wilde, Lord Palmerston and Prince Kropotkin, Mr Charles Dickens and the Countess of Bradford, the pale pianist and . . .

But not the Duke of Wellington, who'd left the room, presumably to answer a different kind of call.

'You must *all* answer your calls!' she cried in a kind of agony.

Still Agutter didn't dare to respond . . . nor did anyone else. But when she gave him a strange, tremorous smile, he knew he had no option.

'What do you mean?' he asked hoarsely. '*They?*'

La Bruce pointed mutely up at the sky.

With the clear sense of his fate upon him, Agutter took his phone from his pocket and touched the *Receive* cell.

'Yes,' he said, breathing deep . . .

And he heard Gillian's disembodied voice, faint and crackly.

'Dad,' she said, 'It's time you joined us. Now, listen . . .'

27.
Lark Descending

What now? Carmody wondered, leaving the party with the Iron Duke's eye like a spear in his back. No way was it chance that Hector Rae, no party-goer, was at La Bruce's. Someone had talked. It had to be a set-up, and fear gnawed at him as, collecting H.G.'s cape and bowler, he called for the lift (he hated lifts) in the brocaded, securiscanned foyer, where from hidden speakers Vaughan Williams's *The Lark Ascending* softly rose.

But this bird's going down, he thought grimly. Discreetly he felt the tape in his pocket. The Khufu tape. He knew what was on it, and about the Radio Shangri-La bust. He also knew Rae capable of arranging a mugger's knife in the guts of anyone who got in his way. Channel 3 execs hadn't forgotten the fate of the comic Harry Toombs who'd made Death Rae jokes on the air. Now Harry was busy building the Maghreb Motorway. No cards from him . . . and no more Death Rae jokes on the air. At least he was, presumably, still alive – luckier than Marc Lamotte and Blue Jones of Radio Shangri-La. Carmody knew what had happened to them – what might soon happen to him, and to Agutter, if not for whom he'd be in a cell already. Amazing. Maybe *too* amazing? He'd always seen Agutter as a fence-sitting jerk. Now it seemed he played a double game. But who didn't? And how double? *We all wear masks in the Met,* he knew. *We can't be ourselves without 'em. Hilarious.*

The lift arrived; the door opened. Within was a tight little velveteen cage. He got in, so scared that his sinuses were clear for the first time in days. A wall-mirror showed not Carmody Cee but H.G. Wells. *Welcome to my time machine!* Wells seemed to whisper as the door closed. Trembling, he shut his eyes, the old claustrophobia seizing him, unable to press the *Down* button. *Lark Ascending? Lark about to be bloody well shot!* Wildly opening his eyes, he sought the securicam, but couldn't spot it.

Taken your Chance at last, have you? asked a mocking inner voice.

And by God he had! It hadn't taken John Lloyd to convince him!

'I've waited all my life for this,' he muttered at H.G.

'*Waited for what?* his mask demanded sceptically. *Morlock Dawn? The red tide that sweeps all before it? The End? The Parousia? The pole-shift?*

'Call it what you like,' he whispered, 'All I know is Arianrhod's in the sky. The dumbest Nazi knows the game is up. No more free lunches.'

And if they don't know? Wells enquired sweetly.

'Then I'll tell 'em,' he muttered, 'That's why I'm doing this.'

First you have to get out of here, Wells advised politely.

Carmody shivered. 'You're just my mask!' he hissed, finding courage to press the button that committed him to the ground-floor security gate, 'But I'll find a way, because *it*'s coming . . .' – with a jerk the fall began, and he gasped – '. . . and it doesn't matter if you're a saint or shit, because . . .'

. . . *Nobody'll be around to see it? Splendid!* His mask grinned wickedly at him; he stared dizzily back as his sense of helpless fall got worse.

Six, he heard the floor indicator hiss, *You know it's just a fix.*

What if it is? he wondered, sweating, *What if Rae's thugs just do me in at the bottom? What if nothing ever changes and I'm killed for nothing, just like a bloody fool! That scares me worse than Hector Rae ever could.* And in sudden rage he shouted, 'Okay, you bastards! So let's have it! The End! I didn't ask to be born! I didn't sign a bloody contract!'

Five, the floor-count told him quietly, *Better dead? – or alive!*

'I'm crazy,' he told himself. The cage fell faster. Appalled, he tore off the mask. He stared at the naked, hollow, dissipated middle-aged face in the mirror. 'Who's that?' he whispered, and saw his mirror-lips move as a flat, harsh voice answered him. 'A bloke like the rest,' said the voice he didn't recognize. 'Thinks himself special, same as the rest. Death can't happen to him, so he embraces it. He fucks up his life and calls it success. Could have been out on the hills watching the coming glory but instead gets himself into the worst bloody fix imaginable! A clever guy!'

Four, said the eye on the door. *Who wants a war?*

It is sweet and good to die for any shit the bastards sell you! he thought wearily. *And John says the Big One's only four months away. So why worry?* At which his showman's inner voice again began ranting: *Step right up!* it roared in him, *Step right up for the Big One! Fire and flood, as guaranteed by astrologers, mystics, seers and Chancers! Plus we have many scientific testimonials! Why did the dinosaurs die? Why sea-shells in the Andes? It's written in the rocks! Written in the Great Pyramid and at Stonehenge and on the hills and wherever the Death Rae seeks to stop you seeing! Scared to lose a world? So Take a Chance to gain your soul!*

He felt a crazy glee. *Hey, that sounds good! Lemme see. How to do it? Pole-shift due to build-up of South Pole ice? Stuck by a meteor? We can do it. Incinerated by nuclear fire? Smothered in CO_2? Burned in Sodom and Gomorrah? – which, incidentally, we hit because they was getting out of line on their tax, it was no morals rap at all. We can arrange it. Or maybe you wanna be pulled out of orbit by giant planetary conjunction? Or all of the above, plus fire and flood as a Special Free Bonus!*

HIs voices – for suddenly they were many – grew to a crescendo.

Step right up! Ride the Death-and-Rebirth Express – You've done it before, you can do it again! It's writ in the rocks!

Bewildered he eyed the wet-eyed, laughing face in the mirror even as the descending light flashed again. *The Beast's got me!* he thought madly.

Three the red light breathed, *Is that really what you want to see?*

'Yeah, it's written in *our* rocks,' he muttered, dizzy and desolate. 'We've got no option. Must be that "selfish gene", or Original Sin, or something,' he went on, remotely perplexed by his state, for he'd done no dope or booze tonight; there was nothing unusual but for . . .

. . . his fear that he was trapped and about to die . . .

. . . And Arianrhod . . .

. . . Arianrhod . . . sailing in the sky, two-faced . . .

He laughed. 'Those Siberian mammoths had bigger balls than we do,' he babbled, 'and see what happened to them! One moment chewing their grass; the next – frozen steak! Hey, Hector Rae,' he cried, 'why're you such a prick? Who do you think you are? People like you and . . .'

Two, advised the floor-counter, *Who do you think is true?*

And he stopped the name on his lips . . . but not the thought.

People like you and . . . that bastard Agutter?

'Why's he doing this?' he muttered, 'What's he got to gain?'

Abruptly he saw, with chilling sobriety, that Agutter and Rae had set him up, that this was a plot to get rid of him, to kill him or send him off to the Sahara and ensure that he broadcast no more rebel material – ever.

Why didn't I see it? he asked reasonably. *Why would a bloke with the brownest nose you ever saw suddenly turn into a hero? Why did I buy it?*

Arianrhod! came the distant answer, a song beyond the blood-redness on his mind now as he plunged, but in his thickness he didn't hear it.

Because now it was obvious. Entrapment.

He groaned. He could see Disraeli and Wellington congratulating each other over a drink as they called the security gates with orders to . . .

'I *am* crazy!' he wailed, ripping the Khufu tape from his pocket, trying to break it in half as if that would save him. 'Why do this, you idiot?'

But the cassette, of modern unbreakable plastic; would not be broken, and there was nowhere to hide it as . . .

One! Now it's done!

And the lift slammed to a halt. The gate began to open. Hurriedly he recollected himself and thought, then thrust the tape back in his pocket and replaced his H.G. Wells mask. But through it his eyes said: *Why didn't you listen to Esther? They're going to kill you!*

He was right. They were. But . . .

That was when the phones all rang.

That was when La Bruce's phone rang.

That was when Agutter's pocket-phone rang.

That was when Hector Rae's pocket-phone rang.

That was when Carmody's phone rang, and the phone in the guard cubicle by the security gate, and the phone in the grimy pocket of the hot chestnut seller out on the street, and the radiophone on the belt of one of Rae's Special Duties agents, at that moment waiting in the silence and darkness of Carmody Cee's flat in Kentish Town.

That was when the phone that sat on the gauntleted hand of the armoured knight on the first floor landing of Lionel's house in Closed Area N4 rang; rang with all of them back in the house, and a blazing row going on in the kitchen between Bobbie and Ruth; a row which Diane in the front room was trying to ignore. She was trying to play Monopoly with Justin and Grace. This was hard. After last night she had no idea who to trust, she felt ready to explode. The headache was worse all the time. It was like a live thing writhing in her skull . . . and the horror was that this (she knew now, and knew everyone else knew it too) was exactly true. A *thing* squatting in her head, a thing planted in her at Peterborough, a *thing* broadcasting not only whatever anyone said in her hearing but – worst of all – her own innermost feelings. It was the ultimate humiliation; an inner nakedness she'd resisted for a week only by remaining determinedly ignorant of it and because Lionel had turned aside all talk or thought about it. *Lionel!* But since he'd betrayed her last night it was impossible to bear it any longer; the only reason she hadn't already taken terminally drastic action was that she couldn't think straight enough to know how to end her life. For it was intolerable, it was . . . *Probably no worse than what we're all going through*, she told herself exhaustedly, her rigorous self-denying female habit of a lifetime triumphing as from the kitchen she heard –

'Ye stupid auld bag!' Bobbie was bellowing at Ruth.

'You're just shit shaped like a man!' Ruth was screaming back.

'For Chrissakes, the pair of you!' Lionel was shouting at both of them.

Diane winced. 'Ignore it,' she told the kids. *Sick old witch*, said their frightened looks. They hadn't been told but they knew. 'I'll buy a hotel on Mayfair,' she said faintly. Sick? Yes. Very sick. Sick in brain and body. How could she trust Lionel now? What was he up to? Why wouldn't he say? Ruth of all people had rescued her and Bobbie from the pub last night. 'Come on home,' she'd said flatly. 'God knows what he's up to. Too bad if it gets us all busted, but I won't be turned out of my house.' And Lionel not back till dawn – slinking back, pale and drawn, saying only: 'Just a few more hours! Just wait!' But wait for what? And Bobbie still mum about Gruinard. *And the way they look at me!* She felt so unreal . . . here in London, in these last hours of 1999, playing Monopoly with that thing singing from the sky and herself stuck here going mad with pain. *Chrissa!* she implored, *Sam! Get me out of this. Please.*

Yet even as she shook the dice (voices shouting in the street outside) she knew she was abandoned. What could Chrissa and Sam do, even if they still existed? All she had was memory of the Sam-voice croaking through poor Gussie (Only eleven nights ago?): '. . . *Wait . . . phones all ring . . . on New York's Eve . . .*' *Well*, she thought grimly, *They'd better ring soon.*

She shrieked and nearly fainted in shock as the phone began ringing . . .

And it was then that in Sussex Carol Agutter turned over in bed and stared blearily. The phone was ringing. She let it. There was nobody she wanted to talk to. She sank back into her stupor leaving it unanswered.

And then too that Jessica, utterly relieved at finding herself at last through Heathrow Customs and Immigrations, stepped into a pay-phone booth on the Terminal 1 concourse to call a number which Mo had given her. Lionel's number. But as soon as she was in the booth, fumbling with an unfamiliar mechanism, she flinched with shock. For even as she slotted her newly-purchased plastic and was about to lift the receiver, the pay-phone rang.

In her hyper-tense mood it seemed at first like some sort of insult – the Met Brits sticking their tongue out at her, or something.

She stared at it. But it went on ringing, insistently.

Then she grinned at it, as if calling its bluff.

But it still went on ringing . . . ringing . . . ringing . . .

For that was when all the phones rang, all round the world.

Whether radio, laser, or wire-based, all the phones in the world rang at the same moment, exactly at 21.47 hours GMT on 31 December 1999.

They rang from Graham Land to Point Barrow to Dunedin; they rang in Moscow, Madrid, Melbourne, Madras, Maracaibo and Mexicali; they rang in the White House; they rang in the bordello where Abe spent his evening; in the tent where the Mahdi prayed for victory over the infidel; in Mecca, Minsk, and Mali they rang in mosques, churches, police stations, gymnasiums, youth centres and private homes; they rang for company receptionists; bypassing switchboards as extensions rang too; for executives, vice-presidents and heads of state; for firemen, nurses, Samaritans and priests; for grieving mothers and lonely salesmen in motels; for the pregnant girl contemplating the overdose; for the Datsun cowboy on the range and the tiger chef in a Hong Kong bar – a billion people answered the phone when it rang; in their private or public places a billion people picked up the phone to hear what shocked them . . . well-known voices . . . very well-known voices . . .

The phones rang and were answered, or rang and rang . . . they rang for up to fifteen minutes before the world's telephone switching systems and their computers began to fail. Engineers were awestuck. For despite the great sophistication of the global system, there was no way on earth it could handle such a volume of calls. But it did. Before overloading it handled many more than the theoretical maximum number of simultaneous calls.

No way on Earth . . . as Arianrhod sailed serenely above the world, shining on the chaos below. Emergency services everywhere were crippled. There were enormous power surges. Complex data-systems guaranteeing the economic security of entire populations were scrambled. Defence systems failed: in Strategic Air Command bunkers sirens wailed and red lights flashed; but the operators received their private calls too; no Launch keys were inserted.

Later some historians compared (speciously, said critics) the terrible chaos of the event with the various burnings of the Library of Alexandria, and concluded that, in terms of data lost, what happened at 21.47 hours GMT on the last night of the twentieth century knocked all previous information losses into a cocked hat . . . even if back-up systems meant that 99% of lost material was recovered by dawn of the new millennium.

Maybe a billion people answered the phone. But five billion did not, for they had no phones to answer.

Perhaps they were lucky. It was hard to know. The subsequent chaos of power-cuts and scrambled data-banks proved traumatic, but more damaging by far was the terror caused by the messages received and the apparent source from which they were received. The calls upset belief in all traditional truths, in all the supposed laws of cause and effect, of life and death.

For most of those answering their phones heard the well-known voices of relatives and loved ones who, to their certain personal knowledge, had been consigned to earth, fire, air or sea weeks, months, or years previously.

In short, one-sixth of the world's population picked up their phones and heard the voices of those they knew to be dead.

Of course . . . it had to be . . . it *was* a trick.

Only a few knew it was no such thing.

28.
Death Rae's Call

One of the few was Jessica Bright.

Jim? she wondered, half in hope and half in horror in that booth at Heathrow as she summoned the courage to answer her call.

'Yes,' she said in a whisper.

But it wasn't Jim.

'I will have a beer, Jessica,' said the accented voice in her ear, a faint hint of humour in it. 'You sell beer in here? Yes?'

'You!' She flinched. '*Pierre . . . Belot!*'

'Yes,' said the voice, 'It is I . . . with a message from Jim.'

'Why can't he talk to me himself?' she heard herself cry.

But the last time I saw this guy he was walking with the whales!

'So I was,' said Pierre, 'And because it is not possible for him.'

He's reading my mind! Then she laughed. *So what's the big deal?*

'But he's been in my dreams!' she exclaimed. 'I keep hearing him in my head! Talking like some . . . I don't know . . . English yokel, or something.'

'He talks like that because he went through one gate,' said Pierre's voice obscurely, 'and now he is back through another . . .'

'So why can't he talk to me himself . . .?'

'. . . But he did not go through the higher gate,' the voice explained patiently. 'Like you, he remains fixed in a way that . . . we of the Company have escaped. In time and space, so to say. He cannot manifest in this manner . . . any more than we can manifest in the flesh – yet.'

'But who *are* you?' Jessica cried.

'No matter,' said Pierre's voice, 'for now. There is not much . . .'

'Of course it matters!' she insisted angrily. 'I like to know who I'm dealing with. So I'd be fried chicken if not for you, but how do I know it's not the devil's bargain? How do I know you're the good guys?'

'By doing as your son says when you meet him.' Pierre's voice grew steely. 'It took trouble to save your life, Jessica. We are not all-powerful: there is work to do if the Beast is to be flushed from his lair in time. Hear me! Jim says: Meet him on the bottom level of Aladdin's Trezure Kave at Oxford Circus. Near the Loony Lolly. In an hour.'

'Near the . . . what?' she asked feebly.

Pierre Belot's voice repeated the instructions.

'Take a cab,' it added, 'If you go now you will have the fortune of an honest driver who will not . . . what it is? . . . "rip you off". Go. Now.'

There was a click.

In shock, Jessica replaced the receiver and wandered out of the booth. She was not alone in her shock. No planes were taking off; she reached the cab-rank before realizing she'd left her bags at the booth. *No matter*, she thought vaguely, *I won't need them where I'm going.* She was halfway into London before, with a chill, she began wondering what exactly that meant.

Within a second of the phone ringing Diane shrieked; Bobbie and Ruth stopped their squabbling . . . and Lionel had the receiver in his hand.

'Yes?' he whispered, and then, sweat beading his brow, fell

silent, just stood listening with Diane staring at him from the living-room door, Justin and Grace behind her as Bobbie and Ruth came to the kitchen door.

Bobbie strained but couldn't hear a thing coming through the receiver at Lionel's ear. 'Whit is it?' he demanded into the silence.

'Sssh!' Diane raised a hand, her pain-dulled eyes expectant.

'Okay,' said Bobbie, 'Okay.' Biting his nails, he fell silent.

Lionel nodded slowly. Whatever he was hearing, he seemed not at all surprised. At last, with the receiver still in his hand, he eyed Bobbie grimly . . . then silently gave Diane the receiver. 'For you,' he said.

Diane knew who it was even as she said, dully, 'Yes?'

'Hullo, Mum.' Chrissa's voice was remote and crackly as if the connection was poor. 'It's me and Dad. We said we'd get in touch. Now listen. Your memory was always bad, so write it down, because there's not much. We've got a friend called Jim. You almost met him in the pub a week ago. He wants you to go with Bobbie and Lionel – you'll need them – and meet him on the bottom level of Aladdin's Trezure Kave at . . .'

Diane's head pounded worse than ever. 'Aladdin's *what?*'

'Trezure Kave, Mum. Write it down. At Oxford Circus. By the Loony Lolly. Got it? Good. Get there fast. I can't say more – it'll be plain to you soon. Now we have to talk to Bobbie.'

'But, Chrissa . . . this headache . . . I can't . . .'

'Just bear it, Mum. It's not for nothing. Now get Bobbie.'

So Diane learned nothing about the CSU bug, nor that soon they'd meet the lost soul who'd tried to kill Sam in his Fool's grove four thousand years ago, and Chrissa at Carcassonne six hundred and sixty years ago. There were enough complications. Arianrhod's power wasn't unlimited. It was a tight operation, as Sergei Bilibin already knew.

'Bobbie?' Diane whispered, calling Bobbie Aird to the phone.

'What is it?' Ruth begged, Justin white-faced behind her, Grace in tears in the kitchen where Lionel sat staring out at the ruddy, riotous, millennial night. But Diane could only shake her head, remotely wondering through her pain if that had really been Chrissa.

Or something just . . . pretending to be Chrissa?

Bobbie eyed her thoughtfully as he took the receiver.

'Aye,' he growled, 'So who the hell is it?' Then –

'Bobbie, ye daft fool!' the voice of his brother Ronnie bellowed in his ear, and for his ear alone, 'It's me. Ronnie! Yer brither!'

Bobbie jerked as if electrocuted. 'Aw, no!' he roared, as Ruth behind him gasped, 'Ah'll no be gabbin' wi' the deid!'

'Aw, haud yer tongue!' Ronnie bellowed back, 'Ah hae a message frae the Big Yin! Bobbie, ye fooked up. I ken ye meant well, but ah nivver meant ye tae blaw up the whole boat! Ye cannae get awa' wi' shite like that. The reckoning awaits ye, Bobbie – an' afore the nicht's done. So get those toff's breeks aff and find that teuchter gear ye fecht in, an' get that ponce Lionel tae fit ye up wi' a good shairp sword wha winnae wince when it bites intae a neck or jaw – because ye'll be needin' it soon, Bobbie boy! At the Temple. And a' the deid Knichts o' the Temple'll be watching' ye – an' if they like the way ye fecht then soon ye'll join them a' in Valhalla. So mind ye dae it richt this time! It's that Beast ye want – an ye'll ken him fine when ye meet him! Now get aff yer arse an' get movin'!'

There was a click. The phone had gone dead.

Bobbie whistled, shook his head, and replaced the phone with a slam.

'Some folks have nae gratitude,' he complained.

But Diane saw the grief-stricken wilderness in his dark eyes and feared the worst. So did Lionel, coming out of the kitchen as Diane asked, in a whisper that only he heard, 'What's Aladdin's Trezure Kave?'

Lionel nodded slowly. 'I know it,' he told her, eyeing Bobbie. 'And about the ferry,' he told him, indicating Diane. 'She knows too?'

'Get lost!' Bobbie glared at him. 'I'll pay in full the nicht. At the Temple, whitever that is. Onyway, ye telt me not tae say a wurd.'

'What is this?' Ruth demanded shakily, and on realizing she was being ignored her voice rose to a shriek. 'Why won't anyone talk to me?'

'You're lucky they won't,' Diane said, realizing through her headache: *Lionel knows about Gruinard! What else? About Jim Bright? Jessica?*

'Yes,' she told him faintly. Her skull felt as if crabs were eating it from inside. 'I know about it.' *But what's Bobbie on about?* she wondered.

'We'd best get you kitted out in your gear,' Lionel told Bobbie.

Bobbie stared at him with pained, hostile, dangerous eyes.

'Wis it Ronnie that telt ye aboot Gruinard? Ma brither?'

Shrugging, Lionel started upstairs after another look at Diane. She was clearly on her last legs. *She knows it too,* he told himself wearily. *But the Old Man was right last night. We haven't been busted. So the game's changed, like he said. But who's the third contact?*

'Come on up,' he told Bobbie. 'I've got stuff you can use.'

'Ah'll need a twa-hander,' Bobbie rumbled grimly, 'Dinnae want a Dinky Toy. Ah'll need weight tae swing . . . when we meet the Beast in the Temple.'

'The Beast?' Diane asked anxiously, following them. 'The Temple?'

'*Shut up!*' Lionel hissed at Bobbie. 'Or we'll never get there – and you'll never die proud. Isn't that what you want?'

Bobbie shrugged angrily at Diane. 'Ye'll mind soon enough.'

'And . . . what's Aladdin's Trezure Kave?' she persisted at Lionel.

I shouldn't ask, she knew amid her pain, *But how can I not?*

'In a minute,' he muttered back, pointing up, 'In a minute.' And Ruth stared helplessly as they vanished upstairs to the armoury.

In Carmody Cee's flat the thin-lipped man who worked for Hector Rae also took a call . . . but not on Carmody's phone. He said not a word, but by the end of the call his lips were thinner still. He nodded to himself in the darkness of Carmody's kitchen. Flickering on a torch, he sat at a table with notepad and pencil, and in large, shaky capital letters wrote: *Sorry, Mate. I got it wrong. Won't bother you again. Watch Rae.*

Sighing, he unholstered his silenced Walther, unclipped his radiophone, and laid both precisely across the sheet of paper. Leaving them there, he climbed out onto the fire escape and vanished into the night.

But from Carmody's point of view the most important call was the one Hector Rae received behind the locked door of La Bruce's bathroom.

Rae had sought that privacy as soon as H.G. Wells alias Carmody Cee left, not to answer nature's call, but to make three of his own.

One to the security gate.

One to the sergeant on the street.

And one to the assassin in Carmody's flat.

Not to the chestnut seller. He didn't know about him.

He locked the door, nose wrinkling at the alarming female smells of powder and potion. But his hard eyes were triumphant through Wellington's mask. He had not only Agutter but that media perve where he wanted them.

Yet even as he slid out his phone from under the shining buttons and Peninsular Campaign medals of Wellington's scarlet tunic, it rang.

'Damn!' he said. Only Harry Fisher (at Number 10 instead of Chequers because of the crisis) had tonight's number. Angrily he thumbed *Receive.*

'Prime Minister!' he barked. 'I thought I made it clear that . . .'

'Hector!' a well-known, hated voice chided him. It was gentle but very insistent, and the scent of attar of roses came with it.

Under the mask his face turned purple. He tried to speak.

'Who – is – this?' he croaked, La Bruce's bathroom spinning.

'Hector!' said his mother sternly, 'You're a bad boy!'

He couldn't take it in. He made incoherent choking sounds. All his life she'd tyrannized him with the whip, spur and reins of moral virtue. So he saw it. Only her death ten years ago had freed him so that at last he'd begun to fulfil himself, rising to his present eminence, known and feared throughout the Met as 'Death' Rae. And that foul scent she'd always used! 'No!' he cried, gagging on it, glaring at the phone, outraged by his own fear. *A Chancer trick?* 'We can't have this! Stop it at once!'

'Remember those dreams you had as a child, Hector?' her voice went on inexorably. 'The nightmares? Wild women tearing you to pieces? A mad friar burning people in France until he chased that girl and lost his . . .'

'*Go away, Mother:*' he cried, now mortally afraid, holding the phone at arm's-length. But it was too late. Those dreams! Only dreams? He hadn't thought so forty years ago – and now as he swayed in La Bruce's bathroom the blood-roar returned to cloud his vision, the cloying scent of roses made him gag . . . and even as he tried to thumb *End Call* the phone seemed to writhe and turn into a snake as, gasping for breath, forgetting himself, he plunged through forgotten centuries, plunged through memory back to . . .

. . . back to that grove in the ancient time where She keeps Her Fool whom Her people must not touch nor harm . . . that naked Fool riding his Ailma, his love; Ailma who's broken taboo to spite him, who lies with the Fool. The Fool called Samjoyce. 'Father, give me strength to aim true!' he howls in his rage, spear raised high as he charges, meaning to kill both with one strike . . . but his spear turns into a serpent that writhes and bites him, and then the Wild Women seize him and begin tearing him until he's a flayed, bloody, dying mess . . . and then SHE comes, the Watcher Tiy Herself, a great red bird of prey looming over him in triumphant contempt as . . . as he dies, as . . . as he plunges through the abyss to a new incarnation, the new birth of his unappeased hate in the time of women-fearing men who worship the God of Love, the Christ . . . for now he's Brother Jean, the black friar, writhing in his cell in Carcassonne in the year 1240, infested by worms, consumed by the guilt of dreams that he can never quite face nor dismiss; his dreams of Hoel's death . . . and Ailma too is reborn, reborn as Joana the heretic maid, the hope of the Cathars whom he's sworn to exterminate – and he has her almost at the stake, but – SHE ESCAPES HIM AGAIN! Madness takes him; he escapes Carcassone; for four long years he tracks her, vowing revenge – until at length he comes to the dragon's head of heresy, the chateau of Montségur where the heretics make their last stand, where for months he lurks about the camp of the

besieging army, until at last the chateau is taken and . . . BUT AGAIN SHE ESCAPES HIM! Yet he pursues her and the shepherd Pierre Belot who got her out of Carcassonne, he follows them deep into the caves at Tarascon; with blood roaring he crawls after them through the maze to Her Gate – to Tiy's Gate – and too late, TOO LATE he realizes just how he's been fooled again as through the teeth of Her Gate he stares into the blinding radiance of the inner chamber . . . and sees her! Joana-Chrissa!

'*You're here just in time,*' she cries, *twisting the lever that closes Her teeth even as, throwing himself at her, he screams: 'You killed me once! Now . . .' But too late. Far too late. Even as he leaps through the Gate at Joana-Chrissa-Ailma, Her teeth clash together on his neck, and . . .*

Then Hector Rae found himself crying on the floor of La Bruce's bathroom with the phone still at his ear and his mother lecturing him:

'Hector! Wake up now or you'll lose your head again – and this time will be the last! Now listen to me, you cretin . . .!'

It was ten minutes before he got her off the line. By then fists (accompanied by hysterical cries) were hammering at the door.

'Who's in there! I need to go to the loo! For God's sake!'

But Commissioner Rae, numbly staring at Wellington's face in La Bruce's mirror (gilt frame shaped like the shell in Botticelli's painting of Venus) heard only that plaintive voice which had tortured his childhood dreams.

'*Hoel! Poor Hoel! Nobody ever listens to poor Hoel.*'

Carmody's phone buzzed as the lift door opened and he stepped shakily onto the shining red-and-black zigzag tiles of the bare, bright-lit ground-floor foyer, facing a metal-grilled cubicle by the locked security gate.

The door to the outside world lay beyond the gate.

The phone in the cubicle was ringing too: behind the grille a jowly middle-aged guard eyed the man in the H.G. Wells mask, shrugged . . . and answered the phone even as Carmody uneasily unclipped his own insistent buzzer from his belt. Two phones ringing at once? He thumbed *Receive.*

'Yes,' he said with a premonition of . . .

'Kenneth,' said a precise, silvery, reed-thin voice in his ear, 'Take off your mask and walk through the gate.'

'What . . . who are you?' Carmody whispered, sure he was dreaming.

'He whose warning words rest in your pocket,' the voice said, 'What must be said must also be heard, by all. Remove your mask. Walk through.'

But, Carmody thought, unable to speak, *The gate's locked.*

'Not for those who dare it,' the voice assured, 'See the gatekeeper!'

Carmody looked . . . and saw the man behind the grille swaying on his feet, phone clamped to his ear, open mouth working slackly, wet eyes unfocused as he crossed his uniformed chest repeatedly. And the voice said: 'Now! Off with that mask. You cannot pass with a false face.'

Phone at his ear, Carmody dreamily peeled off his mask. Barefaced he approached the man who guarded the locked gate. The man was weeping, and at the sight of Carmody grew even more terrified. He stared at Carmody as if at a ghost. 'Uh . . . Uncle . . . Jack!' he stammered inexplicably.

'Say, "Bless you, me boy, if you let me through,"' said the voice.

'Bless you, my boy, if you let me through,' Carmody managed.

The guard turned whiter. Shuddering, he crossed himself again.

'Aunt Peg in my ear, yourself on my eye,' he croaked, 'and both . . .'

'Say, "It's a fine woman she was, and a finer one now!"'

Carmody bit his lip but managed to get this line out too.

'God bless her!' the guard said in a daze as, crossing himself again, he stabbed at a button, missing it twice before managing to open the gate. 'And God bless you too, Uncle Jack,' he said, tears rolling down his leathery cheeks as Carmody, shaky on his feet, dreamed that with phone to his ear he passed safely through. 'Bless yourself too, me boy,' he heard himself say as he gained the door to the outside world.

And found himself out in the night on gaslit steps above the cobbled street. Overhead wild shreds of cloud still flared with fire. Below him, cabbies stood silently round their mates who were taking calls. A number of Rae's bully-boys were similarly occupied. The only human sound came from over the road where a shabby man at a hot chestnut barrow wailed in private rage, phone at his ear. Nobody paid him any mind. Other than that, not only the street but the city beyond was oddly quiet, at least to the ear. No traffic roar. Only the wind. But there was another, weirder note. For, as Carmody stood there, from the night beyond this enclave he sensed something waking up; something strange, deep, and very dissatisfied. As if some raw unknown aspect of human mind had begun to stir but as yet knew not how to express itself. The sense of it was so strong and primal that his lips drew back from his teeth, so that as he faced the hansom ranks he seemed to smile . . . for it was a note that stirred the blood . . .

At that moment his producer at Channel 3 was taking a call apparently from Carmody himself. 'Listen!' said a voice that sounded like Carmody's, 'I'm at Aladdin's Trezure Kave at Oxford Circus. Know it? Right! Get a crew here in thirty minutes – to the Loony Lolly. It's a scoop!'

Carmody knew none of it. He stood on the steps in a dream.

'Walk to Marble Arch,' the voice in his ear advised him quietly, 'then stay in a hotel for the night. Do not go home. Wait for morning.'

Carmody flinched. He'd forgotten the phone still at his ear.

'But,' he asked plaintively, 'Who *are* you?'

'Your father, my son,' said the voice – and the tone of it stressed the new note Carmody sensed; the new note that made him grin like a jackal. He felt ancient engines in him stir to life. He shook. He began to remember.

'Hi, Dad!' he whispered as a long-forgotten light shone . . . *and for an instant under the desert sun he sees the thousands of men toiling, heaving on the ropes of the sleds on which great dressed blocks of stone are rolled to* . . . then it was gone, and that calm old voice spoke again. 'Broadcast it tomorrow, my son. Fight the Beast. Let the people hear my words.'

There was a click. And he knew Khufu was gone.

'I can't build as well as you,' he said soberly, 'But I'll try.'

Nobody tried to stop him as he started walking towards Marble Arch.

Minutes later Hector Rae, at last pulling himself together, left the bathroom to find La Bruce's party in chaos and the lift jammed, Agutter among those who'd fled already. *Hoel!* wailed the voice in him. *Poor Hoel!*

'Mr Smart-Arse Agutter!' he growled, Wellington mask impassive, 'So the perve got away. But you won't!' And nearly he spoke the truth.

For outside, the chestnut seller was waiting.

29.
Hot Chestnuts

'*Hot* chestnuts! *Hot* chestnuts! Get yer luvly *hot* chestnuts!'

This monotonous cry was the first thing Agutter heard from the street as amid a batch of La Bruce's terrified guests he stumbled out of the lift, past the security gate and through the front door, both of which the guard had left wide open as he fled in Carmody's wake.

'*Hot* chestnuts! *Hot* chestnuts! Get yer *hot roasted chestnuts here*!'

The panic in the salon had spread as if by chain reaction of instinct fear and bewilderment as La Bruce's guests joined Agutter in obeying her command to answer their calls, their fear already palpable, masked faces of the phoneless fixed on the masked faces of those who were called. Even as La Bruce wept and Agutter gaped at Gillian's voice, Florence Nightingale alias Marie Hudson had loosed a shriek of terror, for the voice she heard was that of her late husband Dieter, blown up by some freedom faction or another while imprudently including Belfast on a concert tour in 1993.

'Oh God, no!' she shrieked, dropping her phone and tearing off her mask as the lighting flickered, once, twice. It steadied again, but that was enough to trigger pandemonium and a rush for the door so sudden and violent that Agutter nearly didn't get out. For as it began he, like others, was lost in rapturous horror, so overwhelmed by his daughter's voice on the line that it was as if a veil of idiocy had fallen on him.

'Listen again, Dad,' she was pleading, and he knew she was telling him to meet some people at some place, somewhere, something to do with Oxford Circus. And there was something else, about an immediate danger.

Oxford Circus? he asked, childlike in his confusion, vaguely aware that people were screaming; that he was being pushed and shoved, *But wasn't it Billy Smart's we went to? Or Bertram Mills'? When the Big Top was . . .*

'Dad!' the ghost-voice implored, 'Dad, get going! Now!'

'Get going,' he muttered dully as his line went dead, not knowing what this meant as he found himself stupidly caught in a tidal wave of shrieking humanity that soon got itself stupidly jammed in the exit from the salon, clawing and punching its way to the lift. He stubbed his foot on a fallen body; it was the balding Jeeves, knocked down, bloody-mouthed and now feebly trying to rise. Cursing the obstruction without looking down he met the terrified, unthinking eyes of Lord Palmerston alias Chancellor Peter Wood.

'You brought it on us, you bastard!' Wood screamed, and punched Lord Beaconsfield alias the Home Secretary hard on the nose.

'Hey!' Agutter shouted angrily, about to strike back.

Then in the bulging eyes of the man who'd hit him he saw his own near-madness reflected. He flinched. His whole nervous system jolted as the veil of idiocy tore . . . and then he remembered. *Carmody. The tape.*

And what Gillian had told him that he couldn't quite remember.

Suddenly urgent, he tore off his mask and fought his way forward.

He never knew how he got into the lift as the sixteenth and last member of the fourth downward overload since the panic had begun. *Warning!* read the sign in the lift that nobody heeded. *Maximum load 6 persons.* Nor did he know his luck, for after disgorging these sixteen the lift gave up the ghost and refused to rise again. Many guests were stranded in La Bruce's salon. Hector Rae was one. Security had decreed no stairs in these modern Victorian properties, and the fire escape system (an extending ladder each section of which unrolled from balcony above to balcony below) was not for humans to control but automatically released by the in-site smoke-detection system alone. Lift break-down didn't trigger the fire-escape, being a Jap model deemed never to break down, unless abused by uncouth people unable to read warning signs. In emergency it was the job of the *concierge* (required by Met law to be a Domestic Electronics Ph.D.) to fix it; the *concierge* was also the only human in the building who could override the smoke-detection system and release the fire escape manually. And usually the middle-aged *concierge* in La Bruce's building was reliable. But years ago he'd marched with the Militant Tendency; he'd never quite reconciled himself to what he did now, and the stinging call he'd just received from a bloke he'd thought murdered years ago by the CIA in Greece had him so fired up that when the lift malfunction light started flashing him, he gave it two fingers, poured himself a beer, and ignored it. A minute later the in-house phone rang: it was that bloody Bruce woman, ponced up as bloody Queen Victoria. He gave her two fingers too, right there onscreen. 'Stuff it, aristo,' he growled. 'Wait till the revolution comes.' Then he remembered his phone-call and he laughed in her face. 'But it *has* come!' he cried triumphantly, cutting her off and settling back in his chair, smacking his lips, happy at last.

So Hector Rae was stranded, and could only watch from a window in frustration, fear, fury and hope when Agutter met the chestnut seller.

'*Hot* chestnuts! *Hot* chestnuts!' Get yer luvly *hot* . . .'

In a rush sixteen scared, bruised individuals burst from the lift and out into the night. Agutter among them, to face a lurid rioters' sky and utter gas-lit confusion among the hansom cabs at the kerb. Guests already out on the street, deranged by too many years of play-acting and now dazed by their calls, had no idea which cab or driver was theirs; in their panic they were fighting each other and the drivers and peelers; nervous horses whinnied and pranced; the odour of equine excrement hit Agutter's nostrils as he burst out into the cold air, and so too did . . .

'. . . roasted chestnuts here! *Hot* chestnuts . . .'

The voice's blank, mechanical quality stopped him. *What's that?* he asked, pinned to the spot, the hairs on his neck bristling, feeling not only a terrible familiarity but an irresistible morbid curiosity. He had to know. Still wondering what it was Gillian had told him he used elbow and knee to push clear of the mob. A frightened horse tried to bite him as he ducked past it too close. He didn't recognize his own cab, nor hear the blanketed Sergeant Grant on the high seat who, staring down, called out:

'Mr Agutter! Watch out! Mr Ag . . .!'

'. . . *here! Get* your *hot* roasted chestnuts here . . .'

Then he was facing the chestnut seller.

'. . . Get yer luvly *hot* ches . . .'

The chestnut seller saw him . . . and fell silent, staring back.

Agutter saw a creature in shadow and rags, its jaws and brows and spiky white hair underlit by the burning coals of the brazier in its barrow.

A hunched and bent old creature; surely an old, old man.

But those eyes! Agutter instinctively drew back. He knew that zombie gaze. It filled him with pity and disgust – and fear. Another Pseudodeath victim. Brain sludged by too many Reely-Show battlefield shocks for snuff-show ghouls. *Pseudodeath times three means prosperity.* A year ago he'd tried to ban Pseudodeath Reelies, backed by growing public concern about ever-more Pseudodead dragging their wealthy, witless feet through London. And by concern about 'Pseudodeath Paradise'. For some pseudo-dead had begun muttering about a strange lotus-land of immortality they visited while 'dead'. Oddly, their tales matched accounts by people surviving clinical death on the operating table. So who knew? But their mumblings of meeting 'a loving being of light' were encouraging too many down-and-outs and fools to sign up for or identify with what the hype sold as 'the final frontier'.

'A terrible sickness!' he'd called it during the Commons debate. So it was. But the vote had been lost on a three-line Government whip.

'Know how you feel,' Harry Fisher had privately commiserated later, 'Feel the same myself. It's a rotten business . . . but we need the cash.'

'*Hot* chestnuts, sir?' the seller chanted softly, '*Just* 3.45 a bag.'

And suddenly, staring into those empty wet eyes, Agutter felt as frozen and helpless as a hypnotized rabbit. He felt the known world vanish from under his feet as everything turned to slow motion. *I – know – something – about – this*, he told himself with huge difficulty as the hot chestnut salesman, apparently trying to smile, palmed something – a pill? – into his wizened mouth. *That – dream – last night. It – was –*

Then the smile split into something else even as the cry from Ted Grant behind him distracted him and turned him round . . . just as the attack came.

Colin Cooper was his name, Loving Death was his game, and he did not think himself sick, though he was twenty-five and looked eighty. Colin was a pro. He'd been in the illegal SAS cavalry charge at Bannockburn in '95 that caused Bobbie Aird and the Knights of the Purple Heather such huge damage. So now those glory days were gone . . . but unlike most who'd signed up for the quick Pseudodeath road to guaranteed tax-free Met income-for-life, he'd endured the regulation three Pseudodeaths with his wits mostly intact. Broken in health and emotion maybe, but unready to retire to Bognor's sea-front deckchairs, full of Pseudodead pensioners aged thirty or less. For during his last Pseudodeath (as Banquo in a jazz *Macbeth*) he'd entered the Realm of the Loving One . . . and the Loving One had given him a mission.

Colin! The Light had blinded him. *You are a Loving Death-Bringer! Return to the half-world and feed Me, and you shall rest here forever!*

Colin Cooper, ran his business card, *Creative expediting.*

'Creative expediting' meant 'assassination undertaken'.

So he'd found his road in life, and luckily the Met encouraged any activity that could afford a good legal programme. Which his could. He'd done well. No longer had to tout. Punters came to him. Like last night, in his sparse Bermondsey flat (no carpets, chairs, not even a bed) he'd taken a call from a male voice so flat it could have been a Pseudodead, or maybe a man hypnotized. Directed to a public phone in the corner Tandoori House, he'd rung a complex number answered by the same voice. Identifying itself by name (surprising: few clients did that unless making frames) the voice required the Home Secretary to take a trip. Also surprising. But he was never moved by surprise. More important, the request came with a large advance instantly okayed not only by his bank circuit but by Law-Prog too.

Having recorded instructions, time and place, he'd asked: 'Are pain and terror required, sir? That of course is extra.'

In his dragging voice the client had laughed.

'Just get him. The pain and terror come later.'

Colin knew exactly what he meant.

'If you don't get him,' the voice had continued, 'steps will be . . .'

'Your threat is unnecessary,' he'd said, 'I do this for the Loving One. I am not influenced by fear of death or suffering.'

'That is why I called you,' the voice (maybe drunk?) assured him, 'Like vultures we need Untouchables. Have a Lamb Of God Vindaloo on me, mate.'

But he fed on other meat. He went back to the empty room and pretended to sleep. In the morning he set it up, ensuring that the security would turn a blind eye. Only when Agutter came in his Disraeli gear and went up to the party did he wheel out his barrow and start his cry.

'*Hot* chestnuts! *Hot* chestnuts! Get yer luvly . . .'

Among those who came to buy (he was well briefed) was Agutter's MI6 minder. 'Licensed, are you?' Ted Grant had demanded, cop eyes boring.

'9.95 for the Family Pack, 3.45 to you!' he chanted.

'I'll take some for the guv'nor,' Sergeant Grant muttered, dropping his eyes as he slotted plastic for 9.95. Colin felt his usual cold triumph. The living always dropped their eyes before the likes of him. 'Chestnuts! *Hot* chestnuts!' he cried, showing the fool his permit as he turned away. And of course the living man had bought it. They always did. They were all scared. Yet to be a Loving Death-Bringer was hard. Always the ghost of feelings to fight. For Colin cared. Hits were holy only if his marks saw their fate in his eyes as he struck. That brief contact of love and terror before termination guaranteed the loving-kindness of the act.

Without that . . . the money's nothing.

So he was telling himself as his phone rang on the business circuit.

'Colin Cooper, Creative Expediting Undertaken,' he said routinely.

And heard the Loving One, radiant, vital, ever-effervescent!

'Oh My Son and Lovely One! Glad am I to know that soon you'll be with Me forever! Your time in the half-world's up! Soon there will be no more insults! But before you win your reward, first see what you may gain!'

It was then he lost control. For like a Hashishin assassin he tasted the delights of the Old Man's paradise garden . . . he swooned with delight as senses long dead were awakened on the lawns and by the streams of sweetness where the skilled women and flowing cup attended to all his needs . . . then from it he was suddenly kicked, dragged by brute hands, torn screaming back to this half-world, and he was in a terrible rage, caught in a storm of emotion such as he'd never known since his first Pseudodeath, since the first time that brainstem bug had fired him into the screaming Pseudodeath overload. For long minutes, even as Carmody Cee came and went, he stood there howling . . . ignored by the cabbies, by the peelers, and by all but Ted Grant amid the common dream and separation that fell on everyone on the street during the lonely strange time when all the phones rang.

He forgot that now. He stared at the man he was about to

expedite so lovingly. He tried to remember how to smile (for frozen in him was great gratitude) as he palmed the Nervo, ready in his hand, to his blue lips.

'You want *hot* chestnuts, sir?' he asked softly . . . as his victim, hearing a voice crying from a cab, turned away . . . as the Nervo hit, and he attacked.

'Watch out! Mr Agut . . .'

Ted Grant's warning almost killed Agutter.

Steady, perched up on the hansom, reminded of his duty by the call he'd just had from his old headmaster, Sergeant Grant had been keeping one sharp eye (and something more effective) trained on the chestnut seller, and his other on the door as La Bruce's guests flooded out. But he wasn't feeling one hundred per cent himself, not after meeting the creep's eyes, especially not after the call from his dead headmaster, and though when his boss came out he'd tried to warn him, Agutter was as loony as the rest, jumping past him like a man possessed, somehow drawn straight to the creep, and in Ted's line of fire too. To spend seconds staring at the creep. Then by gaslight he saw the creep palm something, and shouted, and knew instantly that he'd screwed up. For even as Agutter turned, the killer moved so fast from behind his barrow that Grant instantly lost him from his sights.

Slim blade gleaming, the Creative Expediter accelerated and stabbed at Agutter's back all in one. A Nervo blur. No wonder he looked so old.

But just as suddenly Agutter's back wasn't there.

What saved him was a natural product of neo-Victorian panic-fantasy, for as he turned he stepped into a freshly-deposited load of what was not often found on London streets these days; with an angry cry he skidded and cartwheeled on the horse-shit even as the Loving Death-Bringer stabbed.

Colin Cooper, Creative Expediter, came as near to real surprise in that moment as it was possible for him to feel. Every other time he'd popped a 15-second Nervo he had successfully hit, killed, and been well away before the acceleration faded into the week-long agony of cellular reaction.

Nervo set all synapses firing, sent you flashing through a grey-black world where even a racing car seemed to move like a snail. It was hard to miss on Nervo. Targets loomed as big and slow as houses. But he did miss; though not completely, for as Agutter skidded off his feet the knife ripped through cape, frockcoat, shirt and singlet, slashing his right shoulder.

Agutter crashed to the cobbles with no idea what was happening. Grant fired a sleeper that missed. The assassin, off-balance and carried on by his unchecked momentum, almost falling over himself, crashed into the horse harnessed to Agutter's hansom, and began witlessly, mindlessly, to stab.

The horse screamed in terror; La Bruce's squabbling guests falling back as it reared and began to kick, sending Grant tumbling from his seat – and Colin Cooper, losing the support of the heaving flank he stabbed, slipped and fell under front hooves that lost no time in trampling his skull.

Then, dragging the hansom behind, the horse bolted. A wheel lurched over the killer's prone body. The clattering, whinnying, and screams told people who hadn't noticed that there was real drama. Fights forgotten, an interested audience gathered as the empty, out-of-control hansom clattered away down the street and the mortally-wounded man writhed on the cobbles.

'Get back, get back!' cried a peeler automatically as Sergeant Grant ran first to Agutter, who was kneeling with hands and knees in shit.

'You all right, sir?'

Agutter felt incredibly ponderous and slow. His shoulder was just beginning to hurt. He felt the slash, the blood seeping through.

'What the hell was that?' he asked wonderingly.

But the siren voice in him said: *You know very well.*

'Don't know, sir. Let's see if we can get it out of him.'

'Right!' Agutter muttered, kneeling clumsily forward to his feet.

Within the peeler-cordoned circle of onlookers the Death-

Bringer was still alive – just. His back was broken. From the crushed right lobe of his skull a ropy mess of blood and grey matter spilled onto the cobbles. His face (a jumping, bug-eyed grin) and body twitched not only from the massive trauma of his injuries but from the acute pain of Nervo deceleration. But this time, he knew, it didn't matter.

This time the dying was real. Even as his fade began he'd awoken; so that now Agutter, looming dazed over him, was further taken aback by the intense humour blazing from eyes which seconds earlier had seemed dead.

'Who sent you?' Agutter demanded in a hiss. 'Who wants me dead?'

The dying man giggled. Filmy bubbles of blood foamed from his mouth and nose. The intensity began to fade from his eyes.

Agutter seized and shook him, his slashed shoulder throbbing. 'Who sent you? Tell me! I must know!'

A terrible smile briefly lit the ruined face.

'Put . . . ear . . . to . . . mouth . . .' the bloody lips demanded.

Agutter mastered his fear and his throbbing shoulder to do as he was told . . . and felt the blood-film of each word burst softly against his ear –

'You . . . did . . . Mr . . . Agutter . . .'

'What?' Starting back, Agutter stared in utter – not disbelief, but horror. *That dream I had last night. No! I couldn't have!* 'When?' he demanded, ignoring Grant and the crowd as he put ear to mouth again.

'Last . . . night . . . you . . . rang . . . I . . . rang . . . back.' The soft words burst, felt, not heard. 'You . . . hired . . . me . . . to . . . kill . . . yourself . . .'

'What number did you ring?' Agutter whispered.

The blood-bubbles broke on the first four digits of a code; faded into a rattle, then a sigh, and then – nothing.

The Loving Death-Bringer was dead. But it was enough.

'Last night's number,' Agutter muttered, unsteady on his knees above the dead man he'd hired to . . . 'I'm the only one who knew it.'

Yes, he realized, flummoxed and terrified, *It must have been that dream last night. I called him. Why would he lie? But why would I?*

The enemy within. Too much. Feeling sanity slipping away, he began to laugh as he looked up at Grant, at all the uncomprehending faces. 'We have wonderful security here in the Met!' he cried, 'We don't even know our own secrets! And what just saved me from mine? Huh-huh-*horse*-shit!'

With the siren-song mocking him he scrambled to his feet, laughing at it all – at the dead man, at Ted Grant, at the fake cabs and fake people – at Arianrhod and his own futile plot. *What's left? Where did Gillian tell me to go?* And still laughing he pushed through the amazed crowd, Ted Grant hurrying behind. Lifting his head, he saw Wellington alias Rae glare down from a high window against the ruddy sky. 'Too bad!' he shouted, 'Couldn't manage it myself. Too much horse-shit. Why don't you have a go?'

'Mr Agutter!' Sergeant Grant insisted. 'Sir, just slow down!'

But Agutter ignored him and kept walking east towards Oxford Circus, a whirl of insane circus images competing with the pain of his wound and his lost daughter for his attention, so that when his phone buzzed he was slow to answer. For he no longer cared. This turned out to be a mistake.

30.
Oxford Circus

For at CSU Console 77 Joe O'Brien was, despite the chaos of the last fifteen minutes, still on the job. Claudine had called him with another goodbye-cruel-world-if-you're-not-here-FAST number, but he wasn't buying that again. Yet even as he'd cut her off he'd realized that about him the entire op room had fallen into utter confusion; operators abandoning their consoles and wandering about muttering or crying or laughing; and from the street below the screech of traffic piling up. Turning grimly to his work again he realized that all over the city his contacts had suddenly shot up into the red. Chancer mental break-out all over the place. 'Jeeze, you poor bastards!' he cried, trying to damp down the amygdaloid level in half-a-dozen implantees at once, almost feeling their violent headaches himself, 'Slow down!' And then, CSU in turmoil, all lines jammed and no clear sense of what was going on, he saw that several contacts were now in real-space motion. Worms wriggling, going places. Particularly 76-E-678-DEJ.

Diane Emily Joyce. Code Blue Five-Oh-One-Alpha-Zero-Five. Agutter's so-called secret Ghost Project. *Idiot!* Joe thought scornfully, eyes fixed on his monitors, *Him and his crew of old lefty liberals pull it off? Sure, personal interest, his daughter . . . I see it, I guess*

. . . but why a stupid plot that leaks like a sieve? Or is it martyrdom he wants?

For last night during Carmody's broadcast 76-E-678-DEJ had gone right off the top in response to high-level Chancer neurogenics at *very* close range. Joe had instantly called Chief Super Macdonald, a channel meant to lead to the Home Secretary and nobody else: in fact other ears heard it all down the line, which surely Agutter knew even as he squashed the raid.

'No,' he'd insisted. 'Wait 24 hours and we'll net more.'

Which was rubbish. Chancers knew what sudden headaches might mean, and right at that moment Diane Emily Joyce must have been wailing for Anadin.

But Agutter wouldn't listen. He'd stood the assembled snatch squad down. Death Rae was said to be very pissed off. Afterwards Joe had spoken with the Super who, with a heavy nod and wink of the Say-No-More variety, let him know that the Home Secretary's hours were numbered.

Yet 76-E-678-DEJ hadn't been dumped. She was still alive . . . and still in Chancer contact. And now she was moving, her amygdaloid net screaming at an intensity higher even than last night. Joe knew grimly that the time had come. What as he saw as the deadly chaos the Chancers represented was now strong enough to invade even this secure bastion of law and order. The evidence was all about. His partners in punishing mind-crime milling about like bleating sheep. Hardly any of the consoles were occupied. Even Super Macdonald, on a visit when the phones rang, was standing in a daze.

'Super,' Joe cried, 'Big action here. Code Blue Plus again.'

That meant: confidential to the Home Secretary.

Chief Super Macdonald, now fifty-three, was a Mancunian. He'd been ten when the Manchester United team crashed at Munich Airport; a tragedy convincing him forever that life is a bastard. Now he was shaking and undone. He'd just had a call from his boyhood hero who died in that crash; the electrifying Scot Duncan Edwards who, had he lived, might have been as great as Pelé.

'You're on the wrong side, Mac,' Duncan had told him, among other home truths, so that now he was sleepwalking round the CSU op room, unable to recognize it or anyone in it. He didn't even hear Joe.

'For fuck's sake,' Joe muttered, and tried the call himself. He wasn't meant to have Agutter's code for today, but he did. You didn't get to the top in the Met without knowing things you shouldn't.

The direct call produced only a whine. He tried the switchboard.

'Anyone there?' he barked after five seconds of no reply.

'All lines . . . still closed,' said a faltering voice.

'So try this one for me.' And Joe gave Agutter's code.

Ten seconds later it rang. And rang and rang.

At last Agutter answered. But he sounded odd. Remote, somehow.

'76-E-678-DEJ, sir!' Joe barked, 'Diane Emily Joyce! On the move! From N4 south-west! I'm tracking her! We've waited twenty-four hours, so now . . .'

But Agutter just laughed and in a spooky, breathless voice said: 'Call me when she stops somewhere. I'll decide then.' And added strangely:

'You've got my number, eh? Didn't have it last night, did you?'

'Nossir. This is an emergency. The Super's . . .'

But the line went dead. Joe cursed.

'Okay,' he muttered, 'You don't want to know. So who does? I don't mean to be unconstitutional, but I need a chain of command.

But he waited before calling another number he happened to know. He waited half-an-hour, until Agutter had twice more rejected him. By then he knew 76-E-678-DEJ's location exactly. Sighing, he called the other number.

'Yes,' growled Hector Rae, still stranded at La Bruce's.

Darkness, darkness. She knew Bobbie was ready to kill, ready to die – ready to run amok. It came off him in waves. No love in the human maze. The echo of their feet on the slick broken pavement. Diane, lost in trance of pain and unreality as they soft-footed along deserted Stroud Green Road, followed Lionel's quick shuffle. He wore a black anorak and balaclava and sneakers. Then the quick, precise, nervous tic-tac-toc of her own steps. And the limping fast-slow swagger of Bobbie behind her. He limped because of the sword strapped to his side under his cape. Lionel hadn't let him leave the house without the cape. *He's ready to die*, she knew, then weary with pain reminded herself: *But so he was the night we met. It's all he can do now. To do it well. But what does it mean to him? Or to me?*

She no longer knew. Pain had killed her perspective.

Yet under the cape the gear he wore was so bizarre – Roman gladiator crossed with Scots clansman plus a dash of American footballer – that up in Lionel's workroom, watching him dress, she hadn't known whether to laugh or cry. For over a makeshift philibeg (tartan blanket torn into two strips fastened end-to-end by leather thongs) had gone a steel breastplate, steel shoulder plates, and a heavy leather piece over his gut and thighs. In the bag over his shoulder he'd packed a steel bonnet and a small round shield; into his belt he'd stuck various poignards and dirks; and last but not least he'd strapped to his side the sheathed two-edged cross-guarded sword, one of Lionel's best – though not what he'd wanted, any more than he'd wanted the cape that now hid him and his gear but for his bare hairy ankles and the flat leather brogues (slap-*limp*, slap-*limp*) on his horny feet.

'And the cape,' Lionel had insisted steadily.

'Why're ye baith sae feart?' he'd grumbled, glaring at them. 'it's bludy Hogmanay. Ah'm nae aboot tae fecht in a fookin' pinstripe suit!'

'You want to do it right?' Lionel had asked softly, a coldness in his eye which Diane hadn't seen before. She'd been watching Lionel as closely as her headache allowed. She knew he was hiding a lot from her. Maybe he had to. Maybe not. 'So why draw attention before it's time?'

In a spasm of rage Bobbie had grabbed Lionel by the shirtfront.

'Ah'll answer soon enough, shiteface – but nae tae you!'

Unimpressed, not scared, Lionel had just stared back at him.

'Stop it,' Diane had howled, 'What are you both on about?'

But though they'd obeyed her, though Bobbie had reluctantly worn the cape, neither would tell her what they knew that she didn't . . .

'So I'm bugged!' she cried. 'So why bother with this?'

'So probably you are,' Lionel had said flatly.

'But you knew that from the start, didn't you!'

'I suspected it,' he'd agreed. 'Last night my stupidity confirmed it. That's why I got everybody out of the house, and the pair of you into the pub. While I went . . .' – he hesitated – '. . . for instructions.'

'Well, why can't you . . .?'

He'd raised his hand. 'Let's go.'

Her wrath was nothing compared to Ruth's.

It had taken them a while to get out of the house.

'And don't come back, any of you!' Ruth had screeched after them down the strangely empty street, a woman betrayed, as ever, forever.

Diane didn't feel like a traitor to her sex. She'd been through too much already. Darkness, darkness. Her head pounding like metal beaten on a forge. It was 10.15 pm, sky lurid above the black angular edges of nineteenth-century brick and steel, wind still wailing over rooftops, but the road was unnaturally quiet; its cracked pavements deserted but for litter and broken bottles. Since the phones had rung a chill silence had fallen on the city. There was no traffic. Not even the usual cop patrols. Riot and ruction had died instantly. Just thirty minutes ago the road had been full of folk as disorderly as you'd expect in a Closed Area on New Year's Eve; spaced not only on booze or dope but on a mounting wave of millennial fear – this despite the fact that all day long the tv had been parading tame vicars, sociologists, and politicians all insisting that the crisis was imaginary, purely calendrical; the world wouldn't end when Big Ben struck midnight; this wasn't supersititious AD 999 when end-of-world fever sent Europe crazy, rich men throwing away their silks and ill-gotten gains only to wake next morning to AD 1,000 and realize they were just medieval neurotics suckered by chiliastic hope and fear of The End. *We're not like that now,* the experts insisted, *We're rational beings, so stay in tonight, don't risk it!*

Few had listened. What about *it* invading everyone's dreams? What of the crazy events everyone knew about? Who could be sure it wasn't The End? Best have fun before it's too late. Get out there and party; get out there and burn the place down. And even as night fell the streets had filled, the fires had begun and soon, in London as elsewhere, matters were out of hand.

Then the phones rang . . . and even in areas like N4 where few had phones, the word spread like lightning. *It*'s speaking to people! *It*'s ringing the phones; nobody can stop *it*! This is the beginning of the . . .

So the chill had fallen. Bottles cast aside. People gone inside. Now N4 and its inhabitants were like a vast animal, waiting, locked in the grip of increased expectation and fear as Lionel and Diane and Bobbie came past Wells Terrace. Through her agony and doubt Diane saw the dark silhouettes of homeless people hunched round their scrapwood fires. None of them had phones to answer . . . yet she knew they knew about it . . . their very stillness and silence said that they were waiting – but for what?

To *Take a Take a Take a Chance!* pulsed her pain and briefly, as she threw back her head, she passed beyond pain into a blinding river of light streaming down into this dark hidden world . . . streaming into what last night she'd heard called *Arianrhod*, the *Whirling Castle* (with all its half-sung half-memories of the visions that Chrissa had brought her; visions of the world of the Elohim; visions of hope and disaster . . . visions of the Beast).

For who else could make the phones all ring at once?

Who, she thought bitterly, *But the false lord of this world!*

Signs and miracles! So, through Gussie he'd spoken!

As for Jim Bright, and Aladdin's bloody Trezure Kave, and the Temple Bobbie and Lionel wouldn't tell her about . . . she felt like a hymn-singing Christian martyr en route to the lions. *I won't break!* she told herself, clenching her teeth as they entered a greater darkness under the Finsbury Park railway viaduct crossing Stroud Green Road. *Politicians give human beings a bad name*, ran a foot-high graffiti on the dirty brick wall. *No I won't!* But she shuddered. Not with cold. She wore two sweaters under her old brown coat. It was the silence, the echo of their feet on the rubbish-strewn pavement as they came to lights at the junction with Seven Sisters Road. And still no traffic. It was so unreal. It felt like being on some vast stage-set. Any moment now and the scenery would be swept away; some huge voice would yell: '*Cut! That's it! Okay! You can all go home!*'

'So what's Aladdin's Trezure Kave and where are we going?' she asked Lionel dully as they crossed the empty road. But what he told her only increased her sense of trance as they started down Blackstock Road. For he told her about Jim.

'Jim . . . Bright?' She stared at him. 'Why didn't you tell me before?'

'I didn't know myself until last night,' said Lionel flatly.

'Why does he want us to meet him in the . . . Trezure Kave?'

'Who *is* this guy Jim Bright onyway?' Bobbie asked suspiciously.

'So what's with the Temple?' Diane demanded, but Bobbie just shrugged and glowered in silence, Lionel watching them both very closely as Diane went on angrily: 'Won't you say? You big bold man! Cat got your tongue?'

When Bobbie still refused to speak Lionel suggested softly: 'Diane, it's best we just stay calm till we get there.'

She felt stupid with pain. 'Why?' she demanded petulantly.

Sighing heavily, he came to a door and rang a bell.

'I'm just doing what I'm told,' he muttered.

'But who the hell's telling you to do it?'

'Same people who sent you here, I guess.' And when he pointed up at the sky she groaned. Through her pain she saw his face and Bobbie's swim before her in the darkness. *Masked faces. I don't know anything about either of them*, she realized, and snapped: 'I'm sick of both of you.'

Lionel grimaced at the agony in her eyes. 'Just try to hang on,' he said roughly. 'We'll be there soon enough.'

Then the door opened.

Meanwhile Jessica had problems of her own. The cab she got at Heathrow was as honest as Pierre had promised. No rip-off.

Big joke! The cab was automatic. No human driver.

She didn't realize it until her journey was nearly over.

Still shocked by her call she'd entered the cab without seeing a driver or hearing the message about this week's Reely preview (*Battle of Britain*, Louis Black as Douglas Bader, the Legless Air Ace, full SI available). She assumed that the voice telling her how to slot her plastic was human, and that she'd duly be delivered at her given destination: *Oxford Circus.*

So she was. And in retrospect it wasn't as bad as the night Shasta blew. It was just that her nerves were too frayed for the succession of fresh shocks about to strike her. Bad enough to land in a foreign city and step in a call-box, only for the phone to call *you* with a personal message from a ghost, telling you to meet your long-lost son at some place with a crazy name. Aladdin's Trezure Kave? The Loony Lolly? Worse to realize, as she did after some while, on swimming out of her daze, that she'd left her bags behind in the airport, deliberately, in the crazy belief that she was going someplace where she wouldn't need them, never ever again.

That was the first new shock.

'Jim,' she asked uneasily. 'What's going on?'

Looking about the cab's plush interior, she grew aware of the blaring holoscreen before her. She turned to the window. It was as opaque and blank as milk. She sought the catch to open it . . . and slowly realized that it was not to be opened. Dazed, she stared instead at the holoscreen.

Flame leaped from a street-long Victorian terrace.

'. . . Here in Stockwell,' the voiceover cried, 'fire still rages . . .'

The voice, the too-bright 3D colour hurt her head. She didn't want it. How to turn it off? She sought and found armrest controls; tried another button. A game-show host wearing disastrous purple lurex and a broad fake grin jabbered: '. . . And *now*, here on the *Cream Dream* tonight we welcome back last week's winners . . .' With a growing sense of nightmare she went rapidly through all available channels:

'. . . and Al-Khash tonight said that if the West will not . . .'

'. . . Watch it, Skipper! Hun in the sun at nine o'clock!'

'. . . Reports from all over London of an unprecedented . . .'

'. . . *Rotley's! The brew that gets your rocks off like . . .*'

'. . . south-west depression. Light rain followed by . . .'

'. . . reports of increasing panic. Unfortunately nobody here at Channel 16 can tell you what this means. It seems that all the phones . . .'

Then briefly she thought she had it. There was a crackling, a hissing, and for a moment the screen went blank.

But even as she sighed in relief a face appeared before her – a hook-nosed face, desert-dark, with the most piercing eyes she'd ever seen.

'Good evening,' said the quiet, calm voice, a sense of immeasurable age in it. Jessica sat transfixed. *It's one of them*, she realized in a dream, *One of the Elohim, or the Company, or whatever they call themselves.* 'By now you will all be asking what is going on,' the calm voice said, flowing like spring water in her mind, 'Good! This is why we intervene with these tricks, to stimulate your curiosity. For if you fail now to ask the right questions, if you fail to find the right answers, soon none of you will be able to ask questions ever again. For the Shift approaches. But it is not necessarily fatal. Therefore we ask you, please, to tune in the same time tomorrow night.' The eyes pierced her. 'Thank you and goodnight.'

The screen went briefly blank. Then normal programming returned.

Jessica sat staring, her brow beaded in sweat.

'Jim,' she muttered, 'Jim, for godsakes . . .'

Then she knew she'd had enough. 'Hey!' she cried, hammering on the bulkhead above the screen, 'Driver! How do I turn this damned thing off?'

'Sir or Madam, you have a problem?' a voice murmured, and it was very polite, very British, and very . . . *mechanical.* 'To change your destination, comment on in-service facilities, or seek information, please consult the panel to your right and programme your taxi accordingly.'

'Goddammit!' she insisted in a panic, 'Just turn this thing *off!*'

'Sir or Madam,' said the polite mechanical British voice, 'We am not permitted by Metropolitan law to disserve you media-wise. The time is now 22.18 GMT. We are now overpassing Chiswick. Your ETA at Oxford Circus is 22.33 GMT. Temperature outside is 3°C, windspeed 25 kph, and may we wish you a very Good New Millennium. Thank you for choosing Aquarius Taxis.'

Only then she knew she was riding in a robot.

'Jim!' she cried in a futile, fearful rage, 'what the hell have you got me into? Where am I going? Can't I even look out of the window?'

To this at least she received a positive response.

'Sir or Madam, to facilitate extra-vehicular vision please consult the panel to your right and programme your taxi accordingly.'

Angrily consulting said panel, she saw a touch-cell labelled: *Window – Vision/Opaque.* She touched *Vision* and the window promptly cleared.

Sighing with relief, trying to ignore the holoscreen, she gazed out at London. A computerized map-display one side of the holoscreen told her the cab had left the Chiswick Flyover, was now on the High Road to Hammersmith and Kensington. Innumerable cute little red-brick side-streets branched off; the wet sidewalks – *I mean, pavements,* she corrected herself – were almost empty; the traffic seemed very light for a major city on New Year's Eve, but it was increasing now. Above, the stormy sky flared orange with the fires reported on the holoscreen, yet through gaps between buildings to the east she glimpsed patches of clear sky. With a mild shiver she knew: *It'll rise again soon.* She looked at her watch. 10.25 pm GMT.

Only another 95 minutes (local time) of 1999 left to go.

Fifteen minutes later AD 2000 was closer and the traffic denser, stunned Londoners emerging onto West End streets again as the cab, past Hyde Park and Marble Arch, slid into the neon swirl of Oxford Street. Bright rivers of spectral light poured through the cab windows, strobing and confusing her. Briefly she found herself back on 101 that hellish night when Shasta blew; she seemed to hear Mo. '*They want you in London – that means you'll get there.*' And Jim, in his weird accent: *Come to London. Ma. I'm waiting for you.* And here she was! Her heart beat hard. *Are we really going to meet? Impossible!* She wrung her hands together. *He's waiting? Sure! In Aladdin's Trezure Kave. By the Loony Lolly.* She heard a hollow laugh. It came from her throat. Insane! And what had the ghost-voice meant, saying Jim hadn't gone *through the higher gate*; that, like her, he remained *fixed? Fixed in what?* she wondered, *The physical body? But how?* Dazzled and very confused, she flashed back to that blazing moment in Death Valley fifteen years ago. *Nothing left but his buckle! I'm mad*, she decided, tears in her eyes as the cab inched forward past Selfridges through the thickening traffic, signs blazing all round. A gang of kids, bald heads dyed purple with gold zigzags, ran out of a door (*Electrohit Hotel! Only 29.99 a hit!*) and into the traffic, rapping her window as they passed, their eyes crazy. *Return of the creature from the Black Lagoon! Come on, Jessica, Take a Chance!* And even as the cab inched out of the one-way flow approaching Oxford Circus and drew in at the kerb, she saw it up ahead.

The biggest, brightest, most garish sign of all.

Aladdin's Trezure Kave! London's Most Exotic Medina!

Automatically the door opened. The street-roar leapt at her.

'Thank you Sir or Madam for choosing Aquarius taxis. May we wish you a very good New Millennium, and allow us to hope that your stay . . .'

But as she got stiffly out what she heard was not that taxi's farewell but, through all the blare of traffic and music and people, a honey-soft voice insinuating itself into her dazed mind:

'. . . *come on in just come on in you lovely people I'm yours to please to please you and I'm waiting yes I'm waiting in Aladdin's Trezure Kave . . .'*

There she stood before the low mysterious tunnel of entry to the vast Aladdin medina. The broad irregular tunnelmouth was sickly luminous green, chaotically plastered to represent a natural rock outcropping. About and above it, dayglo jets of colour fired each other up to the vast hologram of Aladdin which, bare-chested and sensuously moving against the black-and-red urban night, grinned lasciviously down at her as it rubbed the golden lamp from the suggestive spout of which coiled a luscious, smoky, steamily-naked houri. And Jessica slowly realized that it was the houri's milk-and-honey voice that breathed so invitingly through the traffic-roar and the human rapids of hustle-babble and neighbouring attraction, whispering from throw-speakers on high window-ledges and up the tall, slender lamp-posts:

'*. . . come on in please come on in and rub my lamp and get your three wishes tonight because I can't wait so come on in please come on . . .*'

And Jessica stood there, utterly lost, in the middle of London.

Jim, she implored her son silently, *Jim! Where are you?*

31.
Aladdin's Trezure Kave

In fact he was just ten yards away, casual by the Trezure Kave door in jeans, denim jacket, and cowboy boots, arms folded, legs crossed, black hair neatly combed – just another face amid the thickening crowds.

For now in London as everywhere else people were hitting the streets, shocked by the phone-calls; by the hook-nosed spectre who'd hijacked the media. With Arianrhod's song breathing in their brains they sought bright lights to dazzle the dark dream, loud noise to drown it out; some sought riot and mayhem . . . and in London as elsewhere the police didn't stop them; the law too was paralysed, without philosophy to comprehend the how and why of the increasing chaos. In London the Salvation Army, St John's Ambulance Brigade and other voluntary groups, foreseeing the panic ahead, were soon out and about to help as best they could. But they were few, couldn't be everywhere at once, and they certainly weren't at the mouth of the Trezure Kave as Jim Bright saw his mother get out of a cab barely ten yards away.

Her distracted gaze didn't even linger on him. Then he nearly broke. Fifteen years; four hundred; what odds? For he knew her rightaway. She'd hardly changed. Maybe plumper, more lines round the eyes, but her hair as glossy black as ever: he knew her, and the lost child in him grieved that she didn't instantly know him and run forward, crying: 'Jim! Jim!'

Emotions and memories he'd thought gone forever surged up. He clenched his fists. *Back To The Future!* he thought bitterly. The last movie he'd seen. And so much else lost that moment lightning had struck in Death Valley – sunshine, skateboards, chocolate malts – it all came back.

But to call her now would ruin it. Somehow he restrained himself. It had to be done right; the Chosen One was ready; Jessica was here – but the others had yet to turn up – and the tv crew. He didn't know why They chose it like this. Twice he'd been through lower gates, but not through the higher doors. His understanding of the Company's purpose was vague; he did only as the Old Man and the Doctor's good angels commanded; he was here only as a guide. Yet ignoring his mother now was the hardest thing he'd had to do since spilling through the Templar Gate ten days ago; harder even than standing here amid the crowds. For this age to which he'd . . . returned revolted him. Born in California, sure, but that was vague now; he'd got used to rural Warwick in Armada-time; to the scent of woodbine, horseshit, oxlip. From all that the Doctor and Mr Francis, who'd sent him to Warwick "for your own good, Jim", had lately called him back to Mortlake. And how eagerly he'd gone, thinking his long exile over! No more bumpkin taunts that he was strange, witch-touched! It was a miracle he'd survived the stocks, far less the stake, his tongue being as long as his temper was short; he'd never suffered fools gladly, and Warwick then had been as full of fools as London was now. Yet now he couldn't believe how glad he'd been to leave. 'Best go now,' his "father" and protector Will had said – and off he'd gone like a shot! Even his Emma had been soon forgotten that May morning he'd set out for London, fully expecting that now at last he'd be admitted to the Doctor's secret work; work involving Europe's best minds – Mercator, Ralegh, Harvey, Gilbert – imagining the intrigues to which soon he'd be privy; secrets that his bum-scratching, ale-swilling tormentors in

Warwick would never grasp in a thousand years! He'd thought himself about to be recruited into Mr Francis's work of Philanthropia as one of his "good pens", with cot and desk in a garret (the meanest would do!) in that fine palace at Twickenham! Mr Francis himself had hinted as much the last time he'd come, incognito, to see Will. As to the gossip about milord – how the Queen had set him up in Twickenham, close to her palace, to keep him in her fond (none dared hint it aloud) *maternal* eye – should it concern a simple scribe like himself? He'd dedicate himself (if the Doctor approved) to the laying of what Mr Francis called *Great Bases for Eternity*.

So he'd hoped. What a fool! Yes, indeed, they *had* called him to help with the laying of *Great Bases for Eternity* . . . but not as he'd expected.

It had taken the Doctor time to get to the point. The old man had been embarrassed. And when Jim had learned what was intended, he had resisted – uselessly. That very night they'd taken him to the Temple. Howling into the Gate he'd plunged . . . and out again, into 1999, to meet the Old Man . . .

Now here he stood shivering among these modern . . . English?

No! he thought hotly, *Not English, but poor slaves!*

Now he mourned what he'd been glad to leave. Warwick had been crude and dirty; it had taken him years to find his feet after the shock of his inadvertent arrival due to the Doctor's angel-summoning rituals – but the folk of that time were heart-strong and open. This mob of mean and pallid geeks? He thought little of this cold, frantic, modern London.

'Oi knows how ye feels, Ma,' he muttered as he saw her so reluctantly enter the Trezure Kave, 'Oi'm a bumpkin 'ere too. But soon Oi'll speak with thee . . . when all's ready an' the others are here . . .'

So he waited. All the players had to be onstage for the diversion. He saw the Channel 3 crew arrive, as the Old Man had said, and dully saw the team rush into the Trezure Kave even as another known face approached – the strained white face of the woman who'd eyed him in the inn where the Old Man had sent him some nights earlier. He breathed deep and drew back.

That's her! Her with the Beast in her brain!

And the other two with her. That tall thin fellow, Lionel, who'd come like a hounded hare to the Old Man's door last night, asking what to do. In his eyes Jim saw a scared man. And the Scotch lunatic – he limped past, emanating rage. Jim drew further back; the Scotchman looked ripe to go berserk. Yet Jim was less interested in him than in the woman. Such pain in her! He knew who she was. Diane Joyce. Wife and mother of Sam and Chrissa – Last Days folk, now Shining Ones – who, through contact with the Doctor, had kidnapped him from the sunshine into . . . this madness!

He fought to stay calm, to show nothing, but he breathed hard. He knew about the worm and how (though not why) it was so crucial. But her obvious agony made him doubt Their motives as the three passed him into the Trezure Kave, and he wondered if he was a coward or fool, to be obeying Them when so obviously They didn't care a fig about human suffering.

Then the third contact – a manic figure in the Victorian cape and top hat that Jim had been told to expect – also arrived, face glowing neon, muttering to himself. Blood stained his cape. He ran into the Trezure Kave crowds. A man behind him cursed and followed, also at a run.

They were all here now. Jim could feel Arianrhod rising.

He sighed and followed them into the depths of the Trezure Kave, down to the place of the Loony Lolly where the Chosen One waited.

By Oxford Street Agutter was in a bad way, lunatic voices and visions tormenting him as he lurched along, hissing in time to the throbbing of his slashed shoulder: 'Who sent you? Who sent you? Who sent you?' For before him swam a bloody smile, street-wide and as faceless as the Cheshire Cat's.

Again and again the Loving Death-Bringer hissed in his ear: '*YOU did, Mr Agutter. YOU sent me.*'

Sergeant Grant, doggedly following, heard him cry:

'And where are we going tonight, Mr Agutter?'

The Home Secretary laughed raggedly amid the human torrent.

'To the circus!' he shouted like an excited child.

Then Grant saw him flinch in astonishment as –

'... NO! NOT THE CIRCUS,' cried Carmody Cee before him, now wearing an Eamonn Andrews mask, 'PHILIP HENRY AGUTTER! THIS – IS – YOUR – LIFE!'

– and gasping in amazement he found himself onstage:

'YES! PHILIP HENRY AGUTTER! THIS IS YOUR LIFE! BORN IN GRAVESEND IN 1953, NOW METROPOLITAN HOME SECRETARY! GREAT TO HAVE YOU WITH US, SIR ...'

'But who sent you?' he demanded frantically.

'*YOU* DID, PHILIP HENRY AGUTTER!' the mocking voice roared, and now it was the Iron Duke before him; 'SO CARMODY'S GOT THE TAPE AND DEATH RAE'S GOT THE WIND UP! HEAR THIS VOICE FROM YOUR PAST!'

'*Who sent you?*' cried a familiar voice, off-stage.

'Carol!' He threw up his hands in amazement. 'Did you ...?'

He saw her betraying him, on the phone to ...

'YES! YES! YES!' cried Carmody. 'AND NOW HEAR THIS!'

The Iron Duke sang in a monotone: 'SO HEAR WHAT SISTER RAE SAID ...'

Grant, plagued by his own voices, saw Agutter flinch as a gang of kids ran out of a neon waterfall: ELECTROHIT HOTEL! ONLY 29.99 A HIT! From the neon blasted a dreary old rock track, something about Sister Ray. Seeing Agutter in his top hat and bloodstained frockcoat the kids paused to jostle and jeer. What Agutter saw and heard was a crophead Greek chorus cackle:

'DID YOU THINK YOU COULD DO IT? DID YOU REALLY BELIEVE THAT LOVE AND INSPIRATION CAN BE CENSORED AND CAUGHT IN A NET?'

Ted Grant moved in. The kids took one look and got lost; but as they fled into the circus crowd Agutter heard a buzzing.

'Mr Agutter!' Grant snapped. Agutter seemed to see him. Confused, in a plaintive voice he asked the sergeant: 'What's that?'

'Your phone, sir. Your phone! Answer the bastard!'

Agutter briefly came to his senses and answered the CSU tracker who illegally had his number. Grant eyed heaven and stepped back.

It was the third time Joe O'Brien had called him.

In the CSU op room matters had gone from bad to worse.

Chief Super Macdonald had organised a team of soccer fans like himself. With a ball of taped-up scrap paper they were busy being Denis Law, George Best, Bobbie Charlton and other late great Man United stars. The Super of course was Duncan Edwards. 'Goal!' he cried, side-footing the ball into Console 77 as Joe called Agutter.

'She's at Oxford Circus, entering Aladdin's Trezure Kave,' said the edgy voice. 'We HAVE TO send a squad to take her – RIGHT NOW!'

Agutter had forgotten about the Ghost Project. He thought the voice meant his daughter. Gillian.

'Why's she here?' he muttered, in his agony spinning through visions of Gillian as toddler, teenager, young woman who'd gone to the Pyrenees to research Catharism . . . and vanished . . . into nothing . . . until . . . Oxford Circus! He looked about. 'This is where she told me to come!' Ted Grant heard him exclaim in amazement, 'To the Circus! This is where . . .'

Then he forgot the call. His mouth fell open in shock. He swayed.

'*. . . come on in and rub my lamp*,' Gillian whispered down at him, licking her lips, rubbing her thighs together, '*. . . because I can't wait I . . .*'

Ted Grant groaned to see his boss stare up at the hologram issuing from the spout of Aladdin's lamp on the wall above. 'Sir . . .' he started.

'STOP it!' Agutter cried in terror, face streaked by neon colourfalls as he cut the caller off. 'Gillian!' Ted Grant heard him roar, 'Stop it!'

Then Joe O'Brien gave up. With Agutter clearly mad and half the CSU about him engaged in an insane football match, he called Commissioner Rae.

At that moment Hector Rae, still trapped not only in La Bruce's flat but in visions of Hoel and Brother Jean d'Aubigny, was trying to swing off La Bruce's window-ledge into a net suspended from an erratically hovering police chopper. Life was getting no easier. But his sense of duty was strong. He answered the call.

'GOAL!' cried voices in the CSU background.

But Hector Rae got the message and gave appropriate orders.

Agutter didn't know that.

'*. . . come in, daddy, and taste my . . .*'

'STOP IT, Gillian!' he wailed at the Aladdin holo-houri, only Ted Grant watching him as he was distracted yet again by the poison dwarf:

'BUT SEX IS A SALEABLE COMMODITY, SIR!' crowed the death-clown, 'SHE'S GOT IT, SO LET HER FLAUNT IT! PAY THE BEAST HIS DUE! – EH?'

'Bugger off!' he bellowed . . . and Grant, his own senses swimming in the tide of STEP RIGHT UP AND TRY YOUR LUCK, saw Agutter flap his hands at the sea of demented faces that swam about.

'BUT I'M JUST ONE OF YOUR FACES, SIR! WHY GO ON CENSORING YOURSELF?'

Then Agutter knew: *So that's what Arianrhod's here to tell us!*

He laughed . . . but promptly lost the insight as –

'*. . . so come on in just come on in I'm yours to please to please you and I'm waiting yes I'm waiting in Aladdin's Trezure Kave . . .*'

Biblical wrath and terror seized him. 'Whore of Babylon!' he cried, shaking his fist at the hologram, 'Creature of the Beast!'

Then (maybe it was the shock of his rage) briefly he came to his right mind, to find himself on a cold neon-drenched pavement, blank crowds all about. In horror he knew: *We're all asleep. That's why I'm here. To. . .*

'TAKE A CHANCE, SIR. THAT'S RIGHT! BUT. . .'

'. . .come on in just come on in and free yourself and. . .'

His blood roared. *The Trezure Kave. Of course. But. . .*

'YOU HAVE TO BE SLY, SIR. WHY IS THE WISDOM HIDDEN?'

'Don't look round,' he told himself, remembering Grant.

'. . . *just come on in*,' Gillian breathed, '. . . *eat me, daddy* . . .'

I must lose Grant, he thought groggily, voices and visions swimming together, '. . . OR HE'LL WIPE THAT SMILE OFF OUR FACE FOREVER . . .'

'Don't look,' he whispered craftily, 'don't let him know you know . . .'

'BUT IF RAE KNOWS? AND THE CSU?'

Gillian, are you really here? he asked in agony, staring past the holo-houri at the blood-red sky beyond the high city roofs, grippping his bloody shoulder but noticing it no more than he noticed the slim dark man watching him from a doorway. The dwarf tugged urgently at his elbow.

'QUICK!' cried the death-clown, 'LOSE HIM! ARIANRHOD RISES AGAIN!'

He swayed; heard the song of Arianrhod rising in the east: then, taking Grant by surprise, he whirled and ran into Aladdin's green mouth, barging past the crowd, not knowing what he sought as he vanished into the depths.

Grant cursed and followed him . . . but Agutter was already lost in the swarm of trezure-kavers as Arianrhod rose again over London.

It was 10.50pm. Seventy minutes until the New Millennium.

Terrified she descended to the depths of the Trezure Kave, Lionel in front and Bobbie behind, her headache worse than any other pain she'd ever known. It went beyond pain into a sort of ecstasy that removed her from all accustomed human feeling. She had only dim memory of leaving Stroud Green Road, of being driven to the West End by a man who'd spoken not a word. None of it mattered. The pain had torn her from the world into a light-headed realm of memory, fantasy, vision and dream. Maybe it was no more than due payment for her sins. So much guilt over Sam and Chrissa. Losing them at Gairloch so many years ago, too scared to follow them into the Gate, throwing that ring of moon and horns into the sparkling lochan after seeing Chrissa consumed by the writhing bloody worms. And all the years since. Looking after Sam's dad till the old man died. Then the Church of the Second Coming. Gussie's empire of false hope. That night at Waverley, getting off the bus, hearing Sam's voice. And then the dreams. Chrissa visiting her nightly from the Cathar lands so long ago. Embracing a philosophy horrifying not just because for so long all those who embraced it had been killed by the Church of Love, but because it was so very hard!

To think this world owned by the Beast, and procreation damnable because it dragged down more free souls into hell. What a belief!

Yet all round her now that hell was plain as the three of them flowed down the curving tunnel to the Trezure Kave's depths, past bars, 5-star restaurants, video-parlours, roulette-halls. Through tinted tunnel-front windows she saw the come-on fun of society lost to hope and direction, advertise itself – semi-darkened Reely-lounges in which she saw, as in a nightmare, ranks of Sensory Identifiers couched in dead rows as from every side barkers, human and electronic, waging war for the punters' plastic in Aladdin's Trezure Cave tonite. LIVE NOW PAY LATER they were all chanting, the epiphany of the 20th century. But now LATER was just an hour away.

'Hey! You want Mindswitch? Wanna be Napoleon tonight? Or Josephine? Or ya wanta be Adolf? Or Josef? Or Pol Pot? We can arrange that too!'

'Hey! Whatever you want, I kin git it fer ya!'

People spinning, hands grabbing, Artful Dodgers everywhere –

'Jist fook aff!' she heard Bobbie behind her cry. 'Git lost ye fookin' shites. Boogar aff or I'll fookin' do ye!'

And the voices jeered.

But Lionel never turned round, his face was set forward and

down, down to the depths, and though she still doubted, she followed, his seeming calm amid the uproar providing direction even amid the scream of the worm in her brain . . . and the scream was a wave hurling her up to the realm where Sam and Chrissa waited, so that the deeper she went the more clearly she saw them, heard them, reconnected with them in her pain.

'*Soon, Mum!*' she heard, and, '*Hey, Diane, I didn't mean to mess you up like that, but if you'll just hang on another . . .*'

Thirty minutes. That's what the voices said.

Thirty minutes! Just hang on that long!

Yet she was racked by pain so fierce she doubted if it was possible.

So they reached the Hall of the Loony Lolly.

Jessica was already there, wandering in jet-lagged amazement.

The Hall of the Loony Lolly, offering the most intense Trezure Kave experiences, had been developed from redundant Oxford Circus Underground facilities. A vast domed space, the Hall was disguised as a natural cave. Lit ghostly green by pulsing electronic stalagmites and stalactites, its atmosphere was euphoria-enriched, its platforms, nooks and ramps tonight crammed with glittering, nervous celebrants, many masked in period costume, fancy dress, or drag. But it was too hot. Jessica felt faint, coat slung over her arm, head swimming as she passed a holoshelf where the Watchers belted out: '. . . *Aw ma mind's bin murdered by Mars . . .*' Then she stopped dead at what she saw before her, unsure whether to laugh or be outraged.

There stood the Loony Lolly itself.

Like a giant Maypole, a hundred feet high, twined about with luminous ribbons, the Loony Lolly was a big prick, complete with glowing purple glans. All round its bulging base the Loony Lolly maidens, voluptuously naked but for moulded frogheads, moved among the punters breathing the approved Aladdin message. One of them fingered her:

'. . . *Get yer Luvly Loony Lolly here . . . get your rocks off with the Luvly Loony Lolly . . . suck this stick and you don't need no . . .*'

She was still staring when a voice behind her said:

'Jessica? You *are* Jessica, aren't you?'

. . . as in an Edgware Road hotel room Carmody Cee angrily wrenched the so-called Khufu tape from the cheap cassette player he'd just bought.

Suckered. Of course. Because the tape was blank. Both sides.

'Big joke,' he muttered. 'And Muggins here went for it.'

His phone buzzed. He hesitated before thumbing RECEIVE.

'Carmody? We've got the boys down there, but where the hell are you?'

'What are you talking about?' he demanded, suddenly cold.

'To the Oxford Circus Trezure Kave! Like you said!'

'Like I said . . .' Carmody stared. 'When did I . . .?'

'Half an hour ago.' Joe sounded puzzled. 'When all the phones were ringing. You said meet you there in thirty minutes.'

'When all the phones were ringing,' Carmody repeated, thinking fast, 'and a voice sounding like mine told you to . . .'

'Oh.' His producer seemed stunned. 'But I don't . . .'

Carmody sighed. 'Tell them to go ahead without me.'

'You mean, live? But what's the story?'

'Don't ask me,' said Carmody, 'Ask Khufu.'

'Ask who?' Joe asked, very tentatively.

'The bloke that built the Great Pyramid,' he said harshly, and was about to sign off when the voice the other end said:

'By the way, that tape – broadcast it tomorrow night. As it is.'

'But it's . . .' Carmody started, then froze. 'What did you say?'

'I didn't say anything,' said Joe. 'Look, what's . . .?'

'Don't worry about it.' Carmody shook his head in wonder. 'Just put the Trezure Kave on the air – now.' Ending the call, he gazed through the window . . . then turned on the hotel room's holoset. To Channel 3.

He didn't have long to wait . . .

. . . as Hector Rae at last jumped from La Bruce's window-ledge into the net hanging from the chopper which, lurching this way and that, had seemed likely at any minute to hit the house. He'd paused to take the CSU call and transmit orders. Now, as he was drawn safely into its belly, the chopper crabbed up and away into the blazing night.

'You okay, sir?' asked Chief Super Fisher, dusting him off, 'Are . . .'

'Right as rain,' Rae snapped, tearing off his Wellington mask. But under it his own face looked like a mask too, livid and tight. Fear was in his eyes. Setting his jaw, he snapped: 'Get to Oxford Circus, that's all. Are those squads there yet?'

'Be another five minutes. Traffic's building up and there's trouble on the streets. Sir, we're losing control; we need explanations before we . . .'

'Screw explanations.' Rae glared. 'Just get those bloody Chancers. They're behind this. Somehow. My guess is ELF.'

'ELF, sir?' The Chief Super looked worried.

'Extra Low Frequency transmissions making people hallucinate all this crap,' Rae grunted. 'Find the transmitters and we'll kill it.'

The Chief Super eyed the sky where Arianrhod shone.

'It's not there,' Rae muttered through clenched teeth. 'It's induced hallucination. When we nail those bastards you'll see for yourself.'

He called Joe O'Brien at CSU, who told him 76-E-678-DEJ was putting out Chancer neurogenics from the Trezure Kave. As the chopper crossed Hyde Park he settled back grimly. *Ghost Project!* he thought with contempt. *Agutter's been with them all along. We'll get him now.*

But, the Chief Super saw, Hector Rae was trembling.

32.
The Sacrifice

Wild in top hat and bloody black cape, Agutter ran deeper through the Trezure Kave crowds, determining to lose his shadow. But though he'd lost Ted Grant he still saw the death-clown capering before him and knew he was rushing into his own mind-depths like everyone else: everything censored was erupting now. 'THAT'S RIGHT!' cried the dwarf, 'ONCE WE ONLY CAME OUT TO PLAY WHEN YOU WERE ASLEEP, SIR!' Delirious, he passed a sweating media crew manhandling its gear into the depths. 'That's Agutter!' a voice cried as he ducked through electrohit and reely parlours, clutching his shoulder. He looked back. There was no sign of Ted Grant. 'Who sent you?' he hissed again. The dwarf's black eyes gleamed. 'THE SHINING ONES, MR AGUTTER.'

'Who are they? From where?' he demanded.

The dwarf pointed a leathery finger like a wand at his head. A shock of light burst in his brain. 'You mean we're doing all this to ourselves?'

Abruptly the dwarf vanished. Agutter ran blindly on through the crowds and burst into a crowded, green-lit hall. Electronic stalagmites pulsed. Dazed, he collided with a huge black-bearded man wearing a cape that flew open to reveal a wicked looking sword. Grabbing him with ham-like fists, the Rob Roy type fixed him with homicidal, whisky-blurred eyes.

'Ye fookin' cripple!' roared Bobbie Aird as Lionel's eyes widened on this unmasked, wounded, shit-stinking man, 'Cannae ye look whaur . . .?'

Then came a second interruption. 'Well met,' cried a broad strong voice. 'We're all 'ere now, eh? Jim Bright at your service, mistresses and maisters – and past time ye got here!'

Lionel turned. So did Diane beside him, and Bobbie. Facing them they saw the man they'd seen in the Cumberland a week ago, the black-haired man in jeans and denim jacket. He sounded like an Olde English rustic . . . and amid her pain Diane was seized by a sense of recollection and imminence – a sense that grew as her tired gaze moved from Jim Bright's dark eyes to the black-haired woman standing just behind him. And Diane knew who she was.

'Jessica,' she whispered, pain beating so fiercely through her she felt she was burning up. '. . . *Get yer Luvly Loony Lolly here . . .*' she heard as the glittering demented crowds swam about them. 'You're Jessica!'

For Jessica it was almost too much. Barely a minute since the young man with his outlandish accent – *Is it REALLY Jim?* – had accosted her: she hadn't even had time to get her breath back, and now . . . now here was the woman she'd seen in dreadful vision that night she'd fled Nome Valley.

Jessica hesitated, insisting to herself: *This IS real! It IS! This IS Jim! It IS!* – then asked haltingly: 'You're . . . Diane? Diane Joyce?'

Agutter flinched. He stared. At *Diane Emily Joyce.* This frail grey woman, 76-E-678-DEJ? Obviously in acute agony. Agony caused by . . . he choked and tried to look away, but Bobbie's grip on his collar didn't allow it. It was the first time he'd seen the pain of a wormed subject –

'But . . . but . . .' he croaked, 'Don't you realise you're all . . .'

'And who the fook are ye?' Bobbie demanded. 'Count Drac?'

Lionel glared at the man in the bloodstained Victorian gear.

'I know you?' He shook his head in disbelief. 'I'm sure I . . .'

'. . . He's the fine gentleman that done the dirty deed what lets us join the Company,' said Jim Bright grimly. 'Come on! Time we went to church.'

'But,' Lionel stuttered, 'this is . . . Philip Agutter – aren't you?' he demanded angrily. 'You're the Home Secretary, right?'

Lightheaded, Agutter laughed as Lionel cried: 'This bastard runs the CSU! He planted the worm in you, Diane, it's him that . . .'

Bobbie's face darkened, his free hand went to his belt . . . but before he could draw the dirk Jim Bright was between him and Agutter.

'Hold on!' Jim Bright roared. 'Hear me! Company wants this man too, for his daughter is gone through gates like . . .' – he faced Diane's distress – '. . . yours did, ma'am. And like I did too! They needs us all! Alive!'

I'm dreaming, thought Agutter, staring at the angry green faces round him, Gillian singing in his skull. 'TELL THEM, DAD! ADMIT IT!'

Stuttering he heard himself tell Lionel. 'Yes, I . . . Alpha-Five-Zero. Worm. But I'm . . .' – it sounded so feeble; urgently he eyed Jim Bright – '. . . with you. But the CSU's tracked you here. Me too. They'd have raided you last night. I stopped them.' He couldn't face Diane Joyce. He felt her eyes on him. He felt fire in his skull. 'My daughter, Gillian,' he croaked, '. . . she sent me. I was looking for someone who . . . Oh God . . . she vanished in the Pyrenees . . . but when the phones rang she . . . told me to . . .'

'In the Pyrenees?' said Diane, in a dragging, wondering voice.

Twisting in Bobbie's grip now, he stared at her. 'She was . . .'

Then through the seething crowd he saw the Channel 3 crew. 'We must get out,' he said urgently, 'My minder . . . I lost him . . . but Rae . . .'

'Now, maisters,' demanded Jim, 'It's time we . . .'

Lionel was totally confused. *Agutter* their contact? Why would They? Then he too saw the Channel 3 crew, and belatedly realised what Agutter had said. 'Bobbie,' he said, struggling to think, 'Swap his gear for yours. And you . . .' – he eyed Jessica – '. . . get one of those frogheads. Quick!'

To Jim in a choked voice he said: 'Is the Chosen One ready?'

'Ready this hour past,' said Jim grimly. 'I do give 'er the word now. And you will meet me over in the door to the railway . . .'

'Got it,' said Lionel, sweating as Jim left them. 'You two – change your capes. Come on, Bobbie – please, man!'

In a daze Jessica bought a froghead from a Loony Lolly salesgirl as Bobbie reluctantly swapped capes with Agutter. With a sneer he snatched the top hat and stuck it on his head.

Lionel grabbed the froghead and tossed it at Agutter.

'Put it on, fuckhead. Bobbie, stick him if he tries anything.'

Wincing, Agutter pulled on the latex froghead. Bobbie laughed.

'A fookin frog-prince, eh?'

'Let's go.' Lionel started off. A knife pricked Agutter's back even as, squinting through the froghead eyeslits, he saw Grant just yards away, hunting through the mayhem of masked faces and babble . . . and then passing without spotting him. He sighed, knowing he'd just made his decision.

'Move it, froggie,' Bobbie growled.

'I'm coming,' he said, feeling oddly relieved.

Past the Loony Lolly they pressed, Jessica beside Diane. 'I don't know what's going on,' she told Diane breathlessly, 'but Jim . . . vanished fifteen years ago. Struck by lightning. In front of my . . .'

She realised Diane wasn't listening.

She followed Diane's glazed look . . . and saw the woman.

On a ledge high up the grotto wall the Chosen One stood in a flowing white robe, lank hair framing a pale face. Raising a megaphone she cried:

'TAKE A CHANCE! TRY TO DANCE. TAKE A TAKE A TAKE A . . .'

The amplified voice roared through the hall. The hustle-babble ceased; the crowds froze, staring up in amazement.

'It's for us!' hissed Lionel, 'We have to get to the tube.'

'. . . CHANCE! FOR THE SHIFT IS NIGH! THROUGH

PAIN WE'LL . . .'

Diane couldn't breathe. Raging fire consumed her. King's . . .

'. . . FLY!' cried the Chosen One, Channel 3 live broadcast cameras now rolling as the five of them, Lionel and Jessica supporting Diane, Bobbie prodding Agutter, met Jim at the entry to the Underground. Agutter looked back . . . and saw what the Chosen One was doing. 'Move it!' growled Bobbie. He did. But he was trembling. For he'd seen it . . . and couldn't believe it!

Carmody saw it on the hotel room holoset; saw the white-robed Chancer step off the ledge onto thin air and . . .

'Oh, God!' he muttered, rubbing his eyes. Impossible. But he saw it. So did everyone in the hall of the Loony Lolly. There were shrieks of disbelief, then total silence fell, save for a child crying:

'Mummy, why doesn't she fall?'

For the Chosen One floated in mid-air with no visible means of support. High above their heads she floated even as Hector Rae landed on the roof above the Trezure Kave and his squads charged down the walkways to the Hall of the Loony Lolly. Then she broke the silence and began chanting again. 'FORGET YOUR NAME!' she cried as she'd cried at King's Cross a week before; amid that escorted bunch of flagellant crazies Rae had thought tagged and harmless. 'FORGET THE GAME! TIME IS SHORT!' she cried, impassioned voice echoing round the Hall of the Loony Lolly as a police squad burst in and stopped dead, staring, as in the CSU op room (7-3 to the Busby Babes now) O'Brien saw that 76-E-678-DEJ was on the move again.

The six on the run reached the southbound Bakerloo platform as a train came in. Uniformed police leapt out and charged past them as Hector Rae, eyes gleaming, mind maddened (*Wild Women tearing him to pieces in a sweet green glade*), ran into the depths, ignoring his phone. Joe O'Brien cursed. Carmody and all other Channel 3 viewers saw what happened next: the trance-like ecstasy on the face of the levitating woman as she cried: 'THE WORLD'S BEEN BOUGHT BY THE BEAST! BUT THE SHINING LIGHT IS COMING TO . . .'

Then the camera swung to the cops. Carmody heard the shrieked order; saw the gun that came up, the flare of fire leaping to halo her in the middle of the air even as Hector Rae reached the Hall of the Loony Lolly and the southbound train departed. For a moment her body jerked, her hair stood on end as the fire ate into her. Then in mid-air she collapsed, she seemed to shrivel, her white robe caught fire, her hair flamed, her face blackened . . . and like a broken rag doll she fell. She was dead before she hit the floor. Then the screaming and the panic began as Rae at last answered the buzzing phone and cried in a congested voice: 'WHAT?'

'They're on the move again!' cried Joe O'Brien, 'Towards Charing . . .'

Rae bellowed with rage. He tasted blood in his mouth. '*Hoel! You're a fool!*' cried the blazing woman in birdfeather robe who stood above him – and an ancient panic seized him as with faces agape about him in the green gloom he turned and started running. 'Come on,' he shouted. 'Quick!'

33.
The Temple

She flew! Agutter told himself, propelled at knife-point into the coach vacated by the cops. Other coaches were full; people heading to Trafalgar Square: this one was empty but for a subdued couple at the far end. In a cold sweat he found himself wedged between Bobbie and Jim, facing Diane, Lionel and Jessica as the train rattled into the tunnel: the mad Scot beside him trembling with murderous tension; Agutter's top hat askew on Bobbie's unruly head; dark eyes burning on Diane who stared through them all.

Dumbfounded, Jessica gazed at Jim. It WAS Jim. She was sure. Her blood told her; her hand in her bag held the belt-buckle he'd left in Death Valley and her tingling fingers confirmed it. So why wouldn't he look at her? He sat sphinx-like and blank, fists clenched so hard the knuckles showed white. *You called me here!* she cried silently, *Here I am! Why won't you talk to me? Jim! What's happening?*

Only Lionel seemed calm, reading a paper he'd found on the seat beside him. POPE CALLS MILLENNIUM CRISIS SUMMIT was the headline.

'Where are we going?' Jessica demanded.

'Charing Cross,' he murmured, not looking up, 'then the Temple.'

'The Temple?' Panic seized her. That fire! She stared at Jim, but still he seemed petrified. 'You mean the . . . round church with stone knights on the floor and weird heads round the wall?' she asked faintly.

Lionel looked surprised. 'You know it?'

'Jim,' she begged, 'What's going on?'

'BART, Ma.' Jim, struggling to speak, found the Californian accent of the boy she'd known. 'Remember? Aunt Mary. Going to . . . Oakland. BART.'

Yes. She *did* remember. One day in 1985 they'd gone to Oakland to see Aunt Mary. Under the Bay on Bay Area Rapid Transit. And he'd screamed and screamed! Staring at him now, she laughed in disbelief. 'All this and you still get claustrophobia?' she whispered, but he said nothing.

'I *insist*,' interrupted the froghead, 'what the hell is . . .'

Bobbie twisted Agutter's arm hard. 'Shut it, frogface!'

'Bobbie,' said Lionel tersely, but Bobbie ignored him.

'See her?' Increasing the pressure, Bobbie made Agutter face Diane. She sat upright, hands limp in her lap, wide-open eyes seeing nothing at all . . . at least in this world. 'That's Diane, an' ye an' yer goons . . .' – suddenly wordless with disgust he spat, adrenalin pumping. He knew that soon he'd go for broke. Ronnie's words rang in him. '. . . *And a' the deid knichts o' the Temple'll be watchin' ye – an' if they like the way ye fecht then soon ye'll join them a' in Valhalla. So mind ye dae it richt this time! It's that Beast ye want – and ye'll ken him fine when ye meet him.*' The Beast? Surely this creep Agutter was the Beast, or the Beast's agent. Angrily eyeing Diane he found his voice again. 'Ye've tortured her wi' yer fookin' worm! *Worm!* Yer the worm . . . an' I'm right sorry I cannae cut ye up an' shove ye back in the earth like ye deserve, ye piece o' shite!'

'It's okay, Bobbie,' said a dreamy voice. He started with shock. It was Diane who spoke; though still she stared through him, through the walls of carriage and tunnel; through the walls of the world itself. 'It's okay,' she repeated, so calm that all of them, even Jim, stared. 'He did as he had to. We need the . . . worm to go through the Gate. Isn't that so . . . Jim?'

Then she retreated back to remoteness, to the shining heights beyond pain where Sam and Chrissa waited. Fearfully Jessica eyed her son.

'It's so,' he muttered. 'It's as Them wants.' He scowled at Agutter. "Im only does as Them wants, if 'im knows it or not.'

With the train slowing down into Piccadilly Circus Agutter laughed in Bobbie's face, pulled off the froghead and cast it away, his face pale and oddly exalted. 'You don't have blood on your hands too?' he demanded. 'I don't need you to kill me. Last night in my sleep I hired a man to do it. Rang him up! He damn near succeeded. If I hadn't slipped in the shit . . .'

The train stopped. The doors opened. People flooded in, many drunk and loud. Lionel scanned the platform. No sign of cops. The doors shut. The train pulled out again. Glaring, Bobbie let go of Agutter's arm.

'Aye,' he admitted roughly, 'So my hands isnae clean. But that disnae mak ye nae hero neither.'

'But what's going on?' Jessica demanded, her heart beating too hard. 'Why did we have to meet in there?'

'Harder to track in a crowd,' said Lionel, 'And . . .'

'But what do They want us to do? Why are we going to the . . .'

'You mean you *don't* know?' Lionel asked.

'I've had enough,' Jessica hissed, 'Guys who vanish, Shasta blowing up, born-again airlines and . . . and . . .' – she stared at Jim – '. . . Jim, I saw you in this Temple place! On fire with a guy called the Doctor watching, and it's all Olde Englande, then . . . here you are . . . I mean I dreamed it, then saw it in a book. Now we're going there. Why?'

'To go UP,' whispered Diane, startling them all with her spooky smile. She pointed up with a trembling finger. 'That's where we're going. UP. You, Jessica, and me and . . . you there . . . Mr Agutter . . . your daughter . . . she went . . . where mine went too. Did she have dreams about the . . . the Cathars?'

'What?' Cold fingers clutched Agutter's heart. 'Yes, she was writing a . . . but how . . . for heaven's sake, TELL ME: WHY US?'

'Why us?' Diane's eyes were wet. 'Because we can bring back those who wish to return,' she whispered. 'Our children! We're the closest to them! But the Beast that rules this world doesn't want us to win! Mr Agutter . . .' – her smile froze him – '. . . you say in your sleep you hired a man to kill you?' She sighed. 'That was the Beast in your heart! I listened to him too – I almost went over a cliff to my death, but Bobbie . . .'

'And I almost drowned!' Jessica stared at her. 'I got drunk and had a bath and . . . something was pushing me under, it must have been me, the death-wish in me – I see that now – and I'd have died, but Pierre Belot . . .'

'Pierre?' Diane whispered, 'He came to you too?'

'You know him?' asked Jessica, spellbound. 'He said he came from . . .'

'The Pays d'Oc,' said Diane, looking up, 'Chrissa met him there.'

Agutter shut his eyes. Sensing the fire ahead, Jessica shivered.

'I still don't see why we have to go through . . . this whatever . . .'

'The Gate,' said her son harshly. 'You must do it, Ma.'

Jessica stared at him. 'But . . . you're coming too . . . aren't you?'

'Yes, Ma,' he said gently, his accent less strange now. He seemed to have beaten off the claustrophobia. He squeezed her hand.

'But . . . what *is* this Gate?' She was terrified. 'This . . . Temple?'

'Ma, there be places, special places, power places, where the walls between the worlds be thin. The Temple be one. It were built by . . .'

Jessica felt sick. The train was jerking, slowing again. Platform lights ahead. Spinning. Faces staring, silent. 'I've got the whirlies!' she groaned, leaning forward. 'I'm sorry, but I'm going to . . .'

An arm hugged her. Dizzy, she met Diane's eyes. They alone were alive in that paper-white face. They burned; reflecting Jessica's own pain and fear. But there was such kindness in them that instantly she felt relief. 'Don't fear,' Diane whispered. 'It's like going to school again. Dear Jessica, they've shown me! It's nothing to fear! We have to learn who we are and . . . how to help them. Your son's been through it! Yes?'

'Only part of it,' said Jim harshly. 'Not as far as some. Not as far as them as calls me 'ere. Not as far as your . . . Sam and Chrissa . . .'

'Can't all do it . . . at once,' Diane whispered, her look embracing the man who'd caused the pain that now crucified her, overloading her nervous system and shifting her out . . . out . . . and up. 'That's why we're going . . . to the Temple. To get to where . . . we can meet them face to face . . . so that . . .'

Then her strength failed and she fainted as the train pulled in.

'Help her!' cried Jessica. Bobbie jumped up . . . and between the two of them they raised her. People were staring. 'Come on,' said Lionel quickly as the doors opened. He felt smaller . . . even jealous of these chosen ones.

'But I still don't see . . .' protested Agutter. Yet he followed amid the crowds flooding off the train, bound for Trafalgar Square and the millennial hour. Briefly he saw the dwarf capering: 'Who sent you, Mr Agutter, eh?'

At the foot of the escalator sat a ragged old violinist, sawing out the last movement of Beethoven's 9th. His playing was awful; his case held enough plastic for a bowl of soup and a doss-house room for the night . . . yet as the six of them neared he eyed them, stopped playing, cased his violin, and came with them . . . and Diane, recovering from her faint, dimly recognised him as the Old Man who'd led the whipping parade at King's Cross.

'. . . TAKE A TAKE A TAKE A CHANCE!'

Crowds surged through the barrier at the top. Police were visible, but not many. Near an exit Lionel told them to wait. The Old Man limped by without looking at them. Thirty seconds later Lionel said: 'Let's go.'

Outside, the Strand was packed. To the east Arianrhod had risen above the rooftops. Agutter's head rang with siren voices. A helicopter hovered above. 'No shite, now!' Bobbie hissed in Agutter's ear as Lionel led them to the cab rank. They stood in line.

'Not this one,' he said, 'Nor this one either . . . okay! Here we are!'

Into the cab behind the unseen driver they climbed. The cab took off up the Strand past Aldwych to the start of Fleet Street. Dark imperial buildings – the Inns of Court – lurked like dinosaurs. Jessica shook: Jim gripped her hand. Bobbie's hand caressed the sword. 'Sure this is guid metal?' he demanded as the cab stopped. But Lionel was peering out up at the hovering helicopter. 'They're on to us,' he said. He eyed Agutter suspiciously. 'How precisely does the worm fix position?' he asked softly.

Agutter shrugged, mouth dry. 'To within a hundred yards.'

'We'll have to be quick, then,' said Lionel as the doors opened.

'Good luck,' whispered the unseen driver as they got out.

Through a covered close Lionel hurried them. Round a corner. Then there before them it loomed in the Arianrhod-bright night.

The Round Church the Knights Templar had built.

Rae was in the chopper, zeroed in by continual updates from O'Brien, Wellington tunic torn open, his heart pounding, sweat pouring off him. It wasn't just that his ground-based squads couldn't get through the packed West End streets; it was those damned eyes in him, glaring at him, laughing at him. *Hoel!* cried his voices, *Poor Hoel! Nobody loves poor Hoel!* Worse still, that damned eye in the sky. He was sure it laughed at him too. But that was impossible. It wasn't there. It was an illusion, a Chancer plot, a sophisticated use of ELF by crazed enemies of society. What they sought was beyond him. He only knew they had to be stopped. And Agutter was one of them? Amazing. Rae had already been onto Fisher at No. 10. 'Philip? That can't be so!' the PM had moaned, before bowing to Rae's demands. *The fool! If only he'd acted tough we wouldn't be in this jam!* Rae was sure of that. He had to be. He had no time for people who weren't sure. Doubt was weakness. Look what had happened to the world since Einstein and Heisenberg and all those German Jews had got people thinking that nothing was sure! Hector Rae shuddered.

'They've stopped, sir,' O'Brien reported. 'They're at the . . . Temple.'

'The Temple?' he bellowed. He was right above it now. 'What the hell are they doing there?'

Not O'Brien nor anyone else dared offer any suggestions. They simply waited. He felt so alone now!

'Where are our boys?' he demanded.

'Caught up in the traffic.' The uneasy Chief Super – Barlow? Jones? – shrugged. 'Maybe we should wait for them to . . .'

'Wait?' roared Hector Rae. 'No, dammit. Pilot. Set down. Quick!'

Even as the chopper settled by the Round Church he saw, perfectly lit by the light of what didn't exist, a figure guarding the South Door. And more. From the Temple's clerestory windows a weird silver glow pulsed. As soon as he saw it, pain blinded him. He groaned and bit his lip.

'Sir? What is it?'

Rae knew what it was, but he refused to admit it.

'Your gun, man!' he gasped, fists clenched. 'Give it to me!'

'Sir, I'm not carrying a gun,' the Chief Superintendent told him.

'Bloody fool! Who's got a gun?' He glared through the starlit cabin. His bulging eyes said he'd gone barmy. But who wasn't barmy tonight? Nobody. The phones had rung. The screens had been hijacked. And being barmy was no crime – not if you were the Law – and Hector Rae was the Law.

'Here, sir.' A shadowy Detective Sergeant handed over his Walther.

Hot and feverish, Rae snatched it, worked the action, flipped off the safety. As someone threw open the door he fired a shot into the night. Up at that shining light. Just to check. *Yes, Hoel!*

Just to check. But as he jumped down to the ground eyes met eyes and the Chief Super shrugged.

Through the clerestory windows the strange glow was increasing.

'Come on!' he roared, turning briefly to wave them after him. 'They've got one of their transmitters in here!'

Then he charged the door where Bobbie Aird waited, Arianrhod's silver light mocking him, driving him on as he ran without thought, ran to embrace the same ancient fate . . . yet again . . .

'*Hoel!*' hissed Her voice, '*You fool! Won't you ever learn?*'

He heard. But the answer was no. How could he heed what he couldn't believe? How could he stop? For he saw blue eyes and golden hair; he saw She who'd killed him twice already, in other places, other times. Modern London blurred and faded; and it was a spear he held, not a gun.

'Father, give me strength to aim true!' he screamed, charging Bobbie Aird, charging through a sweet green glade. 'One strike for two lives!'

. . . as high above Arianrhod whirled, masked in light . . . watching him . . .

34.
In the Whirling Castle

Sergei Bilibin and Marie Nelli dreamed . . . and they watched.

'*Freude! Freude! Freude, schöner Götterfunken* . . .' Klaus Micus had wailed – then the fire had consumed them; hurled them into soul-abysses where gods and demons ravished them. From the flash of Clear Light down to the blood-depths they'd plunged, not knowing what had happened, for neither belonged to a culture that knew. They had no Books of the Dead to say what lay beyond the world they'd left behind. Like fish scooped from a tank they learned too late that the tank was not the universe. Yet as they strangled and floundered into Arianrhod, they were helped – helped like fish netted and thrown into an oxygen-rich pond.

Bilibin and Marie Nelli alone survived. They survived because neither believed the descriptions by which the world explained itself. The others on the *Gogol* did, and died in fear on entering Arianrhod. Only later did Bilibin and Marie Nelli learn not only that the *Jefferson* had vaporised when Bill Dodd had tried to blow out the Mystery that birthed him, but that the rest of the *Gogol*'s crew were dead too. Yet Derebin, Kuchinikov and Klaus Micus had all entered Arianrhod alive, entered a mystery permitting biological survival – given flexible reaction to the Unknown. But none of them made it. Their imaginations failed them. They could not cope. Micus died first, screaming Schiller's *Ode to Joy*, doing so because (all unknown) that's what he chose. Chose because surely that flaming light consuming him was God, who did not exist. His intellect signed his death-warrant. What he experienced did not exist, thus he could not exist. And so Micus, by his own intellectual design, was quickly, cleanly, logically dead.

That was his own triumph. To embrace eternity as fast as the crew of the *Jefferson*, who had no chance. Bill Dodd saw to that when he obeyed his generals and pressed the button. Whoever and whatever they might have been or done, they were instantly gone. . . .

As for Derebin, he died for his belief in myth. His heart failed when (not unlike Micus) he saw, before him in the Light, the . . . Staring Goddess. *Ishtar!* Her eyes consumed him and he died. In ecstasy. But he died.

Kuchinikov met an old drunk in the gutter; a drunk called Stalin. He cursed that drunk for murdering his grandfather then walked happily on down the shining street – and never knew it when he was stabbed in the back. He died bitterly cursing his nation's history.

And Marie Nelli and Sergei Ivanovich?

It was in a room within the maze behind the mask of Arianrhod that they awoke to a situation both awesomely strange yet . . . oddly familiar.

Yet before they knew themselves again, they dreamed, and perhaps it was the dreaming that let them make the transition.

What they dreamed was this:

Through the blinding light on wings of fire they fly hand-in-hand (Why? They barely even know each other) through gates that clang shut behind them and hurl them on past agitated stars, until abruptly they're plunged into a deep ocean world circling (How do they know it?) a dark star of the Sirius system. Entering this ocean their bodies change, growing sleek and smooth. Down through shining deeps they swim, past vast gleaming grey forms that dance before them. Who are you? they ask, wondering, both as one.

The answer comes: WE WATCH YOUR WORLD.

What do you want? Why are we here?

LISTEN NOW. WATCH. AND LEARN.

Then the Great Grey Ones tell them: We Elohim set the Whirling Castle above your world as a way-station. Here we put on the dense bodies that let us walk among you. But when we left, you Lullu forgot us, and lost sight of our station. For generations none saw it. The Beast who was once one of us kept your world in darkness. Now he hopes to destroy it, winning the oblivion he desires. It is a sign of the Shift's approach that again you see what for so long you forgot. But we cannot help you now. You must help yourselves. Your world is a trial; many wish to end the project.

What project? How can you . . . ?

LISTEN. HEAR HOW COUNCIL DISCUSSES YOUR WORLD.

Then they see how amid the dance of the Great Grey Ones those who wish to end the Hidden World Project are clearly in the majority.

Admit it! their speakers demand. We are all ultimately subject to the Law of Economy. We cannot bear the cost of this war. Too many minds have been corrupted. Too much has been lost. If the Lullu cannot drive out the Beast themselves, let Azazel have them.

But that's not fair! Bilibin cries hotly in his dream.

WAIT! HEAR HOW THOSE FROM YOUR WORLD WHO LIVE AMONG US ARGUE!

Then they see amid the dance many great-souled human beings who since the last Shift (a vision of flood and fire, the world turned upside down) have made their way through the higher gates. Like fireflies in the ocean they dance before the wall of pink and yellow coral in which is set the Emerald Gate. Through it, in the depths below the space-and-time twisting of the Sinking Ways, they see the threatened world, furious clouds rolling about it; the Beast's ever-shifting image squatting on it as the Shift begins and its fabric begins to tear. And they hear the human cry:

One more chance! Let us go back and try again!

But the dance of the conservatives is sceptical:

– Why waste more energy with so much wasted already?

One more chance! That's all! Reactivate the platform. We'll give up the subtle body to fight this war. You know we're not all rotten! Why abandon a world just because it causes you trouble? Do you want children who simply bow down and agree with all you've already decided?

Council seems moved. The dance speaks of willingness to listen. But still the conservatives hold sway.

— But we've been through this! How often has the Hidden World endured the Shift without waking up? How often has Fire and Flood necessarily wiped out bestiality before it bursts up the Sinking Ways to corrupt us all? Is it any better now? Children, we sympathise, but we cannot continue a Work that lets Evil grow stronger. Surely you understand?

Yes! Yes! Yes! But our world! Our families!

— The Beast loves such argument. If we accepted your attitude we'd be bailing out every damned cinder-ball between here and . . .

Do you willingly lose our world? the Flaming One who leads the Lullu demands. Where's your courage? You've had it easy so long you forget that Good needs Evil to sharpen and define it! The Beast in us came from you when you changed us! So we're still children — but the world you've cared for so long is worth another chance! Whatever you say, we're going back!

Then Council enters discussion and reaches a verdict which, though the conservatives grumble about weak-minded sentimentality, all agree.

— Very well! Enter madness again! Reactivate the platform. But find help from those you left behind. This is your last chance. Wake up your world now — or die with it.

Then Sergei Bilibin and Marie Nelli see the Company of great souls turn to the two of them. Are you with us? the Flaming One asks, Or will you stay here with the Elohim while our world hangs in the balance?

Even as they give their answer a vortex opens below them. There is huge pain, a sense of dizzy vertigo and weight, and a crushing sensation of loss, as if they are falling from light to eternal night.

They forgot. But not entirely.

Suddenly they're heavy in their bodies again, stretched out on their backs in pain, in a room of unsure colour and dimension.

An old man stands before them, hawknosed and desert-dark. Behind him stand other, vaguer figures — a woman with corngold hair, a man with a cynical face, another man who looks like he'd slept in a haystack, another woman who . . . in fact a multitude of glimmering, semi-formed figures.

Who are you? Bilibin asks in bewilderment.

'I am Khufu,' the old man said.

Slowly Bilibin realised he lay on a hard floor. Groaning, Marie Nelli stirred, her head pounding as if she'd been struck. Neither of them knew what had happened; time passed before it grew clear to them that the voice they'd dreamed was a real voice, and that its owner spoke to them now:

'I am Khufu,' they heard, 'with you in the Whirling Castle, our house below the Sinking Ways over the Hidden World. Here we exchange the subtle body for the dense form that lets us walk on Earth. The Law is: Do as you would be done by. Who destroys is destroyed. Those who live in fear die in fear. Those who build are built up. So you live. So the others died. So we return. But we need your help.'

Bilibin blinked, trying to focus. Shapes came and went. He seemed to be in a small round room. It was warm. Beside him he made out the prone form of Marie Nelli. Her eyes were shut. She was rubbing her brow. He thought she was beautiful. He remembered a shining ocean. He remembered a great Council. He remembered a journey.

Remembering something, someone else, he looked up.

Above him, blurred, stood a spectral, shining figure.

'A cruel law,' Sergei Ivanovich heard himself whisper.

Khufu shrugged. 'The Law is the Law.' His voice echoed in Bilibin's head, 'Curses strike those who curse. The Shift is close. If we cannot alert you to help us uncurse this world, then the Beast has won.'

Bilibin raised himself painfully up on his hands.

'Are you really there?' he whispered, 'Or am I just . . .'

'We are here,' said Khufu. Humorously the old man gestured at the vague ranks of those who waited behind him. 'But none of us can walk the world. Not yet. We need your help. Do you remember your dream?'

Marie Nelli opened wide, frightened, perplexed eyes. She too saw the shimmering figures before them. She eyed Bilibin questioningly.

Bilibin shrugged and shook his head.

'How do you mean?' he asked, 'Help you.'

'Look,' said Khufu, pointing behind them, and as he did the wall behind them seemed to . . . dissolve, to corkscrew into a whirling tunnel filled with smoky silver light. At the far end of this tunnel, as if seen through the wrong end of a telescope, tiny human forms played out a strange drama.

'Look,' the apparition repeated.

Struggling to his feet, fighting dizziness and the sense that surely he was dead, no longer himself, Sergei Ivanovich Bilibin looked . . . and saw . . .

Near midnight they entered the silent Temple. Arianrhod shone through stained glass above the east altar, through the clerestory windows of the Temple Round in the west. Above, the roar of the police chopper said there was no time to waste. Lionel had opened the South Door with his purloined key. Leaving Bobbie ready outside, he stood under a heavy Norman arch, one eye on Bobbie, the other on Jim who quickly, using a flashlight, chalked a five-pointed star on the flagstones at the centre of the Round. Beside him Diane stood on a World War II memorial plaque amid a pool of Arianrhod's light. It rendered her ghost-like, singing in her mind: she was trembling as she endured these last agonising seconds. Near her the stone effigies of long-dead knights lay prone, some with hounds at their feet. Her eyes filled with tears. In her pain she felt as if only the inconvenient weight of her body kept her from lifting entirely off the ground up to the source of that silver light . . . up to the suns so far behind it, beyond the Sinking Ways. She didn't know she was in the Temple, or even in London. She was elsewhere and elsewhen. Flying the Sinking Ways with Chrissa. Seeing brilliant, violent things that tore at her mind. A tall woman in a robe of bird-feathers, stalking an underground place. Hundreds of subtle bodies soaring from an inferno where pain consumed itself. Moaning, she shook like a leaf, for the thing crawling in her brain was eating her alive: she had so little body left; all she awaited now was the end.

'Dear Chrissa,' she whispered, 'Chrissa . . . are you ready for us?' And in the silver light that poured through the clerestory windows and lit up her face she saw a smiling, wraith-like face. '*Yes, Mum,*' she heard, '*Yes, you're about to join us and bring us back! Just a little longer.*'

Beside her Jessica eyed Philip Agutter in a horror he shared. Both felt frozen in a nightmare which, like a continually-rising tide, would never stop rising until it had swept them entirely away – a tide from their depths; a force which had always been there in them, deprived and subdued by society, and all the more potent now that it erupted without warning or defence against it. Yet it had always been known: the knowledge of it was blatantly visible in the terrified grimaces of the grotesque stone heads in their cold purgatorial niches all about.

This is what Dante described, Agutter thought, now in a state of dreamy wonderment that made independent action impossible. *Is this how you feel when sentence is pronounced and you're about to be shot?*

For though he was terrified he felt no fear. He felt nothing familiar at all. His wounded shoulder throbbed, but that hardly mattered. For the terror was as pure as the light flooding the windows above. It possessed him but he did not possess it. The universe watched him: he knew he had no defence. All he had from the familiar world were his images and memories of Gillian, and the sense that somehow she was with him, waiting for him.

Jessica no longer knew where or who she was: she thought maybe she was still in Nome Valley that night Shasta blew, following Coyote through the woods up to the rocky seat where old Taikomol brooded on a world which had lost its heart . . . watching Coyote turn into Egyptian Anubis . . . watching the bright star suddenly JUMP; watching the shimmering rivers of fire hiss over the heavens even as Jim's transformed face appeared before her; Jim's face blazing as he stood here in this place where –

'. . . *At the Templar Round . . . at midnight . . . tonight, like . . .*'

But the blaze was so bright that she could not see who . . .

Vaguely she heard the chattering roar above grow louder.

'Ma . . .' – Jim took her arm and she flinched – '. . . Come, now.'

In a tremulous voice Diane said to the terrified pair:

'Come on, both of you. They can't wait any longer.'

With the sense of watching himself enact some absurd and awful ritual Agutter joined the other three within the five-pointed star. He felt the 20th century slipping away from him. He felt his reason die. He felt the ghosts of Paracelsus and Nostradamus and Cornelius Agrippa there beside him as Jim made them wrap their arms round each other's shoulders . . . and then Jim cried out, his voice echoing out through the pillared Temple Round:

'Good Doctor. Dost thou hear me? What thy good angels have commanded is done! So send us on the paths that lead from Malkuth to Tiphareth and even to Kether the Crown and Shining Light; send thy guardians to protect us on our journey from this sphere; bring us safe to those that call us forth . . . in the Name of Adonai and Enoch; in the Name of the Elohim!'

Then Philip Agutter heard no more words; only the singing of the siren voices and the throbbing of his heart; all he saw and felt was the burning fire of their transformation . . . first a heat in his bones, and then, bit by bit, a terrible agony that tore him apart . . . and the last he heard was Diane Joyce cry out, and the last he knew was what it was like to carry that worm in the brain . . . and there was a frightful humour in the knowing: that the worm had always been there, in everyone – it was a condition of existence in the Hidden World; technology had only rationalised it into new areas of frightfulness. And in the agony that seized him as the siren song flooded him he bit through his lower lip and never knew it as Jessica screamed – but her scream quickly turned into an odd warble, for it seemed that a hand of fire had clutched her throat . . . a hand that had reached up from her own gut. Then she knew, and Agutter learned what Diane and Jim already knew –

the fire that took them came from themselves; a spontaneous combustion which all the ritual preparations like five-pointed stars did no more than focus.

It was not from outside them at all.

It had been there all along.

It was a natural power of the Earth-born, star-born human mind.

And Arianrhod shone down as they fled up the path of its silver light; and Lionel under the archway watched, breathing hard as the transformation began, amazed to find that he had an erection. But why be surprised? What more natural than that the fire was Eros itself? Yet it was hard to bear. It was hard to stand and watch it, to be left behind so cold and lonely. He felt like a voyeur of some vast act of cosmic lovemaking as he watched. He felt like a 20th century fool for being able to watch at all; for being so capable of rationally defining what he saw . . . even as the chattering roar of the descending police helicopter filled the sky above.

But the Light! The Light!

For first he saw that Diane seemed to elongate, as if her body was being stretched and pulled up the path of the silver fire that fell from Arianrhod . . . and then somehow the four of them merged into a weird twisting upward movement that . . .

Something lurched in his mind. Something he couldn't handle. To know it would be to die. His gorge rose. He turned away and staggered through the South Door, locking it clumsily behind him and joining Bobbie Aird even as the helicopter landed on the open space on the south side of the Temple.

He threw up violently. It felt like he was throwing up his life.

Then through tear-blurred eyes he met Bobbie's gaze and saw that Bobbie too was gone, though not in the same way as the four inside.

For Bobbie had cast aside cape and top hat, the steel bonnet was on his head and the round targe on his left forearm; the philibeg was thrown back over his left shoulder; he waited in a crouch with the sword gripped two-handed before him. He looked a dead ringer for the Hollywood version of Rob Roy, and Lionel, madly, was tempted to laugh, but –

Bobbie's eyes. They were like twin burning pits, smouldering fires that competed with the silvery blaze in the sky and the other fire glowing through the clerestory windows of the Temple Round above them. Chilled, for a moment Lionel feared Bobbie no longer knew him, was about to . . .

'Bobbie,' he said, a quaver in his voice, 'They're away . . . they're . . .'

Grinning mirthlessly, Bobbie Aird acknowledged him.

'Then get away yersel', ye stupid bastard. Ye've done yer bit. Now let me dae mine!' And when Lionel didn't move, Bobbie grabbed him and shook him. 'Go on!' Bobbie cried hoarsely, 'Back tae yer wife an' bairns. Go on, Lionel! Ye dinnae wantae die an idjit like Bobbie Aird, eh? So fook aff! Go on! Run, man! Live tae fecht anither fookin' day!'

Turning away, he pushed Lionel violently towards safe shadows.

The light from the clerestory windows pulsed brighter still as a big man in the dress uniform of a 19th century English general appeared at the helicopter's hatch brandishing a pistol which, insanely, he pointed and fired up at Arianrhod the instant before he leapt down to the ground.

'Come on,' Lionel heard the lunatic roar to his men in the helicopter behind him, 'They've got one of their transmitters in here!'

That's Rae! Lionel realised as he saw the Commissioner charge at Bobbie Aird, who waited for him. But nobody followed Rae from the chopper.

'Father, give me strength to aim true!' Rae howled, pointing the pistol as he came, 'One strike for two lives!'

Lionel couldn't know it, but the man who charged was no longer Hector Rae, but another man long ago, called Hoel, and he was leaping into a sweet green glade, spear upraised, meaning to kill the naked loving couple before him on the grass . . . but even as he charged, Bobbie bellowed with laughter.

For Bobbie too was elsewhere and elsewhen; up on Arthur's Seat again, jumping down to the path where Diane struggled with the Beast-wind, with the slit-throated blue ghost of David Riccio.

'So here ye are, ye Beast, ye Lord of Illusion, ye bastard Watcher!' the Knight of the Purple Heather bellowed, braced with back to the locked South Door of the Temple, sword raised, glaring at the charging man and meaning to make one strike do it all . . . but as Hector Rae closed with him Lionel heard a shot, then a second, and a third . . .

Forgetting his own safety, he ran back to see –

All three shots, fired at close range, struck Bobbie Aird.

Lionel's armour deflected the first two. One made Bobbie stagger, and spanged away off the steel breastplate; the second pierced his shield and struck his shoulder plate, spinning him half round as Rae fired a third shot from less than six feet away . . . and this time the armour didn't help.

The bullet struck Bobbie under the right arm-pit. Lionel heard him cry out in fury, saw him stagger . . . then, bared teeth gleaming in Arianrhod's light as the fire in the Temple windows grew dazzling, sending out shafts that lit the roofs and upper storeys of the elegant Georgian buildings about, Bobbie blew blood out of his mouth and raised the sword and with all his strength swung it in a flat, hard arc.

The blow was perfectly timed.

Or maybe it was just that Hector Rae ran into it.

Whichever, it worked better than the blow Bobbie had struck on Arthur's Seat eleven nights earlier. It caught the Commissioner's neck just above his braided scarlet collar, and sliced through as clean as a whistle.

Panting, Bobbie lowered the sword.

Hector Rae stared at him.

Blood filled his mouth.

His eyes bulged. He dropped the Walther.

'Not . . . ag . . . ain . . .' he started to whisper in disbelief –

Then, like an ungainly ball, his severed head tilted and rolled off his neck, bouncing heavily onto his right shoulder before falling to hit the concrete with a dull thud. But, saw Bobbie as blood flooded his own mouth, life remained in those bulging eyes. He looked down and grinned as Hector Rae's eyes stared incredulously up at their body still standing above them.

The lips blew blood . . . then those furious, amazed, aggrieved eyes glazed and grew dull. Rae's body crumpled from the knees and fell with a crash, to twitch and jerk a second longer before lying still at Bobbie's feet.

Then Bobbie Aird bellowed a blood-strangled roar of triumph. Dropping the sword he clutched his chest and bent. He picked up Hector Rae's head by the hair, turned stiffly to the Temple Round, (from which the weird light was now fading), and heaved the head up against one of the windows.

'Here's anither heid fer yer collection!' he croaked as blood burst from his mouth, as Hector Rae's head bounced off a window and rolled into shadows. 'Now take me . . . tae . . . Valhalla wi' ye!' Lionel heard Bobbie rasp as he swayed on his feet. 'Did ye . . . see it . . . Ronnie? Did ye . . . see it . . .?'

Then like a felled tree Bobbie crashed to the ground, falling over the body of Hector Rae alias Brother Jean d'Aubigny alias Hoel.

He heaved a giant, contented sigh.

Then he rattled and lay still.

There was a long silence.

Lionel stared. The helicopter crew stared. The clerestory windows were dark again. But Arianrhod still shone from the night sky as from Fleet Street came the wail of approaching sirens.

'TAKE A . . . TAKE A . . . TAKE A TAKE A TAKE A CHANCE!'

And Lionel slipped away into the night . . . even as Big Ben began to sound the chimes of midnight . . . the chimes of the new millennium . . .

And he looked up at Arianrhod and laughed . . .

35.
The Masks of Arianrhod

A dream within a dream within a dream . . .

After the terror there's no fear or pain or thought.

First the fire, then a song singing ever higher, then lightning motion up a long dark tunnel to a grid of shining strands that intersect in knots vibrating with a pure cold energy. It's blinding, this grid, and briefly there's fear again, fear of an awful barrier beyond which nothing familiar lies; of desire for the world left behind – then: CONTACT! TRANSFORMATION! CONVERSION! *And it's done, like that! – chrysalis discarded; the released one entering the formless, dimensionless, egoless realms beyond the Hidden World, above the Sinking Ways. And first is a sense, not of strangeness or alienation, but of utter familiarity.* I'VE BEEN HERE BEFORE! I'VE ALWAYS BEEN HERE! *Then, chagrin; chagrin at long wasted years of blind cowardly refusal to embrace the still small voice of the soul for fear of the death of what it had called its 'self'. And then it sees the black self-imposed joke. For this process is not soul-death but the stripping of the mask of personality's false mask; the joining of the great dance . . . and now with deeper chagrin it remembers that blinding river of light it had seen (in some other sadder, heavier realm) pouring into this blazing void from a gate so bright it hadn't been possible to face it.* 'WE ARE THE COMPANY OF THOSE WHO RETURN TO TIME FOR THE SHIFT! BUT WE CANNOT TAKE FORM

IF YOU WON'T HELP US!' It remembers that heart-beat voice and realises: Now I'm part of the Dance! Part of the Company! I always belonged here!

Yet still that awful regret that it let the mask blind it so long.

I failed, it tells itself, I . . .

– Don't despise the mask, advises the little voice. In the Hidden World our masks are like clothes; protection against the weather, like egg-shells before the bird bursts free. Are you ready for the truth now?

Yes! Yes, yes, I'm ready! cries the released one . . . then to be shocked as the small voice calmly insists:

– Good. For you can't stay here. You have work to do. You must help us return in the flesh. We can't do anything unless you go back.

Go back? I don't want to go back! Go back to . . . THAT?

A scream. Looking dizzily down in horror at the Hidden World below; at a charnel-heap of tears, impermanence, pain and loss. A sense of acute claustrophobia, of being shut up in an awful subterranean place where no light penetrates the slow eternity of bloody fires and massacres. And the voices and scenes from long years of a well-lost life all clash together amid a din of banality and self-accusation –

'. . . I mean, lately he's been really difficult. He's hardly ever home and when he is his mind's somewhere else.' –

'. . . The truth is you just want to run away again! You won't remove that ring because you don't want to face the world!' –

'. . . Chrissa! Stop it! You're talking to thin air!' –

'. . . Mum? Mum? Can you see me? This is Chrissa!' –

'. . . No! I've seen enough! I've had enough! I don't want any more! Why don't you both go away and leave me alone?'

'. . . She called it betrayal. We got a lecture on loyalty from Iain when she found out you'd changed your number.'–

'. . . I've been having the most awful nightmares – you know I lost my husband and daughter years ago but it still seems like yesterday and . . .'

'. . . taking us now to Northern California for a further update on the catastrophic eruption of . . .'

And more of it, much more of it, a million movies all playing at once, each distinct and horrible; and amid them all a mouth screaming, a wailing round O as black as the maw of the pain-flooded Hidden World below where the Beast squats laughing, fed by pain and despair –

TOO MUCH! TOO MUCH TO BEAR! BEAST-BABBLE! YOU CAN'T SEND ME BACK!

Struggling against invisible bonds wrapping tighter; fighting the foul weight and darkness; tears streaming down a universal face –

I WON'T GO BACK TO THAT! I REFUSE! I . . .

But amid the panic the little voice speaks again:

– None of us want to go back. But we must. Would you condemn children to darkness and unbirth? Do you want the Beast to win?

No, but . . . what can I do . . . ?

– You can remember this. You can bring it back with you.

But . . . but must I go back so soon? Can't I . . . ?

– You're already going back. Don't you feel it pulling you back?

She can. She can feel the thickness and weight of her body again. She knows her name. HER name. Diane. Diane Emily Joyce. She groans. But . . .

I'm damned if I'll go back! How can you trick me like this?

– There's no trick. You go back by your own choice, as do we all.

But I don't choose it! How could I?

– You do. If you didn't you wouldn't be arguing like this.

But I only just got here! she thought, dull and aggrieved.

– You've always been here, the little voice said softly.

But . . . but why bring us here just to send us back?

– It's the same for all of us. We're all going home. Back to THAT!

Back to that! Diane agreed dully, dizzy and sickened as the dark smoky turmoil of the Hidden World below fastened its hooks of forgetfulness and pain into her again . . . and that turmoil seemed many times more horrible now for having been so briefly escaped. She groaned.

– Do you think we like it? It's frightful. Yet we must go down . . . but we cannot if you won't remember your part in this.

What part? Part in what? I chose no part!

– Diane, we cannot return without your help.

Who are you? Diane shrieked. I DEMAND to know!

– Diane, you already know who we are.

'Yes,' Diane admitted dully, the blissful light fading. And with the

sense of eternity lost she added, with the sigh of a woman coming home from a night out to find the sink full of unwashed dishes, 'I do. So what now?'

– This! said the little voice that was Chrissa's, was Sam's, was her own . . . the little voice of hope through which the entire Company spoke . . .

There was a roaring, a sudden sense of physical tumult. It was like being hurled down rapids, torn to pieces by wild beasts.

There was heaviness, pain, pulsation, despair . . .

Moaning, Diane found herself sprawled on a hard floor, her body aching, her head throbbing, but . . . it was an ordinary headache.

The worm was gone.

That was the first thing she realised.

Her eyelids felt like steel shutters bolted down. Blind and crawling, she felt about her. She felt her naked body. With trembling fingers she touched her face, her legs, her arms, her . . . She felt something on a finger on her left hand. Wonderingly she forced open her eyes – and saw it –

The ring.

The bronze ring with the emerald set in it, set in a raised boss, the strange bronze sigil of moon and horns set in the emerald's topmost facet.

The ring that Sam once wore, and Chrissa too; the ring that had taken them through the Gate . . . the ring that in her despair she'd thrown away into the Fairy Lochs at Gairloch nearly fifteen years ago.

Staring into its dizzy green depths she wanted to give way to hysteria. Her first impulse was to tear it off her finger and hurl it away. It had caused so much pain! She loathed it! Yet now, not wanting to, she found herself caught by its dizzy green depths, looking down into . . .

Fury seized her. She wrenched at it, she . . .

'No!' a quiet, sharp voice insisted. 'Wear it! You must! Or you'll never be able to lead us down again.'

Diane looked up to see the vague, shining figure of a tall young woman with hair the colour of ripe wheat; and behind

Chrissa floated a multitude of other spectral human forms, as insubstantial as dream-beings who did not yet belong to the waking world of shape, weight and density. In her very perception of them Diane felt caught between sleep and waking, and though part of her wanted to see them more plainly, another part did not – yet.

'Who said I want to lead you down again?' she asked harshly.

There was no reply. Now the shining figures seemed no more than a trick of the light. The ring, throbbing on her finger, drew her to more prosaic things. She realised she lay on the floor of a small round room. She was not alone. Numbly she counted five other – people? Yes, real people. *Solid* people. Three she recognised. She saw Agutter unconscious beside her, face waxen and twisted. She saw Jim Bright sit up, helping his mother, Jessica, who was groaning as she floundered back to consciousness.

And there were two others – *human* beings – who squatted, watching her.

One a woman, thirtyish, with cropped hair, a Mediterranean complexion, and a nervous, intelligent look. The other a man, fortyish, with refined features, dark eyes, a high forehead, and a look as uneasy as the woman's.

Both wore astronaut coveralls. On the man's chest, the USSR's hammer-and-sickle insignia. On the woman's was the French cockerel.

Diane stared at them. Shook her head to make them vanish. But they stayed. They eyed each other. The man sighed.

'Welcome to the Mystery,' he said in accented English. 'I am Sergei Ivanovich Bilibin, lately pilot of the *Gogol*. We have been put in here by the . . . the . . .' – he shrugged wryly up at the vague, shifting light-forms – '. . . The *Company*. My friend here is . . .'

'Marie Nelli.' The woman laughed shakily. 'Professeur d'Anthropologie, Université de Toulouse.'

'Oh,' said Diane faintly. 'But what . . . but who . . .?'

'We have been asked,' said Bilibin with heavy stress on the *asked*, 'to welcome and . . . reassure you.' Struggling with his

English, he eyed Marie Nelli. But she seemed even more at a loss. 'We have been *asked* by those who rule this place to say that . . . that . . .'

Again he turned to Marie Nelli who, with a scared grimace, said:

'Ils sont nos amis.' Dubiously she smiled at Diane. 'Hi!'

'Where are we?' Diane asked bluntly. 'And who are you?'

Bilibin made a face. It said: *We'd like to know that too.*

'They want us to stay here. They say many will come soon . . . friends, mothers, fathers of people in the Company, to lead them all down through gates into the world, and we must stay here to . . . interpret . . .?

Diane sighed. 'We're your first customers?'

'Yes!' Bilibin's fingers knotted tight together. 'We have . . . a job to do. We have seen what they are. We think they are . . . good?' Screwing his eyes shut in agony at the difficulty of translating not only language but intention he added: 'They say now many will come from above and from below – meeting from Sirius, and our world, and we must tell them that . . .'

Again in despair he looked to Marie Nelli – '. . . What must we say?'

'Merde!' Marie Nelli cried. 'Je suis fou! Je ne sais RIEN!'

'Me too,' Diane said. She stared into the ring's dizzy emerald depths. Anger seized her. She stood up and cried:

'Sam! Chrissa! Stop playing with us! Show yourselves!'

'Mrs Joyce!' The voice came from behind her.

Gasping, she swung round. As she did she saw Jim Bright do likewise.

Together they stared up at the hawk-nosed old man who eyed them as if they were stupid children. His edges flickered smokily, he wasn't quite solid, but the light in his eyes was hard to face.

'Who's that?' Jessica whispered, awestruck as she awoke.

At least it's not just me! Diane told herself grimly.

'Who are you?' she demanded, the ring burning her finger.

'I am Khufu,' he said, unsmiling . . . at which Agutter sat up.

Diane didn't notice that. 'Your lips didn't move when you said that,' she said carefully. 'But . . . who . . . I mean, are you one of the . . .?'

'Khufu?' Agutter's laugh was a moan. 'He built the Great Pyramid.' And suddenly he was up on his feet. 'Where's Gillian, you bastard?'

Trembling, Diane looked down from Khufu to Agutter.

'You know who he is? You know where we are?'

'But I saw him on tv!' said Jessica shaking like a leaf as she stared up at the apparition that called itself Khufu.

'If it was really you on that bloody tape,' Agutter interrupted in a violent voice, 'then you can tell me where Gill . . .'

'Where are we?' Diane demanded again, twisting the ring on her finger, her voice rising. 'What's going on? I heard Chrissa – where is she?'

'Why do we have to go back?' Jessica chimed in.

'Come on, Ma,' Jim scolded her softly. 'Do not forget so easy!'

Khufu waited, smiling faintly as Bilibin interrupted all of them:

'We are in orbit,' he said flatly, 'between nine thousand and thirty-five thousand kilometers above the world. The . . .' – he paused – '. . . poor *Hidden* World. Our home, my friends. Our home!' He laughed unhappily.

They all stared at him. Agutter said:

'You mean we're *in Arianrhod*?'

Bilibin said patiently, 'We are in the satellite that appeared a week ago. Mademoiselle Nelli and I were on the *Gogol*, sent to examine it. The rest of our crew is dead. The Americans who came too are dead. They tried to destroy.' He smiled wanly. 'We have seen strange things. This Khufu is among those who now return because catastrophe comes. He has shown to us how you come here from . . . London. It is our task to help them back into bodies to the world to fight the . . . the Beast. They want our help, to . . .' – he sought the English word – '. . . to *earth* them.'

'It is so.' Khufu smiled. Diane wanted to pinch him to see if he was really there. 'Yes,' he said, 'I am here. So are you. But I am only one of many from all the world's ages in the Company. You are six among many from these Last Days. I use energy we have gathered from your belief in us and have taken on this task because . . . you will see soon . . .'

'But it's all on that bloody tape!' cried Agutter.

'You are correct, Mr Agutter,' said Khufu.

'So John Robinson really did see you!'

'We showed ourselves to him.' Again that dry spectral smile. 'We tried to deliver a message which we hoped might help.'

Agutter scowled. 'I gave it to Carmody Cee,' he said.

'Fortunately you did not,' Khufu told him.

Agutter gaped at him. 'But I . . .'

Khufu smiled. And in that smile Agutter saw himself at home in Sussex, sleep-walking, not only calling the Loving Death-Bringer but also, with great care, placing the tape seized from Radio Shangri-La in his reel-to-reel . . . and wiping it out entirely, leaving only blankness.

'But . . . but . . .' – and he scowled, and shrugged, and –

'Look,' said Khufu, still smiling as he turned, lifting a hand –

The wall of the tiny round room seemed to dissolve. They were looking down a whirling tunnel . . . into the world . . . to see . . .

Carmody was arrested when he entered the Channel 3 centre next day. The tape in his pocket was seized. But later he was released . . . not just because of his lawyer and his connections . . . but because the tape was blank.

No evidence. No proof. Nothing subversive in a blank tape.

'We'll play it,' he told Joe Daniels as they set up the New Year Show.

'But it's blank,' the producer said. 'What the hell are you . . .?'

'We'll play it,' said Carmody, grinning.

And on his show that night he did.

And the world heard . . .

'But how do you control all this?' demanded Philip Agutter.

Khufu sighed and said slowly, like a teacher to his class:

'We humans are limited. We believe what we see, and deny what we do not. Here we are in a device that some call Arianrhod.

It is a refractive resonator of energy fields still denied by Last Days science. It unifies electromagnetism and gravity, and creates what Einstein, our brother from your age, spent his life trying to discover. But he worked in the Hidden World, which is Plato's Cave. He could not proceed beyond the theory – an old problem. Yet millenia ago we who then lived on Earth had advantages. We were visited openly! The Elohim descended in visible form. This is the platform – Arianrhod! – that they used as the transitional medium. We had the chance to *See*! Yet the gift was two-faced. Not only could few of us appreciate it, but with the Knowledge came the Beast. Worse still, the Elohim are not gods. It is 6,000 years since the pain of a star that blew up – faraway and long ago – struck our world so fiercely that the Elohim left, and have never – openly – returned.'

He shrugged. 'The Elohim too are subject to the Law. They cannot rule the activity of the stars. That power lies Above. Like us they are limited. The evil that comes from knowledge of life is in them too: they don't want to fight for our world any more. We must do it ourselves. For we Lullu that they bred so long ago have caused them trouble: trouble they deserved, by developing us. We are a pain in the arse to them – full of potential, yet refusing to accept their wisdom on trust. This some see as the Beast's perversity. Myself I think it a fine quality – if harnessed. And so here we are, in this device that converts us from high to low, low to high. The conversion occurs with our conscious co-operation, or it works willy-nilly on our unknown depths, leaving us angry and confused and . . .'

He paused, sensing dissatisfaction.

Agutter eyeing Bilibin, Diane eyeing Jessica.

'What's the matter?' Khufu asked with a tinge of irony.

'Are we here just for the lecture?' asked Philip Agutter.

And Diane said angrily: 'I came here for Sam and Chrissa.'

Khufu smiled and nodded. He seemed inexplicably pleased.

'Exactly. You tire of listening. You assimilate the extraordinary so fast that already you're bored. You want something new to happen.'

Forestalling their protests he raised his hand again.

'You've heard enough,' he said, 'So look – over there!'

Diane opened her mouth, but stopped as, behind Bilibin and Marie Nelli, light flared, the wall of the round room dissolved, and before them they saw the entrance to a tunnel – dark, rectangular, precisely engineered, lit only by the faint glimmering of mica and quartz in its granite walls.

Diane felt the ring on her finger pulsing.

'There's your path!' Khufu's voice, suddenly harsh, echoed like a dream-voice, already receding. 'Find truth by walking through it and out to the world again. Find the Gate and bring us back! What I built was only a reminder – a reflection of this very device in which we have met. This is the hidden upper chamber your archaeologists still seek. Why can't they find it? Because it isn't on Earth! But the passage from it leads down to Earth! So lead us down! Start with your loved ones! They're why you're here – every new movement starts with sympathy and love!'

Then the light faded as if swallowed by the darkness emanating from the tunnel-mouth. Without realising it they were all on their feet.

'Bon chance,' Diane heard Marie Nelli murmur.

'But remember,' echoed Khufu's voice, 'we need each other. Remember the Light. Call us down, or the world will die, and all of us with it.'

Agutter laughed fearfully as the darkness sucked them in.

'That's what you said on the tape!' he cried back.

'Call us down now,' said Khufu's vanishing voice. 'Call down those you came to find. Take them with you . . . through the Gate I built . . .'

Then they were alone. All six of them. All six Hidden World humans from the Last Days. In darkness between the glimmering ancient walls.

'What about you two?' Diane cried.

'We stay here,' came Bilibin's faint voice. 'Mademoiselle Nelli and myself. We stay here in orbit for those who follow you. Good luck!'

Whispering encouragement to each other the four crept down the tunnel, feeling their way, followed by those they'd come to find. Diane heard Sam and Chrissa whispering in her, saw glowing animal-masked faces hovering before her . . . and all four sensed electric currents moving through them.

Agutter began laughing and couldn't stop. Jim told him to shut up, but he only laughed louder. 'Gillian!' he cried, his voice resonating in that dark, claustrophobic, downward-sloping tunnel, 'I had a great job – but you had to do this to me!'

'Shuddup!' Jessica cried, the shadow of Pierre Belot at her heels, his bright eyes gleaming. 'We're scared enough already! Why make it worse?'

But Diane, twisting the emerald ring of moon and horns round her left index finger, said nothing, for now. Looking back, she thought she saw Sam and Chrissa following, and they told her to keep quiet. Which she did.

In time they emerged through an opening in a granite wall and stood in a cool dark chamber. Agutter, feeling behind him for the opening through which they'd come, found it closed. There was only the smooth wall.

That, and the barely-perceptible lights that flickered about them.

'I was here once,' Agutter said, his ebullience at last cowed, and again, almost plaintively, he asked: 'Don't you know where we are yet?'

'*This is it, Diane,*' a voice whispered for her alone.

'*This is the Gate, Mum,*' another familiar voice added.

'Don't you know where we are?' Agutter demanded again.

Nobody answered him. Jim, seeking a way out, felt a draught and walked ahead but crashed his head against the hard stone of a low lintel.

He cried out in pain – then ducked cautiously through the door.

'Forty-one inches,' whispered Agutter, 'That's the height of it. For just a few feet. Then an open space. Then another head-banger. So watch it!' He grinned in the darkness. 'Then another platform, and then . . .'

'No!' On Diane's finger the ring was on fire. 'Go any lower and we'll come out in Egypt – alone! Here is where we do it.'

'That's right,' said Agutter, impressed. 'So you know where . . .'

'Forget it!' Diane snapped. 'What about Gillian? Don't you want her back? This is the Gate. Look!'

Emerald fire was leaping out of the ring. It lit their faces, lit the ancient chamber in which they stood . . . and in the light, flickering along the granite walls, shining shadows writhed, halfway to form, recognisable enough for the four who stood there to see –

'The Doctor!' Jim muttered. 'Doctor Dee! You . . .'

And Jessica beside him saw Jim with the old man in the black robe and skull cap, standing by the table with the Solomon Seal on it, and the book with the Latin title – *Monas Hieroglyphica* – lay nearby . . . and now here they all were . . . but the Doctor was Jim's business. For now before her amid the emerald light she saw her own link. There before her he stood at the bar, waiting in his drenched olive cape, eagle-feathered hat on his head.

'*Jessica,*' she heard him tell her, '*There are many gates in this world – gates to other places and times.*'

'Pierre,' she whispered. 'Pierre Belot.'

The half-formed phantom grinned at her and tipped its hat.

'As Above,' it said, 'So Belot.'

Philip Agutter had lost his voice too.

For now as the emerald light drenched him he found himself in his study in Sussex, working too late again, Carol asleep upstairs, confronted by the ISO monitors yet staring not at them but at the gilt-framed holo placed by the whisky bottle – and from the holo a young woman was smiling at him from a sunny mountain meadow – and as he faced his lost daughter hopelessly she stepped out of the holo, flickering with light, and asked:

'Dad? Won't you bring me back? Isn't that why you came?'

And Diane – before her now she saw –

She swallowed. She whispered: 'Is this real?'

'Oh come on!' said Sam, disgusted and impatient – and he looked just like the Sam she'd known, but for the white streaks in his hair and the new lines on his face – 'Are we going to hang around here? Do it, for heaven's sake. Get us down through the bloody Gate before we lose our nerve!'

'Yes, Mum, PLEASE!' Chrissa implored, 'Let it GO! NOW!'

'But why?' asked Diane quietly. 'Is it really so important?'

They both stared at her – flaming ghosts in the King's Chamber.

They looked at each other, and Sam deferred to Chrissa, who said:

'Yes, Mum. IT IS. So take us back – NOW!'

And looking into Chrissa's eyes, eyes which had seen the fate of those who'd preferred death at the stake to defeat by the Beast, eyes which had looked upon the dance of the Great Grey Ones – eyes which, the last time she remembered seeing them in the flesh, had been those of a naive London schoolgirl – looking into those eyes, with their knowledge of depths and heights, Diane knew she had to bring them all through the Gate. Back to the suffering Earth. Back to fight the Beast. And she did. She did.

Epilogue:
The Gairloch Gate

Ian Mcgregor lay abed in his bungalow by the shore at Shieldaig, staring through the window at the new star which had appeared on Christmas Eve, wondering about mysteries which, he was sure, had no answer on Earth.

He was 86 now, three years a widower and on his own. Life had grown hard for him since Mrs Joyce had first come with her family to Cuilchonich, the old farmhouse he still rented out every summer. What with his failing wit and strength and the loss of the pension (he couldn't afford tv or the phone any more) and the rising tides which had ruined his beloved garden in March and his kitchen last October, he was glad to know he wouldn't be here much longer. Why live in a world where nobody seemed happy any more? The shoreline holiday homes, all bought up by southerners during the property boom 12 years ago, were now abandoned. Their temporary owners had fled, leaving the local folk (as he saw it) fatally corrupted. His son had tried to make him move out to a croft on the high safe ground above Gairloch, and maybe he was a fool, but he was damned if now he'd abandon the home he'd built with Jean. Why worry if one night the sea washed him away? He still ate his black pudding and beans, which were supposed to kill you, and had his dram each evening

– and that was supposed to kill you too – the truth was that EVERYTHING (or so he gathered from the papers) you ate or drank was going to kill you. For the life of him he couldn't see why folk were so concerned about what killed you, instead of what nourished you and kept you alive. Like black pudding for breakfast and a stiff dram at night. Anyway, why bother if you were 86 with your wife dead and the world clearly gone to hell? So Ian Macgregor stuck to his bungalow and his black pudding and his nightly dram . . . and to his memories; including those of Diane Joyce.

Now as he lay awake staring at the wild faery light of the New Star he was wondering why Mrs Joyce hadn't been back since '96 for her annual visit to Cuilchonich, where in – was it '85? – she'd come from London with her husband and daughter. *It was so strange!* he thought. *Sam and . . . Chrissa – that's what they were called!*

Yes! Sam and Chrissa! During her visits in the years after their disappearance up by the Fairy Lochs, Mrs Joyce had told him so much by them that he'd come to know them almost as well as his own family. *But never*, he thought now, *was I able to comfort her. What could I say?*

For though he'd seen it (and John his grandson too) he'd had to look after himself and his own when the police and tv and newspapers all came asking what exactly they'd seen up there on the moor that morning they'd driven Mrs Joyce up in the Land Rover.

He knew he'd seen it. Chrissa, that young girl, vanishing amid the old stone circle amid a flood of fire where no fire could be. And that ring Mrs Joyce had hurled into the lochan. Of course he'd denied what he'd seen, and so had John – it didn't do to let folk think you crazy. Yet it hadn't made him happy, to have to deny it. The denial had seemed like flouting the Law of God! Yet even Jean hadn't believed him. All he'd been able to do, to salve his conscience, was to insist (and John had backed him up) that they'd seen the girl vanish into the peat-mire, and got there to late to save her. The result? Mrs Joyce had been judged insane, but not criminal – at least she hadn't been brought to trial for murder.

Mrs Joyce had been grateful . . . and obsessed. Annually for ten years thereafter she'd returned to Cuilchonich, to spend a week walking the moor where she'd lost her family, and Ian had never charged her a penny.

'You're too soft, Ian!' Jean's ghost told him now as he stared through the window at the new star, and he muttered: 'Get away with you, woman!'

For Jean had never liked that free week he gave Mrs Joyce each year – and was it or was it not strange that Jean had died the same year that Mrs Joyce had not returned; had refused even to answer the letter he'd sent to her Edinburgh address asking where she was?

Now tonight, on his own in bed in the sea-threatened bungalow, old Ian gazed through the window at the New Star and saw Mrs Joyce.

She was smiling at him, and she said:

'Ian, you've been a good friend. You never betrayed us. Now I want you to know: we're coming back! I've found them at last, and we're coming back tonight, with our friends! The Beast can't stop us! We're coming back, Mr Macgregor – please be there to see us return!'

Ian groaned. His bones hurt. He tried to pretend he was asleep. But he wasn't. Rising from bed, he knew this night was his last . . . yet he felt privileged. 'I'll go out going up,' he muttered, wheezing as he struggled into his clothes, his heart struggling as he stumbled out under the bright night to the old Land Rover – the same in which he'd driven Mrs Joyce and John up to the Fairy Lochs that morning so long ago. It was rusty now, and had maybe no more than a pint of diesel in it, but as he started the engine he knew it would get him up there. And suddenly he felt like a boy again as under the bright winter night sky the engine coughed and fired.

He started up the rough track from Shieldaig to Loch Bráigh Horrisdale. He didn't turn on the headlights. It wasn't because he was scared of the neighbours seeing him – they'd all gone – but because tonight the New Star shone bright enough to light his way up the bare steep slope to the moor that undulated inland all the way to the ancient Torridon peaks. And every upward yard he drove was like a year peeled from his life; each well-won then lost . . . until at last he was on the top.

He turned off the engine with a sigh of relief. His heart was pounding horribly. He got out of the Land Rover and patted the door. 'I won't see you again, old friend. You'll rot into the earth here.'

The sea was spread below him. It shone silver, the Outer Isles mere dark humps interrupting its passage into the eternal West . . . to Tir Nan Og, the Isles of the Blest where the heroes lived forever.

Ian laughed. 'To believe that could damn a man!' he cried. 'Isn't that so?' But the New Star shone in his eyes . . . and, suddenly reckless, he plunged into the heathery peat-mires that lay between him and the Fairy Lochs. He felt urgent now. *No more time!* And as before him he saw the bare low height of Sidhean Mor, the hill below which lay *the* place, he began to *run*. He hadn't run in forty years. Over the moortop he ran through the quiet still night, the heavens blazing with a million candles, the new star dominating all; and with each yard he felt his strength failing but his spirit rising; he felt like a boy again as he gave himself up to this stumbling race; and tears were running down his cheeks when at last he came to the Fairy Lochs, to the old stone circle amid which he'd seen Mrs Joyce's daughter Chrissa vanish amid a flood of the fire that –

'Just in time!' he cried, suddenly stopping in his tracks, raising his arms up to the suddenly flaming night. 'Thank You!'

For now, not twenty yards from the circle, he saw all he'd lived for come to pass and knew he would die happy. He saw the New Star flash so blindingly that the tears burned from his cheeks as the moors lit up in emerald and turquoise and diamond; he felt the fire race through his old bones with such incandescent energy that he was dancing even as he knew that his own dance was over . . . as amid the fire, at the heart of the circle, twisting shapes at first like shining vapour, then like capering skeletons joined bony hands in witchfire reel and rout, sucking denser form from the fire amid which they danced. One . . . three . . . six . . . *nine* of them he counted, *nine*; increasingly recognisable as human beings – but as the land below him bucked (or was it his heart?) suddenly there shot up from their midst a plume of violent scarlet light which HISSSSED, and –

He saw a huge blue cockerel-headed shape loom above them, forked tongue flickering from a quivering beak, and knew who and what it was even as the Beast screamed: 'NASSSTY! NASSSTY NASSSTY NASSSTY'; even as Azazel swept his wing over the dancers so that an utter darkness fell . . . yet as it fell, from its heart speared an intense emerald beam, and old Ian saw Mrs Joyce, a golden-haired woman and a thin, dark-haired man standing beside her, and he knew that she'd found Sam and Chrissa and brought them back, and others too, whom he did not know; saw too that the emerald fire leapt from the ring she wore, and knew it was the same ring she'd hurled away into the lochan that long-ago morning when Sam and Chrissa had vanished –

The emerald light pierced the Beast, and with a scream that echoed the scream of the world, the Adversary lost shape, dissipated, and fled.

'I'll be back!' wailed Azazel, 'Don't think you've won yet!'

Then, as his heart gave up and he died to the world, Ian knew that the world was not in fact lost, no matter what the jeremiahs said – knew that life would go on, in flower and humming-bee, in struggle and change . . .

'I LOVE YOU!' he cried as he died, not knowing who or what he meant as the Company returned through the Gate and the World stood in the balance.

THE END